THIS LIMITED AND SIGNED FIRST EDITION OF

# INMATE
# 1577

# Alan Jacobson

HAS BEEN SPECIALLY BOUND AND PRODUCED BY THE PUBLISHER

*Alan Jacobson*

# INMATE 1577

# NOVELS BY ALAN JACOBSON

*False Accusations*
*The Hunted*
*The 7<sup>th</sup> Victim*
*Crush*
*Velocity*
*Inmate 1577*
*Hard Target (late 2011)*

For an updated list of current and future
Alan Jacobson novels, please visit
www.AlanJacobson.com.

# ALAN JACOBSON

# INMATE 1577

A KAREN VAIL NOVEL

NORWOOD
PRESS

Thomas White and William Post Leavenworth quotes used by permission of Pete Earley, author of *The Hot House*; Roy Gardner Alcatraz quote used by permission of Michael Esslinger, author of *Alcatraz: A Definitive History of the Penitentiary Years*, and his publisher, Ocean View Press.

Text set in Garamond 12pt; italics and chapter subheaders in Californian FB 11pt; chapter numbers and title pages in Futurex Distro-Survival 36pt/48pt; text messages in Candara 10pt; notes, signs, and dedication in Hypatia Sans Pro 10pt/11pt.

ISBN-13: 978-0-9836260-0-8

10 9 8 7 6 5 4 3 2 1

For Mark Safarik

Nearly 20 years ago, a chance phone call led me to a blood spatter pattern analysis course that was being attended by FBI Special Agent Mark Safarik. Mark and I started talking one day, and a strong and deep friendship was born.

Over the years, on book tours and in interviews, I've discussed the research I've done with Mark in his position as a senior profiler at the FBI Behavioral Analysis Unit. But as fascinating as that education has been, and as impactful as it's been on my career, my friendship with Mark has been that much more rewarding. In many ways, Mark is like a brother to me.

Early on, Mark coined a phrase that he began using as a footer in the emails he wrote to me: *Knee Deep In the Blood and Guts*, or *KDITBAG*. It was a reminder that, while writing my novels, I should "keep it real" to respect the victims of these heinous crimes and the work the profilers do.

When I look back on that phone call nearly two decades ago, I had no way of knowing that KDITBAG, and the person who gave birth to that saying, would have such a long-lasting professional—and personal—impact on my life.

Mark, this one's for you.

# AUTHOR'S NOTE

This is a work of fiction. While there were actual people named Leonard Williams, George Whitacre, Arthur Dollison, Marvin Hubbard, Frank Morris, Bernie Coy, Allen West, Clarence Anglin, Joe Cretzer, Billy Boggs, John Anglin, and Clarence Carnes, this novel is not intended to be an accurate portrayal of their personalities, nor is it intended to be a complete or factual account of the actions these individuals took in real life. All other characters in this story are entirely fictional and any resemblance to actual persons, living or dead, is coincidental.

*When you are small and need help, you run to your parents. When you get older... If someone threatens you, you call a cop. In prison there is no one to turn to, no one to solve your problems for you. If you go to the guards, you will be known as a snitch and that can get you killed. Believe me, the guy demanding that you drop your drawers isn't going to be a good sport and simply let you walk away. You must be willing to fight or you must give in.*

– Leavenworth Chief Psychologist Thomas White, PhD

*Sometimes, I think about what it would be like to just go into a bank and blow the head off the first teller I see. I know that I am capable of that; I mean, any criminal is capable of that, and long-term prisoners can kill easier than most people, because you are around the dregs so much and for so long that you forget the worth of a human life. You think all humans are dregs.*

– Leavenworth inmate William Post

*The hopeless despair on the Rock is reflected in the faces and actions of almost all of the inmates. Watching those men from day to day slowly giving up hopes is truly a pitiful sight, even if you are one of them.*

– Roy Gardner, Alcatraz inmate #110

*Nobody ever did, or ever will, escape the consequences of his choices.*

– Alfred A. Montapert

# 1

*37 W. Rosedale Avenue*
*Northfield, New Jersey*

Henry sat deathly still in the corner watching the life drain from his mother's body, knees drawn tight against his chest, arms wrapped around his shins. He stared at the blood seeping from her pulpy head wounds, poking forth from between strands of matted hair.

The seven-year-old boy had told the policeman in so many words about the man in the black knit mask who came up from behind and struck his mother several times, then disappeared out the back door. Afterwards, Henry had sat frozen, unable to move, unable to comfort her in her last seconds before her body stilled, her eyes rapt in death.

A bottle of maple syrup, the lone weapon his mother had grabbed to fight off her attacker, lay shattered on the floor, oozing across the kitchen linoleum. In halting sentences, with shock-laden tear-filled eyes, Henry described how the masked man had knocked it from her hand before she could raise it.

It now sat impotent on the ground, like a cold revolver stuck in the deepest reaches of a holster, never given the opportunity to be of service.

Henry had finally eased forward, inching across the floor until the tips of his toes were a fraction of an inch from the pooled blood that encircled his mother's head. He reached over and touched her ashen face, then poked it, despite the policeman's admonishment to stay back from her body.

At his tender age, the finality of death was little more than an innate concept, like when an animal in the wild knows that one of its own kind is no longer among the living.

THE POLICEMAN, AFTER HAVING WAITED in the living room with Henry, walked outside into the winter evening. Moments later, he pushed open the door and then stepped aside so another man could enter.

Walton MacNally's eyes instantly settled on the center of the kitchen floor, taking in the violence laid bare before him. A grocery bag dropped from his hand, glass bottles within shattering as it struck the hard floor.

"Doris?" He rushed to her side, caressed her face, felt for a pulse, couldn't stop staring at her head wounds.

"Sir!" the cop said. "Mr. MacNally. Don't touch the body—"

MacNally's Adam's apple rose sharply, then fell. Ignoring the cop's directive, he lifted Doris's hand and brought it to his lips, kissed it, and then started whimpering. He became aware of his son and pulled his gaze from his wife's irreparably injured and abnormally still body.

"Henry—what…what happened?"

The boy's eyes coursed down to his mother. His lips made an attempt to move, but no sound emerged.

But there was little doubt as to what had transpired. His wife had met with severe violence, the overt damage to her head and brain unquestionably fatal.

A parched "Why?" managed to scrape from MacNally's throat. "Who?"

"A detective should be here any minute," the policeman said.

MacNally scooted over to Henry and took the boy into his arms. His life had been turned upside down, destroyed…his mother, his maternal presence, ripped from him like a doe taken down by a lion while her fawn watches.

MacNally swallowed hard. A whimper threatened to escape his throat, but he fought it back. A pain unrecognizable to him, unlike anything he had ever felt, emerged from deep in his soul and manifested as a plaintive, silent moan. He balled a fist and shoved it between his front teeth. He did not want to further traumatize his son by losing control.

Now more than ever, Henry needed him. He needed him to be strong.

A DETECTIVE ARRIVED TWENTY MINUTES later. Dressed in a charcoal suit with a narrow tie and a black fedora tipped up off his forehead, he stepped into the kitchen through the back door and surveyed the room.

Henry was seated in his father's lap on the floor, against the far wall. The side of the boy's head rested against his dad's chest, a gathering of shirt stuffed into the palm of his left hand.

"I'm Detective George O'Hara. You're Walton MacNally?"

"Yes, sir."

O'Hara knelt carefully beside the woman's body and felt for a pulse. "So what happened here?"

"I came home about, about twenty-five minutes ago. Henry—"

"No," O'Hara said. "Your son. I want to hear from your son." O'Hara took a knee in front of the boy. "You okay, Henry?"

Henry's eyes moved about the room, then finally came to rest on the detective. "My mom's not gonna wake up."

"I know. I'm sorry, son." O'Hara glanced at MacNally, then swung his gaze back to Henry. "Did you see what happened? Did you see who did this to her?"

Henry sucked on his bottom lip. Dropped his gaze to his lap. Nodded.

"Did you know the person?"

Henry spoke without looking up. "He had a mask."

"What kind of a mask?" O'Hara asked. "Like the Lone Ranger?"

"Bigger. All over his face."

O'Hara nodded. "Did he say anything? Did you know his voice?"

Henry shook his head. "He didn't talk."

"How big was he? Was he—was he as tall as your dad?"

Henry twisted his lips. "Same."

"Close your eyes for a second, son. Go on." He waited for Henry to comply, then said, "Imagine the man is right here, right now. I'm here, so he can't hurt you. Picture him, look right at his face. Can you tell me anything more about what he looks like?"

Henry kept his eyes shut but shook his head.

"If your dad was wearing a mask, would the man look like that?"

Henry nodded.

"What kind of a—"

"Quiet, Mr. MacNally," O'Hara said. He rose, sucked on his teeth a second, and then looked over at the woman's body.

Henry tightened his grip on his father. MacNally shifted his weight and cuddled the boy. It was now just the two of them. Henry had been such a blessing that he and Doris had started discussing another child. But times were tough, and he had lost his job as a welder for a commercial building contractor three months ago. They were existing solely on Doris's lean secretarial salary, so they decided to put off the idea of another child, at least until he had found employment. He began drinking to escape the pressures and feelings of inadequacy.

Then came a break: a week ago MacNally heard of a shipping company that needed an able-bodied man to work the docks unloading cargo. It was a waste of his artistic talents, but he needed the money. Though it had only been six days, he hadn't had one drink and his boss took notice of his work ethic. Tonight he was going to tell Doris they should consider that second child.

Those plans were now gone. Forever lost, like the life that had drained from his wife's body.

# 2

O'Hara pulled a long, narrow pad from his vest pocket and jotted some notes. He clicked his pen shut, and then stole another look at the body of Doris MacNally. "I'll be right back. Gotta go find out what's keeping the coroner. Don't touch anything. Best if you two go wait in the living room."

The door swung open and closed, a blast of frigid air blowing against MacNally's face. The police officer who'd been there earlier stepped back inside and folded his arms across his chest.

MacNally did as he was told, taking Henry into the adjacent room and waiting on the couch. He cradled Henry against his perspiration-soaked body, oblivious to the chilled draft that swept through the house...the cold emptiness mimicking what he was now feeling.

"What's in your hand?" MacNally asked softly.

Henry splayed open his fingers, and an opal brooch stared back at him. It was the only keepsake Doris's grandmother had left her, and it was something Doris cherished and wore often. MacNally knew it was Henry's attempt to be close to his mother, to have something of hers that he could hold onto. Emotionally, MacNally could relate: he wasn't prepared to let go of his life companion yet either.

O'Hara was gone for several minutes, during which time MacNally numbly stared ahead at the wedding photo that sat in a wood frame on the fireplace mantle across the room. He stroked his son's back, an action that felt pathetically inadequate. But he didn't know what else

5

to do. He had just turned twenty-four—what could he possibly know about helping a young boy deal with the loss of his mother?

In the space of mere seconds, the lives of Henry and Walton MacNally were shattered beyond repair.

But MacNally did not—could not—know just how much of a difference his mate's death would make in their lives.

DETECTIVE O'HARA WALKED BACK INTO the house. His cheeks and the tips of his ears were red from the blistering cold, and his face was stern. The creases were more prominent, the brow rigid, the lips taut.

But it wasn't until O'Hara was fully inside the kitchen that MacNally realized that the man had his service revolver in hand, at his side, poking out from behind his thigh. Concealing it.

"Mr. MacNally, can you please let go of your son and come over here for a moment?"

MacNally's gaze was fixated on the tip of metal peeking from behind O'Hara's leg. Whatever the detective had in mind, it was not good. But MacNally had nothing to hide, so he gave Henry a gentle pat on the back. "Son, I need to get up for a second."

Henry unfolded himself and flopped down beside his father as MacNally pushed up off the sofa. He walked over to O'Hara.

"Sir, I'm placing you under arrest for the murder of Doris MacNally. Please put your hands behind your back."

MacNally leaned back. "Arrest? For— Are you out of your mind? I loved my wife. We were going to—"

"I'm just following orders, sir. Now turn around and give me your hands."

"How could you th— What could possibly make you think I did this?"

"Once we get to the station, we can talk about it in more detail, get it all straightened out."

MacNally did as instructed. As he turned, he locked eyes with his boy. "Everything's going to be okay, Henry. I'm going to clear up this misunderstanding and be back home as soon as I can. I promise."

# 3

Walton MacNally soon learned not to make promises he could not keep. Because as it turned out, all would not be okay. MacNally was questioned at the station for hours. His alibi was thin at best—he repeated what he had told O'Hara outside, when he first arrived at the house—that he had gone shopping for groceries but then made a stop somewhere. He claimed it was a bar for his first drink in nearly a week to celebrate his new job—but couldn't recall which establishment he'd visited.

O'Hara questioned the owners of local taverns in the vicinity, but none recalled seeing MacNally during the hours in question.

That lent credence to the prosecutor's theory that the defendant had hired a prostitute, had sex with her in his car, then drove home and killed his wife when she confronted him with some form of evidence—errant lipstick, foreign perfume, or suspicion brought on by a pattern of such behavior.

Although Henry—the sole witness to the murder—had stated to O'Hara that the attacker did not speak before beating his mother, the prosecutor pointed out that it was only natural for a young boy to "cover" for his father, particularly once he realized the weight of the situation facing him: with his mother gone, his dad was his only remaining family.

And making the defense even more difficult was MacNally's history—his father's, to be exact—convicted of murdering a woman with whom he was accused of having an affair. That trial had made the newspapers, too, nineteen years earlier. And although MacNally's defense attorney objected to the prosecutor's mention of that old case during his opening arguments, it was a seed planted in the jury's minds. More importantly, however, it brought his father's legacy once again to the front pages of the newspaper and painted the MacNally family name with such distrustful strokes that it became a dirty image the public could not easily discard.

Henry MacNally, living temporarily in a local orphanage, was unable to provide any further description of the assailant...a description that could very well have been his father. Or—as the defense attorney claimed—it could have been thousands of other men of similar build.

Ultimately, Walton MacNally was found not guilty. But the job that MacNally had won in the days before his wife's death was long gone. A man whose face had graced the local papers was a pariah, despite the prosecution's failed bid to build a convincing case against him.

MacNally and Henry packed their belongings into two large suitcases and headed south. Where it would lead MacNally did not know. But perhaps it was better that way. Because had Walton MacNally known the turn his life would eventually take, he might very well have committed suicide. At least it would have eliminated years of incomprehensible pain and suffering.

# 4

Present Day
July 26
11:01 PM

*The Marina District*
*San Francisco, California*

San Francisco Police Inspector Lance Burden greeted the first officer on-scene with a firm nod. "What's the deal?"

The man tipped back his cap and shifted his weight. "Pretty disgusting, if you ask me, Inspector."

Burden yawned wide and hard, then said, "I did ask you. Can you be a little more specific?"

"Victim is an old woman. I didn't want to mess up the crime scene and shit, so I'm just eyeballing it, but she looks like she's in her eighties."

"Okay. Go on."

"Kind of looks like my grandmother."

"She's old. I got that. What else?"

"Her pants and underwear are pulled down to her knees. She's…uh…she's been penetrated."

"Penetrated—how? You mean sexually?"

The officer rested both hands on his utility belt and hooked fingers around the gear. "Yeah. There's something rammed up her, up her anus." He looked away, shook his head, then continued. "Like I said. Disgusting. I mean, who'd want to rape and sodomize an old woman?"

Burden's eyes widened. "Wait here."

"Don't worry. I'm not goin' back in there," the cop said with a sardonic chuckle.

Burden lifted his two-way and got an ETA on the criminalist: fifteen minutes, best case. His partner was en route, as well, but he decided not to wait. He pulled a pair of blue booties from his pocket—he'd learned first day on the job as a detective years ago to carry the things with him. And they'd come in handy on more than one occasion.

He walked into the townhouse. A sour-stale odor flared his nostrils. It was a scent he'd experienced a number of times over the years—the way homes of elderly individuals can sometimes smell, particularly when mixed with the putrid cologne of death.

The place was well kept, orderly and clean. Oil paintings and dated knickknacks betrayed their age about as blatantly as the yellowing black-and-white photographs that sat on a bureau in the living room.

And then, in the bedroom…two bare feet visible from the doorway. Burden walked another couple of yards and had enough of a view to get a sense of what he was dealing with. He bit the inside of his lip.

"Inspector."

Burden did not look away from the body. "What is it?"

"The criminalist made better time than he thought. He'll be here in five minutes."

"Yeah. Right. Send him in when he gets here."

"See what I mean?" the officer asked. "What kind of monster would do that to a poor old woman?"

Burden sighed deeply. "I think I know just the kind of monster we're looking for. And I know who to call to help find him."

# 5

July 27
12:07 PM

*George Washington University Hospital*
*900 23rd Street, NW*
*Washington, D.C.*

FBI Profiler Karen Vail walked the hospital hallway with her son, Jonathan, and DEA Special Agent Robby Hernandez. Vail and Robby were both off duty, a rare Saturday when they had time to decompress, grab lunch at Charlie Palmer's, and then a late afternoon movie. They left their case folders on their desks, their problems neatly tucked away in a file drawer, and all concerns of serial murders and drug cartels out of reach of their collective consciousness.

Robby's shoulder was still in a sling, recovering from a gunshot wound he had sustained two months ago. But the injury had an unforeseen, nonmedical side effect: Jonathan got a kick out of handily beating the one-armed Robby in every videogame in the teen's arsenal, so they played together at every opportunity. Robby represented the positive male presence Jonathan lacked, and Jonathan gave Robby the father-son relationship he had wanted but not yet experienced.

With various bruises and lacerations now healed and a knee that finally felt whole following recent surgery, Vail had found peace being at home after a tenuous two weeks in the Napa Valley. What started as a dream vacation had degraded into a recurring nightmare that, for a while, Vail had difficulty awakening from.

But Vail and Robby were not at the hospital for their ailments; they were visiting a friend and colleague, Mandisa Manette, who had been shot in front of the White House just before Vail and Robby left for Napa. It had taken three surgeries thus far, but she was making steady progress and had begun rehabilitation.

Jonathan insisted on waiting in the hall, choosing instead to trade text messages with his friends.

"We won't be long," Vail said.

Jonathan already had his phone out, eyes riveted to the screen. "Take your time."

Robby reached out to pull open the Physical Therapy department door, but Vail slapped her hand against the wood panel. "You think she'll be glad to see us?"

"Why wouldn't she be?"

Vail bobbed her head. "Every time she and I get together it turns into a major ordeal."

"I could say the same thing, but that doesn't stop me from seeing you."

Vail elbowed him in the side. Robby pulled open the door.

Gripping two wooden parallel bars was Detective Mandisa Manette. Her normal cornrowed hair was pulled back into a bun, disheveled and in need of a shampoo. Rather than the lithe, athletic detective, Manette was having difficulty negotiating the normally automatic movement of walking. The therapist's gaze snapped up— causing Manette to stop and twist her body.

"Jesus Christ. Kari, what the hell are you doing here?"

"Good to see you, too," Vail said. She turned to Robby. "See what I mean?"

"Robby," Manette said. "You still dating this crystal ball psychic magician?"

Robby grinned broadly, then stepped forward and gave Manette a hug. "How are you doing?"

"Better than you," she said. "What's up with the sling?"

"Same as you. GSW. No big deal, I'm back on the job already."

"Sequestered in this hospital, I tend to be a little out of touch. Especially when people don't visit you."

"I was here last week," Vail said.

"I don't consider you 'people,'" Manette said. "I mean real flesh-and-blood humans."

"Sounds like you're doing well," Robby said. "Getting back to your old self." He gestured toward her with a raise of his chin. "How's your hip coming along?"

"I got me a brand new one, titanium or some shit like that. Bionic space-age technology. I'm going to be faster, stronger than before."

"Yeah," Vail said. "And she'll be able to leap tall buildings in a single bound."

"I got a doc who's got a bedside manner just like yours," Manette said. "I slapped him upside the head. He's much nicer to me now." She shifted her weight and grabbed the parallel bars. "If he wasn't such a hunk, I'da fired his ass the first day."

Vail's phone rang. Her hand sprung to the holster and silenced it, then pulled it free. Glanced at the display and said to Robby, "It's your father."

Robby rolled his eyes. "Will you stop saying that every time your boss calls you?"

Vail feigned innocence.

"What's that?" Manette asked. "Vail's ASAC's your father?" She looked back and forth at both of them. "Man, Kari. You don't tell me nothin'. Sounds like I missed some juicy shit wasting away in this here hospital."

"Juicy shit, indeed." Vail turned and answered the call.

"Karen," Thomas Gifford said. "Sorry to bother you on a Saturday. But something's come up."

"I think this is the part where I make believe there's static on the line and then press the END button."

"I'm serious, Karen. I've got something here."

"And you've got at least eleven other profilers you can call."

"The one I really need has retired. And he's out of the country so I can't even give him a shout. So you're it."

"Robby and I have plans with Jonathan for a movie later."

"Take a rain check. A detective just called the unit with a fresh eighty-two-year-old female, sexually assaulted and murdered."

"So you want Mark Safarik. He's the world expert on the sexual homicide of elderly females—"

"Yes, yes," Gifford said. "But like I said, he's unreachable. And I know you worked with him before he retired and coauthored his last paper."

Vail sighed. "So I'm the pinch hitter."

"For lack of a better term, yeah."

Vail looked at Robby and gave him a thumbs down sign. "Where and when?"

"We've got you booked on a flight to San Francisco leaving out of Reagan in two hours."

"San Francisco? Wait, I get it. This is a joke, right? I had the nightmare of my life in Napa, so you're sending me back there a few months after I got out of that godforsaken place. Good one, sir." She pressed END and disconnected the call.

"Problem?" Robby asked.

Her BlackBerry rang again seconds later. Vail looked at the phone, then at Robby. Brought the handset to her ear. "You weren't kidding, were you."

"No, Karen, I wasn't. I'm emailing you the flight information. Pack whatever you need and get over to Reagan ASAP."

"Fine."

"And—please, promise me one thing."

"Only *one* thing, sir?"

"Only one thing," Gifford repeated. "But it's a big one. Stay out of trouble. This one time. That's not too much to ask, is it?"

# 6

Karen Vail arrived at San Francisco International Airport at 11 PM. Her connecting flight in Atlanta was delayed due to weather somewhere over the country, so she'd picked up a copy of Nelson DeMille's latest novel at an airport bookstore and devoured half of it by the time she touched down at SFO.

Robby had turned her on to DeMille. He'd said DeMille's main character, John Corey, was a lot like her—a sarcastic, wise-cracking former detective. She told Robby he had his head up his ass. But now that she'd read DeMille's novels, she realized that maybe she did share a few similar characteristics with John Corey—but she wouldn't give Robby the satisfaction.

"First of all, I'm not a wiseass," she started. He merely squinted at her. *Fine, that wasn't too convincing an argument. I wouldn't believe that one, either.* "Second, I'm a lot better cop than Corey."

That was when Robby tilted his head and said, "You're comparing your skill set to a fictional character?" And then he delivered his zinger, designed to put her in her place: "Besides. Come to think of it, I think maybe Corey's a little smarter than you are."

At that point, Vail fell back on the only card she had left to play. "Who would you rather sleep with. Fictitious John Corey, or me?"

Robby didn't have a comeback for that—or he chose to keep it to himself. *Wise choice.*

Vail took a cab to the Hyatt Regency in the city, left a message for Inspector Lance Burden that she had arrived later than she had anticipated, and told him she would meet him at 8 AM at the Hall of Justice's Homicide Detail on Bryant Street. Then she sent an email to her friend, Roxxann Dixon, an investigator with the Napa County District Attorney's office, who served with her on the Crush Killer task force a few months back. Vail didn't know if they would be able to coordinate a dinner together, but she wanted her to know that she was working a serial killer case in the city in case they had a chance to see one another.

The wind coming off the Bay struck her as she got out of the cab on California Street. Vail walked past the cable car, loading passengers in front of the Hyatt, and strode up to the hotel's entrance, where the escalators carried her up to the third floor. As the moving stairs lifted her toward the lobby, the grandness of the central atrium left her jaw slack. Ahead, a massive sculpture—it looked like a swirling copper sphere—sat atop a black marble base with water cascading down its sides. To her left, thousands of tiny lights, suspended from above, stretched what must've been a hundred feet in length by a hundred feet in width.

"Wow," she said under her breath.

After so many sleepless nights on this coast, Vail was relieved to enjoy a restful evening, in a comfortable bed and no middle-of-the-night pages, texts, or calls. She dreamt of Robby and was disappointed when she awoke early to find that he wasn't beside her. Despite the momentary letdown, she felt refreshed and ready to go to work.

After showering, while still wrapped in a bath sheet, she pulled open the curtains and peered out the window for the first time. Her view was the finest she had ever seen: the room was on the fourteenth floor and overlooked the Embarcadero and Port of San Francisco. *Maybe this trip won't be so bad after all.*

To her right stood the steel blue Bay Bridge, stretching from an island on the left all the way to the furthest reaches of her window's field of vision on the right. A cargo ship marked *Hanjin* in enormous white letters set against a dark body ferried blue and red containers on its back. An escort tug tailed it a safe distance astern as both vessels passed beneath the farthest span of the bridge.

The sky was a thick gray, remnants of fog hanging low in the distance. While pondering the weather and what to wear, her wakeup call came, the automated voice welcoming her and informing her that the high temperature was expected to be a nippy 52 degrees. Actually, the recording omitted the adjective.

In her haste to pack—Gifford hadn't left her much time—she'd neglected to check the weather. She pulled out the pair of form-fitting jeans that she had worn on the plane and snuggled into a tight-knit black sweater. She stepped into the cylindrical, windowed elevator and again marveled at the curtain of hanging lights as the car descended to the lobby. Curbside, she was about to hail a taxi when a text message from Inspector Burden hit her BlackBerry. He wanted to meet instead at the crime scene, in an area he called the Marina District.

Vail gave the cab driver the address and asked how long till they arrived. It was only a few miles—a ten-minute ride, traffic permitting.

She arrived as promised, in front of a well-appointed line of charming row houses, decked out in muted colors of butterscotch and sapphire, each sporting their own variation of wrought iron-wrapped balconies.

Standing out front of a creamy avocado building marked with a brass "114" was a tall, thin man chomping on a slice of gum. Vail paid the taxi driver, then walked up to the house. "Karen Vail. Are you Burden?"

The inspector extended a hand. "With a lot of things, yeah."

Vail took it. His grip was soft and quick. "A sense of humor. A bad one, but a sense of humor. That's good."

"My kids give me shit too."

"About the weak handshake or your bad jokes?"

Burden drew back. "Man, you're a fiery one. Give me a few minutes to adjust to that, okay?"

"Only a few minutes? You're in danger of impressing me, Inspector."

He eyed her cautiously. "Maybe a few days."

Vail broke a smile. "That's more like it. But if it helps, I'm told I grow on you once you get to know me."

"I wanted Mark Safarik."

Vail nodded. *Hey, if it was me, I'd want Safarik, too.* But she kept that to herself. "He's not available. You get me."

Burden pulled his leather jacket tighter as the wind whipping off the Bay blew through his thin shirt.

Vail shivered. "What's up with your weather? It's July. If I'd known it was gonna be this goddamn cold, I'd have packed a jacket and gloves."

Burden pulled a key from his pocket and unlocked the door to the house. "Don't you know the famous quote?"

Vail frowned. "I know a lot of famous quotes, Inspector. You have a particular one in mind?"

"'The coldest winter I ever spent was a summer in San Francisco.' Mark Twain. Well, some think Twain said it."

"Never heard it."

Burden moved inside the house. "The city's weather is kind of like Australia, all messed up calendar-wise."

Vail eyed him. "Okay. Right. San Francisco is Australia. Got it." She followed him in through the door and up the stairs.

"Any security other than locks on the doors?"

"Nope." Burden led her inside, to the mouth of the living room. "That bedroom there," he said, gesturing down the hall with a nod of his chin. "That's where the body was found."

"Got another piece of gum?" Vail asked.

"It's Nicorette."

She lifted her eyebrows. "In that case, I'll pass."

"By the way. You can drop the Inspector crap. Guys in the unit call me Birdie."

Vail eyed him. "Birdie."

Burden shrugged a shoulder. "Yeah, I didn't like it either at first. But after twenty years, I've kind of embraced it. Burden works, too. Don't really care for Lance. No one calls me by my first name. Except my mother."

"What about your wife?"

"She calls me jackass." He apparently noted Vail's confusion. "We're divorced."

Burden led the way to the bedroom. "What do people call you?"

"Depends who you ask. Asshole. Bitch. But those are just my friends." Vail grinned. "Karen's fine."

Burden nodded. "Why don't we start with Karen, and as I get to know you we can graduate to Bitch?"

"I think I'm going to enjoy working with you, Burden."

"Hey, I was born in New York. I understand sarcasm."

"Good. You're likely to get a good dose of it." Vail indicated the bedroom. "Shall we?"

"I was trying to avoid it."

"I can tell." She pushed open the solid-core wood door and stepped in. A queen bed sat in the middle of the room. Unremarkable furniture lined the wall to her right, below a large bay window that gave her a third-floor view of the top portion of a fog-obscured Golden Gate Bridge tower peeking out between the crests of nearby low-cut trees.

Dried bloodstains soiled the left side of the mattress.

"Vic was eighty-two. Maureen Anderson. Married, haven't been able to reach the husband. William. Last seen yesterday morning."

"Who called it in?"

"Neighbor came by for dessert and coffee. She didn't answer the door. Maureen was apparently very reliable, so an hour later, when she still wasn't answering, the woman got concerned and dispatch sent out a well-check."

"Any evidence her husband left on a trip?"

"Nothing we've been able to determine. Still following up with airlines, family, credit card records. The usual. Put out an APB as soon as we found the body. He's the obvious prime suspect."

Vail winced. "Not so fast. And not so obvious. What do we know about him? About their relationship?"

"Good, according to the neighbors. The usual bickering, but from what we've been told, looks like they genuinely loved each other."

"What was his occupation?" Vail asked. "What level of education?"

"He retired about five years ago. He was a lawyer with a firm here in the city. Last five or so years, he was 'of counsel,' picking the cases he wanted to work on."

"What kind of cases?"

Burden scratched at his forehead. "White-collar defense."

"What about the place. Ransacked? Anything missing?"

"Nothing, far as we can tell. Money, jewelry, valuables. All here."

Vail glanced around. "It's harder to notice something missing than something added. But there's a fair amount of dust. Did you—"

"Check all the flat surfaces where the dust is missing, like if an object's been removed? Yeah, we know what we're doing, Karen. We thought of that. Like I said, nothing appears to be missing."

"Forensics? I see some blood spatter on the wall—"

"Castoff, from a shoe, most likely. He kicked her. Looked to me like he kicked her while she was on the floor, then got her up on the bed for the second act of his horror show." Burden shook his head in disbelief, then continued. "Forensics are still being processed. But from what I'm told, he didn't leave a whole lot. We came up with fibers, hair, that kind of stuff, but whether any of that belongs to the offender remains to be seen."

"And this blood. Here," she said, pointing at the pooled stain on the bed. "If she was lying with her head in the usual spot, this bloodstain would be about where her vagina would be. I know she was raped, but—"

"The scumbag sodomized her, too. With an umbrella. It was brutal. That's what got me thinking that we were looking at something far more complex than what we're used to dealing with. That's why I asked for Safarik."

"Understood. Not likely a white-collar criminal would be good for this. Unless there was a really bad thing done to him and he snapped and crossed the line. Even then, the anger and ability to become violent would be in his repertoire of behaviors. It'd be there, even if it hadn't yet manifested in a way we'd have seen publicly."

"So not our first choice for a theory."

"Definitely not," Vail said. She knelt down and examined the area underneath the bed. "Any semen?

"Looks like he used a condom. ME found spermicide."

"Tell me more. Cause of death? She didn't die of rape."

Burden bit his lower lip. "ME thinks she was tortured before she was killed."

"Tortured how?"

Burden turned away. "Electric shocks."

"Like a stun gun or a Taser-type device?"

"ME said no. More irregular, like nothing she'd ever seen before. She said she'd read about a case in a rural town in the Midwest where some guy had taken an electrical cord and snipped off the end, then splayed apart the exposed wires. He shoved the plug into a wall outlet and then shocked the vic. And those burn patterns matched the burn marks on Mrs. Anderson's body. Electrical burn marks."

"I'll want to see the body."

"Figured you might. But I thought you should see the crime scene first, so I told the ME we'd be by around eleven."

Vail pointed at the bed. "This is where you found her? Facing the doorway?"

"Yeah. Like she was peacefully at rest. Even though, well, she wasn't." He shook his head. "Legs were spread. Like I said, he used an umbrella. Lots of vaginal and anal tearing, all the way up into the abdominal cavity."

"Bodily fluids? DNA?"

"Working it up." He nodded at a spot on the carpet. "There were four deep impressions at the far side of the bed, near the window. And drag marks leading away."

"A chair? Someone was watching?"

"My partner's guess? *Forced* to watch."

"The husband."

"Possibly," Burden said. "Assuming he's not the killer."

Vail nodded thoughtfully. After a long moment, she said, "Okay."

"So COD, to answer your question. Multiple. Heart attack, probably from the shocks she sustained. But there was also substantial head trauma. Like I said, she was kicked. Repeatedly. Hard. And there was some cutting on the body, but not deep."

"I'll want to see your photos."

"Being printed this morning. My partner's putting together a packet for you full of what we've got so far."

Vail stepped over to the window and peered out, taking in not the scenery but whatever was there to see. Routes of escape, views that passersby might have had. What the neighborhood looked like from this vantage point.

"How long have they lived here?"

Burden pulled a notepad from his interior sport coat pocket. Flipped a couple pages. "In the neighborhood, twenty-two years. In this place, nineteen."

"We'll need a list of all residents in a six-block radius, with ages and occupations of the males. Contact info, too. Flag any with prior violent acts or arrests of any kind."

"In this neighborhood?"

"Is that a problem?"

"Nope." Burden pulled out an older model BlackBerry and began typing. "I'll have my partner start on it. It'll take a while to get that together."

Vail turned away from the window. "What can you tell me about Mrs. Anderson?"

Burden shrugged. "People liked her. She had her circle of friends, many for a couple decades or so. But she wasn't overly social."

"Let's check into the Andersons' finances…were they involved in any shady deals? Were they the subject of a scam? Were they involved in any failed business or real estate partnerships that might've gone south?"

Burden began typing again. "Don't know. Nothing that came up."

"Ask the neighbors, family members. Let's be thorough." Vail crouched down to peer under the bed. "I take it you haven't had any other elderly female sexual homicides in the region the past few years."

He pocketed his BlackBerry. "Correct. I checked before calling. I knew we hadn't had any up till '06, when Safarik was here for that Violent Crimes conference the BAU put on for us. That's why I was concerned. Somebody like this, I think he's gonna hit again. We need to grab him up quickly."

Vail thought a moment before responding, because she knew her answer was not going to be one that Burden wanted to hear. She decided to withhold her opinion until she had gathered more information and examined the body. "Are any of the lamp cords missing or cut?" Vail asked.

"What?"

"You said it looks like he used an electrical cord to torture Mrs. Anderson. Did anyone check the appliances, lamps, anything with a power cord?"

"I don't see—"

"Did he bring it with him, or did he use what was here? If he brought it with him, that indicates premeditation. He planned this out. And that typically points to—"

"An organized offender."

Vail tilted her head back. "Very good. There's a very recent shift away from using that term and classification system, but I'm impressed."

"I remember that from Safarik's session at the conference. But don't get all excited. A lot of it went in one ear and out the other. Wish we'd recorded it."

"What, and put me out of a job?"

Burden looked at the night table. "We didn't check the appliances. Guess we should do that."

"Guess we should." Vail and Burden began inspecting every outlet and powered device in the townhouse.

Vail pulled back the nightstand closest to her and peered over its back for an outlet. "Was she naked when you found her?"

Burden yanked the mattress aside to check behind the bed. "Nightgown was pulled up."

"Over the head?"

Burden thought a second. "No, why?"

"Offenders sometimes cover their victims' faces with an article of clothing or a pillow. A lot of times they pull up the dress and drape it across the eyes. Think of it like an apology, embarrassment at what they're doing to an elderly woman. Maybe they don't want to look at the face they've just beaten the hell out of. But if we're dealing with a psychopath, they don't feel anything. No remorse, embarrassment, guilt. Nothing."

"It's hard to think of these monsters being embarrassed about what they're doing."

Vail moved over to the dresser in front of the wall opposite the bed. "Like a lot of the behaviors we see, it's symbolic. Psychologically, they're not aware of why they're doing what they're doing. It just feels right to them. It gives them a sense of power; it's sexually gratifying, exciting."

"Exciting, huh? Man, I just don't get that."

"Then congratulations, Burden. You can tell your ex you're not just a jackass, you're a normal jackass."

"Thanks." He glanced sideways at her. "I think."

"Don't mention it."

Vail was back on task—and headed into the living room to look at the lamps' electrical cords. "Based on your knowledge of the neighborhood and your discussions with the neighbors, do you think the UNSUB made conscious efforts to avoid detection? That's Unknown Subject—"

"No shit. I know what an UNSUB is." Burden grabbed hold of the paisley patterned velour couch and pulled it away from the long living room wall. "To answer your question, I'd say absolutely he did. No one heard anything. No signs of a struggle, no evidence of a forceful break-in."

"So whatever method he used to gain entry, it was smart—and effective."

"Judging by the results, it appears so."

Burden followed an electrical cord along the length of the wall to a clock on the side table. "What are you thinking?"

"I'm trying to build the offender profile."

"And?"

"And I'll let you know what I think as soon as I have something intelligent to say."

"So that could be…never?"

Vail swung to face Burden. "Ooh. Good one. I think I'm gonna like you." Then she walked into the kitchen where multiple appliances stared back at her. "Any marks on the wrist?"

Burden followed her in and shifted the blender aside. "Restraints were used, if that's what you're getting at. Figured it was part of the torture ritual."

*Just torture? More like sexual torture.* But Vail absorbed that fact, and assumption, without comment. After a moment's thought, she said, "First thoughts here...but it looks like we're looking for a sexual sadist."

"So," Burden said, "that would be the first intelligent thing you've said?"

*Boy, this guy's good. He's definitely got game.* "Yeah," Vail said. "That'd be it."

"And you're saying he's a sexual sadist because of the torture?"

"Because of the *sexual* torture. The scumbag's inflicting physical or emotional pain—to elicit a response from the victim. It's a response he finds sexually gratifying. Now you can have torture without sexual gratification, but a sexual sadist, by definition, has to have a living victim. Make sense?"

Burden's face was contorted. "So he did this to her while she was alive?" He shivered, as if he had bitten into a lemon rind. "Honestly, none of this shit 'makes sense' to me."

*I know how you feel.* "The husband," Vail said. "You said he's an attorney. I assume he's got no criminal record."

"I'm sure there's some crude joke here about lawyers, but no, Mr. Anderson's got a clean sheet. Like I said, we've got an APB out on him."

"I'm trying to eliminate him as a suspect."

Burden pushed the toaster back in place, then gave a final look around the townhouse. "Looks like all plugs and appliances are intact. Which means he probably brought the electrical cord with him."

"So," Vail said, "he's either killed before or he intends to kill again. He might also be keeping the tool as a reminder, kind of like a trophy. A way for him to relive the murder."

"I thought a trophy was something of the victim's, like a lock of hair or a photo."

"It can be anything," Vail said. "Something that has psychological significance to the offender that allows him to relive the kill. I'm not saying this electrical cord is a trophy, but it could function for him like one. Or it could be that it's a tool in his murder kit."

Burden sat down heavy in a soft overstuffed living room chair while Vail walked over to the bay windows. The fog was lifting a bit. She could now see more of the Golden Gate's tower.

"You think this UNSUB will kill again?"

Vail watched the fog roll by. It moved swiftly, tumbling and swirling, like time-lapse photography.

"Unless there's something else you want to see here, we should get over to the morgue."

She pulled herself away from the window. "Drive me around the neighborhood a bit so I can get a feel for the area."

"One thing'll be obvious," Burden said as he pushed out of the deep chair. "This isn't the kind of place you'd expect something like this to happen."

Vail chuckled. "Thing is, Burden, this shit can happen anywhere. Anytime. To anyone." Vail glanced back at the bedroom. "Even, unfortunately, to old ladies."

# 7

January 20, 1958

*366½ Service Creek Road*
*Independence Township*
*Aliquippa, Pennsylvania*

Walton MacNally blew on his hands, then replaced his worn leather glove. He looked over at Henry, who was fiddling with the radio dial. "Shut the radio, son. It's time."

"But it's Elvis, Dad."

MacNally tilted his head but did not reply. His stern look said enough. Henry reached over and turned off the radio.

"This isn't exactly the way I thought we'd be spending your tenth birthday," MacNally said. "I figured we'd have a party, with candles and friends and lots of gifts."

"But I don't have any friends."

MacNally felt a deep sadness wash over him. Henry was right. They had moved so often it was impossible to forge meaningful relationships. Just when he'd settled into a school, they had to uproot and go somewhere else to find work. It was a process they had done more than a dozen times over the past three years, and it was getting tough to continue the trend. He didn't want Henry to grow up without friends, because they gave depth and meaning to a child's youth.

He was no expert on children, for sure. Henry was his one and only source of knowledge. His experience was limited, and god knows he'd made a ton of mistakes. But he always did everything within his power to give his son a happy childhood.

MacNally had seen a headline in a local paper a couple of years ago that the police had charged a man for Doris's murder, a drunkard who had robbed another neighborhood home and killed the man who lived there. MacNally wanted to see the guy, shake him, spit on him— yell at him, maybe. Tell him the pain he had caused. But what would that do? Doris was gone, and his and Henry's lives had been irreparably changed.

In the intervening years, MacNally had become Henry's one and only friend. They fished together, hunted together, bowled together and, more recently, even snuck into a few Pittsburgh Pirates ball games at Forbes Field. But he knew that was no substitute. It was simply the best he could do.

Lately, though, his best was not enough. Money was short, food was scarce, and work was not just sporadic, it was almost nonexistent.

"I know you don't have any friends, son. And I'm sorry about that. If we didn't have to move so much, things'd be different. A lot of things."

"I don't need friends. I've got you."

Tears formed in MacNally's eyes. He turned away so Henry wouldn't see him cry. His thighs were so cold they were numb. He rubbed his gloved hands across the threadbare denim of his Levi's to get some feeling back into his legs. It gave him something to do while he composed himself.

"I wanna turn the radio back on," Henry said.

"We need to go through things one more time." MacNally pulled at his muffler, straightening out the folds in the thick wool where it crossed his neck. "Do you remember what you're supposed to do?"

Henry rolled his eyes. "Sit here and wait for you to come back. Keep a watch on the bank's entrance. When I see you come out, I put the car in drive. You get in and I floor it."

"Yeah, but don't press the pedal too hard too fast. Do it just like we practiced, okay?"

Three weeks ago, MacNally had taken Henry to a parking lot in a Pittsburgh suburb, where he taught his son how to handle a Chevy just like this one. Henry was tall for his age, just like his father, and had no difficulty reaching the pedals. They practiced for a solid week in secluded parking lots until he had demonstrated good control of the vehicle, then graduated to streets, after dark, that saw little traffic.

When they abandoned that Chevy—they'd stolen it in Florida and had been driving it too long for MacNally's comfort—he was intent on finding as close a match as possible to ensure Henry would be able to handle it properly under pressure.

"It's important we do this right. It's dangerous. But we need the money for food. We don't have much of a choice. Besides, banks have a lot of money, they aren't gonna miss the few bucks we're gonna take." He reached over and brushed back Henry's dirty blond hair. "And I'm gonna buy you a birthday present. Tomorrow, as soon as we get to a safe place." What was safe, MacNally didn't know. But he didn't want his son to be nervous. "What do you want?"

"I don't want nothing.'"

"*Any*thing. You don't want anything."

"Okay. Sorry."

"So c'mon. What would you like?"

Henry looked around a moment, thinking. "An Elvis record."

"Nah, we'll get you something better than that. It's your tenth birthday. How about a bike?"

Henry sat up straight. "Really?"

"If we do this right. Yeah. I'll get you a bike."

"I never had a bike. Can it be a Royce Union?"

"Sure."

"A black one?"

MacNally smiled. "If that's what you want. Black it is." He looked at his watch, then leaned forward in his seat and let his eyes roam the street ahead and behind them. "I don't know how long we can sit around in this car. And I don't know how good the cops are in this city. We've just gotta do it and get as far away as fast as possible. You ready?"

"Ready."

MacNally pulled his gaze over to his son. "Okay then. Just like we planned. I'm going to pull up in front and when I get out, you move behind the wheel." He got a nod from Henry, then he drove a block east and took an open curb spot in front of Township Community

Savings Bank. He shoved the gear into Park, then looked out the window at the blue and black TCS logo on the brick building.

MacNally took one last glance at Henry, gave the boy a smile and a wink to mask his own building apprehension, and then popped open his door.

# 8

V ail followed Inspector Burden into the Hall of Justice, home
to the SFPD Homicide Detail. They passed through the
metal detectors, then walked across the vast seventies style
lobby, which was appointed with green marble walls and a thirty-foot
ceiling.

After reaching the fourth floor, they hung a right toward Room
400. Above a set of opaque glass doors, anachronistic metal Helvetica
lettering spelled out Bureau of Inspectors.

Inside, Burden led Vail through the administrative area, where
several blue-walled cubicles were arranged behind a maple countertop.
Mounted over the entryway that led to the office space where the
inspectors worked, a hand-carved wood sign, with irregularly shaped
letters, read Bureau of Investigation.

"The facility is tired but the people are top notch."

"Tired," Vail said. "That must be California-speak for 'old and
desperately in need of renovation. Ten years ago.'"

Burden chuckled as he led her to his cubicle. "No argument from
me. Money's tight, so we put it into stuff that helps us clear cases."

"Money well spent, for sure."

"Have a seat." He motioned to a black fabric chair, then sifted
through the messages on his desk. Off to the side sat a thick
paperback book of sudoku puzzles.

Vail picked it up and thumbed through the pages. "Don't tell me you're into this."

Burden moved a file, then found an envelope and pulled it out. "Some people are addicted to cigarettes. Drugs. Booze. Me? I'm addicted to sudoku. Keeps my mind sharp. Maybe that's why I wanted to be a detective. What we do, it's like solving complex puzzles, right?" He handed Vail the envelope. "Your copy of the case file."

Vail took it and removed the folder. "Thanks."

Burden's phone buzzed. He consulted the screen and said, "Mrs. Anderson's waiting for us. And she's getting cold."

"To quote Twain, it's summer in San Francisco, right?"

"That's not the quote, Karen."

"Yeah, whatever. I got the gist, didn't I?"

VAIL AND BURDEN WALKED INTO the morgue and met the medical examiner, Dr. Beth Chow. She disposed of pleasantries with a wave of her hand, then pulled back the sheet on the chilled Maureen Anderson.

Anderson looked surprisingly good for her age. That is, if you could get past the severe bruising and wounds.

"The discoloration, the ecchymoses all over the face," Vail said. "Would you agree that indicates Mrs. Anderson was still alive when the trauma was inflicted? And that she lived for a bit after the beating?"

"That'd be correct," Chow said.

The ME was a stout woman, thick in the neck with the puffiness of adipose tissue smoothing out the normal age-induced facial wrinkles.

"Inspector Burden tells me she was tortured. With the electrical cord."

"Yes. I think it may've caused the heart attack that ultimately killed her. Disrupted her heart rhythm, which wasn't good to begin with."

"How do you know that?" Vail asked.

Chow moved back a step and pointed to a bulge below the woman's left collarbone. "Implanted pacemaker."

"I thought it was a multiple COD," Burden said.

Chow flexed her gloved fingers. "Yes and no. We're splitting hairs, really. The blows to the head were so violent that the trauma caused a great deal of bleeding between the surface of the brain and the bony skull—which obviously can't expand. So the bleeding compressed the brain tissue, causing massive dysfunction. And all that was happening around the time that her heart stopped. Regardless, the damage to the cortex from the pressure it was under would've been deadly on its own."

"Brain damage," Burden said.

"Rather severe."

Vail leaned over the body to view the head wounds. "And the penetration?"

"The sexual penetration came first. Condom, no semen. And she was sodomized, rather brutally. Substantial injury to her internal organs. It was an angry attack."

Vail looked up at Chow. "I think we should refrain from classifying it as emotional, or not, for now."

Chow chuckled. "Her uterus was torn to shreds. All her sexual organs, for that matter. And the liver, too. I don't think it was a friendly act."

"The liver was damaged?" Vail asked, straightening up. "That's like...what, a foot up into her abdominal cavity?"

"He used an umbrella, Agent Vail." Chow said it with disdain, then shook her head. "Whether anger was involved on the killer's part, you're right. I can't say. I'll let you people determine that. But what I can tell you is that for Mrs. Anderson it was, unequivocally, an extremely unpleasant death."

Vail clenched her jaw, trying to wipe the violent image from her brain. A moment passed before she asked, "Which came first? What did he do to her first?"

"Based on the bruising and capillary bleeding, I'd have to say he raped her first, then sodomized her, then he kicked her, then he burned and shocked her with the wires."

"Jesus Christ," Burden mumbled. "This guy...when we catch him...if there ever was a guy who could serve as the poster child for the death penalty, this one'd be it."

Vail could not pull her eyes from the corpse. "Couldn't have put it better, Burden."

The three of them stood there a moment before the inspector's cell phone began vibrating. He answered it, listened, and then said, "We'll be right there." He hung up and turned to Vail. "My partner found the husband."

# g

Walton MacNally felt the glass door behind him close, springing against his buttocks. It nudged him forward, as if it were the survival portion of his brain urging him on, telling him that if he did not complete this act, he and his son would go without food.

Could it really be that simple? Was the money in Township Community Savings there for his taking?

Yes. Sometimes society provided for those who were less fortunate. Wasn't that in the Bible? It had to be. It made so much sense.

MacNally let his eyes roam around the bank's interior. Women with reading glasses perched on their noses and coifed beehive hairstyles counted money, stamped slips, and chatted politely with their customers. It was a small institution, with wooden desks to his right and doors along the far wall ahead of him.

MacNally walked in slowly, glancing around, looking for security guards. Were they armed? He had no idea. He realized now that he had not thought this through very well. He had been so focused on how he would get away—and preparing Henry for driving the car— that he hadn't devoted any time to figuring out how he would even get the money. Could he merely go up and demand it? Can it be that simple?

He walked over to a desk that stood thirty feet from the wall of tellers. The nameplate read G. Yaeger, but Mr. or Mrs. Yaeger was apparently on a break at the moment. Next to a blotter that sported messages and notes along its edges sat a flyer that read, Introducing New Rates for 1958, with the text below urging customers to place their money in a certificate of deposit. At the edge of the blotter in front of him lay a gold Cross ballpoint pen. He picked it up, turned the advertisement over, and scrawled, in nervous caps:

THIS BANK IS BEING ROBBED. I DON'T WANT TO SHOOT ANYONE BUT I WILL IF I HAVE TO. PUT ALL YOUR MONEY IN A BAG. DO IT QUICKLY AND DON'T SAY A WORD.

MacNally looked around again. There—about a hundred feet away, an overweight man with graying hair wearing a uniform and octagonal cap stood near the end of the line of tellers. His head was down, reading what appeared to be a newspaper. From this angle, MacNally couldn't tell if he had a sidearm.

He turned back to his note and reread it. The threat of shooting them was good. MacNally did not have a gun—he had never even held one—but the woman with the money didn't know that. Still, to "sell it," he had to convince her with the look on his face. Anger was the key. He needed to channel the pain he felt most nights as he lay awake in bed picturing his wife lying on the floor of his home, murdered. He closed his eyes and thought of the man who had killed her, who had turned his life upside down.

His heart raced. Perspiration prickled his scalp.

He really did not want to do this. He had never taken anything from anyone that didn't belong to him. Yet so much had been taken from him, and Henry, what was a little money? Money was replaceable. Doris was not.

But they needed food and shelter, and MacNally had to take care of it. He didn't see a choice.

He opened his eyes, tightened his lips, tensed his hands.

MacNally scooped up the note and marched over toward the other customers and took his place in line. As he stood there waiting, he realized he didn't have anything to wrap across his face. Did that matter? He was going to leave town right away. Still… He should've thought of this. What if the teller described him to police?

His eyes darted around for something—a hat, a kerchief, anything that would cover all or a portion of his face. *His muffler.* He pulled it off his neck and tossed it over the opposing shoulder, draping it across his nose and mouth. It was cold out, so he wouldn't look out of place, and although half his features were still visible, it was enough to provide doubt in a witness's mind.

"Next," called a smiling woman in her late fifties. She was ten feet away. All he had to do was hand over the note.

MacNally clenched his jaw, put his head down, and walked forward.

# 10

urden pulled his gray Ford Taurus into the parking lot that served the Exploratorium and Palace of Fine Arts entrance. Vail swung her legs out of the car and rose, then craned her head skyward. Ahead of her were groupings of thick, Corinthian columns that stretched more than thirty feet into the sky.

"What is this place?"

"The Palace of Fine Arts. Part of an exposition the city had in 1915."

Vail knew that voice. She turned and saw a man in a black overcoat sporting a crew cut, a Marlboro dangling from his lips. "Inspector... Friedberg, right?"

The man grinned and approached with his right hand extended.

Vail took it and shook. "My personal historian."

Burden came around the vehicle. "You two know each other?"

"I was out here a couple of months ago on another case. Friedberg helped out on a cold case of his."

"More like frozen. And she cleared it for me. Ain't that a goddamn kick?" He pulled the cigarette out and expelled a wisp of smoke from the side of his mouth. "A dozen years working the case, I got a big goose egg. Then she blows into town and in a week, she solves it."

"The task force solved it," Vail said. "I was just part of the team. But let's hope we clear this one just as fast."

"Speaking of which," Burden said, "what's the deal with the husband? Where is he?"

"Follow me." Friedberg led the way through the path between the two large stands of columns.

"You said this place was the Palace of…what?"

"Fine Arts," Friedberg said.

"What's it for?" Vail asked. "And don't say 'fine arts,' or I'll have to kick you where it hurts."

Friedberg glanced at her over his shoulder. "The way you say it, I think you're capable of doing just that."

*You wouldn't be the first.*

"Ten of these buildings were built to celebrate the rebirth of San Francisco after the 1906 earthquake. They weren't supposed to be up more than a year, so they made 'em out of wood, plaster, and burlap. But people really liked them. I mean, they were freaking gorgeous, right? So they raised money and collected a gazillion signatures, and the city eventually made castings of the original structure. Around 1964, I think, they tore the whole thing down, then rebuilt it in concrete."

Burden, striding to catch up, shook his head. "I don't know how he keeps all these facts crammed into that brain of his."

"Is he like this with everything?" Vail asked.

"*He* is right here," Friedberg said. "And it's just Bay Area stuff. For the most part. What can I say, I like history. Shoulda gone into teaching. Instead I carry a gun and badge and try to teach lessons to the scum of San Francisco."

They had walked through the colonnade and were headed toward a large rotunda. Vail stopped and brought her hand to her forehead to shield her eyes against the bright gray, glaring sky as she looked at the columns. They were conjoined by a walkway of sorts, with what appeared to be female figurines standing with their elbows draped across the top of the portico, as if peering over its uppermost boundary.

"It's quite beautiful." She swung her gaze to Friedberg. "But where's the husband?"

"In here." Friedberg led them into the rotunda, a large structure that dwarfed the pergola and served as its centerpiece.

"What's he afraid of," Burden asked. "That the killer's going to find him?"

Friedberg stopped walking. "Nope, that's definitely not a concern of his."

"Then why meet us here?" Burden asked. "Why not the local Starbucks?"

"I think the answer to that question'll be evident in a minute."

Vail peered up and around the vast structure, which she figured stretched over fifty feet into the air. Half a football field ahead, there appeared to be a body of water. "C'mon, Friedberg. You interrupted my morgue visit, and you just gotta know I cherish my time in those places. Where is this guy?"

Behind them, footsteps. Vail turned and saw a man dressed in a county uniform marked CSI. He was carrying a kit. She looked at Friedberg.

Friedberg took a long drag on his Marlboro, then pulled it from his lips and watched the smoke swirl on the breeze. He then tipped his head back and gestured above them with the cigarette. "Agent Vail, meet William Anderson."

Vail and Burden craned their necks and saw, twenty feet above them, an ashen elderly man. Tied to the base of a massive wine-red column.

"That's William Anderson?" Vail asked.

Friedberg brought his eyes down to meet Vail's. "Yes ma'am."

"But he's dead."

"Right again."

Vail looked away. "Shit."

# 11

MacNally pulled his shoulders back, shoved his right hand in a pocket, then looked up and met the teller's eyes.

"Good afternoon," she said with an absent-minded glance down at her watch. Then, with rote skill: "How may I help you?"

The woman's nameplate read, Mrs. Wilson. MacNally slid the note forward, keeping his gaze locked on the woman's face. Looking for a gesture toward the security guard, an unfriendly movement of any kind.

Her eyes rotated from her watch to the note, then quickly up to MacNally's face.

"It's real easy," MacNally said, hardening his brow. In a low voice, he said, "Do it. Now. Fast, or I start shooting. You'll be the first I kill."

Mrs. Wilson fumbled for her drawer, then pulled it open. Her hands were instantly unstable, trembling as she reached for the neat stacks of bills. "This is a very dangerous thing you're doing, Mister."

"I don't want any kinda commentary. Put it in a bag. Do it real quick. That's all I want you thinking about." He moved his arm, as if he was tightening his grip on the phantom weapon in his pocket.

"I don't have a bag," she said.

"And I don't want excuses. Put it in something. Fast." Fact was, though, he had zero leverage here. If she refused, or called his bluff, he could only run out empty-handed.

It was a moot point because Mrs. Wilson began stacking the bills in front of her. But she was moving slowly, as if stalling for time.

MacNally was trying to look calm, but how could he? He was perspiring from having the wool wrapped across his mouth and nose, and the pressure of the moment was no doubt making things worse. He stole a glance at the guard to his right. The man was folding the newspaper. He tossed it aside and looked up. MacNally swung his head away, back toward Mrs. Wilson.

Jesus Christ, hurry the hell up!

She grabbed a brown bag that was pushed to the side, removed a container, an apple, and a bottle of Coke. She stuffed the money into the sack, which was bulging from being so full, and attempted to roll the top closed.

"That's good," MacNally said. Glance at the guard. He was headed toward him. "Give it to me."

He snatched it, then took a breath to relax. He didn't want to look guilty, but he needed to get the hell out of there before Mrs. Wilson flagged the approaching man.

In five long strides MacNally reached the glass door. He pushed through, then continued to the curb, where Henry was sitting and the Chevy was idling. MacNally got in, Henry pressed the accelerator, and the heavy car swiftly left the curb.

Lacking skill, Henry hung a right faster than he was able to control. The rear of the sluggish vehicle swung wide, but he recovered control and seconds later they were speeding down the side street.

MacNally tore open a seam in the bag. "Whoo-hoo! We did it, son."

"Did we get enough?"

MacNally flipped through the combination of used and new bills, watching the twenties and hundreds as they fluttered by his eyes. "I...I don't know. Must be like a thousand. Something like that."

"A thousand *dollars*?" Henry asked, turning to steal a glimpse of the money in the remaining strains of twilight.

"Hey, hey," MacNally said, pointing at the road ahead of them. "Keep your eyes where I taught you." He shoved the bills back in the bag, then leaned back. "Yes, son. Dollars. Lots of dollars."

# 12

Vail shook her head. "Inspector, forgive me if this is a dumb question. But why the hell didn't you tell us he was dead?"

Friedberg squished his Marlboro against the outsized cement brick that made up the adjacent wall of the rotunda. "You didn't ask."

"It's not you," Burden said to Vail. "He sometimes gets like this."

"I forgot. You like puzzles. Guess you and Robert were made for each other."

"It does help," Burden said. He followed Friedberg, who was climbing a semicircular set of stairs that led to the column to which Mr. Anderson was fastened.

"Scene's yours," said an SFPD officer as he pushed away from the fifteen-foot concrete urn that he was leaning against. "ME's en route."

Behind them, the CSI set down his kit, then brought a Nikon DSLR to his face and began fiddling with the lens.

Vail looked up at the body. "COD?"

"Blunt force trauma to the head," Friedberg said. "Maybe kicked. But as to what actually killed him, there are bruises on his neck. I'd guess asphyxiation."

"How'd you find him?" Burden asked.

"One of the ice cream vendors saw him. As he got closer, he realized the guy wasn't moving. And he was, well, he looked kind of awkward just standing there like this."

*Yeah, no shit.*

Mr. Anderson's back was pressed upright against the square face of the column's base, his shoulders pinned back and his head erect. His right knee was slightly bent, but the left was locked straight.

Burden took a couple steps closer. "Is that—yeah, he's tied up with fishing line. Significance to that?"

"Too soon to speculate if there's a psychological component," Vail said. "Obvious first thought is that he didn't want anyone to see the bindings. He wanted it to look like the vic was just standing here."

"And why would that be?"

Vail shrugged. "Don't know. Maybe he liked the way it looked. Who knows…it could be significant, could mean nothing. If you're going to tie someone to a pole, or a column, the first thing you reach for is *not* gonna be fishing line. So, yeah, common sense says there might be something behind that. What it is, we don't know. Yet." She turned her body and took in the scene from their elevated perch. "Nice view up here."

"Are you trying to be funny?" Burden asked.

"I'm serious. The view, that could be significant, too. For now, we note it. Could just be that he was posing the vic and this seemed to be an intriguing spot to place him."

The CSI had taken all his photographs from ground level, and had now joined them near the body. "Did you see the drag marks?" He shifted the camera to his shoulder and shook Vail's hand. "Jackson. Rex."

"Vail. Karen. What drag marks?"

"Here, and down there." He pointed at two streaks in the disturbed loose dirt that lay atop the cement. He then led them to the steps they had climbed. Pointed. "See?"

Vail tilted her head. "Yeah. So he dragged the body." She walked back over to Mr. Anderson and looked up at it. "How much you think he weighs?"

"He's an old guy," Friedberg said. "And only about five-five. I'm guessing he's 135."

Burden nodded. "Seems about right. So, fireman's carry, over the shoulder. Not that big a deal to get him up here. Not the easiest thing in the world. But not impossible."

"Hold that thought a minute," Friedberg said. He pointed to something lying behind the column. "Rope."

Jackson had finished placing markers and a ruler beside, and then shooting photos of, the drag marks. He joined Friedberg, snapped pictures of the coil of yellow rope, and then the inspector gathered it up in gloved hands and examined it.

"Looks like the kind used for climbing, or search and rescue," Jackson said. "Braided nylon sheath, probably over a nylon strand core. And it's frayed." He looked around and said, "If you're going to use a rope, you need a pulley-type system. Or an anchor."

A moment later, Burden knelt in front of the massive concrete pot. "I think I found that pulley."

Jackson shot photos of the lower portion of the urn, which was round, slightly ridged, and narrow at its base. "I'm guessing these yellow particles here are nylon fragments."

They looked at the rope, then at the colored specks dotting the rough surface of the pedestal.

"So," Friedberg said, "the UNSUB wrapped the rope around this thing and pulled the body up from below. Then what about the drag marks?"

"Sometimes we see what we want to see," Vail said. "And sometimes we don't have all the answers to reach a valid conclusion."

"Right," Jackson said. "Maybe they're not drag marks. Document and figure it out later."

"Pretty ingenious, if that's what he did," Burden said.

"Given the type of rope he used," Friedberg said, "any chance this guy's a mountain climber?"

"Yeah," Vail said. "There's a chance. But I'd say a small one. Without other hobby-specific equipment, like those anchors Jackson mentioned, the kind climbers hammer into the rock face, or footprints from special types of climbing boots, I think we just have to look at this rope as, well, rope—sturdy, reinforced rope. The kind that'd help the offender accomplish his task."

Vail stood there a moment working the scene through her mind. She swiveled a bit, looking around, then said, "From what I'm seeing here, it's safe to conclude this offender planned the kill—and the location and positioning of the body. So if he scoped out the place, he's been here more than once. Maybe someone saw him, a regular— you said an ice cream vendor found him. If the guy's here a lot, maybe he saw someone looking around, doing things the typical tourist doesn't do." She swung back to Burden. "Cameras?"

"I'll have to check on that. Maybe in the parking lot. Nothing in here, I don't think."

Vail stepped over to the body. A large number 37 was scrawled in black marker across the man's forehead. "Any San Francisco relevance to the number 37?" Vail asked.

The inspectors thought a moment. "There's a Pier 37."

"What's there?"

"It's on the Embarcadero, near North Beach," Burden said. "Other than that, not much. It's small, not commercialized like 39 and 35 are."

"What else?"

"Golden Gate Bridge was completed in 1937," Friedberg said.

*That's not it.* Vail sucked on her cheek. "Anything else?"

"It's a MUNI route," Burden said. "Public transportation. Starts at the Haight, I think."

"The what?" Vail asked. "The hate?"

"H-a-i-g-h-t," Friedberg spelled. "Famous area of the city. It's kind of considered the melting pot of the sixties hippie movement, when it was a haven for drugs, cheap rooms, and plunging property values. It's had a mixed history. It's still kind of bohemian."

"Bohemian," Vail said. "Hippies." *This isn't helping.*

Burden moved in front of the body and looked at the forehead marking. "Don't forget the painted ladies."

*Painted ladies.* "Is that an old case?"

Burden grinned. "Victorian homes. Colorfully painted rowhouses. They're called painted ladies. They're really kinda nice."

"I don't think so," Vail said. "Thirty-seven's gotta have some other meaning." A moment later, she tapped Jackson on the shoulder. "Rex, can you process Mr. Anderson so we can cut him down? I want to get a look at his back. If he was pulled up with that rope, we're going to see scrape marks on the skin and the clothing. His front looks clean."

Friedberg had gone quiet. He was staring out at the Bay, his back to them. "This doesn't look right to me."

"How do you mean?" Vail asked.

He turned to face them. "Well, think about it a minute. If you saw this body here, and his wife's body at their townhouse—but they weren't husband and wife—would you think it was the same killer? Or just two unrelated murders, killed by two different killers? Point is, is it the same guy who offed both Andersons?"

"Maybe we've got two killers," Burden said. "Working together, each with his own—what do you call it? Signature?"

"Ritual," Vail said. "And that scenario is certainly possible." She stopped, thought a moment.

Burden tilted his head back. "Ritual. I remember that term from that violent crime symposium you people did out here in '06."

"I'm sure it was discussed," Vail said. "Ritual refers to those things the offender does with the body, things that aren't necessary for him to pull off the crime without getting caught. They're the things that tell us the most about the killer. It's not stuff he does consciously—well, I should say that he knows he's doing it, but he doesn't know why. To him, it's sexually gratifying. It fills the need to be powerful and in control. That could manifest as cutting off a body part or writing numbers on the face. Those peculiar behaviors form what we call ritual. So if we've got two psychopaths, each with his own deep-seated needs, yeah, we'd probably see two different crime scenes like these. But not necessarily."

"But if there were two of them," Friedberg said, "you wouldn't need the rope to hoist Mr. Anderson here up to the column. Much easier to just carry him. Really, the vic's so slight that even if there was only one of them, he could've still been able to carry him over his shoulder."

"I think there were two killers," Burden said. "Two different rituals, two different killers."

Vail winced. This was dangerous territory for a profiler. Behavioral analysis was a science, yes, but it was also dynamic, based on the totality of what you know at the time. You took the information, compared it to what you knew of other crime scenes and behaviors and killers, analyzed the psychology behind the actions taken by the killer and the victimology of your victims, and drew conclusions based on your assimilation of all those factors.

Asking for a quick and dirty analysis at this early stage risked forcing her into making incorrect assumptions. She didn't want to lose their confidence—or, worse, send the investigation in the wrong direction.

Vail crouched near the victim's feet. "Look at the raw facts. Husband and wife. Both murdered, both exhibiting blunt force trauma. The time frame is important, too, but for the moment, I think it's best to assume it's a single killer until proven definitively otherwise. Besides, despite the glaring differences in the scenes, we don't have anything solid that tells me we're looking at two offenders here. There are other explanations for the disparity."

"Such as?" Burden asked.

Vail frowned. "A high degree of variation in a series of crimes could also be because we've got an offender with a tremendous amount of impulsivity. Another thing to factor in is that psychopaths get bored. It's part of who they are. So they might vary their crimes just to keep it interesting."

"Fair enough," Friedberg said.

"Until we know what the emotions, or motivations, are behind these murders, we can't know if the offender's making a statement by brutally raping and torturing the woman and doing far less to the male—yet still killing him. It could simply be that his real target was the wife, and the husband got in the way. He could've knocked him unconscious, had his way with the wife, then decided to make a statement by displaying him here. Or maybe he tied the guy up and made him watch, like you thought back at the townhouse. Once he was done with the wife, he couldn't leave a witness, so he offed the husband."

"I'm not convinced," Burden said.

A bluster of wind snaked through the loose knit of Vail's sweater. She drew her arms in close to her body. "An important determination will be whether or not he planned out the husband's murder. Looks like he did. And if he did come here once or twice to sketch it all out, then we're looking at something more involved than what it appears to be right now."

Jackson folded up his kit. "I'm ready to cut him down. I'll need a hand."

"You got gloves?"

Jackson pulled two from his kit and passed them over to Vail, who unfurled them and shimmied her fingers in as Burden and Friedberg helped the CSI lower the body carefully to the ground.

"I don't think he's even one-thirty-five," Friedberg said. "He's pretty freaking light."

Jackson collected the nylon fishing line while Friedberg and Burden rolled the stiff corpse of William Anderson onto its side.

Vail tugged on Anderson's shirt and examined his back, then his neck and head. "Right here," she said.

Burden pointed to a spot lower on the body. "And there. Abrasions on the pants. The buttocks, and down by the shoes. The black leather's pretty chewed up. Probably from scraping along the cement facing as he was pulled up."

"How does he do this without anyone seeing?" Friedberg said. "I mean, it's gotta take a good three to five minutes to pull the body up with that rope."

Burden, still kneeling beside the body, swiveled around and took in the lay of the land. "Unless he did it at night, or the early morning hours. No one's around."

"If he's a psychopath," Vail said, "and I think that's likely, they're not nearly as affected by stress like you and I would be. So interacting with a dead body, out in public, wouldn't cause the UNSUB the kind of anxiety we'd feel. And that's why we often see a boldness to a psychopath's behavior, a brazenness. They just don't experience fear to the same depth that we do." She curled some hair behind her right ear. "Do we have a TOD on the wife's body?"

"About three hours before I called your boss," Burden said.

Friedberg adjusted the glove on his left hand. "So either the UNSUB kept Mr. Anderson around for a while, or he killed him at the same time and stored him somewhere till he was ready to...do this. Transport him here and tie him up."

Burden grumbled, "If it's the same guy."

"Doesn't make sense he'd kill the husband at the house," Vail said.

"Because…" Burden said.

"Because I'm assuming he planned all along to display the guy here. This was part of his plan. So why kill the guy at the house, then have to lug a dead body around? But if you could incapacitate him, tie him up and gag him, then have him walk wherever you want him to go, kill him closer to where we are, then pose him. It becomes a logistics issue."

"How so?" Friedberg asked.

"Transporting a dead body bears a high degree of risk for the offender, right? He's gotta drive around with a DB in his car. He gets stopped by a cop, he's got a big goddamn problem. So where's he gonna put it? Not in the backseat, in plain sight. Generally, the more risky it is, the more thrilling it is for these guys. So while he'd probably get off on the risk, there's a difference between it being thrilling and just plain stupid. So he'd have to put it in the trunk."

"Yeah, but lifting a DB out of a trunk isn't fun, and it isn't easy," Burden said.

"Right. So that's what I was saying. The best way to do this is to control him somehow. Using a gun, or a drug to make him drowsy, you can do pretty much what you want. Control is the key."

Friedberg looked up at the column where the body had been fastened. "Soon as the ME gets us a time and a definite cause of death, we'll be able to piece this all together. For now, we should look into the vics' backgrounds."

Vail lifted Anderson's right hand and examined the fingers. "No defensive wounds." She reached across the body and checked out the left. "Hmm." She stood up and looked out, through the columns ahead of her. "What's around here, in this area?" Vail asked.

Friedberg pointed. "Out ahead of us is a man-made lagoon. They do lots of weddings there. Navigating the seagulls can be a challenge."

As if on cue, a cacophony of birdsong built to a crescendo. Vail ducked as several gulls sped past her head and swept through the rotunda. "What the hell's that?"

"Every once in a while they go nuts. Hundreds of them." He gestured out over the expansive, irregularly shaped pond, where the large gray birds were diving and climbing, darting and swooping. "Lasts a minute or two, then they quiet down."

Over the water, the cloud of gulls eventually calmed, as Friedberg predicted.

"As I was saying," Friedberg continued. "There are homes along the perimeter. Expensive ones, well maintained. That building you saw when we parked, directly adjacent to the property, is the Exploratorium. Kind of a hands-on science museum."

*A science museum. Perfect.* "Let's head back there, I'll bet they've got some expensive equipment in there. With expensive equipment comes security cameras."

"Hang on a minute," Jackson said. "You may want to see this."

They gathered around the criminalist. His gloved fingers spread the hair on the back of Anderson's head, toward the base of his skull.

"Blood?" Burden asked.

"Looks like it. Bruising of the cranium. And over here," he said, gesturing at the throat. "Those marks you were talking about, anterior C-spine. I don't think they're finger impressions, but we'll know more once the ME examines him."

Friedberg said, "Just like the wife. Assuming it's the same UNSUB."

"Or," Vail said, "he could've struck his head on the cement while he was being pulled up on the rope. Or he could've fallen when he was killed. We don't know at this point."

Leaving Rex Jackson to finish his work, they headed back toward their cars.

As they entered the small parking lot, Vail stopped. "There." She nodded at a panoramic lens mounted atop the tall adobe-tinted Exploratorium building, near an inside corner overlooking the arched glass doors of the museum. She traced the line of sight to where she was standing, at the mouth of the Fine Arts entrance. "But that might be a problem." Below and in front of the building was a grouping of three gnarled and heavily leaved trees, partially blocking the view.

"We'll take what we can get," Friedberg said. He headed toward the entrance. "I'll get started on securing the tapes."

As Friedberg walked off, a bushy-haired man with iPod earbuds plugging his ears strolled in front of them. His hands were curled around a long bar that protruded from a rectangular shaped, three-wheeled cart, colorful stickers dotting its surface: Good Humor chocolate chip, Big Dipper, Popsicle Shots, Pink Panther, Scribblers, Snow Cone.

*An ice cream vendor discovered the body.*

"Hey, Robert! This the guy?" Vail asked, tipping her head in the direction of the vendor.

Friedberg cricked his neck, snatched a look at the man, and nodded.

Burden stepped in front of the man and held up his shield.

The vendor, who looked no more than twenty-two, pulled his right earbud free and, as he turned his head to reach for the left ear, his gaze found Vail. His eyes slid down her body. And his demeanor transformed. He straightened up. "Can I—do you need help with something?"

"Yeah. You are—?"

He narrowed his eyes and held out his hands palms up, indicating his cart. "An ice cream vendor."

"No," Vail said. "I got that. I meant, what's your name?"

"Oh. Oh. Alex Montague."

"Mr. Montague," Burden said, taking back control of the interview. "We understand you found the body in there."

Montague reluctantly pulled his eyes from Vail. "Yeah, dude was just hangin' out there. Looked kinda weird. As I got closer, I was, like, what the fuck. He ain't movin'. So I wheeled up far as I could, and well, it looked to me like the dude was dead. I mean, I'm no expert or nothin'."

"That's right," Vail said. "The dude was dead. You're a sharp guy. Expert or not."

He didn't like that retort, because he stopped looking at her with lust. He was actually frowning.

"So," Vail said. "We'd really like to know if you saw anyone in the area the past few days who didn't look right."

"Didn't look right?"

Burden shoved his credentials case into his jacket pocket. "Yeah. Like he didn't belong. Or he was doing stuff that a typical tourist doesn't do. Not just a tourist. Anyone, really, who might come around here."

Montague shrugged.

"You been doing this a while?" Vail asked. "Selling ice cream here?"

"'Bout a year."

"Good. Then you've seen thousands, if not tens of thousands of people, visit this place. Based on what those people look like, have you seen anyone lately who looked out of place?"

"Out of place, how?"

*I wonder if brain cell transplants are possible yet. This kid needs some. Badly.*

As she was pondering how to get some meaningful answers from Alex Montague, a woman nudged up to the cart, brushing Vail aside.

"Excuse me," Vail said, not bothering to hide her annoyance. She tilted her head. "Can I help you?"

The woman lifted her eyebrows. "Oh. Yes. I'd like two snow cones and a chocolate sandwich. But if you've got lemon popsicles, I'll take that instead of one of the snow cones."

Montague opened his mouth to speak but Vail beat him to it. "Yeah, thing is, we're all out."

"Out? Of which?"

"Everything. Go find another ice cream cart."

The woman eyed Vail warily, then turned and walked off.

"What the fuck?" Montague said.

Vail stepped forward. "We're in the middle of an important conversation, Mr. Montague. We can have it here, and be done in a couple of minutes, or we can do it downtown."

"Downtown?" Montague said. "But we are downtown."

Vail clenched her jaw. "Just answer the question."

"Which question?"

Burden must have sensed Vail's building consternation, because he held up a hand. "Mr. Montague. Focus for a second and we'll be out of your hair. Did you see anyone suspicious the past few days? Maybe he was looking at the area around the rotunda, scoping things out, like maybe he was looking for a place to put a dead body."

"Oh," Montague said. "Oh, I see what you're gettin' at." He looked off a moment. "Mind if I?" He held up his iPod.

"Do we mind if you listen to music?" Vail asked. "While we're talking to you?"

"It'll help me remember."

Burden motioned with some fingers. "Go ahead."

Montague plugged his ears and glanced around. His head began bobbing with the beat.

"This is a new one on me."

Burden shrugged. "If it helps him concentrate, what's the harm?"

"I'm not a very patient person, Burden, and this—"

"There was a guy." Montague yanked the earbuds and said, "He was up in that same spot, looking around. And I remember thinking that it was strange. I mean, he didn't have a camera and he wasn't with anybody. Lots of times people will put their kids up on those steps and take pictures of 'em. And sometimes they'll go up there to get a different view of the columns—but again, they have cameras."

"What'd the guy look like?" Burden asked.

"Tall. He had a hoodie on." Montague stuck one earbud in and listened a few seconds. "Navy."

"He was in the Navy? Was there a logo on the sweatshirt?"

"No, no. His sweatshirt was dark blue. You know, *navy*."

"Right," Vail said. "Navy. Anything else you can remember? How tall was he?"

"Hard to say, because he was like up on that platform, or whatever you call it. He looked tall and kind of thin."

"Beard?" Burden asked. "Glasses? He walk with a limp?"

Montague shook his head. "I don't know, I kinda was trying to sell ice cream. Not the easiest gig in San Francisco in the summer."

Vail chuckled. "Mark Twain once said something about that."

Burden frowned at Vail and said to Montague, "Call us if you think of anything else. Or if you see the guy again."

As Burden handed Montague a card, Vail backed away, keeping her eyes on the entrance to the Palace of Fine Arts pergola.

Burden joined her a few seconds later. "What are you thinking?"

"Trying to figure out how he got the body in there without anyone seeing. Even late at night, or early in the morning, there's risk. I'm thinking he backed his car right into that parking spot," she said, pointing at an area at the mouth of the entrance.

"Open the trunk, pull out the body and drag it the fifty yards or so to the place where he wanted to display it." Burden glanced back over his shoulder at the security camera.

"If he really did plan this out, and if he knew about the camera, it's possible he could've hidden himself behind the car so the camera wouldn't pick him up. But we might be able to get a plate. Or at least a make and model."

Friedberg pushed through the front door of the Exploratorium. In his hand was a DVD envelope. He held it up as he approached. "I've got a week's worth of footage."

"Let's take it back to your place," Vail said, "break out some popcorn and watch some movies."

# 13

January 31, 1958

*Columbia, Alabama*

Their take from the Township Community Savings haul was seven hundred and ninety dollars. Although it seemed like a lot of money, it did not last as long as MacNally had hoped or planned. After ditching the car in an abandoned lot fifty miles outside town, they hitchhiked with a trucker and spent a dozen or so quiet hours traveling south as both father and son fell asleep against one another, despite the chatter of music that poured from the radio. It was a selection Henry found to his liking: Elvis, Chuck Berry, the Shirelles, and some Tommy Dorsey thrown in. MacNally finally convinced Henry to lay his head down, and shortly thereafter both began snoozing.

Upon awakening, they found themselves sitting in a small-town gas station as the driver tended to his rig. MacNally chatted up the attendant and discovered they were in Alabama, a place he had seen once in a newsreel at the movies, but never visited.

He placed his hand on his jacket pockets, where he had shoved the money they had appropriated from the bank. He patted them down, and satisfied he had not dreamt their haul the night before, asked how far it was to the nearest city.

The man estimated it was only about a mile or so down the road, so MacNally told Henry he thought it was best if they thanked the trucker and walked the rest of the way.

Two weeks after arriving in town, MacNally began plotting out their long-term plans. He had landed a job cleaning a local elementary school, but it fell short of being enough money to pay for room and board. They found a dive of a place to rent, a converted garage that had no heat and no plumbing.

Through one of the school parents, he heard of a local construction company that needed a hard worker who was good with his hands. MacNally had always prided himself on his sculpting abilities but had no formal training and had never found a way to channel his skills into a money-producing occupation. Building would be a cruder form of sculpting—but he would be utilizing his natural gifts and it figured to pay better than his current job.

That afternoon, he asked for some time off to tend to a family emergency, and went to the construction site to talk to the foreman. He ended up speaking with Mr. Flaherty, the owner, as it was a smaller company than he had envisioned. The man explained that he had won the bid to build an addition to a home that belonged to a government commissioner in Dothan—and if he executed well, Flaherty could then tap the inner circle of a more affluent customer than usually sought his services, allowing him to elevate his business to the next level.

But Flaherty needed two additional workers and he had to find them fast. The architect had drawn plans and Flaherty was compelled to complete the renovation before the owner started in his new position at City Hall.

MacNally explained that he had never worked construction, but he was good with his hands, he possessed a keen attention to detail, he was a hard worker who learned quickly, was always on time and never left early. Flaherty asked him a number of questions, and then, apparently satisfied with MacNally's responses, said, "Be here tomorrow morning, seven o'clock sharp, ready to work." But then he pointed an arthritic index finger and said, "Don't disappoint, me, boy. Screw up, put me in a bad way, and I'll see to it that no one in town hires your ass again. You hear?"

MacNally took the threat in stride and assured Mr. Flaherty that he would not regret his decision. He quit his maintenance job and reported to the construction site at 6:45. It was then that he learned that the government official was someone far more important than he had figured: the recently elected mayor.

MacNally took a moment to gawk at the mayor's personal effects as he and a few other workers hung tarps to seal off the rooms where they would be working. MacNally had never met a politician, let alone been inside the home of a person as powerful as this man.

"Let's go, MacNally, get your ass moving," Flaherty called to him as MacNally's gaze roamed the bedroom with its woven lavender comforter, plantation shutters, and ruffled plum drapes. Such grandeur. Such wealth.

"Yes, sir," MacNally said.

The next two weeks passed quickly. MacNally learned to dig and pour foundations, and made friends with one of the other men, who specialized in two-by-four framing, ventilation ducting, and electrical work. MacNally figured that in the coming months, he would become proficient in a variety of skills that could translate into other jobs. The more he learned, the more valuable he would become to an employer—whether that be Mr. Flaherty or someone else. He spent his lunch times chatting with his new friend, and had already gathered more practical information about construction than he remembered ever learning about any subject in school—the sole exception perhaps being mathematics.

MacNally felt like a contributing member of society again. Standing trial for his wife's murder was becoming a distant, though still vivid, memory. The bank robbery was behind him, and he had received his first paycheck.

But on the third Monday of his work with Flaherty, the boss whistled him aside. And he did not look pleased.

"Sit down," Flaherty said, and pointed at a tree stump that was due to be removed from the ground later in the day. Flaherty remained standing. "The mayor called me into his office this morning," he said, his arms folded across his thick chest. "Wanna know why?"

MacNally did not know what to say. He nodded but said nothing.

"He asked me when we started this here job if I knew my employees real good. I told him all 'cept two, new men I recently hired. He asked me for their names. Yours was one of 'em."

MacNally felt a sense of dread building deep in his belly. He tried not to show it on his face. "So?" he asked.

"So the mayor had someone look into y'all. And it seems you were arrested for—get this—*murdering* your wife three years ago."

"Yeah, but—"

"I'm not interested in excuses, MacNally. I told you, you do anything that screws me over—"

"But I didn't do anything, sir. I was not guilty. A jury cleared me. And they arrested someone else last year."

"Mayor don't care. He don't want no murderer, or even a guy accused of murder, workin' on his house, 'round his family. Almost fired my ass. I had to beg him not to. You hear me? I coulda lost this goddamn job. I need it, I need the money."

"Me, too."

"Well that's too doggoned bad, ain't it? You shoulda told me."

MacNally rose from the stump. He threw his arms out to his sides. "Told you what? I didn't kill my wife and they let me go. A jury said I wasn't guilty."

"Yeah, but they didn't say you was *innocent*, neither, did they now?"

MacNally furrowed his brow.

"Here's your pay," Flaherty said as he dug around in his pocket. He pulled out a wad of cash and peeled off a bill. "For this morning. Now leave. Don't come back no more. I need to tell the mayor you're history."

*History.*

History was cruel for Walton MacNally. And, as he was learning, history was not easily purged.

MacNally first went back to the school and asked for his maintenance job back. But it had been filled, and they were pleased with their replacement. They did not appreciate being shorthanded for a week while they sought for, and interviewed, new applicants.

After spending the two-plus weeks' earnings MacNally had made working for Flaherty, and then dipping into their savings—from the bank haul—MacNally was becoming increasingly frustrated at his inability to land another job. Flaherty had kept his word, and had let it be known that MacNally had nearly cost him a customer that was vital to his company's survival...and that he had stood trial for murdering his wife.

In a small town, MacNally did not stand a chance of escaping the wrath of a well-liked and established business owner who had been burned. And killing your wife was…well, frowned upon, even if no one bothered to ask about the details of something remotely important like a jury's verdict. He was guilty in the municipal court of public scorn.

With no other work history MacNally could lean on for references—even the school would freely tell a caller he had left them without notice—he realized he needed to use a bogus identity to prevent a prospective employer from finding out about his prior arrest. The truth and disposition often did not matter; he was a marked man and would be so for a long time, if not the rest of his life. Not having experience with such things, he didn't know what to expect—how long it'd remain an albatross, or if someone would be willing to invest the time and thought to truly evaluate his particular situation.

Flaherty's retort that a not guilty verdict did not mean innocent was a distinction MacNally did not fully grasp at the moment, but in the subsequent days, as he thought about it, he saw where the man was coming from. But seeing the difference did not matter. No amount of talking was going to persuade Flaherty, he knew that. Going back to the man was out of the question. And he did not dare attempt to speak with the mayor.

MacNally was also concerned about getting Henry an education, as he was certain his son was falling behind in his schooling by now.

MacNally did his best to work with Henry on his reading and math skills using the local library's resources. But he had to be careful not to call attention to themselves—one person had already asked Henry where he went to school, which led to a very uncomfortable silence while MacNally stammered something about being new to town and there being a delay in getting him "signed up."

Three weeks after losing his construction job, MacNally explained to Henry that unless things changed soon, they would likely have to leave and find a more affordable city where, even if he couldn't land a decent paying job, their money would last longer.

Days passed, yet they did not discuss it again. MacNally figured it was easier to stay where they were than to move into a new place with more unknowns than they had now. For the time being, it was better to remain in Alabama and continue trying to better their situation.

He resorted to going door-to-door, offering to do odd jobs as a handyman for cash. This worked at times, and at times not. His tax-free pay was less than it had been when he was working at the school, forcing them deeper into their savings.

One day, MacNally came home to find Henry sitting on the floor against the wall with his mother's brooch in one hand—and a bar of soap pressed to his nose. It was round and tinted pink, with a beveled, decorative edge. The soap they used was a plain white square bar.

"Where'd you get that?" MacNally asked.

Henry's brow furrowed. He moved the soap behind his back. "Somewhere."

"Somewhere?" MacNally moved closer. "Where'd you get the money?"

"I didn't need no money. I took it. From a store. That one in town, Chuck's Five and Dime."

MacNally knelt down in front of his son. "Henry. Taking things from stores without paying for them isn't right."

"We took money from the bank. No difference."

"There is a difference." MacNally thought a moment, searching for a way to explain it. Was there really a distinction? He sat on the dirt floor beside Henry. "We stole that money because we had to. We need to eat, we need a place to sleep. There was no choice. I don't want to steal. But..." He did not know if Henry could comprehend the concept of having an unfair and soiled reputation hung around your neck without the ability to remedy it.

He flashed on the irony of being a handyman—with the capability of fixing a variety of things—yet being unable to repair his own reputation.

"Son, we had to rob that bank. You didn't need to steal that soap. We've got other soap. And even if we didn't, you could live dirty. But you can't live without food. You understand?"

"I needed the soap."

"No, you wanted the soap." Could a ten year old comprehend the difference between "need" and "want"?

"No. I needed it."

MacNally extended a hand. "Give it to me. I'm going to bring it back to Chuck's."

"No!" Henry scooted away. "You're not takin' it from me."

MacNally leaned back. What was going on with his son? His body language, the constriction of his pupils—over a bar of soap? "You said you need it. Why? What's so special about it?"

Henry slowly brought the bar from behind his back, then wrapped it between two hands. He held it up to his father's face.

MacNally sniffed. And he instantly understood. The scent was nearly identical to the perfume Doris had sprayed on herself every morning. "You smell Mom."

Henry brought it back to his nose and closed his eyes.

MacNally fought back tears. He composed himself, took a breath and then said, "You can keep it. But we're going to go over to Chuck's and pay him for it."

TWO MONTHS PASSED. ON AN uncharacteristically sunny day, Henry asked if they could go downtown to look at bicycles. Although MacNally had not brought up his birthday promise to Henry, it bothered him and he felt increasing pressure to make good on it.

Money was a daily concern, and the last thing MacNally was planning to spend it on was a bicycle—unrelenting guilt or not. "We move around a lot, Henry. Sometimes we have to get up and go, without a lot of planning. Having a bike isn't a good idea."

"But you promised. My birthday present. Remember?"

"We can't take it with us if we have to leave."

Henry looked down at his hands, where he was rolling a Bazooka bubblegum wrapper between his forefinger and thumb.

"You won't be happy if we spend our money on a bike and then have to leave it when we go."

Henry narrowed his eyes. "Then it's about the money."

"No. Yes. It's both."

"You didn't say 'if' we had to go. You said 'when.' Are we leavin'?"

Henry was a bright kid—smarter than MacNally remembered being at this age. "I don't know. But I think it's likely we're going to have to move on. I will get you a bike, just not now. Maybe when we settle down. When I find steady, good-paying work. We can buy one then. Okay?"

Henry twisted his lips, but did not reply.

Three weeks later, as MacNally and his son were finishing supper at the rickety wood table that served as both a dinner table and desk, MacNally set down his fork. They were going to move again, he told Henry—but before they left town, they needed some traveling money because their savings had nearly been exhausted.

"There's a bank," MacNally said. "First National—"

"I've seen it," Henry said. "When?"

MacNally was surprised that his son was keyed in on their needs and the means for obtaining that which would efficiently deliver the solution. Henry was not only smart, he seemed wise—and practical—beyond his ten years. "I have to go by there to check it out. But maybe tomorrow night if it looks good."

Henry thought a moment, then said, with a shrug, "If that's what you say we gotta do, we'll do it."

MacNally had, indeed, decided that that was what they had to do. They lived and died by his decisions…it was a concept he found frightening. He was responsible for their well-being—for providing food. Money. And shelter.

He cleared the plates from the table, then began planning their next job.

# 14

Vail sat at the counter in front of monitors in the Photography Lab at the Hall of Justice. On-screen, a static camera angle displayed images of the Exploratorium parking lot. At its upper rightmost edge was the Palace of Fine Arts entrance.

"This gives us a pretty decent view of the area that leads down the path into the rotunda," Burden said.

Friedberg stuck an unlit cigarette between his lips. "Assuming he came in this way."

An hour later, Vail rose from her chair. "I used to have more patience for this. Let's fast forward to the most likely times for him to have come by. If we don't find anything, we can always rewind."

"Fine," Burden said. He pressed the remote and the digital tape sped forward to 2:00 AM. "So just curious. Is boots-on-the-ground, grind-it-out police work below your pay grade?"

Vail focused on the screen. "You're trying to pick a fight with me. Not a good idea. You'll lose." She pointed. "Look. One of those ice cream vendors."

On-screen, a hooded man was pushing the multistickered carts into the entrance to the colonnade.

"Well that's a bit bizarre, huh?" Friedberg asked.

*Just a bit.* "Selling ice cream in San Francisco in the frosty cold of summer is strange enough. But at 2 AM?"

"I think we got us a suspect," Burden said.

They watched as the man disappeared off-screen.

"Devil's Advocate," Friedberg said. "So the guy's an oddball, pushing around the ice cream cart at all hours of the morning. How does that make him a suspect?"

"It doesn't," Burden said. "Unless he's got something of interest inside that cart. Like Mr. Anderson."

"Fast forward," Vail said. "Let's see if we can catch him coming back out. Maybe we'll get lucky with a face shot."

Friedberg grabbed the remote and seconds later the numerals on the digital readout were morphing faster than the eye could discern. He stopped when the front of the cart appeared again, then backed it up ten seconds.

"What's the time code?" Vail asked. "How long was he there?"

Friedberg consulted the screen. "Nine minutes forty-nine seconds."

"Nine minutes. Is that enough time to use that rope to raise the body up to that ledge?"

"Plenty of time—it's a lot longer than you think. You can get a lot of stuff done in nine minutes."

Burden gestured with a finger at the screen. "Run it in slow motion."

Friedberg manipulated the remote. The image slowed to a jerky, nearly frame-by-frame progression.

"Face?" Vail asked. The hood of his sweatshirt covered the man's entire head, except for the tip of his nose.

Burden leaned back, keeping his eyes on the screen. "I can ask if our guys can clean that up, lighten it. But it's a grainy image. You know what they say."

"Garbage in means garbage out," Vail said. "That what you mean?"

"Right. We can't create detail and resolution if it wasn't there originally."

"Sometimes if you play with the different exposure settings, things that were hidden suddenly pop out at you. I've seen it done with that photo software. Light-something."

"Photoshop?"

"No, it was like Photoshop, but—Lightroom. That's it. It had all these sliders. When the tech moved them, things appeared in the picture that weren't there before."

Burden cricked his neck in doubt. "I'll see what they can do. This is video, severely compressed and shot in low light. And it's not a jpeg file. I'm not sure the same image data is there."

Friedberg backed up the tape to the point where the suspect entered their field of view, then froze the image.

"Forget about the technology for a minute," Vail said. "What can we tell about the guy?" She took her seat again. "He's what, over six feet? Can't say much about his gait, because he's bent over a bit pushing the cart and we're only seeing a couple of strides before he moves off screen. Age?"

"Hard to figure," Friedberg said. "Definitely not a teenager. Other than that, he could be thirty to eighty. It's impossible to say because he's pushing that cart. And if he's already gotten rid of Mr. Anderson, that cart is empty and on wheels. It can't weigh that much. With that bulky sweatshirt on, we can't even really tell much about his build."

Vail looked at the frozen image of their mysterious suspect. "You think this guy's really an ice cream vendor?"

Friedberg set down the remote and pulled out his pad. "I'll find out who these guys are—if they're employees or if they're franchisees, if they're licensed...the whole deal. Then I'll get a list of names and addresses. We can track 'em all down and eliminate the ones that don't look like the guy on the tape—the fat ones, the short ones, the ones that limp. The rest we put in a room and sweat, see what we get."

"When you've got your list of suspects, I might be able to help narrow it down further."

"Good," Burden said. "But I don't want to wait. Let's nail some things down right now. What can you tell us about the type of guy we're looking for, based on Safarik's research on the sexual homicide of elderly females? Maybe that'll give us a foundation to build on."

"Normally, it would." Vail pushed her chair back. She was not looking forward to this discussion.

"I'm not sure I like the way you're starting your answer."

"That's only because you're not going to like what I have to say."

"Karen," Burden said, inching closer in his chair. "I need some valid direction for this case. When word gets out we've got an elderly couple murdered in the city—one savagely violated, and the other left in the Palace of Fine Arts...SFPD's gonna come under intense pressure to solve this, and solve it quickly."

"And that's something you're going to have to manage," Vail said.

"We brought you in here to help us."

"I get that. But with one rare exception, this case is unlike any of the cases Safarik studied and profiled involving elderly females."

"How so?"

"There are distinct characteristics of the typical offender who sexually murders elderly women. And this UNSUB just doesn't exhibit them."

Even in the muted lighting of the video room, Vail could see Burden's face shade red.

"Since this is my case, why don't you let me be the judge of that?"

"It's not that easy," Vail said.

"Karen, I think I'm getting close to being comfortable enough with our relationship to call you what your friends do."

The reference seemed to confuse Friedberg, but he apparently sensed it was not a flattering remark. "Hang on a sec," he said, pulling the cigarette from his mouth. "Let's take it down a notch. We've got two very upsetting murders. Let's keep our heads clear and work together."

"There are going to be others," Vail said.

"How the hell do you know that?" Burden asked.

"Yeah, I don't think that notch was quite as low as your partner suggested. But to answer your question, this UNSUB is skilled at what he's done. He appears to do lots of planning. He's thoughtful, cool under pressure, and engages in high-risk behavior without the anxiety one would expect to see. He shows preplanning and a certain level of comfort that doesn't come the first time out of the box. He's brought his torture weapon with him, meaning he's either done this before to others, or he's thought a lot about what he wants to do and how he's going to do it.

"Based on what I've seen at the crime scenes—the way he gained access to the vic's house is one example—I think he's intelligent, and if I had to guess, I'd say he's got formal education. He's physically agile to some extent. He's aware of police presence—the hooded sweatshirt might be one indication, though I'm not entirely sure of that yet. We'll see if tracking down the ice cream vendors pays off. I'm betting it won't. From what I've seen so far, this guy is smarter than that. He wouldn't expose himself that way. And there's definite purpose in how he posed Mr. Anderson's body. Why, what it means, we don't know yet. But when we figure it out, I guarantee you it won't have been random."

*Shit. I just gave them a profile...well, a bit of a profile. I should've kept my mouth shut. But I'm not very good at that, am I?*

They sat in silence for a moment, absorbing that information. Finally, Burden spoke. "So it seems like you've already got a decent feel for this guy."

"I'm in for a dime, so might as well make it a million bucks. Here's more to consider. Leaving William Anderson in the middle of San Francisco...he's flipping off the police, the FBI, and the victim. In the unit, we call it a '360 degree Fuck You.' It's extremely arrogant, risky, and shows a complete lack of empathy. The point is that all of these factors are indicative of psychopathy. This type of psychopathic individual would likely be more of the interpersonal type versus a white-collar psychopath."

"Interpersonal type?" Friedberg asked.

"The lack of defensive injuries implies he was able to use his verbal skills to get close enough to the victim to take control. We call that type of psychopath interpersonal for obvious reasons. Contrast that with the bully type, which would hit the victims over the head with a club—no talking, just *bam!* and he's in."

"So you're saying he's a social guy," Burden said.

"Not exactly. He has advanced verbal skills that allow him to appear less threatening to his victims."

Burden looked over at the frozen image on the screen. "So we've got a glib serial killer who'd just as soon as ram an umbrella up your ass and tear up your internal organs as chat you up in engaging socially stimulating conversation. This just keeps getting better."

*Now you're starting to see what we're up against.* "Our offender has physical violence in his repertoire of behaviors—behaviors that I believe he's used in the past, maybe even more than his verbal skills. His anger is intense and he sustains it. But here's the thing—even though he can experience anger, it's not like the anger you and I feel. His comes and goes—it's very intense, then suddenly it's gone. Jekyll and Hyde."

"But the crime scene," Friedberg said. "The blood, all the torture, all the physical damage to the victim—he obviously lost it. No?"

"No. A guy like this, their scenes can be at the extreme end of the injury scale, but they can be very composed on the inside. So he can appear to be in control because he doesn't experience emotions the way we do." She scooted her chair forward. "Not only that, but he likely ejaculated. That suggests what I just described—that he's capable of losing his anger enough to experience sexual arousal and then go back to acting out aggressively."

"Are you sure we're dealing with a psychopath?" Burden asked.

"There was a study done by Safarik, O'Toole, and Meyers on simultaneous states of arousal. An offender can't be in a state of rage and sexual arousal at the same time. So at a scene where I see a lot of physical injury to the victim, and she was sexually assaulted and semen deposited rectally or vaginally, it strongly indicates a psychopath. They're the only ones who can go into a heightened 'emotional' state like anger, then lose it quickly and then get sexually aroused. That's just not normal.

"In terms of practical application to our case, we'd likely see this as a hallmark of his in his past crimes. Interpersonal crimes of violence. And—it's probable that he's had contact with law enforcement before because of this anger."

A long moment passed. The two inspectors appeared to be absorbing the information.

"Well," Friedberg finally said, "you've totally ruined my day, Karen. Sounds like this is a seriously bad dude we're after."

"I'd have hoped you would've already known that from what he did to the wife."

Burden cleared his throat. "So why do you say it doesn't fit the typical elderly female sexual killer?"

Vail sighed deeply. She looked over at the hooded offender on the screen. "Okay, here's the deal. There are a number of similarities here. I'll be totally honest with you so you can make your own assessment. When we're talking about an offender who sexually murders elderly women, the mean age of the victim is usually around 77. So we're in the ballpark here. And the vics they choose are overwhelmingly Caucasian—about 86 percent. Our vics are Caucasian. And more than 70 percent of the typical vics have lived in their place of residence for ten years or more. The Andersons have been there nineteen. And like the Andersons, over 70 percent of the typical elderly vics did not have better home security than simple locks on their doors."

"You saw the crime scene," Friedberg said. "No alarms and no forced entry."

"Right. And we see that in about 60 percent of the cases, where the offenders enter through unlocked doors or windows—"

"So that fits."

Vail bobbed her head. "Yes—but maybe not. For the moment, let's stick with the similarities. The injuries inflicted on the victims appear to be consistent with what we would expect to see. The typical injury severity in an elderly sexual homicide is much greater than what'd be necessary to cause death."

"Overkill," Burden said.

Vail nodded. "We're getting away from the term 'overkill' and starting to call it an 'excessive injury pattern' because it's more accurate. But yes. The vics often suffer multiple severe injuries. Strangulation is the most common, somewhere around 65 percent of the time. Blunt force trauma is second, in the high thirties. But broadly speaking, that's really where the similarities end."

"These guys who do this to old women..." Friedberg said. "I remember Safarik talking about a specific motive, but I can't remember what he said it was."

"Safarik found that, on the surface, it's all about power, or anger, or both. In a deeper sense, though, it's really about punishing, dominating, and controlling his victim. This offender's assaults are rarely about sexual gratification. Physical force is the predominant form of violence they use—often involving their hands, fists, or knives." Vail leaned back in her chair. "But the most interesting thing—and I think this makes a hell of a lot of sense—is that these offenders, who tend to be younger men—see the elderly female as representing an authority figure. Or they may even be the actual woman who was the source of the anger he's feeling. And that's obviously why he wants to exert power over her. With these sexual homicides, sexuality is the method he uses to get his revenge or to transmit his hostility."

Friedberg placed both elbows on the desk. "You said the UNSUB we're looking for doesn't look like the typical offender who rapes and murders elderly women. But everything you've said so far sure looks like the kind of guy we're looking for."

"Like I said, there are similarities. But they're mostly similarities relative to victimology. If we look at offender characteristics and the behaviors left at the scene, it's a different story. The offenders who sexually abuse and then murder elderly women are criminally unsophisticated. It's a spontaneous act, with little or no planning. They leave behind a fair amount of evidence and the scene is sloppy and random.

"He doesn't make efforts to hide or protect his identity. And he uses a blitz attack to gain control and disable his target. While our UNSUB's attack was brutally violent, it wasn't blitz-like. Like I said before, it was controlled anger. And it doesn't look like he had any trouble controlling Maureen—or William. We'd also see property taken, money or valuables. Far as we know, nothing was missing. There's more about these offenders I can tell you, but unless we're convinced this is the type of guy we're looking for, it's senseless—"

"Like what?" Burden asked. "Share it all so we can make an informed decision."

Vail frowned. "Fine. These offenders tend to be alcohol or drug users. They have lower intelligence and are what we used to classify as disorganized. They're often unemployed and have a poor work history. Not surprisingly, that goes with a diverse arrest record, for a variety of unrelated crimes. And they also tend to be antisocial and/or socially incompetent—which doesn't appear to be the case with our UNSUB because, unless the Andersons were easy marks, it looks like our offender was able to talk his way into the townhouse with no signs of difficulty."

"You're holding back on us," Burden said. "You said there was an exception to all this."

*Indeed I did.* Vail sighed. "I didn't want to confuse things because—"

"Confuse things, or confuse us?"

*Keep calm. Count to ten. Hell with that—who's got time to count to ten?* "Safarik did have a case like Maureen Anderson. Robert Mark Edwards tortured an elderly woman to death. Rammed things up her vagina and ruptured her uterus and internal organs, then pulled her fingernails off with pliers and did the same to one of her nipples. Edwards was a sexual sadist who was also a smart guy. But he's an outlier."

Burden spread his hands apart. "So our UNSUB could be an outlier, too."

"Sometimes you have to go with your gut. You've been a cop a long time, you know that. And I know Mark Safarik and I've discussed all his cases with him. And if Mark were here, he'd tell you that guys like Edwards are exceptionally rare, that our UNSUB is a different animal than the animals in his research."

"Well, he's not here to tell me that. I've gotta take your word for it. Regardless, you shouldn't have held that back."

"Burden, listen to me. You know how many serial offenders there've been? I can't brief you on every case that could be similar to this one. Part of my value to you and Robert is to cut through all the fat and narrow things down. Just like if you had a list of fifty suspects, my profile would pare it down to a handful who are most likely to be our UNSUB. That outlier case is so rare, it wasn't worth mentioning. And there are other things, too, which support that."

There was a silent moment as Burden and Vail stared at each other.

Friedberg cleared his throat. "Back at their place, you wanted a list of all residents within a six-block radius."

"Because these offenders typically live in the neighborhood and walk to their victim's house. They've lived in the area for years, and they may've even seen the victim a number of times in the past. A guy I know does geographic profiling—which is basically the study of where offenders feel comfortable operating from a geographic point of view. The research suggests some offenders create 'mental maps' of an area when they identify one or more victims who interest them."

"Mental maps?"

"An offender catalogs victim information in a mental 'card file' that allows him to find that victim again in the future. Mental mapping."

Friedberg stuck the cigarette back in his mouth. "So much for being safe in your own neighborhood."

"I still think there's too many questions," Burden said. "We can't reach any conclusions yet."

"Honestly, you're probably right," Vail said. "But I strongly believe we're looking at something different here. A psychopath. But the most important point in all of this is that we're not just talking about the sexual homicide of an elderly female. He killed the husband, too. And that may tell us more than anything about this offender, and his motivations."

"Maybe he had to get the husband out of the way. Maybe he killed him first. We don't know yet on the TODs."

"Yes, Burden—but what he did with William was far different from what he did with Maureen. It may not look like it, but there were nearly as many behavioral clues left on William as there were with Maureen."

"How so? William was pretty clean—"

"Think about it a minute. Remember what I said? In placing William in the middle of San Francisco, in one of its beautiful enclaves that symbolized a rebirth of the city, he was telling all of us—SFPD and any other law enforcement who investigated—that he was king."

"Back at the crime scene, you said something about William not having any defensive injuries."

Vail curled a lock of red hair behind her right ear. "It would make more sense to me if he had defensive injuries, which would indicate he was forcefully taken, or overpowered by the offender against his will. But the absence of defensive injuries suggests a control issue. The offender wanted to control William during the time Maureen was attacked. So maybe part of the attack on Maureen was a psychopathic maneuver to get William to talk about something. There was no ongoing assault evident in other areas of the house, right? It seemed to all occur in the bedroom. And there was no ransacking. So it got me thinking, what if there was money in the house, and he was trying to get William to tell him where it was? Or maybe they owned bonds or some other asset that he could steal."

Friedberg pulled out his pad and clicked open the pen. "We can look into that."

"We should. But, that said…because of the type of violence, I really think…" She stopped. "Cold-blooded instrumental violence once again points toward psychopathy. We need some direction here, so I'm gonna commit. We should approach these murders from the perspective that we're dealing with an interpersonal psychopath. And in cases like this we always have to ask, How'd the offender find these people? Why these victims, and why now? If we can answer that last question, we'll have made major progress in solving this case."

"So if we're dealing with a psychopath," Burden said, "in your experience dealing with these monsters, what are the ramifications?"

"He has no remorse for these victims, and like a hardened inmate in a penitentiary, he's got no regard for the rules of society. So he will kill again, it's just a matter of time. The only positive in all this is—and this is a macabre way of looking at it—the more victims he amasses, the more we'll learn from him."

"As the body count rises," Friedberg said, "so does our knowledge base."

*That's a concept I'm all too familiar with.* Vail took another glance at the screen, where their UNSUB stood in shadow. She was likely looking right at the killer.

Yet she couldn't see him.

# 15

May 16, 1958

*Columbia, Alabama*

Walton MacNally adjusted his black fedora. He was standing half a block away observing the First National Thrift building—specifically taking note of the flow of people entering and exiting. Evaluating the quality of the clientele and looking for potential pitfalls and traps.

Last time, he more or less had gone in unprepared and, in the end, that had worked out pretty well. But he knew that it wasn't worth taking such a risk again. He was smart enough to know that he'd gotten lucky.

This time, he wanted to think things through, have a sense of what the bank looked like inside, where the security guards were located, how the tellers dealt with the customers. He wasn't sure what he should be looking out for, but he would keep his mind—and his eyes—open.

MacNally made three trips past the bank on foot before going inside. It was a stately interior, with marble columns and intricately carved wood desks, velvet-looking drapes covering the tall windows. This was a classier outfit than the community thrift he'd robbed last time. Three security guards stood at strategic locations, in a triangle formation: one at each end of the teller's row, and one in the back, amongst the executive desks.

He tapped his foot with nervous energy. This would undoubtedly be a tougher job.

"Can I help you with something?"

MacNally spun around, nearly knocking over the woman who was behind him. "I—I was just looking. I was—I was just thinking about opening up an account and I wanted to check the place out."

The middle-aged woman with poofed beauty parlor-set hair tilted her head. "Are there any questions I can answer for you? Would you like to come over to the vice president's desk and talk with him about the ba—"

"No-no, that's okay," MacNally stammered. "I think I've seen enough."

The woman nodded slowly. "All right. Well, if you think of anything you want to ask, my name is Nancy and I'll be right here."

MacNally managed a half smile and, like he had seen Sinatra do in the movies, he brought two fingers up to his fedora and tipped it back. He then gave one more glance around and walked outside.

MACNALLY SAT AT THE DINNER table, a pathetic spread of food in front of him and Henry. In addition to a hunk of stale bread and a boiled potato, the only thing that held any substantial nutrients were two carrots he'd pulled from a neighbor's garden on his way home.

"I went by the bank," MacNally said. He felt odd discussing this with his son. But he had no one else. And Henry, despite his youth, possessed insight and hardened analysis that never ceased to astonish him. "I've got concerns."

Henry put his fork down. He tilted his head, examining his father's eyes. "You're afraid. I can see it on your face."

"No, that's not it at all." But of course, that's exactly what it was.

"We need the money." Henry looked down at the dinner plate, as if emphasizing his point. "You want me to go by tomorrow, take a look see? Maybe I can think of something."

"No. I don't want you going anywhere near there. I'll handle it."

Henry stared for a moment at his father, then grabbed the loaf of bread and yanked off a handful. He shoved it into his mouth and looked down at the table as he chewed.

MacNally stared off at the wall. Embarrassed. His pride bruised like an apple dropped on a hardwood floor.

"There's this guy a few blocks away who needs somebody to mow his lawn. He ain't got no kids. I can do it, git us some money."

MacNally did not look at his son. "No."

"I already told him yes."

"You—" MacNally locked eyes with Henry, then dropped his gaze to his plate. The hunk of bread stared back at him. "Okay," he said in a low voice.

They finished eating in silence. Then MacNally took an axe out to the yard and began chopping wood. It would be cold tonight, and splitting the logs worked up a sweat—but more than anything, it worked off his anger and frustration.

MacNally would go back to the bank tomorrow. There had to be a way to get at the money. He just had to figure it out.

# 16

Vail and Burden walked back into the Homicide Detail while Friedberg finished with the digital tape and asked the technician to create a still print of their suspect. They agreed that even if it was unrevealing, it still helped eliminate, to some extent, suspects with certain body types, ages and constitutions. He was also going to check on that enhanced image, in case there was any hidden data in the tape that, when modified, could reveal a facial trait not previously visible.

Before Vail had settled into Burden's side chair, Friedberg burst into the suite.

"Birdie. Another vic."

Vail cursed beneath her breath. "Where?"

"Totally different part of the city. At the Cliff House."

"Cliff house?"

Burden grabbed his jacket off the back of his chair. "I'll explain on the way."

SEVEN MINUTES LATER, THEY were getting into a gray unmarked Ford Taurus that was parked beneath a freeway overpass a block from Bryant Street's Hall of Justice. The top of the vehicle was caked with pigeon shit, a clear tipoff to any skel who knew anything about the SFPD and where the detectives parked their cars.

"Love your ride," Vail said. "Don't they have car washes in California?"

"We've got a budget crisis," Friedberg said. "Haven't you heard?"

"I would think you'd call it fiscally challenged," Vail said as she swung her body into the rear seat.

"Ain't that the truth," Burden said with a chuckle. As they turned onto Fulton Street, he said, "The Cliff House is in an area that the locals refer to as being 'out in the Avenues.' West area of the city."

"And what is this place? A house on a cliff?"

"The Palace of Fine Arts really was a kind of palace where fine arts were displayed," Friedberg said. "But the Cliff House isn't a house— at least it hasn't been since the late 1800s. Or maybe the early 1900s. Anyway, it's been rebuilt or remodeled a few times, and has been a restaurant for several decades. But it's not just a restaurant. It's part of the National Park Service and used to have a penny arcade on the lower level."

"Anything else that might make it a prime location for a body dump?"

"It's secluded after hours," Burden said. "But during the day, there's a steady flow of visitors."

"Do we know when the body was placed there?"

"We'll have to find out when we meet up with the first-on-scene."

Vail watched as the terrain changed subtly from city to shoreline. "Something else to think about. If we've got another body left in a public place—"

"What do you think?" Burden asked. "We gonna find a companion somewhere else in the city?"

"If this is our offender's ritual, then yeah. Very likely."

A few blocks later, Burden gestured with this chin. "It's coming up." He headed down a sloped two-lane road, the Pacific Ocean swinging into view directly ahead of them. Off to the right, a sizable low-slung cream-colored structure dominated the waterfront. Large capital Art Deco lettering announced that the flat roofed building was, indeed, the Cliff House they were there to see.

Two San Francisco Police Department cruisers sat at the curb, idling with lights flashing in front of a large, glass-walled midsection of the restaurant. A cop stood out front, a blue SFPD baseball cap topping off his uniform.

Burden brought the car to a stop beside the squad cars. Vail was the first out and caught the brunt of a strong, whipping wind that blew her red hair across her face. "Where's the body?" she managed to ask as she swept the locks away from her mouth.

"Down by the Sutro Baths," the officer said.

Vail turned to her cohorts for clarification.

"Sutro Baths, got it," Friedberg said. "This way." He led them up the steep sidewalk, away from the Cliff House, past a couple of sightseeing telescopes on the left and street vendors selling handmade jewelry on the right. In front of them was a small, family-owned seafood café. But before they reached it, Friedberg turned onto a sloping dirt path.

To their left rolled a gradually sloping hillside, tufts of wild grass, scrub, and bushes sprouting from the rocky face. To the right, a steep, nearly barren shale cliff. And directly ahead, abutting the beachfront and the gray Pacific beyond, was a complex of ruins—sans roofs—with half walls divided into what appeared to be rooms, partially filled with pooled water.

"What's that down there?" Vail asked.

"Those are—were—the Sutro Baths," Friedberg said. He tripped on an emergent rock on the increasingly steeper dirt and graveled path, but regained his balance. He stopped and shielded his eyes from the glare. "Back in the late 1800s, I think, there was this guy Sutro, who solved some engineering issues they had with a major gold mine up north. Made him a multimillionaire. He built this complex, which had six humongous, glass-enclosed, indoor swimming pools, a skating rink, a museum, and other shit like that. People came from all over. Anyway, it was still standing after the 1906 earthquake, but ironically burned down a year later. Go figure."

"Indoor glass-enclosed pools," Vail said, looking out at the gray Pacific. "Must've had a magnificent ocean view."

"I'm sure that's why it was such a huge hit. Come on."

They continued down the path. To their right, a large brown and white sign read

CAUTION
CLIFF AND SURF AREA
EXTREMELY DANGEROUS
People have been swept
from the rocks and drowned

"Good to know," Vail quipped. "Watch out for giant, man-eating waves."

"It's no joke," Friedberg said as they passed the warning placard tunnel. "Over thirty ships have been pounded to smithereens against those rocks below us."

"Looks like we found our crime scene." Burden gestured to an area at the end of their path, where an SFPD officer stood guard. "By that hole in the rock face."

"And what is that hole in the rock face?" Vail asked.

Burden shrugged.

"Beats me," Friedberg said. "I've only been here once, for dinner. I read about the Sutro Baths in the gift shop."

"And here I thought you were a scholar, a historian to be taken seriously."

"As a matter of fact—"

"Please," Burden said. "Don't get him started on that."

As they reached the bottom of the path, another brown Caution sign rose from the scattered boulders, warning people of the dangers of falling off the cliffs and into the ocean.

The ruins were now directly off to their left. A pelican was perched on a former wall of the structure; a photographer with a long lens was creeping up, a step at a time, attempting to capture the shot that would add polish to his portfolio.

The wind was appreciably firmer down at the ocean's edge, and Vail wrapped her arms across her chest.

"What've you got for us?" Burden asked the officer, who stood at the mouth of a fairly regular opening in the cliffside, roughened edges encircling its periphery.

"Body's in there," the cop said. "Got a call from a tourist. Kind of hard to figure out what he said—dispatch said he was from Denmark, I think—but he was pretty upset. Something about a body that wasn't moving."

"Is he still around?" Friedberg asked.

"We got here, no one knew anything about him. And he's not answering his cell."

"Okay," Burden said. "Where's our victim?"

"Inside, all the way down."

"Down where?" Vail asked, squinting into the darkness.

"It's a tunnel. He's at the end. Any of you have a flashlight?"

Vail fished a small LED keychain light from a pocket.

"That's useless in there. Take mine. Be careful, the terrain's a little rough."

The upper three quarters of the rock facing surrounding the tunnel's mouth was a creamy, rose-colored tint; the bottom portion was gray and appeared to have layers etched in its surface, like the rings of a tree. A few feet beyond the opening, the walls were black.

Vail suffered from claustrophobia, but it was inconsistent: sometimes she had little difficulty with enclosed places, while on other occasions merely getting in an elevator would fill her with consuming anxiety. She had developed the condition after a recent case that left her in the custody of a killer who traumatized her in a confined space.

Vail took the flashlight and switched it on. The roughened walls and ceiling of the tunnel, which appeared to be about eight feet high, stared back at them. *I can do this.* "Shall we?"

Vail led the way, her shoes crunching on the course, compacted sand. The ground seemed to slope away from her, undulating into the distance as far as the light carried. *So far, so good.* Approximately seventy-five feet away, a semicircle of light blasted through the opening from the tunnel's opposing end. An object appeared to be silhouetted against the glare.

"Is that—" She swung back over her shoulder. "Hey! Officer. Is that our guy down at the end?"

The man bent over and peered in. "That's him," he said, his voice reverberating off the walls. "He's tied up against something."

"That would fit," Burden said.

Vail moved further in. A few steps later, smashing ocean waves echoed somewhere off to their left. The hand-smoothed sheen of a metal railing caught her light beam. They stopped and listened: a sliver of light followed the water into the cave, a tributary that ran below them and perpendicular to the tunnel's main trunk. Vail crouched and looked into the crevasse.

With her flashlight, she followed the water to an area just below them. "High tide, I'm sure the ocean floods this tunnel. We'd better get to that body. CSI on the way?"

"He was dispatched same time we were called," Friedberg said. "Should be here soon."

They walked toward the open end, where, against the gray light of the sky, a shape that resembled the body of a man stared back at them. As they approached, Vail shined the beam on something to the right of the corpse. The reflective coating on a brown Caution sign, similar to the one they had seen earlier on the trail, lit up brightly: End of Trail.

*As if the cable, the abrupt end of the tunnel, and huge boulders ahead weren't clues enough.*

Friedberg rested his hands on both knees to examine the left portion of the body. "Can I get some light?"

Vail complied, illuminating the area.

"Fishing line again. Vic's fastened to the cables that are holding up the sign. But..." Friedberg craned his neck and peeked behind the man. "He's strapped to a two-by-four." He stepped back and gestured with a hand. "Take a look. It runs vertically, from head to toe. It's secured to the two cables that run horizontally across the cave opening."

Burden surveyed the setup. "He needed that two-by-four to keep the body upright."

"And that board isn't from around here," Vail said. "That much is obvious. Meaning our UNSUB planned this. I mean, we knew that already—but this is pretty definitive. It supports what I said back at your station. Organization, planning. He brought the tools he needed with him. And apparently no one saw him."

Behind the body, the terrain changed markedly. Over time, pounding waves had done a job on the rock face, chopping it into pieces of varying sizes. Boulders, large and small, rose and fell in height, leading into the ocean a few dozen feet in the distance.

Vail said, "I can't see how the offender would get in here on this end. He had to have come in where we did. Without anyone seeing him."

Burden gave a quick look, then turned to study the opposite end of the cave. "Coming from the road, it's a long haul. And the terrain's rough. Hard to carry a body. Even using a wheelbarrow, or something like that cart he used back at the Palace of Fine Arts, not as easy to do here."

"Remember," Vail said. "Easiest thing for the offender to do is bring the vic here alive, then kill him in the tunnel." Vail removed a pen from her pocket and handed the flashlight to Friedberg as she separated the ends of the man's Members Only windbreaker. "Wanna hear my theory?"

"That's what we brought you out here for," Burden said.

"This kind of disposal site tells me that this offender has some prior knowledge of what he's getting himself into here. The challenge of the terrain. But he still uses it—which would suggest it holds some kind of symbolism for him. It's more than just being 'in your face.' He wants law enforcement to get the symbolism. And if I'm right, this kind of offender's gonna be the type to monitor the investigation. He'll pay attention to what the media says, so he can find out what we're thinking about his disposal sites."

"Maybe we can use that."

Vail nodded. "The statements we make about these sites are very important. We may even use misinformation. We could totally misinterpret what he'd intended, to get him to contact us—kind of like, 'No, stupid, you got it all wrong. *This* is why I'm doing it this way!'"

"I think we can arrange that," Burden said. "A reporter I know, we can use him. He'll do it."

"Meantime," Friedberg said, "if we can find out who this vic is, we may find another body."

Burden nodded. "His wife."

"Yeah," Vail said, her mind shifting to an image of Maureen Anderson's tortured body. "His wife." Off to the side, amongst the uneven boulders, two parallel rusted metal strips poking up and between the rock caught her eye. "Is that railroad track? Kind of in the middle of nowhere."

"That is what it looks like," Burden said, peering out the opening. "Old. Very old. Maybe there was a gold mine around here."

Friedberg slipped a gloved hand inside the man's jacket. He fished around, then pulled out a wallet and opened it. "Russell Ilg."

Burden pulled out his BlackBerry and started dialing. "Address?"

Friedberg read it off and Burden relayed it to the dispatcher. "Get a unit over there ASAP. Tell them I expect they're going to find a DB. And it won't be pretty. And tell 'em to use booties because I don't want my crime scene destroyed." He listened a moment, said, "Yeah," then hung up. "His wife's Irene. Seventy-nine."

Vail gestured to Friedberg. "Get a light on his face, let's see what we can see. And where the hell's that CSI?"

Ilg's face had deep jowls and a full head of gray hair that had been tousled by the whipping wind blowing in through the cave's mouth. But then the flashlight hit the forehead. A 49 was written in black marker.

"So," Vail said. "First, a 37. Now a 49. Burden, you're the number scrambling Sudoku expert. What's the significance?"

"Hell if I know. But forty-nine is significant to California. Gold Rush in 1849. The football 49ers. There's a Pier 49, too."

"And there's a forty-nine-mile scenic drive in the city," Friedberg said.

*No.* Vail shook her head. "Now that we have two vics with numbers, we have to start looking for a pattern or some relationship between the digits." *And why is it only on the male vics?*

"I'll think on it," Burden said.

Friedberg ran the beam over the length of the body. "No overt signs of trauma."

Vail leaned over the cable. "Let's see the back of his head."

Friedberg brought the light up.

"There," Vail said, pointing. "Looks like bruising. Very substantial. Hard to see all of it because that two-by-four is in the way." She moved around to Ilg's hands. "Give me some light here." She leaned in close, studied all ten fingers. "No defensive wounds. Just like William Anderson."

"Meaning?" Friedberg asked.

Vail stepped back. "Remember I said control is the key? Our offender's got an effective way of controlling them enough to get them somewhere near where he wants to display the body."

"But that doesn't make sense," Burden said. "I mean, the guy's displaying these bodies in public because—what—I assume it's to make a statement. Right?"

"*Could* be. Could be he's going for shock value. Could be these places mean something to him. Or he could be taunting us."

"Taunting us?" Burden asked. "How?"

A whistle echoed in the tunnel. The three of them turned and saw the silhouetted figure of a man headed toward them, carrying a toolkit.

"Our CSI," Burden said. He turned back to Vail. "What do you mean? How is he taunting us?"

"Could be taunting us. I don't know. But it's a possibility. Like I said. The symbolism. We're supposed to see something here, with these vics."

"Yeah, but we ain't seeing shit."

"And that," Vail said, "could be a potential problem. But think about it a second. He could pose or leave the bodies in any public place, places that don't require the same level of effort and risk. But no. He picks these places for a reason. It's more than just for shock. And while I don't doubt there's some taunting involved, it's probably much more than that, too." Vail turned to face Russell Ilg's body. "Maybe we need to shed some light on the subject."

Burden gave her a look.

"I don't mean that as a joke. We need more information. Now that we've got three, and likely four bodies, we can fine-tune our theories. Hone the profile."

"What happens if you're right, and he really is leaving us clues that we're not seeing?"

"One possibility is that he's going to get frustrated. He'll keep killing until we 'get it.' No matter what, he's going to contact us somehow, somewhere. You may want to tell your office staff and operators to be aware of any suspicious calls."

"On it," Friedberg said. He lifted his phone and started dialing.

"You really think that's what we're dealing with here?" Burden asked.

Vail tilted her head, looking at Ilg's face, which was oriented straight ahead. "Unfortunately, we're going to find out. Sooner or later."

# 17

MacNally returned to First National Thrift twice more that week, pretending to request information on opening an account. Fortunately, no one had noticed that he was wearing the same clothes—he owned only one pair of dress slacks and a single button-down Oxford.

On his second trip, he decided on the woman he wanted: Emily September. He had never known anyone named September—had not even realized it could be a real name. She was pert and on the younger side of thirty, with well-styled blonde hair and a tight knit sweater hugging her chest like it didn't want to let go.

MacNally made small talk with her, then realized he had better leave before she—or anyone watching—would realize he hadn't transacted any business.

He walked out and returned a couple of days later. Now, as noon approached, he watched Emily September push out the double doors of First National Thrift and turn left, headed toward the parking lot. MacNally followed her around back and watched her get into a light turquoise Ford Thunderbird. He didn't know a whole lot about cars, but he did know that a T-bird was an expensive luxury car—and a sharp one at that. It was a convertible with a simple, elegant curved windshield, clean lines, and broad whitewall tires.

MacNally started the sky blue Buick Century he had stolen outside town and followed Emily as she maneuvered the vehicle onto the main drag. Blonde hair flowed back off her shoulders in the breeze.

A Thunderbird? For a bank teller? She had money. Or, at least, it looked like she did. This presented an interesting dilemma: go after pretty Emily September when she arrived at home and steal what she had in the house, or go after the more risky—but potentially higher reward job—the bank.

He followed a good forty yards behind her, wondering if it was too great a distance. If she made a light and he did not, he would lose her. And how long could he keep this car before the police would discover it was stolen? Before they would find him and Henry?

He made sure to narrow the gap between them, taking care not to get too close: she had seen him—spoken to him—in the bank, and he didn't want to risk her seeing him again. It could make her suspicious, or she could think he was following her around. Worse still, if he did rob the bank, she would be able to provide an accurate description of him to the authorities.

Ten minutes later, Emily pulled into a well-tended neighborhood with two- and three-story homes lining the green-lawned avenues. She hung a left into a driveway and parked. MacNally drove past her house and parked at the curb. He shut the engine and waited.

Emily went inside and was there for nearly forty minutes before getting back in her car and heading off in the direction of the bank. She must have come home for lunch and was now on her way back to work. MacNally waited until she had cleared the block and then got out of his car. Moving swiftly but cautiously, he walked down the street and into Emily September's backyard.

The landscape was meticulously groomed, with several mature deciduous trees shading the grass from sunlight. A redwood picnic table sat in the center of the plot. MacNally moved past it and stepped up to the back door. He peered into the window, bringing his hands up to his face to block out the light. He looked around but did not see anyone. As expected—there had been no other cars in the nearby vicinity, so it made sense that no one was home.

MacNally balled up his shirt around his fist and looked for the best place to penetrate the door. He would be in and out as fast as possible. But first he would see if he could find some cash—or anything else of value that could be sold with ease.

"Okay, Emily. Let's see what you've got for me."

# 18

Burden, Friedberg, and Vail arrived at Irene Ilg's home on Ortega Street in the Sunset District as a foggy dusk settled in over the city.

While climbing out of Burden's Ford, a man whistled at them.

"Birdie!"

"Allman, my man, how's it hangin'?" The two men met on the sidewalk behind the car and launched into an elaborate handshake.

Vail leaned into Friedberg. "Who is that?"

"Police reporter for the *Tribune*."

"What the hell are they doing?"

"Some kind of fraternity thing."

Vail hiked her brow. "I never took cop reporters as the fraternity type. Rebels. Loners, maybe."

"You've actually profiled reporters?"

"Not exactly," Vail said. "I'm just saying."

Friedberg shrugged. "For what it's worth, I think you're right. But in every profession there are outliers."

Vail gave him a look. "You getting philosophical on me, Robert?"

"Who tipped you?" Burden asked as the two men approached Vail and Friedberg.

Allman sported graying temples but otherwise a full head of wavy brown hair. Small capillaries zigzagged the side of his sharp nose, suggesting he enjoyed his time on a bar stool a bit more often than his physician would recommend. But his smile was broad and infectious, inviting in a magnetic way. A battered tan leather messenger bag was slung across his shoulder.

"You don't really expect me to divulge my sources, do you?"

Burden tipped his chin back.

"Okay, fine," Allman said. "No source. I heard it on the scanner." He noticed Vail and his eyes widened. "Who's the beautiful lady?"

"Oh, please," Vail said. *Please say more.*

"This is Clay Allman, police reporter for the *Tribune*. Clay, this is Special Agent Karen Vail. She's out from the BAU."

Allman's head swung over to Burden, then back to Vail. "You're a profiler?"

"Ah, goddamn it," Burden said. "That's off the record. Got it?" he asked, poking Allman with a stubby finger.

"Sure," Allman said. "Give the dog a bone, then yank it from his mouth. I'm left salivating."

"Now there's an appropriate metaphor," Friedberg said.

"Robert," Allman said with a big grin. He gave Friedberg's hand a firm shake. "Didn't see you there."

"Jeez. Haven't seen you since…well, since the last murder in town."

"You make police reporters sound like the grim reaper."

Friedberg laughed. "Hey, man…if the shoe fits."

"You related to the brothers?" Vail asked.

Allman cocked his head. "What brothers?"

"Gregg and Duane," Vail said. "Allman Brothers. 'Ramblin' Man,' 'Midnight Rider'—c'mon, I know you're old enough to know their music."

"Yes," Allman said. "And no. Yes, I know their music. No, we're not related. But I do play a mean guitar."

"That's true," Burden said. "If by 'mean' you really meant 'horrible.'"

Allman frowned at Burden, and then swung his gaze over to Vail. "So…about the DB."

"What about it?" Vail asked. "This is a crime scene. When homicide inspectors respond, there usually is a dead body."

Allman's eyebrows rose. "Whoa. Do I detect a little…attitude?"

"You detect a lot of attitude," Burden said.

Vail cleared her throat. "I can speak for myself, *Birdie*. Thank you very much." She looked at Allman. "And yeah, I don't believe reporters should be trampling a crime scene before the investigating detectives even get a chance to look things over."

"Okay, okay," Allman said, raising both hands. "I'll wait. I didn't mean anything by it. I just—it's my job to cover crimes."

"I got that," Vail said, "when Burden introduced you as the *Tribune*'s police reporter."

Allman looked to Burden, who shrugged.

"Don't take it personally. Agent Vail treats everyone the same way. She doesn't play favorites." Burden nodded at Friedberg and Vail to follow him. "We'll have a look around," he called back to Allman. "If you're still here when we're done, I'll let you take a look. These days you're not even supposed to have access, so I know you're good with that. Right?"

"Of course. And since I'm a man of words, although it goes without saying, I'll say it anyway: I do appreciate it."

Burden led the way through the decorative iron gate into an arched alley, then up to the townhouse's front door. Friedberg handed Vail and Burden baby blue booties and latex gloves.

As they slipped them on, the SFPD officer gave them a report: "I did a well check, figuring I'd find her deceased, based on…well, based on dispatch's warning. She's upstairs, in bed. I backed out the way I came."

Vail and Friedberg followed Burden through the front door. Inside, off to the left, sat a living room filled with austere antique furniture upholstered in paisley fabrics that were long in the tooth. They moved through the room, then into the dining room and the kitchen.

Vail checked the rear door with a gloved hand. Locked. A small square backyard stared back at her through the window. A well-tended vegetable garden sprouted tomatoes and squash, and what looked like the ends of carrots peeking through the soil.

"No sign of a struggle," Vail said. "No nothing. Everything looks like I'd expect it to."

"Ten-four," Burden said. "Let's go up. After we get a look at the body, we can come back down, take a fresh pass down here."

They moved toward the front of the house and headed up the narrow staircase to the second floor. Two bedrooms and a bathroom sat before them.

Vail led them into the only one with an open door. The odor of death was pungent and flared her nostrils. But as intense as the smell was, it was nowhere near as impactful as the image of what lay before them.

Sprawled out on the bed lay an elderly woman. Vail wanted to turn away but could not. It was one thing seeing the body in the morgue. This one was relatively fresh. And she bore a slight resemblance to her mother. She bit down on her bottom lip.

"Shit," Friedberg said. "I knew what we were gonna see, but does anything prepare you for a scene like this?"

*Maybe a lobotomy.*

Burden backed out of the room. "I've seen enough."

"Are you—you're shitting me," Vail said. "What exactly have you seen?"

"Enough. I've seen enough. Same as before, same as the last one."

"You don't mind if I take a closer look?"

"Be my guest. I'm gonna go check for missing electrical cords."

"You and me, then," Vail said to Friedberg. She carefully moved to the side of the bed and examined the body visually. "Burn marks," she said, pointing at an area overlying the abdomen. "Same as the ones on Maureen Anderson." The woman's blouse had been pulled up over her chest but was not covering the face.

Friedberg smacked his lips, as if trying to hold back an upchuck of bile. "Violated, like Anderson."

Vail stepped back and took a look around, viewing the victim from different angles. Her shoe nudged the edge of something hard. "And I just found his preferred tool." She looked down at her foot. It was touching the tip of a blood-soaked black umbrella.

They remained with the body for another ten minutes, then checked the other rooms. As they were headed downstairs, CSI Rex Jackson was walking in the front door.

"She's upstairs," Vail said.

They found Burden in the kitchen, staring out the back window. "This guy isn't gonna stop, is he?"

"No," Vail said. "Offenders like him, they're going to keep killing until we grab him up. There's a lot going on here. A lot for us to figure out."

"Anything we need to know down here?" Friedberg asked.

Burden hiked a shoulder. "No sign of forced entry. I've got some officers out canvassing neighbors to see who these people were so we can build on our victimology."

"Good," Vail said.

Burden's gaze remained out the window. "The Andersons have a daughter. She's out of the country. Lives in France. We're trying to get word to her. The Ilgs apparently have two kids, a boy and a girl. With families of their own."

"Electrical cords?" Vail asked.

"All here. In fact, this crime scene is a near copy of the other one." He turned to face them. "So what's the deal? Why these people? Another husband and wife. Any significance to that?"

"For now, it's still possible the UNSUB wants something from the man, so he tortures the woman until he gives it up. But..."

"But what?"

"But I'm not sure that's right, or maybe it's not all that's going on. There are a lot of behaviors left at the scene. This guy is a psychopath, that much is clear. It might not be about information or material things that he wants."

"How do we find out what he wants?"

"The answer may be in what he left behind at the crime scene. But we may not know enough yet to interpret it."

Burden's phone buzzed. He lifted it to his ear and said, "Talk to me." He listened a moment, then nodded. "Got it. Thanks."

"Well?" Vail asked.

"Our male vic, Russell Ilg, was an IRS auditor. He retired several years ago and had been working for a consulting company giving lectures to groups on avoiding tax pitfalls."

"Auditors aren't well-liked individuals," Friedberg said.

"What do a white-collar attorney and an IRS auditor have in common?" Vail asked. "Besides brutally murdered spouses and a reservation at the county morgue."

"Irene worked as a librarian," Burden said. "She still goes in—went in—twice a week."

"So did she come into contact with our offender through the library?" Vail asked. "Not sure how we'd track it, but we should see if we can get a list of people who were in the library on the days she worked. Let's go back a few months."

"I'll get on it," Friedberg said, "though I doubt they have any records like that. But who wouldn't like a librarian?"

They fell quiet. Vail used the time to think through what she had seen. "You know…it might not be a personal thing. I'm starting to think these victims are conduits."

"Come again?" Friedberg asked.

"A conduit. It looks personal. The violence, the umbrella, the torture with the electrical shocks. But we've now got four vics and two women brutally murdered. His violence is mostly instrumental. It's cold blooded, predatory, and mission oriented. I don't think it's a personal thing. The vics—the wives, or the husbands, or both—represent someone who wronged him at some point in his life."

"Great," Burden said. "Now we gotta figure out what these people are supposed to represent. Back to that symbolism bullshit. That's fucking great. Where the hell do you go with that?"

"Small steps, Burden. Otherwise it'll overwhelm us." Vail gestured with her head. "Did you look around down here?"

Burden waved a hand. "Nothing of interest. They look like an average old couple. Just like the Andersons. No unusual letters. No computer. Did you find one upstairs?"

"No. It's possible the PC age passed them by. How old are they?"

"Russell was eighty-four. Irene was seventy-nine."

Vail looked around the kitchen. Appliances were used but not original; they had been replaced at some point in the past decade. She moved into the living room. Family photos stared back at her from the walls. The Ilgs had two children and five grandchildren, from what she could ascertain. Everyone looked happy. It wasn't just that they were smiling; it was more than that. Their faces and demeanor looked like they weren't burdened by stress. *That'll change when they find out what happened to their loved ones.*

They remained in the apartment another twenty minutes, then walked outside. Leaning against his car was Clay Allman. He pushed off his Toyota and headed toward Vail, Burden, and Friedberg.

"Okay?"

"You've got three minutes," Burden said. "And leave your bag and phone here."

"You don't trust me?"

"I'd rather not have to answer for missing evidence or unauthorized photos in court."

Allman shoved his phone in the satchel, then slipped his arm through the strap and dropped the bag at his feet.

Vail watched him sprint down the street, then point back at them while talking with the SFPD officer manning the door.

Burden gave the man a signal, and he admitted the reporter.

Vail said, "I'm not sure that's a good idea."

"Years ago he had complete access. These days, it's a no-no. But I've known Clay a long time. He's covered dozens of murders in this city, and I've never had a problem with him screwing us over."

"Then give him a medal," Vail said. "But it's got nothing to do with anything. We need to control the release of information."

"I'm with Karen," Friedberg said. "I don't think it's smart."

Burden turned to face them and shoved his hands in his back pockets. "Look. He's got integrity and he's been a friend of SFPD for—what? Thirty years?"

Friedberg grumbled. "I don't like people going through my crime scenes. You know that. Never have."

"It gives us leverage when we need things in return from him." Burden checked his watch. "This is the guy I mentioned before, Karen. Back at the Cliff House. The one I thought can help us."

"What are the dangers?" Friedberg asked.

Vail cocked her head. "We certainly don't want to say anything in the media that could encourage the offender to continue his killing—or escalate and accelerate. If I'm right about our guy being a psychopath, he's a narcissist. Not acknowledging all he's done, how great and unusual a killer he is, it could piss him off—and even challenge him. Incite him. Years ago, I interviewed Joseph Paul Franklin, a serial sniper back in the late 70s. As he continued to murder, he was aggravated that his 'peers'—Bundy and the Unabomber—were getting all the attention. So he decided to kill two young black boys, figuring that would ratchet things up for him, that he'd get more attention—which is what he wanted. And he was right.

"So back to your question about the press, and the dangers. From what I've seen, the offender's content with the public knowing about him. He seeks it out, like Franklin did. Other than the symbolism, that could be the reason why our offender leaves his male vics in high profile places."

"So what if we just have Clay report the facts and leave out the details? Just that Russell and Irene Ilg were found murdered. Nothing about the Cliff House cave, nothing about the brutal torture."

"You're assuming your buddy would do that. But besides that, it could piss off the offender, frustrate him," Vail said. "And if he's leaving clues for us that we're not getting, that could make things worse. But like I said before, it could also force him to contact us somehow, set us straight by leaving more clues. Like bread crumbs."

Friedberg turned around. Allman was approaching.

His face was taut and his lips thin. "I've seen a lot of violent shit over the years. But...Jesus Christ, Birdie. What the hell was that?" He turned to Vail.

Burden shook his head slowly. "No fucking idea."

Allman swung his gaze back to Burden. "Really?"

"Unfortunately, yeah. Really."

Vail held up a hand. "I wouldn't say that—"

97

"Well that's what I'm saying." Burden's slumped shoulders spoke louder than his words.

"So can I print that?" Allman asked.

"What do you think?" Friedberg almost yelled. "No, you can't print that."

Burden glanced at his friend and gave a slight head shake.

"Birdie. I'm a reporter, remember? We sell newspapers. I write the stories that go in those papers. Give me something I can use."

Vail turned to Burden. "We need to do it right, in a controlled way, saying what we want it to say."

"What's she talking about?" Allman asked.

Burden looked off at the townhouses in front of him. "Fine. Use this: 'SFPD is investigating the death of a San Francisco woman that appears to involve foul play.' Good?"

"The idea is to sell newspapers, not bore people to death. That totally sucks."

"Hey, what can I say? I'm a homicide inspector, not a writer."

"You sure I can't use the 'No fucking idea' comment? Don't worry, I'll leave out the expletive."

Burden looked at him.

Allman turned away. "How about you give me something, I give you something."

"What's that supposed to mean?" Vail asked. "You know something, you'd better not hold out on us."

"Or what, you'll have me arrested for obstructing an investigation, and then we get to play a little constitutional game of chess?"

Vail took a step toward Allman, but Burden placed a hand on her shoulder and gave her a slight push back.

"We already gave you something," Vail said. "Access. Remember?"

"What do you have in mind?" Burden asked.

Vail shrugged off the inspector's hand. "This is not a negotiation, Burden. Besides, he's bluffing."

Allman ran his tongue around the inside of his mouth. After a moment, he said, "Killer from past returns to haunt city. That'd be the headline. Assuming my editor approves."

"What killer from the past?" Vail asked.

"Shouldn't you be telling me?" Allman said. "You're the crack profiler."

"And that shows how little you know about what I do, Mr. *Crack Reporter*. I'm interested in analyzing behaviors a killer engages in with his victims. I'm not a repository of the names of all the killers who've ever murdered someone in every city in the world. So. Who's this killer of the past?"

Allman turned to Burden. "He was never caught. But I saw something in there that reminded me of him. I think it's the same guy."

"You've got our attention," Vail said. "Go on."

"Uh uh," Allman said with a smirk. "Help me, I'll help you."

Vail wanted to plant the bit with the symbolism, but realized they might be able to get more in return if she played it right. She frowned, then turned. "C'mon, Burden. We've got a lot to do and we're wasting time."

"I'll have to clear this with my lieutenant," Burden said. "But you can include the vic's husband. We found him a little while ago."

Allman pulled out a pad. "Where?"

"No, no, no. I gave you something. Now…" Burden said, flexing his fingers in front of Allman.

"Fine." Allman bent down and picked up his messenger bag that was lying on the sidewalk. "There's a key in the vic's bedroom."

Vail blurted a laugh. "A key. Thanks for the tip." She started to turn away.

"A key," Allman repeated. "It's a weird shape, doesn't fit any of the locks in the house, and it's not a car key. And, according to Jackson in there, it was not used to inflict injury on Mrs. Ilg. The key's clean. No blood on it."

"Meaning?" Friedberg asked.

"Meaning," Allman said, "the key has no overt purpose for being there. And I believe Agent Vail can tell you that means it has relevance to the killer's behavior. Isn't that right, Agent Vail?"

Vail turned back. "Potentially. What kind of key is it? Where was it found?"

Allman held up two fingers about three inches apart. "Brass. Big and wide. It looks old, because the brass is tarnished, but it's not worn. I don't know if it's significant, but something's been filed off the top. It was on the dresser across from Mrs. Ilg's body."

"I saw that," Friedberg said. "I thought it was just a key."

"And this ties in to a prior murder, how?" Vail asked.

"Back in '82," Burden said. "A key like Clay's describing was found at the crime scene of a male who'd been murdered, his body dumped in San Bruno, outside the federal building."

Vail tilted her head. "San Bruno—I've seen that. On a sign, I think. Where is it?"

"Near SFO," Friedberg said. "San Mateo County. Ever hear of Keith Hernandez, the baseball player?"

"Wasn't he on Seinfeld a couple of times?" Vail asked.

"One of the best first basemen in history. Went to high school in San Bruno."

"I'm sure tens of thousands of kids did," Vail said. "Why do I need to know this? And why did SFPD get the case if it was San Mateo County?"

"Because," Allman said, "even though the vic was discovered in San Bruno, he lived in the city."

"I want to see that file," Vail said. "Everything you've got."

"Yeah, well…" Burden pursed his lips. "I'd like to give it to you, but a lot of homicide files were destroyed in a fire in '99. What the fire didn't get, the water from the fire department did. We've got some stuff, but it was all dumped in a warehouse. We never had the money to sort through all that garbage. If we need something, we either find the info some other way or one of us spends hours sifting through all that moldy shit. And most of the time we never find what we're looking for."

Allman spread both hands, palm up. "I can help."

"And what's that's gonna cost us?" Friedberg asked.

Allman grinned. "Nothing. I'm offering my services as someone doing his civic duty. Of course, if you find it in your hearts to return the favor at some point in this investigation…"

"How are you gonna help?" Burden asked.

"That murder was the first scene I covered for the *Tribune* as the lead reporter. I'll give you my story, photos, everything I've got that the paper'll let me release. I might even have some other stuff in my archives. And the *Trib* may have something. I'll have to see. We were computerized, but we still used onsite servers."

"Anything you can give us'll be appreciated," Burden said.

"We had full access to crime scenes back then, so I've got a fair amount of stuff."

"When can you get it to us?" Friedberg asked.

"I've gotta file this story—the one I can't say much about—and then I'll dig around and get it all together."

"You can't say anything about the key," Vail said.

Allman jutted his head back. "So let me get this straight, Vail. I give you this all important detail that may provide linkage to a thirty-year-old unsolved case—which all of you missed—and you tell me, a member of the press, that I can't include that in my story?"

"That sounds about right," Vail said.

"Well, it sounds *about wrong* to me," Allman said.

"Clay." Burden stepped forward and placed a hand around Allman's shoulders. "Come here for a sec."

Vail watched as Burden and Allman took ten paces, then turned to face one another. "You have a problem with reporters," she said to Friedberg.

Friedberg's face remained still, but his fingers fumbled in his pocket for a cigarette. He extracted one, pulled out a match, and set it alight. "You really want to know?"

"I'm not just making small talk."

"I've never told anyone this, and if I didn't know you from that Crush Killer case, I'd never be telling you." He took a drag and studied her face. "But I feel like I can trust you." He blew the smoke out the side of his mouth. "Can I?"

"I'm a cop, of course you can trust me. But that's a loaded question. If you're going to confess to a murder, I'm not sure how that would work out." Vail thought of a situation exactly like that, something that had occurred only two months ago. The circumstances were different, but the scenario was the same.

"No, no confession." He held the cigarette in front of him, examined it a moment, then said, "When I was with the county— remember, I was with the sheriff's department in Marin. There was this case. A reporter was covering it for the *Register*. And he was at a crime scene, outside the tape, about twenty yards away.

"He comes over to me and says he has to talk to me about something. I didn't know who the hell he was. Then he introduced himself and I knew of him. He used to be with the *Trib*, taught Clay the ropes. Anyway, he says we should do coffee. I thought he wanted some inside scoop on the case, and I've never been one to leak stuff to the press, and I know you gotta be real careful what you say to them because it may end up plastered all over the front page, and if it gets picked up and runs nationally, it could cause problems. But I figure, hey, this guy's been around a long time in the Bay Area, so sure. I'll give him the time of day."

"So you met with him."

"I hadn't even sat down with my hot coffee before he tells me that he's gonna report me to my boss. For what, I ask. For planting evidence, he says."

"Did you know what he was talking about?"

"No idea. But I gotta tell you, I felt the anger rising in my head, like bile. You know? So I bite down and hold my mouth, because I was ready to rip him a new asshole. Like, who the hell are you to accuse me of something like that? I've been a cop for twenty-three years, and I've never done anything wrong on the job. Never. Goddamn boy scout."

"So what was the deal?"

"He said he saw me put something on the vic. I told him I checked inside his belt buckle, when I was looking for his piece, which we later found underneath him, caught in his jacket. See, the skel got off a couple rounds, I returned fire and took him down. But at first we couldn't find the weapon. I thought it was an automatic, turns out it was a revolver. They never did find any of the slugs he shot, which just added fuel to the fire."

"So this reporter thought you planted the revolver on the vic's body."

"Which is stupid. If I was gonna do something like that—which I would never do—but if I was going to, why would I wait till other cops—and the press—are there?"

"That would be pretty stupid. Unless you didn't have a chance to do it before they arrived."

"I was the only one there. No witnesses to the shooting. I was eventually cleared—that wasn't the issue. But this asshole implied that he had something on me, and that he'd keep it quiet."

"In exchange for something."

"See, that's where it gets muddy. He never asked for anything. But I got the impression that's what he was saying. It wasn't until last year that Clay told me he vouched for me and called off the dogs, so to speak. And that was a big deal because Clay doesn't talk to his former partner anymore."

"And he's never brought it up again."

"Nope. But every time I see him, it's like it's there, under the surface."

"Can it be your imagination?"

Friedberg realized his cigarette had burned a fair amount; he took a long drag, expelled it slowly. "Yeah. Probably is."

"But really, what could he have done to you? No proof. Just his word against yours."

"Something like that, no other witnesses, coming from a longtime journalist... He's not just a Joe on the street who says he saw something." He nodded knowingly. "Would ruin my career. Even if nothing was done about it, it'd be a thing around my neck for the rest of my career. You think they'd promote a guy who's been accused of a bad shoot and dropping a piece on the vic? No question, they'd pass me over."

"Maybe your anger is misplaced. He hasn't done anything or said anything in all these years. Right?"

Friedberg bobbed his head in agreement.

Vail gave his shoulder a firm pat. "I think you're okay. Whatever Clay said to him did the trick. And even if this jerkoff were to say something, all these years later, the focus would be on him and why he didn't come forward as a material witness. Not on you."

Burden and Allman had parted ways, Burden heading back in their direction, Allman toward his car. Friedberg tossed his cigarette to the ground and crushed it with the sole of his dress shoe, then bent over and picked up the butt.

"We're good," Burden said. "He's gonna withhold any details about that key for a while, at least until there's another victim."

"If there's another," Friedberg said.

"I want to give him that symbolism thing," Vail said. She moved around Burden and shouted, "Hey. Guitar man." Allman turned.

"Why didn't you speak up before?" Burden asked.

"We got more from him this way."

Allman stepped up to them and nodded at Vail.

"I just wanted you to know that we do appreciate you giving us that tip on the old case. I'll give you something in return. Interested?"

He pulled out a notepad, then clicked his pen. "You really gotta ask?"

Vail watched as Allman thumbed to a blank page. "The male vic was left in an oceanfront tunnel by the Sutro Baths. There's symbolism in that. The killer's got something against the ocean, so this is his way of saying 'Go to hell' to people associated with it in some way. I think we're gonna find that the vic was a former Marine, or he served in the Navy. Something like that."

Allman looked up from his pad. "He's got a beef with the ocean. You're serious."

"We're serious. Print it or not, your choice." *Print it, goddamn it. Take the bait.*

Allman scanned the faces of Burden and Friedberg, who, Vail thought, gave nothing away.

He flipped his notepad closed. "If you've got something else...more substantive, let me know." Allman nodded at Burden, then walked off toward his car.

When he had moved out of earshot, Burden said, "You couldn't think of anything better?"

"What was wrong with it?" Vail asked.

"Oh, nothing much. Just concerned the department will come off sounding like *idiots.*"

"I'll be sure not to take that the wrong way," Vail said.

"Don't be so sure," Burden said, then stepped into the street en route to his Ford.

Vail looked at Friedberg. "Did you think it was that bad?"

Friedberg shoved an unlit cigarette into his mouth, then shrugged. "Hopefully it won't matter. Maybe we'll get lucky and this asshole won't kill again."

Vail sighed heavily. "If Allman's right, and this offender's the same guy who killed back in '82, it's not a matter of if he's going to kill again. It's a matter of when."

# 19

MacNally closed the door behind him. He stepped over the broken shards of glass and moved to the threshold of the kitchen: and came face to face with a snarling German shepherd.

"Jesus Christ."

The dog sat there, piercing eyes riveted to his own, powerful shoulder muscles tensing. MacNally smiled and forced his body to relax. "Good dog," he said, bringing his voice up a few octaves.

He held out the palm of his hand, low, nonthreatening, then stepped forward. The dog did not move his head, but his eyes followed MacNally as he moved slightly to the right so he could enter the kitchen.

"How's my boy?" MacNally sung. Another step closer. He started to kneel, to get down to dog eye level. He had a feeling this was not a good idea—but he was committed. What was he to do? If he turned and ran, the shepherd would be on his back in half a second. If that.

As he knelt, the dog bared his teeth. Not a good sign. MacNally straightened up and kept his body still, moving his eyes around the kitchen, looking for something—anything—to use as a defensive weapon. Sitting on the stove was an iron skillet. He didn't want to hurt the dog, but if it came down to him or the pooch, there was not much of a choice.

MacNally inched to his right, closer to the stove. The shepherd, teeth still bared, growled long and low. Clearly, he did not care for that move. Fair enough—but MacNally didn't have time to screw around with this. He would have to chance it because he wasn't going to just stand there until Emily returned home and called off the dog. Or told him to attack.

MacNally lunged for the skillet—and, as suspected, the shepherd took offense. He went for MacNally's left arm—and although he grabbed hold, instantly let go when the heavy iron connected with this skull. The dog slunk to the floor.

"Shit," MacNally said. "Shouldn't have done that." He knelt down and felt the dog's chest. He was breathing—just unconscious. MacNally stroked his head and apologized—as if the dog would understand—and found the metal leash and choke collar in the hall closet. He slipped it over the shepherd's head, and then fastened it to the oven handle.

The kitchen was not usually a place people stored cash, other than a cookie jar or coffee can filled with loose change. He wasn't a snob—money was money—but he didn't know who, if anyone, was due to walk in the front door, and when—so he wanted to be in and out as quickly as possible. And that meant prioritizing his objectives.

Emily no doubt had insurance to cover any loss, so he didn't feel too guilty about taking her things. He would not steal anything that appeared to be family heirlooms or otherwise carried sentimental value. His goal was not to cause Emily any harm but rather to improve his own lot enough to enable him to care for Henry until he could find a solution to his employment dilemma. How he was going to do that he was not sure. But that was a long-term plan, and his present concern was more immediate: putting food on the table and clothes on their backs.

The living room offered more promise. The furniture appeared fresh and well kept, with clear plastic covers protecting the gold and brown paisley embroidery from dirt and dust. On the cherrywood bureau along the far wall, elaborate silver picture frames stood proudly facing the room. MacNally lifted the one on the far left and examined the black-and-white photo: Emily in a wedding dress with her husband, both coifed and smiling stoically for the camera.

He set that frame down and moved to the next one. A young boy sat on his proud parents' laps. Emily looked similar to how she appeared when he had seen her in the bank, so this was likely taken recently.

MacNally could not help but mentally draw the comparison to his own life, and what could have been. His own Doris, taken from Henry and him, denied the joy of building memories together as a family. Photos on the bureau. Fancy sofas and wood furniture. A home. His job, an income, a future. Promise. Instead, he had none of that. Taken from him as if ripped from the clutches of hope.

Next photo: Emily's husband, dressed in military garb, with medals pinned to his chest. Apparently, he was a World War II soldier, and had done well for himself—most impressively, he made it home alive. How could a man dodge bullets and bombs, enemy aircraft and ambushes half a world away in a hostile foreign country, and return home alive—yet Doris could be murdered in the safety of her own home in a middle-class New Jersey suburb? It didn't seem likely, and it didn't seem fair.

The final picture showed Emily's war hero soldier wearing a police uniform. The man was a cop. MacNally felt a sense of urgency well up in his stomach. He had better hurry and secure what he needed, then get the hell out of there.

He climbed the plush olive carpeted stairs to the second floor, and moved through the rooms. He learned that the boy's name was Irving, and that Emily's husband was James. MacNally slipped into the master bedroom where furled bed sheets were neatly folded, frilly pillows topping the mattress. Very little mess or clutter.

He checked the dresser drawers and found an unlocked metal box that contained a stack of used bills—twenties and tens, from what he could tell. He didn't stop to count it—he would do that later, in the safety of his car—and continued pulling out drawers.

MacNally ran his hand amongst the clothing, feeling for anything of value that might be hidden beneath. In the fifth drawer on James's side of the chest, his index finger jammed against something hard. MacNally separated the folded sweaters and found another metal box. He pulled it out and popped it open. Inside, a black handgun. It was worn around the edges and sat atop an index card with hand scrawled writing: "Luger P08 taken off the body of a German soldier I killed, Battle of the Bulge, 1/20/45."

MacNally lifted the weapon out of the box and stared at it a moment, then realized it could be of use to him. He slipped it into the waistband of his pants.

In a hinged wooden box, MacNally found a silver high school ring—which he left, figuring it had some value to James—and a gold-toned bracelet with two halves that inserted with a spring lever into one another. Engraved on the face were two block letters: J. and S. He looked at it a long moment—it could fetch him some decent money—but this, too, might mean something to its owner, so he wouldn't take it; he would merely borrow it.

He almost had everything he needed, with one exception: he slid the door to James's closet aside and found a leather satchel on the top shelf. He splayed it open, then selected a few shirts and several pair of pants, estimating by visual inspection that they would be close to fitting him. The saying *Beggars can't be choosers* came to mind—or, in this case, *Thieves can't complain too heartily if the stolen pants are a little baggy.*

He tossed in a few pair of socks, a belt, and sunglasses, and was about to zip the satchel when he saw a cardboard box on the floor marked "Winter." He pulled it out and checked inside: gloves, a knit ski mask—which he shoved into the satchel—wool socks, and two scarves.

Somewhere off behind him, the shepherd began barking. MacNally whirled, his heart rate suddenly galloping, and remembered he had tied down the dog. But it served as a reminder that he needed to get moving. If the animal kept barking like that, someone might call the police—and when they realized which house it was, the cops would double time it over.

MacNally slung the bag's strap over his shoulder and ran out, down the stairs, and was headed to the back door—avoiding the dog, who had now identified the man who'd given him the headache—when he stopped and returned to the living room. He grabbed one of the silver picture frames, shoved it into his bag, and left.

AS THE AFTERNOON SUN STARTED fading and moving toward the horizon, MacNally sat in the car beside Henry, the engine idling. "You sure you've got this down?"

"I'm sure. Do you know what you're going to do?"

MacNally grinned. He liked Henry's confidence. "Sure do." He gathered the items he needed to bring in with him, then pushed open the car door. "See you in five minutes, with a few bucks in my pockets."

"Hopefully it's more than just 'a few.'"

MacNally pushed through the double doors and entered. First National Thrift was a knot of activity, with several people in line and all the teller stations full. Emily September was where she had been when he was last in the bank.

He walked over to the counter and pulled out a piece of paper from a cubbyhole beneath the glass top like he had seen another customer do on one of his earlier visits, and removed the ballpoint pen from its slot. He wrote his note as he had rehearsed it countless times in his mind. He folded it in half and took his place in line.

There were five people ahead of him, which would give him time to get everything sorted out. He removed the ski mask from his pocket and pulled it over his head, leaving it rolled up above his ears. Next came the silver frame he had taken—the beauty was that he was going to return it to its rightful owner—and then carefully slipped the Luger from his pocket, shielding it with his body from the three security guards.

Everything was in place. He looked up and realized he was next. But Emily had just taken a new customer—shit, he had not planned on this. His eyes darted around, analyzing each teller and where each was in her transaction. No—he had to see Emily, or his plan would not work.

"Next person in line," a woman two stations down from Emily said.

"Oh," MacNally said, chuckling. He turned to the man behind him and said, "Go on. I forgot something." He looked down at the floor—at nothing—and pretended to be busy. He no doubt looked foolish, but he continued the charade while the customer walked around him and up to the teller.

He did this once more—had anyone been watching they would've known something was wrong—but Emily was now available, and MacNally nearly jumped when she called for the next in line.

He slipped on the stolen sunglasses as he stepped up to her window. Emily's eyes smiled back at him as if she recognized him, though she likely could not remember from where.

He needed to be efficient and get out of there before the guards took notice and let their gazes linger. Best for him to clear the front doors before they started after him. To speed the process, MacNally placed the frame on the counter in front of her.

Emily squinted, no doubt instantly recognizing the item from her home. The photo of James and Irving. Her eyes widened in fear.

MacNally placed his note atop the frame. It read:

EMILY SEPTEMBER PAY ATTENTION. I KNOW WHERE YOU LIVE. I'VE BEEN IN YOUR HOUSE. I'VE BEEN IN IRVING'S ROOM. I MEAN YOU NO HARM IF YOU DO AS I ASK. I NEED MONEY, EVERYTHING YOU HAVE IN YOUR DRAWER. I'VE BEEN OBSERVING THE BANK FOR DAYS SO I KNOW ABOUT HOW MUCH YOU HAVE THERE. COOPERATE AND I WILL LEAVE THIS TOWN FOREVER AND YOU WILL NEVER SEE ME AGAIN. PUT ALL THE MONEY IN THE BAG. DO NOT LOOK AT THE GUARDS. DO NOT REACT. JUST SMILE. IF YOU CROSS ME, I WILL USE THE GUN IF I HAVE TO. DON'T MAKE ME HAVE TO.

MacNally watched her face carefully. He could tell when she reached the important points in his note, particularly the one where he mentioned Irving. Then she looked up at him. Her eyes riveted to his, conveying a blend of anger, fear, and hate—no, contempt. But he did not take it personally; he would probably feel the same way if the situation was reversed.

MacNally tilted his head, then canted his eyes down to the letter, reminding her she had better follow his instructions. He slowly moved the Luger onto the countertop, in such a way that only Emily was able to see it. Then he lifted the leather satchel, rested it on the frame, and pushed both toward her. She moved the photo aside, with a lingering glance at the image that stared back at her. *Cooperate and I'll leave you and your family alone.* He could see on her face what was running through her mind. Exactly what he wanted to convey.

Emily pulled the satchel's metal hinge apart and began placing packs of money inside. MacNally reached into his left pocket and felt James's ID bracelet. He slowly pulled it out, then dropped it at his feet. If cops later searched the bank, they would find it—and perhaps think that the robbery was an inside job—perpetrated between Emily and her husband. Even if it only caused them to hesitate for a minute or two, it would serve as a welcomed cushion.

MacNally wanted to chance a look at each of the guards, but he did not want to risk making eye contact. Instead, he moved his right hand to the Luger, which attracted Emily's eyes for a moment. She stuffed in the last packet of bills, pulled the satchel closed and zipped it, then hoisted it onto the counter. She shoved it toward MacNally. He pulled the Luger back, then slid the weapon into his belt and grabbed the bag. It was full, and sufficiently heavy.

"Thank you, Emily," MacNally said. "If all goes as planned, you'll never see me again. You made a wise choice."

Her hard facial features demonstrated her emotional shift from fear and contempt to pure derision. She tightened her lips and said, "You'd better keep your word and go far and fast, because my husband's gonna find you if you don't. He's a cop. But you probably already know that."

"I do. And that means he has to follow the law. I don't." With that, MacNally turned and walked toward the exit, wanting to glance at the guard closest to him to gauge his reaction, but he instead kept his face forward, his eyes focused on the door.

He had no way of knowing that the next few moments were going to have a formative effect on the rest of his life.

# 20

Vail, Burden, and Friedberg returned to the Hall of Justice and took the elevator up to four. Friedberg stopped by evidence control to inquire about obtaining the brass key they had secured from the 1982 crime scene, while the others began laying out their case on a large whiteboard that spanned a wall facing the Bryant Street windows.

An hour later, Vail stood back to take in the murder board, and its victims, which now numbered four—five, as soon as Clay Allman sent over his materials on the 1982 murder. The linkage was tenuous for now, but it was an intriguing break in the case. An offender's first kill—if it was the same guy, and if it was his first—often provided more clues about the man than his later crimes. As an inexperienced criminal, he was not likely as careful as he would be so many years later, when he had time, and presumably other victims, to hone his trade.

And if there was a victim in 1982, there were likely others in the intervening years. It was not a certainty, but it was a strong possibility.

Vail looked over at Burden, who was seated at his desk. "We've got four, maybe five vics, and probably a whole lot more we don't even know about. And we're nowhere in finding this guy. And he's not going to stop killing to give us time to catch up." She turned back to the crime scene photos of Maureen and William Anderson, Russell and Irene Ilg. "But I do think he's trying to tell us something."

Burden joined her at the murder board. "Like what?"

"He's placing the male bodies in specific locations, out in public. And he's leaving something at the female vic crime scenes. That key. I think it was meant for us."

"Okay, so what does that mean? What if he's telling us something and we're not hearing him?"

Vail rested part of her buttocks on the edge of the desk. "It could get ugly—I mean, uglier. It'll frustrate him. Remember BTK?"

"Bind, Torture, Kill. How could I forget that asshole?"

"Dennis Rader, in his BTK persona, sent the cops a note basically saying, How many do I have to kill before I get my name in the paper, or some national attention? Part of his positive feedback loop was attaining fame. He gave himself a media-ready nickname, for chrissake."

"So maybe we should let Allman run with his story. Are we making things worse by not mentioning the key, which he's purposely left for us? If he thinks we didn't find it, won't it piss him off?"

Vail sighed. Her eyes flicked over to the brutalized bodies of Anderson and Ilg. *I really don't want to see this happen again. Goddamn it. What's the right call here?* "I'm honestly not sure if I have enough info yet to make an informed decision."

"We've got five goddamn bodies," Burden said, anger lacing his tone. "How many more do you need?"

Vail banded her arms across her chest. "You have five seconds to apologize. I don't fucking deserve that."

Burden turned away and faced the whiteboard. "You're right. That was out of line. I've been a detective for over twenty years. I should be able to work this case without relying solely on your analysis." He thought a moment, then said, "How sure are you about this key?"

"That it was left for us? I'd like to know if the key from thirty years ago matches the one we just found at the Ilg's. If they do…but how do we define match? An exact match? It's the same key, just a copy…or a similar type of key…or same type of lock?" She thought a moment. "If Allman's memory is right, and the '82 key is very similar or identical to the one we just found, then that's significant. Assuming for a minute that it's not an incredible coincidence, it's a very specific ritual behavior. My gut tells me it has meaning to the offender—and because it doesn't appear to have been used to maim or mark the victim, I really do think it's meant for us."

"I've asked Jackson to see if he can get us some info on that key. It's large and its shape is a little odd, with a shaft that's not your usual pin setup. Maybe we'll get lucky." Burden tossed a cluster of papers on the desk. "Knowing what we know now, are you still convinced this isn't the type of killer who preys on elderly women—the offenders that Safarik's studied?"

"I'm more convinced now than I was before," Vail said. "There's no secondary financial component to his act; he doesn't, as an afterthought, take money, jewelry. A typical sexual killer of elderly women is unsophisticated, disorganized, and of lower intelligence. They certainly wouldn't interact with the police. That's an intelligent act, a sign of psychopathy. And displaying the bodies in public places—it's just not their way. Let alone the fact that half his vics are male.

"Safarik found that the killers of older women aren't sophisticated, and they don't mix genders. So, no. Unless I see something that totally contradicts this, this guy doesn't fit. He's a psychopath, and we've got our hands full."

Friedberg walked in. "I heard, 'He's a psychopath and we've got our hands full.' That can't be good."

"It's not," Vail said, sliding off the desk.

"But what does that actually mean—for us?"

"Labeling him a psychopath isn't as impressive as it sounds. Ninety percent of serial killers are psychopathic. That's by far the highest percentage among violent criminals."

"Someone actually studied that?" Friedberg asked.

"Hell yeah. A third of rapists are psychopaths, half of all hostage takers. Two thirds of molesters. Like I said, psychopathy's cornered the violent crime market. If we ever make contact with him—and I think it's only a matter of time before we do—figuring out how to categorize him properly could prove extremely important."

"Categorize him how?" Burden asked.

"There are four types, all with the same basic traits and characteristics. But they're present in differing doses. I've got a decent idea of how to approach him, of how to talk to him, but let's see how he reacts to Allman's article."

Burden sat down at the table. "What if you get it wrong?"

"I'd rather not go there. Let's just say it could inflame the situation."

Friedberg shoved an unlit cigarette in his mouth. "More vics."

*More vics. The story of my life.* Vail looked away. "Yes. To complicate things, psychopathy could be co-morbid with other psychiatric disorders. But psychopathy is king and that's what will resonate the strongest."

Friedberg pulled the Marlboro from his lips. "I've requisitioned the key from the '82 case. Wasn't easy because I had nothing to go on, but I think we found it."

"Assuming the key's the same, or similar," Friedberg said, "what do you think it means? The key to what?"

Vail shrugged. "First thought is that it's a taunt. See if you can find the key to the case. He's left it right there in front of us. He's saying, 'Here's the key. Can't you see it? What's wrong with you people'?"

"What's wrong with *us*?" Friedberg said with a chuckle. "Guy's an insane nut case and he's asking what's wrong with us."

"Lose that thought right now," Vail said. "And don't bring it up again."

Friedberg looked around, his brow crumpled in confusion. "What'd I say?"

"A psychopath is not crazy. He's not insane, and he's not a nut job. He's in touch with reality and knows right from wrong. This is an important concept, especially when it comes time to interview him."

"You sound pretty optimistic that we'll catch him," Burden said.

"We can't take a defeatist attitude. I have to believe we're gonna nail this asshole. I mean, don't you?"

Burden and Friedberg glanced at each other. In unison, they said, "Sure," and "Yeah."

But their body language did not invite confidence.

"Look at it this way," Vail said. "This scumbag's enjoying these murders. And he likes the cat and mouse game he's set in motion. So it's up to us. If we don't figure this shit out, it's gonna be hard to sleep at night. Because he's not going to stop."

# 21

MacNally pushed through the glass doors of First National Thrift. A chill wind slapped against his exposed lips, but he was only vaguely aware of it. He made eye contact with Henry, who was in the Chevy, idling double-parked at the curb. He popped the passenger door open as MacNally slid between the chrome bumpers of the stationary vehicles, then jumped into their car.

MacNally slammed the door. "Go!" But he did not need to say that—before he could finish the one syllable word, Henry had already accelerated hard, shoving MacNally against the seat, his head whipping backwards.

In the corner of his eye, MacNally saw the guard he had passed on his way out of the bank come bursting through the doors, yelling and pointing at them. "Shit." It escaped MacNally's mouth without much thought. He didn't want to distract Henry from doing what he needed to do: Drive. Fast, yet in control. He yanked off the ski mask and tossed it in the backseat.

"Did you get the money?"

"Got the money. Just concentrate on getting us out of here." He looked over at his son. Henry was just a kid. What was he thinking involving him in something like this? But it wasn't like he could've robbed the bank, found his car in the parking lot, and then made a successful getaway.

As had been the case the past three years, he had Henry and Henry had him. That was it. No friends, no neighbors, no one else they could rely on. Fortunately, Henry was tall for his age, and wise beyond his years. Both made this job possible.

"Whoa—" Henry yelled as he swerved to avoid a car that had run a stop sign.

MacNally had to grab the heavy satchel, which had flown off his lap and onto the bench seat between him and Henry.

"How much did we get?"

Clutching the overstuffed bag, MacNally had been wondering the same thing. "Don't know. Don't worry about it—just concentrate on driving." He shifted the satchel on his lap. "A lot. That was a good bank, lots of wealthy customers."

"Guess I won't need to mow any more lawns."

A simple comment, but it was like a dagger to MacNally's heart. He pushed the guilt aside and brought his thoughts back to the road ahead of them. "We need to make a few turns. And we should change cars, too."

Out of MacNally's peripheral vision, a green sign whizzed by: *Welcome to Georgia.*

"Why?" Henry asked.

"Back when we left, I think I saw a guard come out of the bank. If he got a look at the car—"

Before MacNally could complete his sentence, the whine of a siren wound to life behind them.

Henry and MacNally shared a glance. But it was quick, because Henry apparently made his own choice, absent discussion: he floored the accelerator and the Chevy's engine muscled up with a vicious roar, propelling them forward as the speedometer needle wound around toward seventy. On a residential street, it was a dangerous move—but there weren't many options. They had the money in hand, and—something MacNally had not thought of...he had used a handgun. That would make it armed robbery. He didn't know the law, but he had read enough in the newspaper about Machine Gun Kelly and Bonnie and Clyde to know that associating weapons with banks led to long prison sentences.

Such a prospect was something he would have to live with—he was an adult and he had made the decision to move forward with their plan. It was simple. He had to provide for his son. And given his circumstances, this was the only way he could think of doing that.

But despite the wisdom beyond his years, Henry was not even a teenager. MacNally could not stand to think of a life behind bars for him. What did they do with kids, anyway? They couldn't put them in cells with grown men, could they?

All this ran through his head as Henry swerved, swung the car left and right, ran stoplights and generally did a yeoman's job of handling a big, heavy vehicle. Still, MacNally wished it was him behind the wheel. He didn't know if he could do any better, but he felt powerless to control their destiny.

Henry accelerated again. MacNally twisted his torso to look behind them—the cops were about four car lengths off their rear bumper, falling back rapidly as they darted forward.

Before they pulled away, MacNally saw that there were two officers in front. And they did not look happy.

"Shit—"

MacNally swung his head back around to see another police cruiser ahead of them, in the distance, its lights rotating. His eyes darted around, looking for a way out. "There—turn left!"

Thirty feet ahead was a side street. Henry yanked the large wheel toward their escape route and the Chevy tilted hard and fast—slamming MacNally up against the right passenger door.

But their tire struck a pothole and the left side of the hulking vehicle left the asphalt and sent them skidding into the curb and up onto the lawn of a house. They smashed through the front window and came to rest with the hood protruding into the living room.

Something was sticking into MacNally's right thigh, pinning him down. He turned to Henry, whose nose was dripping blood from colliding with the steering wheel.

"Get out. Go on, just run!"

Henry popped open his door and fled. It slammed behind him and MacNally watched as his son darted behind the nearest house, out of sight.

And in that moment, two police cars pulled into the street behind him. He leaned toward the driver's seat, pulling on his leg—but a piece of metal was jammed against it and he was pinned in place.

He looked down at the satchel stuffed with money. He thought of Henry, of a young son on the run. No money, and now no father, no mother. Nothing and no one.

Tears filled his eyes as he heard guttural yells coming at him from both sides of the car.

"Don't move!"

"Hands—gets your hands where we can see them!"

MacNally craned his neck left and right. Officers stood on both sides of him, their pointed handguns staring accusingly at him through the two broken windows.

He struggled to free his arms, then complied with their order.

"Where's the other guy?" one of the men said.

MacNally looked up at the cop. "What other guy?"

"The one who was driving."

"Just me," MacNally said, tears flowing down his cheeks. "I was driving."

"That's a load a horseshit," the officer said to his partner. "His leg's good and stuck, no way he was driving. 'Sides, I saw two men in that car."

"Me, too," said a cop from the other cruiser. "Not a man. A kid. Maybe twelve, fourteen."

"Pete, Roger, search the neighborhood. Stan, call this in and tell 'em we got ourselves a fugitive. Then start a canvass. Find the sumbitch. I'll deal with this asshole." The three men ran off.

So that's what he was now. An asshole bank robber who broke into an innocent woman's house, terrorized her dog, and stole her belongings. For what?

MacNally let his head fall back against the seat. Wondering how this had happened. Three years ago he was an upstanding citizen with a good job, a good marriage to a bright woman, and a young son.

As he lay there, he realized that he no longer had any of them.

# 22

Vail had returned to her hotel at 1 AM—Burden and Friedberg had left three hours earlier, telling her the lieutenant would never approve their overtime and had rules against working cases around the clock. Ballooning state and local budget deficits drove a lot of what happened in California these days, and not much of it was good.

The next day passed uneventfully. They worked the forensics of the case and accumulated usable data—but none of it brought them any closer to identifying an individual or even providing them with a suspect pool to pick from. The crime lab was backed up with cases and evidence, and they did not get an immediate hit on the brass key. Identifying it was going to be a longer slog than they had hoped.

They shifted their efforts toward identifying the portion of the key that had been ground away. Whatever had been stamped or struck in the metal must have contained a clue to where it was made and by whom, or at very least what it was used for. But the filing appeared to be sufficiently deep to obliterate the markings.

Likewise, the video capture of their UNSUB led nowhere. Further analysis of screen shots only told them the killer wore a ski mask. And because it was black, or some other dark color, there was no way to evaluate shadows to discern his facial landscape. Like the rest of the case, his image was stuck in limbo and it became increasingly frustrating to look at the man and not be able to see him.

Friedberg and Vail sat in Homicide staring at the whiteboard when Burden called out from his desk. "Email from Clay. His *Trib* story, photos and notes on the '82 case."

"And?" Vail asked, walking over to his desk and bending over to see the monitor. Friedberg followed, taking up a spot over Burden's other shoulder.

"And I sent it to the printer." He double clicked on the PDF and Acrobat opened. Scans of Allman's article appeared on-screen.

Vail read the headline: Bold killer Leaves Body in San Bruno, by Clayton W. Allman, October 25, 1982. A man was found seated on a bench in front of the Federal archives building, fully clothed. Head trauma. "Head trauma," Vail said.

"I see," Burden said.

Vail continued reading. A shoe was stuffed in the victim's mouth. "That's interesting."

"What, the tie?"

"Haven't gotten to that yet. The shoe. Stuffing a shoe in his mouth is fairly obvious, and it's pretty much what you might think it represents—like the vic snitched on the killer, or said something that offended him. He stuffs the shoe in the mouth as if he's gotten the last word."

"I know the inspector who handled the case," Burden said. "Millard Ferguson. He was retiring when I was promoted. I can look him up, see if I can find him, see what he remembers."

"Anything he gives us is more than what we've got now."

"I'll get someone on it." He rose and walked out.

"The tie?"

Friedberg said, "Read further down. Vic had a silk tie wrapped around his neck."

"Is there another article?"

Friedberg sat down in the chair and scrolled through the document. "Yes. Ten days later."

They both went silent as they read.

Friedberg pointed at the screen. "Cause of death."

"Strangulation. The tie."

"Vic's name was Edgar Newhall. And—"

"He was fifty-seven. Much younger than our current vics."

Friedberg leaned back in the chair. "So you think this case isn't related?"

Vail hiked her brow. "Hard to say at this point. He's an older male, but a totally different victim group. That said, there's a lot more we need to find out about Mr. Newhall. Who was he?"

"Who was who?" Burden asked, a sheaf of papers in his hand.

"The vic," Friedberg said. "Name's Edgar Newhall. A lot younger than our current vics, and I'd like to know why. We need to find out more about this guy. I'll take that, you find Millard Ferguson."

Burden's phone rang. He reached in front of Friedberg and lifted the handset. "Burden."

"He doesn't answer his phone 'Birdie?'" Vail said.

Burden made a flapping motion with the hand holding the papers. *Be quiet.* "Say that again?" he said into the receiver. As Burden listened, his shoulders rolled forward.

*I know that body language. A new victim.*

Burden hung up, then tossed the papers on his desk. "Let's go."


THE TEMPERATURE HAD DROPPED INTO the low fifties and the fog had returned. It blew by the skyscrapers with abandon, American flags mounted atop the buildings stretched tight, proudly displaying the stars and stripes.

"Where are we?" Vail asked, seated in the back of the Taurus, her head rotating left and right.

"You mean the area, or relative to the other murders?"

"Relative to the other murders. I'm trying to figure this out spatially, because I have a feeling that's going to be significant."

"Why's that?" Friedberg asked.

"The male bodies, the ones left outside. Those locations were chosen by the offender for some specific reason."

Burden nodded. "Find the reason, and we may be on our way to identifying the offender."

"I'm pretty sure of that," Vail said.

"From Palace of Fine Arts," Friedberg said, "the new vic's between a mile and a half and two miles. From the Cliff House, about five miles."

*Not as close as I'd hoped.*

"Remember I mentioned geographic profiling? The mental mapping thing? We're dealing so far with a closed city environment. I've got a friend who does it. Could help."

"You can find out who the UNSUB is based on where he kills?" Burden asked.

"Not exactly," Vail said. "By evaluating the pattern and location of the victims, we can learn what type of predator he is, how he searches for his victims, and why he goes after the women he does. And by understanding that, we can zero in on where he might strike next. It's not perfect, but it can be surprisingly accurate."

They arrived at the corner near 700 Bay Street well after sunset. Sodium vapor streetlights gave off an inadequate, orange-hued glow. Headlighted cars moved along the local streets, but traffic was lighter than what Vail envisioned it would be for a city, even if it was near the end of rush hour.

Burden turned right up the adjacent sloping street and left the Ford in a No Parking zone behind a vacant police cruiser. The officer was twenty feet away, standing in front of yellow crime scene tape he had strung around a wide swath of the immediate area, thumbs poking out through the loops of his utility belt as he paced, watching to make sure kids or dogs didn't stray across his makeshift boundary.

Beyond the cop was the purpose for their call: a man standing upright, pinned against a telephone pole.

"Well that's just lovely," Vail said. She swung her body around, taking in the landscape. Off in all directions, homes similar in style to the ones in the neighborhoods where the Andersons and Ilgs lived. Storefront businesses. And a downward angled street running perpendicular to Bay.

A car slowed alongside the crime scene, then parked. Out stepped Rex Jackson, Nikon hanging from his neck and a toolkit from his hand. "This guy's busy," he quipped. "And he's keeping us busy. We haven't even finished processing his last scene."

"When do you think you'll have that for us?"

"This isn't TV," Jackson said. "Just like you don't solve cases in fifty-nine minutes, we can't process a ton of info in a matter of hours. We're running with a thin staff and a thinner budget. You'll have it when we have it."

"No rush—whenever you get around to it," Vail said.

Jackson ignored her dig, setting down his kit and shooting photos. He made an adjustment to his camera and took another test picture. Satisfied, he swung left and began documenting the scene.

"Since Rex is here," Burden said, "let's leave him alone to process everything before we trample it."

Forty-five minutes later, Jackson gave them the thumbs up and they moved closer to the victim.

The body was fastened to the pole with the same type of fishing line as the prior victims. He was dressed in a loose-fitting suit. And a number was scrawled across the vestiges of a scar on his forehead.

"Another goddamn number," Burden said.

Vail tilted her head. "Thirty-five. So, we've got thirty-seven, forty-nine, and now thirty-five. A pattern?"

"None I'm seeing," Burden said. "And it's pissing me off."

"What's the deal with poles," Friedberg asked. "They've all been secured to poles of some kind."

"Phallic," Jackson said as he snapped his toolkit closed.

"You could be right," Vail said. "But it might simply be a means to an end: the act of leaving his victims erect, standing and facing the people who find him, may be what's important to him. The pole is the easiest way for him to do that."

"So this is an attempt to shock?" Burden asked. "Get a rise out of the people who discover the body?"

"We can't rule it out. Let's see if we can find some surveillance cameras in the area."

Burden called to the first-on-scene officer, who was standing near his vehicle, and asked him to look for businesses or homes that had closed circuit systems.

A car came down Bay far too fast. It stopped in the middle of the street and the passenger window rolled down.

"Hey!" It was Clay Allman, leaning across from the driver's seat. "You didn't call me?"

"We're a little busy," Vail said. *And our first call isn't to the press, dickhead.*

Allman parked a few cars down and jogged back toward them. He stood there a moment, outside the crime scene tape, sizing up the victim. "Okay, that's a little weird."

"A little," Vail said.

Allman made a face, then turned to Burden. "You sure this isn't personal?"

"Nah, she's like this with everyone."

Vail frowned. "Sorry. Murders tend to put me in a bad mood. I'm funny that way."

"I accept your apology," Allman said.

"She was being sarcastic," Burden said.

"Whatever." Allman pointed at the body. "Who's the vic?"

"Haven't gotten to that yet." Friedberg reached into the man's suit and felt around. He found the wallet in his trousers, and then flipped it open. "Harlan Rucker." He pulled out his driver's license. "Says here he's seventy-eight."

"Home address?"

"Hmm. Interesting." Friedberg turned to Vail and Burden. With Allman only a few feet away, he was not going to read it aloud.

Vail's phone started vibrating. She reached down and checked the Caller ID: Roxxann Dixon. "Hey, how's it going?" Vail asked as she huddled with Friedberg and Burden around the license.

"I figured I'd touch base with you about doing dinner," Dixon said. "But that's not why I'm calling."

"You're calling because you've got an elderly female who's been brutally raped and tortured, then kicked in the head. And there's a brass key nearby."

There was silence.

"Roxx?"

"What are you, a witch?"

"Nothing so exciting. You've got one of our vics. Text me your address. We'll meet you."

"Where?" Allman asked. "Another vic?"

Vail looked at him, then stepped in closer to Burden and Friedberg. "Got a call from a friend. She's just caught a case in American Canyon, just over the Napa County line. One of our female vics." Vail's BlackBerry vibrated. "And I've got the address." She consulted the screen. "Matches the one on Rucker's CDL."

"Hey," Allman called out behind them. "I keyed you guys in on the '82 case, gave you my files. How about cutting me in on the scoop?"

Vail looked at Burden. "You're not considering it."

"He's just trying to do his job. He's always been fair with us. What's the harm?"

Vail shrugged in resignation. "It's your case."

Burden turned around to face Allman. "Fine. We'll text you the address in half an hour, so we have some lead time. I want to check things out before you get there."

They spent another ten minutes with Harlan Rucker, then released the scene to the officer and trudged back to their car. This case had just taken a turn—which was not good.

They hadn't even figured out what was going on when it was moving in a straight line.

# 23

They pulled up behind an unmarked Ford Crown Victoria. It was the same one in which Vail had spent about ten days driving around Napa while working the Crush Killer case with Dixon.

The American Canyon neighborhood was at the southernmost tip of Napa County, a thirty-five-minute drive from the last crime scene. A bedroom community of both San Francisco and the heralded wine country, American Canyon was a solid middle- to upper-middle-class neighborhood incorporated in the early nineties.

The house was a production home in a residential area. It looked like it had been treated to a fresh coat of paint recently and the front garden appeared to be similarly maintained. Vail greeted the officer at the front door and led Burden and Friedberg into the house. Lights were on in the hallway, and Vail could hear voices in a room off to her right.

As she approached, Roxxann Dixon stepped into the corridor. "Karen," she said with a wide grin.

The two women embraced, and then Vail introduced her to Burden.

"Inspector Friedberg," Dixon said. "How's the city treating you?"

"Not so good these days. These murders are pretty brutal. But I don't have to tell you that."

A man emerged from the bedroom.

"Brix," Vail said. "Good to see you."

"Who woulda thought? I figured when you left Napa three months ago, we were finally rid of you."

"Guess I'm like that piece of chewing gum on the bottom of your shoe."

They all enjoyed a knowing chuckle.

"Detective Lieutenant Redmond Brix," Vail said, "Inspectors Lance Burden and Robert Friedberg—who helped us out with the Crush Killer case, over by Battery Spencer."

"Right, right," Brix said as he and the crew exchanged handshakes.

"So what're you doing here, Roxx?" Vail asked. "Did your transfer go through?"

"I gave it a little push," Brix said. "Guess it was more like a shove. It took the sheriff a little while to free up the cash for another detective, but I told him he couldn't afford to miss out on Roxxann."

"Came through last week," Dixon said.

"Hell of a first case," Vail said.

Dixon brushed back her blonde hair. "No shit. What you described on the phone...it was dead-on. No pun intended."

"Let's take a look," Burden said.

They walked into the sizable master bedroom, where a CSI was bent over a body that lay supine. He snapped a photo, straightened up, and then shot Vail a less than friendly look.

Matthew Aaron. Not a pleasant memory from her time in the wine country.

"Where's that key?" Vail asked.

Aaron reached into his kit and removed a clear evidence bag. It was properly identified and tagged.

Burden took it and held it up so he and Friedberg could get a closer look.

"We've got two others like this," Friedberg said. "Well, one in our possession and one on the way."

"On the way from where?" Dixon asked.

Vail explained the 1982 Edgar Newhall murder. "We don't know enough yet to say if the cases are related, but it sure looks that way."

Burden motioned to the woman in front of him. She displayed nearly identical burn marks, the same gruesome vaginal and anal injuries, and bruising around the head. "What do we know about this vic? I assume her name's Rucker?"

"Cynthia Rucker," Dixon said. "When I saw what we had here, I called Redd. He told me to call Karen. The sheriff went through the FBI's National Academy training, so they felt it was best to find out if we were dealing with a psychosexual killer."

"Kudos to all of you," Vail said. "We're getting away from using that term, but that is what we're dealing with here. And that's not all. There's a lot more to this case. I'm not sure what, just yet, but we're dealing with a very volatile and unstable killer."

"Great," Brix said.

Vail moved around the bed and examined Cynthia's head wounds. "Thing is, his recent murders—if he did the one in '82—have been confined to San Francisco. In fact, her husband, Harlan, is in the city. In case you were wondering."

"We were," Dixon said. "Any chance we can get a sit-down with him? Obviously, we've got a lot of questions."

"He's tied to a telephone pole," Vail said. "I don't think your sit-down would be too fruitful."

Dixon and Brix shared a look.

"Karen thinks there's geographic significance to the killer's choice of victims," Friedberg said.

"Yeah." Vail shifted her feet. "About that. I'm not so sure. This one kind of throws a monkey wrench into that theory." She thought a moment. "But maybe not."

"Worth checking into?" Burden asked.

Vail shrugged. "Yeah. But—this case is very unusual to begin with. Married couples being offed is odd enough—but he's transporting the males and leaving them, in some cases, miles away. To my memory, none of that's ever been done before. I can turn this over for a geographic profile, but it's going to make for a challenging analysis."

"I'm done here," Matt Aaron said, snapping his kit closed.

"The contact at SFPD is Rex Jackson," Vail said. "Can you make sure he gets copies of everything you—"

"I know the procedure, Agent Vail." He rose and faced her, standing a little closer than what would normally be considered a comfortable distance. "You know, it sure was nice not having you around. I already have a few bosses. Don't need someone like you looking over my shoulder."

Dixon placed a hand on Vail's forearm. Calming her. Vail didn't feel calm. But she forced a smile and said, "You must be really, really good on all the other cases you handle in Napa County. Because from what I've seen on the two you handled while I was here, your professionalism left a lot to be desired."

Aaron dropped his kit. "I've had—"

"Okay," Brix said, shoving his arm in front of his criminalist. "That's enough. Matt, if you're done here, you can go." He waited for Aaron to react.

He did—he bent down and picked up his case, then threw Vail a stern look.

"I'd appreciate if you two weren't like two cats in heat all the time," Brix said. "Learn to get along. We're on the same goddamn side."

Aaron frowned at Brix, then pushed his way out of the room, through the crowd of detectives.

"He does have a point," Brix said.

Vail looked at him. "And what point is that?"

"Things have been a lot more quiet in town since you left."

"Don't you remember my nickname?"

"The serial killer magnet," Dixon said with a grin.

Burden shook his head. "Oh, that's fucking great. Couldn't you have told us that sooner? I knew I should've insisted on Safarik."

"What's your procedure?" Dixon asked. "You've obviously got another jurisdiction involved. I'd like to be part of what's going down on your end, help solve this thing together. Does SFPD set up major crimes task forces?"

"Only for drug and gang-related crimes," Burden said.

Vail spread her hands, palm up. "But that doesn't mean we can't work together. Meet in a room, either at Homicide or somewhere else. Not a task force—"

"But a task force," Dixon said.

"Exactly."

Burden shook his head. "The lieutenant won't be happy."

"We can have meetings, exchange info, that sort of thing," Friedberg said. "As long as it doesn't hit his bottom line, if we don't ask for money or staff support, any shit like that, I think we'll be fine. If we're making progress, who's gonna complain?"

"And if we don't get results?" Burden asked.

Friedberg chuckled. "Then we deserve whatever heat the lieutenant sends our way."

# 24

August 6, 1959

*United States Penitentiary*
*Leavenworth*
*1300 Metropolitan Street*
*Leavenworth, Kansas*

"**T**he defendant is hereby sentenced to forty-five years' incarceration in a Federal penitentiary, the location of which shall be determined by the Bureau of Prisons." The judge rapped his gavel, and Walton MacNally's fate was sealed tighter than the animal skin on the surface of a drum.

His arms were engaged from behind by two burly, sour-faced US Marshals. But MacNally was numb, unemotional, and not tuned in to the ramifications of the verdict. He understood the meaning, but he could not comprehend the depth behind the words.

As he was led out of the courtroom, MacNally objectively reviewed the previous week's proceedings in his mind. Unlike his prior journey through the judicial system in Doris's murder trial, this one had not gone well; in fact, there was not one hour during his six days of justice where he felt he had even the slightest chance of overcoming the charges.

His court-appointed attorney attempted to prepare him for the worst well before the trial began. He reviewed each of the pieces of evidence they had against him: the handgun found still tucked in his waistband—a rare brand of an unusual vintage for America— damning in and of itself because the weapon had been documented by a local newspaper when Lieutenant James September returned from his distinguished service in Germany. September had shot an enemy soldier who was attempting to stab one of his fellow infantrymen. The lieutenant then took the sidearm back to the States as a keepsake. The plan was for him to donate it at some future date to the Smithsonian.

That it was found on MacNally, along with the eyewitness identification made by the bank's security guard and Emily September…and, of course, possession of the satchel stuffed with bills that matched some of the serial numbers purported to have been given to Emily only an hour prior, were more than enough to send the jury scurrying back to their room.

But there was more: the discovery of a gold Cross pen in MacNally's pocket, with the name "G. Yaeger" engraved on the barrel, which matched an object reportedly stolen from Township Community Savings during a robbery two months earlier.

Although MacNally's attorney pointed out that the Community Savings incident did not involve a firearm, the local police introduced MacNally's handwritten letter, given by the defendant to the teller during the robbery, inferring the possession of a weapon and his inclination to use it. The writing and linguistic patterns contained in both notes matched, and they appeared to be strikingly similar to an exemplar the prosecutor asked MacNally to provide before the trial commenced.

A minor transgression at the time—the gold pen had some value, of course, to Mr. Yaeger, its rightful owner—but it carried far greater worth to the prosecution. The writing implement implicated MacNally in the earlier robbery and linked the two crimes, indelibly marking Walton MacNally a criminal who had committed multiple armed robberies. But not just armed robberies. Bank robberies. A federal crime.

And an innocuous comment made to a cop at the scene proved equally as damaging—if not the final nail. One of the officers involved in MacNally's arrest stated that he saw another occupant in the vehicle—a young boy running from the scene when they arrived. MacNally did not want Henry's involvement to be anything more than an unwilling passenger, so he initially denied it. But as the manhunt intensified, MacNally attempted to have it called off by telling them that the fleeing suspect had been his son, who was merely along for the ride because he had no place to leave him. He insisted that Henry had known nothing of the robbery, and, in fact, that he hadn't even wanted to go with him.

Based on these admissions, the prosecutor added kidnapping to the charges. And because he had crossed into Georgia from Alabama, the federal "crossing state lines" statute added severity to his crimes.

As far as the jury was concerned, the prosecution's case was as tight as the security at Fort Knox. They deliberated for twenty-one minutes. The verdict was read and the judge imposed his sentence.

Now, several months after being arrested, after watching Henry vaporize into a dusky evening, he was being flown to what would be his new domicile: the United States Penitentiary in Leavenworth, Kansas. Many famous criminals had called the prison home, from gangsters like Machine Gun Kelly to murderers like Robert Stroud. Now, the name of Walton MacNally would be added to the prison's vaunted ranks.

The Boeing 707 taxied to a secluded runway at the recently constructed Kansas City Industrial Airport. The two US Marshals escorting Walton MacNally led their shackled prisoner off the plane and down the stairs before the remaining passengers disembarked. On the tarmac, another marshal and two Leavenworth guards took custody and escorted him to a waiting security van.

MacNally took a seat at a barred window and watched as the vehicle chugged its way through the Missouri countryside. A chase car, containing what MacNally presumed were either more marshals or some other type of federal agent, trailed the van, no doubt guarding against an attack or a coordinated attempt to free him. He found the humor in that: he knew no one, and now, separated from his son, he had no one. No one would care that he was being imprisoned. No one would have the slightest interest in breaking him out.

The prison transport crossed over the Missouri River and into Leavenworth, where Missouri 92 turned into Metropolitan Avenue. As the convoy came to a stop at a traffic light, MacNally could not help but notice the front entrance to Fort Leavenworth.

Ahead on the right, MacNally saw the penitentiary's overbearing silver dome reflecting a sunny haze that hung as thick as the humidity permeating the bus. Beads of perspiration rolled mercilessly down his forehead. With his hands shackled to his feet, which were themselves in leg irons, he was unable to swipe away the lines of sweat as they dripped onto his tan trousers.

As the van began moving again, MacNally shifted his butt in the seat to get a better view of his new home. The dome dominated the structure, which extended in both directions to its left and right. The building was massive and imposing.

"See them columns? That dome?" the guard asked him.

"Yeah." MacNally kept his gaze on the approaching penitentiary.

"Supposed to look like the US Capitol in DC. Funny, don't you think? They built this place and designed it to hold the worst of the worst. Criminals, all of 'em. And they made it look like the place where our senators and congressmen do their business." The man chortled heartily, then leaned forward, inches from MacNally's face. "You should laugh, asshole. Where you goin', may be the last time you feel like laughin' for a long, long time."

MacNally turned to face him but kept his expression impassive. The last thing he needed was to antagonize a law enforcement officer on his way to doing hard time at a penitentiary. He didn't know what it was like inside, but he imagined that the inmates and guards did not get along well. He did not want to make the situation worse.

The van chugged down the road, a wide green median, not unlike pictures he had seen of the National Mall, laid out to his right. Ahead was a tan stone guard tower with a gray-green roof. An American flag flew beside the structure.

As they approached, MacNally had to admit that the place looked like a government structure. He had never been to the U.S. Capitol, though he remembered seeing a photo in a high school textbook. If the guard was right, and it seemed like he was, the Capitol was an imposing edifice.

The monstrosity ahead sported massive columns that striped the front of the building. But they weren't real—they appeared to be carved from the limestone surface, as if in relief. The vertical windows were barred. What looked like nearly four dozen concrete steps led up to the entrance.

At the top of the façade, below the dome, the words United * States * Penitentiary were engraved into the stone's face. As if there was any doubt.

The transport squealed to a stop and a marshal reached over to unshackle MacNally's restraints from the metal bars of the seat. "Up, let's go. End of the line."

MacNally was led down the steps of the van and up the stairs of the penitentiary. The sun's heat tightened the skin on his face as if he had walked into an oven. But it was a wet heat; humidity was a killer at this time of year, in this part of the country.

But as Walton MacNally was soon to find out, that would be the least of his problems.

# 25

The morning gloom hovered outside the large windows of Homicide, bringing a more intense chill than even the first few days of Vail's visit. Roxxann Dixon was en route, toting a packed bag. Vail had invited her to room with her for as long as she was in town working the case.

Clay Allman's *San Francisco Tribune* article made page one. Vail, Burden, and Friedberg huddled over the worktable, reading the paper, when suddenly Vail stood up straight. "Son of a bitch."

Friedberg's eyes darted around the page. "What's wrong?"

"You guys read as fast as a third grader."

"Oh." Burden frowned and pushed back from his desk. "He mentioned you."

"Yeah, he mentioned me."

Friedberg tilted his head. "And mentioning you is a problem... why?"

"It's one thing for the UNSUB to know certain things about our investigation. This kind of offender, he's gonna want that interaction. We have to control it, even fan those flames—but very carefully. I've unfortunately been a part of a few of these cases, and it can really complicate things. I'd rather handle it low key—"

"You?" Burden asked. "Low key?"

"This UNSUB's got a lot of narcissism and grandiosity. He's arrogant and self-assured, the kind that taunts law enforcement. He's posed his bodies in public to show off his handiwork, how great he is.

It's a monument to his skill as a killer. So announcing the FBI Behavioral Analysis Unit is involved turns up the stakes, makes him feel more important. So that's not bad. But mentioning me by name. That focuses things on me. I'd rather be in the background, in a position where I can pull strings the offender doesn't know I'm pulling. But now that I'm on his radar, he's going to be playing to me."

"How's that?" Friedberg asked.

"There's a strong pull between profiler and offenders. Cat and mouse stuff. But the fact I'm a woman…makes it worse. Some of them see it as cool. After their arrest, a lot of 'em want to meet the woman profiler who worked their case."

"And that's bad?"

Vail chuckled. "He's not looking at it as a situation where we'll meet after the arrest. He's going to do his best to find me before then."

"So you want protection," Burden said.

"Me? Protection? No. I'm saying that it adds a dynamic we didn't need, a complication we'd have been better off without. And—it just goes to my point that we need to control the media, what they release. Even the precise wording they use in their reports, their articles—"

"Can't unring a bell." Burden tossed the paper on the desk. "What's done is done. Let's run our investigation based on what we know and what we don't, not what the media knows and doesn't know. Okay?"

"Of course," Vail said, "but to ignore the media's role and how the UNSUB—"

"I'm not ignoring it. But you planted that inane bit about the ocean. You wanted him to contact you. Maybe he will."

"You. I wanted him to contact you."

Burden grumbled something under his breath, then shook his head. "I'm beginning to think that the only thing that's gonna solve this thing is good old fashioned ass-to-the-grindstone police work. Now. I think we need to look at the '82 case and see what it can tell us regarding our current vics."

Friedberg said, "I put out a message to Millard Ferguson."

Vail ground her teeth. *They're missing the point.* "And? Has he replied?"

Friedberg coyly pulled out his BlackBerry and thumbed through it. He tilted his head back to look out the bottoms of his glasses. "He did. Wants to meet."

Burden grabbed his sport coat. "Why don't you two go, I'm going to follow up with—"

"Agent Vail." Before Burden could finish his sentence, a woman entered the room from the outer reception area. "This just came for you." She handed Vail an envelope.

"Who's it from?"

"It was messengered over. The man said it was time sensitive and extremely urgent."

"What man?" Vail asked, heading for the anteroom where the receptionist's station was.

"The messenger. He gave it to me and left."

Vail looked at the envelope, then walked back toward Burden. "But other than us, and my unit, no one knows I'm here." *This is not good. Not good at all.*

Friedberg said, "You mean other than us, your unit, and the entire city of San Francisco."

*Shit, that's right. What did I tell them?* "Gloves?"

Burden stuck a hand inside his coat pocket and pulled one out.

"What do you do, carry an entire supply in there?"

"Boy Scout 101. Always be prepared."

Vail slipped on the glove. "Boy Scout 101, huh? How about Anal Inspector 202."

Burden wagged a finger at the envelope. "Shut up and open it."

Using the tip of a pen, Vail carefully pried open the flap, then slipped out the piece of paper inside. *Yeah. Not good at all.*

Staring back at her was a message. From the offender:

THANK YOU FOR COMING AGENT VAIL.

# 26

August 6, 1959

"Leavenworth's known as the 'Big Top,'" the US Marshal said as he led MacNally up to the administration building's double doors. "It's also been referred to as the 'Big L.' We'll be calling it your new home. But you'll be calling it the biggest mistake of your life."

A heavy steel rolling gate stood there ominously, MacNally's first indication that this place was seriously committed to keeping its inmates contained on the other side of freedom.

The gate slid aside with the speed of molasses, agonizingly pointing out that once MacNally stepped across the threshold, his life was going to change forever. MacNally craned his neck upward to get a last glimpse of the sky as a free man, but the overhang of the building's façade impeded his view.

MacNally tripped on the leg irons and stumbled through the gate into a lobby. To his left, a series of similar steel-barred barriers blocked the hall. To the right, a short corridor led to a couple of rooms.

The marshal grabbed hold of his left arm. "Wait here for the R&D officer." He must have noticed MacNally's confusion, because he clarified, "Receiving and Discharge."

A man with the build and expression of a lumberjack walked up.

He pointed at MacNally. "Face the wall to your right."

MacNally squinted. "What?"

"Face. The. Wall," he said, as if MacNally was incapable of comprehending English. "Eyes front."

MacNally did as ordered.

The marshal handed over a document. "Commitment order."

The R&D officer took the paperwork and began to read it, then noticed MacNally was stealing a look at the text. "What the fuck you looking at? I said eyes front!"

MacNally swung his head back toward the grimy wall.

"Thanks, Deputy," the officer said. "I've got custody. Be back in a few with the iron."

The man grabbed hold of MacNally's arm. "Let's go."

Ahead of him, barely visible through two more gates that boasted inch-thick steel bars, was an oddly out of place, intricately designed rotunda. An officer's desk sat squarely in its center, with dark lines along the floor radiating outward toward the walls. Columns rose in pairs all around him, with hallways leading off the main hub.

The first gate's bars slid apart and the two men walked through. They waited as it slammed shut behind them. The third one then opened slowly, and as they stepped forward into the rotunda, this door also struck metal with a violent echo as it banged closed.

Above him, a hundred, maybe a hundred fifty feet off the ground, rose a dome. Just like his design work on the exterior, the architect honed close to the US Capitol's schema for the interior, as well.

The officer escorted MacNally through the rotunda and down a stairwell to their right that led to Receiving and Discharge. The arm and leg irons were removed and the officer left to return them to the marshal.

MacNally was stripped naked in front of the processing personnel and then searched for contraband and weapons—including his rectum and beneath his scrotum. An intake screening followed: a counselor interviewed him, asking about his work history, his education level, religion, and other such details. A physician's assistant then asked him about his health to determine if he had any special needs. He had none.

He was then given his supplies—a printed manual that outlined Leavenworth rules and procedures; his clothing and bedroll; a towel, toothbrush and Dr. Finks tooth powder.

MacNally looked quizzically at the name on the latter product.

"That's specially formulated stuff," said the man issuing his kit. "After one good brushing, you won't be able to keep your mouth shut."

He said it with a straight face, but MacNally figured it had to be a joke. But he didn't feel much like laughing.

A correctional officer approached, dressed in a tie and jacket, with a stern face and graying temples. His badge read, Voorhees.

"Take him to A&O," the man said to Voorhees.

Voorhees frowned. "This way." He led MacNally back through the rotunda. "Big L has four cellhouses, all joined right here. Centerhall. See those gates?"

MacNally saw them all right.

"Each cellhouse has only one door. Leads right here. Guards need to, they can seal off a cellhouse by slamming 'em shut."

"Why would they need to do that?" MacNally asked.

Voorhees eyed him. "You ever been in prison before, boy?"

MacNally lifted a shoulder. "County, while I waited for my trial."

The officer made no attempt to stifle his laugh. "Really. Well you in for one hell of a fucking rude awakening. Keep your eyes and ears open. Listen. Learn. This is the big time, boy. You're in for a heap a trouble."

MacNally swallowed hard. A font of fear welled up in his throat. Robbing those banks now didn't seem like the prudent thing to do. But it was too late. He'd done it. He got caught. Now he had to learn how to survive.

"That there hallway," Voorhees said, pointing ahead, "the one leading off Centerhall. That's the main corridor. See the floor?" He got a nod from MacNally and continued. "White and red tiles. Walk on the white ones only. Step on the red, a guard's gonna knock you good, back onto the white."

"What's the red for?"

"Staff." Voorhees gestured into the distance. "Lieutenant's office is down that hallway. And that's the rear corridor way down there. The steel grill straight ahead leads to the dining room and the auditorium. The Protestant chapel's located in the auditorium, Catholic chapel's behind the stage. Kitchen, if you got that detail, is by the mess hall.

Those grill doors on either side of the rear corridor down there lead to the hospital, laundry, and the yards. Commissary's located on the yard."

"What can you buy in the commissary?"

"Not much. MoonPies. Snacks, clothing, that sorta shit."

Voorhees examined MacNally's face a moment, then said, "Come with me." He led him into the lieutenant's office, and then closed the door. "Now listen to me. You trust no one here. Keep your mouth shut and do your own time. You go sticking your nose where it don't belong, it could get you killed. Guys here, they're interested in one thing. And that's them and their own interests."

MacNally nodded.

"What'd you do?" Voorhees asked. "To get a ticket here?"

"Armed robbery."

The guard looked him square in the eye. "You do it?"

MacNally bit his bottom lip. "Yeah. But it's not that cut-and-dry."

"Everyone in here's got a story, buddy."

"My wife was murdered and they thought I did it—which I didn't—and the jury found me not guilty. It was a big case, big trial. Everyone knew about it. But as I began to learn, 'not guilty' isn't the same as innocent, and I couldn't land a decent job. Even when I tried to hide it, soon as they found out, they canned me. For years, I tried everything." He looked squarely at Voorhees. "I've got a young son, I had to put food on the table. I didn't have a choice."

Voorhees nodded slowly. "Sorry to hear about your wife. And your troubles. But everyone's got a choice. You remember that. 'Specially here. Guys are gonna talk shit, some may even make you do things. You're gonna have choices to make, choices that are gonna define your life from this point forward. You did armed robbery and they sent you to Leavenworth. That's one choice you fucked up royally, I can tell you that right now. This place'll eat you alive, you let it."

Voorhees opened the door and they stepped out. A rumble emerged in the distance. The odd acoustics of the prison made it appear as if a stampede was approaching.

"The hell is that?" MacNally said.

"Lunch. The cellhouses are released on a rotation."

A wave of men flowed into, and consumed, the rotunda as they moved into the hallway that led to the mess hall, sticking to the white tiles. Many eyed MacNally as they passed, one running his tongue across his upper lip. His gaze remained glued to MacNally even as he followed the moving line down the long corridor.

"What's your name?" Voorhees asked, keeping his face forward, watching the prisoners as they continued on.

"Walt. Walton MacNally."

"Listen here, MacNally. See those guys?" He gestured toward the flow of prisoners, who had moved out of earshot. "Ain't no one of them gonna give a shit about you. It's all about what they can do for themselves." The last inmate in line turned and snarled at Voorhees.

"Turn around, you fucking scumbag," Voorhees yelled after him. He shook his head, and then gestured at the corridor ahead of them. "Don't forget. Walk on the white. Follow the rules and everything'll be fine. If you don't..." Voorhees shrugged. "Choices, MacNally. Remember that." He gave the prisoner a gentle shove from behind. "Let's go get you to your cell."

MacNally moved alongside Voorhees. Had he had choices? He guessed he did. But like everything else, it just wasn't that simple. One thing was certain: it seemed he would have plenty of time to reflect on what he had done. What he could've done differently.

For now, he needed to figure out how things worked here. Because of all the unknowns, there was one fact of which there was no doubt: this was now home. And he didn't care much for the new neighborhood.

# 27

"Let's get that over to the lab," Burden said.

Vail stood there staring at the paper.

"So what does this mean for us?" Friedberg asked. "He's glad you're here?"

"Read the next sentence."

HAVE I SURPRISED YOU? I'VE GOT MORE IN STORE
FOR YOU. YOU'LL FIND OUT SOON ENOUGH

"More what?" Burden asked. "More surprises or more murders?"

"Both," Vail said. "What time did Allman's article come out? When did it hit the street?"

"Heck if I know," Friedberg said.

Vail looked at him.

"What. I'm not a walking encyclopedia. I know history, not mundane facts, like newspaper delivery schedules."

"Let's find out," she said. "And find out when it was posted to their website."

As Friedberg lifted his phone to obtain the information, Burden's handset rang. "Yeah." Burden listened a moment, then hung up. He sat down heavily in his chair. "We've got more problems. There's another article, a reporter with the *Register*."

"Not unusual to have two different papers covering news in a big city," Vail said.

"Except that this article supposedly has details we didn't release to the press. In fact, Clay's the only one who knew any of this stuff."

Friedberg set his phone down. "Allman's piece was posted on the *Trib*'s site around 7 PM. Paper delivery started at 5:30 AM."

"Can you get Allman here? We need to discuss this article. And this guy who wrote the other one, for the *Register*. Let's get a sit-down with him, make sure we're all on the same page. No pun intended." She pointed to the screen. "Can you pull it up?" As Burden played with the browser, Vail continued: "If Allman gives us a hard time and won't cooperate, we might have another hand to play—this *Register* guy."

"Play 'em off one another," Friedberg said.

"I'd rather not—only if we need to."

"Here it is," Burden said. "Give it a minute, the internet sometimes slows to a crawl."

Vail crowded the screen as the *Register* banner appeared, followed by the header and byline. While waiting for the rest to load, she said, "You asked me back at the crime scene what the harm was in letting Allman come along. Well, now you're seeing it."

Burden leaned back in his chair. "He's a reporter, Karen. A really good one, too. Sometimes we use them, sometimes they use us. Mentioning your name went a little too far over the line—from our perspective. He probably thought it was innocuous. It certainly wasn't malicious, right?"

"Probably not."

"I'm not even sure we told him not to mention you. To me, the bottom line when dealing with a reporter, is integrity. If we come to trust each other, both parties benefit. And I've always been able to trust him. So my two cents is that playing one off the other is inviting trouble."

Vail gestured at the screen, then squinted to read the reporter's name: Szczepan T. Scheer. "Whoa," she said. "A *c* sandwiched between two *z*'s. I don't think the human tongue was made to be able to pronounce that."

"I believe it's Stephen," Friedberg said.

"No way." She looked at it again and tried it on for size. "Sztzeepin." She lifted her brow. "Fine...if you say so."

"Oh, c'mon. Doesn't seem so difficult now, does it?"

"Speak for yourself," Vail said. "Looks Greek to me."

"Actually," Friedberg said, "he *looks* like an average Joe Caucasian, but his name's got Prussian roots. Some German and Ukrainian, too. Last name's actually Mennonite."

"Prussian and Mennonite?" Vail glanced sideways at the inspector. "I think that qualifies as a mundane fact, Robert. Not history."

Friedberg grinned. "Okay, fine. You got me. That one I happened to know." He grabbed the mouse and clicked on Refresh.

"Actually," Burden said, "his real name is Stephen but he said he wanted to 'honor his ancestry.' Personally, I think he changed it to make it stand out more so people would remember it. Cops in town just call him Stephen."

"I call him jerk," Friedberg said. "Remember I told you about that reporter who put the screws to me about that phantom piece I supposedly dropped at the crime scene? This is the guy."

The page finally loaded and Vail leaned in close to read:

San Francisco—A series of gruesome murders in the city has baffled local detectives and sent them in search of answers, a quest that landed them on the doorsteps of the FBI's vaunted Behavioral Analysis Unit.

Special Agent Profiler Karen Vail has taken the case and arrived from Quantico sometime in the past week, but sources close to the investigation state that they have yet to make any significant progress, and that no arrest is imminent. That's disheartening news for San Franciscans, as the Bay Killer has now claimed six lives...

"I want to know who his sources are," Burden said.

Vail ground her molars. "I've got a lot more questions than that." She skipped further down the article:

The killer has left an unusually shaped brass key at each of the crime scenes, which the police have, as yet, been unable to identify. It appears to be a similar, if not identical, key to one found alongside the murdered body of Edgar Newhall, a still-unsolved San Bruno case from 1982.

One thing that is known, however, is that the female victims, all elderly, were beaten about the head, tortured with an exposed electrical wire, sodomized with an umbrella and raped before being murdered. An odd twist is that their husbands were also found dead, in some cases miles from the original crime scene, with a number stenciled across the forehead. The only immediately identifiable signs of injury are apparently head trauma from what appears to be repeated kicks...

Vail skimmed—until she hit one particular sentence that mentally slapped her across the face:

It is believed the killer is a man of below average intelligence who has targeted elderly women because they represent his mother, who likely dominated him as a child and young adult.

"Shit," Vail said, backing away from the screen. "I've seen enough. We need to find this *Stephen* Scheer. Right now."

"How the hell does he know all this?" Friedberg asked. "Who's his source?"

Burden splayed a hand. "That's what I was saying."

"This is worse than a major leak in the department," Vail said. "He's incited the killer. I don't know where he got that bullshit behavioral analysis, but it's not only wrong, it's belittling to the offender, and that's likely going to set him off big time."

"How so? Because it's insulting his intelligence?" Friedberg asked.

"Saying we have no leads is like the kiss of death with an offender like this. I'd much rather we imply the killer's made mistakes and that we have a lot of good leads coming in. Someone saw him, heard him, whatever. An arrogant and self-confidant serial killer can't stand the thought that he made mistakes. That could be the most effective button we press that makes him contact us."

"He already contacted us," Friedberg said.

Vail massaged her temples. *Control the media. I told them that. It's so important...* "Yeah, but did he write his note before, or after, he saw Scheer's article?"

"I'll find out if they have a similar release schedule as the *Trib*," Friedberg said. "But we couldn't know for sure if he saw it when it came out—or if he saw it at all."

"Safe to assume this guy's monitoring the media," Vail said.

"Then I'll find out when it posted to their website."

"Could Allman have told Scheer about the key?" she asked.

Burden chuckled. "Stephen Scheer's not exactly on Clay's Christmas list—and vice versa. Remember I told you Clay doesn't talk to him anymore? Twenty-five, thirty years ago they were close friends. Scheer had a three-year head start, built a decent rep in town covering cases. Scheer took Clay under his wing, broke him in, taught him how things are done. They co-wrote articles, covered cases, that sort of thing. But something happened, Scheer got pissed, and ended up leaving the *Trib*. No way is Clay Allman a source for Stephen Scheer."

Friedberg's phone rang. He lifted the headset, then said, "Got it. Thanks." He turned to Burden. "Detective Dixon's on her way up."

"Do you know much about Scheer?" Vail asked.

"A bit of a head case," Burden said. "Other than that, just rumor."

"About what?" she asked.

"Alcohol," Friedberg said. He pulled a cigarette from his pocket and stuck it between his lips. "Did some time in rehab. But I heard stuff about domestic violence. Knocked the wife around or something. He lives in Berkeley. I can call over, see if they've got anything on record. Actually—Birdie, you'd better do it. Because of my history with him—"

"My pleasure. I've always wanted to rattle his cage."

Friedberg shook his head. "He's not gonna give up his source."

"Whose source?"

The voice came from behind them. Vail turned. Dixon had just walked into the unit. As Vail filled her in on the Allman and Scheer articles, Dixon took a seat atop the worktable that was pushed up against the wall where the whiteboard was mounted.

"All right," Burden said. "Let's do this. Robert, how about you go meet with Millard Ferguson about the '82 case. And you two—track down Scheer and see what you can get from him. I'm not too optimistic, but he might tell a couple of women more than he'd tell me."

Vail and Dixon faced each other. "Did he just insult us?" Dixon asked.

"Nah, he's harmless." Vail winked at him. "It's just his way." She led Dixon out of the Homicide unit and into the wide corridor. "Burden doesn't think we can get Scheer's source."

"Then we have to work extra hard to prove him wrong."

# 28

August 28, 1959

*United States Penitentiary*
*Leavenworth*

MacNally spent three weeks in Administrative Orientation, located to the rear of Two Gallery in A-Cellhouse. As it was explained to him, new arrivals were not placed into the general population without being afforded time to learn the rules for each area of the institution and meet with the department heads.

MacNally was given his permanent cell assignment by the cellhouse Number One Officer, who said he knew just the placement for him. "An officer'll be here in a minute to take you to your new home. You got free reign of the cellhouses, but remember: there are five counts a day, and you're expected to be in your cells at that time. The one at 4 PM's a standing count. When you're not working or in school, the rec yard's open."

Voorhees walked in and nodded at the Number One.

"Get him outta here," he said to Voorhees with a dismissing wave of his hand.

Voorhees led MacNally out of processing and toward the cellhouse. "Remember, MacNally. Cons here were sent to the Big L because their crimes were pretty goddamn bad, or 'cause they were problems at other prisons. So all the shit they did out in the street, they do in here. Dealing drugs—heroin's a big one—they smuggle it in from the outside. Guys extort money, run scams on other guys, bankroll poker games. Some get assaulted, some are pimped out."

"Pimped out?"

"You got your homos in here, and then you got your horny fucks who are in for twenty years and haven't seen pussy in a long, long time. For them, they'd rather stick their dicks in your ass than give up sex for the rest of their lives. They're the predators. Weaker guys, their victims, are called lops." Voorhees turned and gave him a quick once-over. "You look like a lop to me, MacNally. That means you're gonna have trouble."

"Gee, thanks."

"Just telling you like it is."

They walked up the steps to Two Gallery. The air got thicker and noticeably hotter.

"Fifth tier's the shits. Heat rises. No air movement, no ventilation up here. Somebody don't like you, MacNally. They gave you a piece a crap cell. What's the saying? Location, location, location." He guffawed at his own joke.

They walked past iron-barred cells, the gates rolled open and the inmates lying still on their beds…no doubt their way of dealing with the intense heat.

Voorhees stopped at cell 511. "This is it." He turned and started to walk off, but stopped. "Good luck."

MacNally eyed Voorhees, then turned to his cell. The lone light bulb was off, his two cellies lifeless lumps on the mattresses. But they suddenly swung their legs off the bed and sat up. Four eyes traversed his body.

Reflexively, MacNally swallowed hard. He knew then that Voorhees's "lop" assessment was probably correct. He put his head down and stepped into his new home, trying not to think about what awaited him.

# 29

Vail and Dixon arrived at the *San Francisco Register* on Mission Street. It was a four-story brick building, built about ten years ago during more optimistic times, before the newspaper industry started crumbling due to declining readership and subscriptions and the attendant slide in advertising revenue. Now the *Register*, like most other dailies in major US cities, was under intense economic pressure to survive.

Vail got out of Dixon's car, then said, "Hold it. What are you wearing under that jacket?"

"Tank top. Why?"

"Good. Lose the jacket."

"It's freezing," Dixon said.

"Exactly."

Then she got it. Blonde, with a body she shaped in the gym several days a week, Dixon often had a predictable effect on male suspects and sources. It was a tactic she and Vail had used once before during the Crush Killer case.

"Not this again," Dixon said. "I thought we're professional women who are proud of our accomplishments and don't have to resort to sleeping around and behaving like sluts to get where we've gotten. We've earned it on merit."

"Yeah. We are. And we did. But we need to use all assets at our disposal. And let's face it, you have nice assets. Honestly, I'm freaking jealous. Now lose the jacket."

Dixon rolled her eyes, then did as Vail requested.

As Dixon was tossing it into the backseat, a text arrived from Burden:

> rumors right. dui '09 and dom vio this year. in custody
> battle over 9 & 13 yo boys. not hard to guess job's in
> jeopardy. complaints never made public.

Vail read the info to Dixon, and then they walked through the *Register's* front doors. They both badged the receptionist, who sat behind bulletproof glass, with surveillance cameras trained on them fore and aft.

"Guess it's dangerous being a reporter these days," Dixon quipped. "Tight security."

Vail covered her eyes in mock concern. She gestured at Dixon's detective's shield. "Jesus, Roxx. Scuff it up or something. It's so shiny and new, you nearly blinded me with the reflection."

"I'm very proud of this hunk of metal."

"You should be. But it's so pristine it makes you look like a rookie."

Dixon pawed the mirrored surface, covering it with fingerprints. "There. Happy?"

Vail playfully revealed one eye, then the other. "Much better."

"You can go on up," the receptionist said, shoving two visitor tags into the pass-through slot. "Third floor."

They clipped the laminated cards, which bore a large red V, onto their belts, and then turned toward the elevator. But as the doors opened and revealed a tiny car, Vail turned away. "Stairs?"

"It's only three floors," Dixon said.

"I don't want to tempt fate. It hits at inopportune times."

They ran up the three flights, then exited at the newsroom floor where a man of about sixty was standing, waiting for the elevator doors to part.

"Just a guess," Vail said. "Mr. Scheer?"

The man turned and his eyes immediately found Roxxann Dixon as if his pupils were made of iron and Dixon had a magnet embedded beneath her chest.

*That's it. Look. Enjoy. Then tell us what we want to know.*

"Yes." He extended a hand, but his gaze slid left and right, from Dixon to Vail...but they always came back to Dixon.

"We have some questions for you," Vail said.

Scheer pulled his eyes over to Vail. "Come on back to my cubicle." He led them through a maze of low-walled dividers. Computer screens, stacks of papers, and file folders covered all available horizontal surfaces. The workspaces looked similar, the only variations being how neatly the materials were stacked, and how many photos the reporters and columnists had pinned to their walls.

Scheer stole two rolling chairs from adjacent, abandoned cubicles and moved them over to his workspace. Vail and Dixon took seats as Scheer fussed with clearing a stack of papers from his workspace.

Vail scanned the photos on display: one of a boy and a young teen, another of Scheer and the same children—presumably his sons—and pictures of what looked like his parents and maybe a sister. Off to the side, there was a snapshot of Scheer dressed in an Elvis costume at some kind of holiday party. There were no pictures of his wife.

Dixon elbowed Vail and nodded at a *Tribune* article pinned to his wall. A handwritten note scrawled below it read, "Wrong again, asshole. Fuck you." Off to the right, two bullet casings hung in a Ziploc bag, skewered by pushpins.

Vail and Dixon shared a perturbed look.

"What can I help you with?" Scheer asked.

Vail wiggled a finger at his wall. "What's up with that?"

Scheer swung his head over. "The article or the casings?"

"Both," Dixon said.

"We get those kinds of notes and emails literally every week, and most of us keep a few hanging around the office as examples of how batshit the readers can be."

"Batshit," Vail repeated.

"And those bullets," he said, waving a hand in their direction, "are from a murder in the Tenderloin. Transit reporters have toy trains on

their desks, cop reporters have toy cop cars. I've got those bullets—
and the Orgy Room key from the Mustang Ranch." He opened a
drawer and pushed a few items aside. "It's here somewhere…."
Anyway, they're mementos of the stories I've written." He shoved the
drawer closed. "Just a guess here, but you didn't come over to discuss
my office décor."

"We saw your article this morning on the case you've dubbed the
'Bay Killer,'" Vail said.

Scheer moved back in his seat. A subconscious but telling action.
"Did you like it?"

"Can't say we did," Vail said. "See, you printed details about the
case that no one knows. And that concerns us."

Dixon added, "If you can just tell us where you got some of that
information, we'll be out of your hair." She sat up straight, bringing
her shoulders back.

Scheer noticed. He turned his head toward Vail, but his eyes
followed a split second later. "I can't—I can't disclose my sources.
I'm sorry."

"We figured you'd say that," Vail said.

"But see, what you did, well, it's irresponsible," Dixon said,
maintaining a pleasing and reasonable tone. "Because you printed
some things that weren't right. And strategically, the things you wrote
were downright dangerous. It's putting the lives of a lot of elderly
women in the city at extreme risk. And we certainly don't want to do
that—and I'm sure you don't want to, either."

"What can I do about that? I'm sorry if that's what happened. But
I can't retract the article. What's done is done. You can't unring—"

"Yeah," Vail said. "The bell. We know. But I'm gonna be blunt
with you. We have a hole at the department. We need to plug that
hole before more information finds its way into other people's hands.
Unscrupulous hands."

Scheer shifted in his seat. "Well, I—I don't want anything bad to
happen, but I've got a job to do, and my job is to find credible
information on a case and report on it. And since you're here, I've
obviously found credible information."

"We've all got jobs to do," Vail said. "And my job is to make sure more elderly women and men don't get killed. Tortured. Raped. And sodomized."

"I understand. But—"

"Is that your parents?" Vail asked. She pointed to the photo.

Scheer did not turn around. His face hardened. "Get to the point."

"They're around the age of the couples who've been murdered. Would you like to walk into a crime scene tomorrow and find your mother tortured, raped, and sodomized? As you were so apt to point out in your article, the killer uses an umbrella, and he shoves it up the woman's rectum. Very hard. He tears her up inside. I don't think I have to tell you it's a very, very unpleasant death."

Scheer's eyes narrowed. His jaw jutted out. "Is this about Friedberg? Is that why you're hassling me? Why didn't he come here himself?"

"You're not getting it," Vail said. "This isn't about Friedberg. It's about the old woman who was brutalized and killed because of *you*."

He rose from his chair. "We're done here."

Vail and Dixon did not move. "I don't think so," Vail said. "We know about your...personal problems. And we know you've somehow managed to keep them under the radar. Maybe you've got friends where it counts. But, see, we do, too. And all it takes is one phone call."

Scheer's face reddened. "Go to hell," he said, then walked away at a brisk pace.

Vail sat back in her chair. "Well, that didn't go as well as we'd hoped. Definitely not as planned."

"Definitely not."

Vail watched him yank open the stairwell door, and then disappear inside. She eyed his desk, the papers strewn across it. The files likely contained information that could be material to their case. But she swiveled her seat away from Scheer's workspace. *I've crossed the line too many times the past few months. I'll get the info some other way. Somehow.*

Dixon rose from her chair. "Just a guess. But I don't think he's coming back until we leave."

Vail stood up as well, then pretended to notice Dixon's outfit for the first time. "Jesus, Roxx. You don't look very professional. Put your jacket on, will you?"

VAIL AND DIXON WALKED BACK to their car in silence, until they exited the building. Then Vail asked, "What do you think?"

"Not to be Captain Obvious, but he's protecting his sources."

"But what source could it be? Remember when we were looking at the wine cave murder a few months ago? I kept saying it was all about access. Who had access to the cave? Let's approach this the same way. Who had access to the information found in Scheer's article?"

"You, Burden, and Friedberg. The people who handle the files—the file room clerk and the guys at evidence storage. The crime lab. The ME. Potentially other inspectors. The lieutenant."

"And the killer," Vail said.

"And the killer." Dixon chirped her car remote and the doors unlocked. They stood outside it. Dixon reached into the backseat and grabbed her jacket, shoved her arms through the sleeves.

"So…what do we do, start questioning all the people involved in this case?"

Vail thought a moment. "Who would have a reason to disclose the information?"

"Unless it's something obvious, figuring that out could take a long time."

"True," Vail said. "Then how about a shortcut? Let's look at the phone LUDs and see who's been talking with Stephen Scheer."

"If you can make that happen, it'd definitely save us some time."

Vail pulled open the car door. "If they used their work phones, or department-issued cells, not a problem. If they use their personal cells for work, too, then that makes our job easier. We get everything at once. I'll send Burden a text, let him know we struck out and see what we can get."

She sat down, and as she hit Send, her phone buzzed. A text stared back at her. "Gotta be kidding me."

"What?"

Vail let her head fall back against the seat. "Another vic."

# 30

MacNally walked into his cell. The two men watched him but did not speak. The one on the top bunk was fat-large and bald, ink-blurred tattoos that appeared to be homemade adorning his neck and shoulders. A red and black bandana was wrapped around his thick head.

The man on the bottom bed was just as massive, but his bulk was the result of weight lifting in the rec yard. Body art also covered his upper torso, which was bare and sweat-moist.

MacNally cleared his throat. "How are you guys doing?"

"What're you in for?" the obese man asked.

MacNally tossed his materials on the bed. "Armed robbery. You?"

"Armed robbery, double murder. Rape. You got a name?"

Double murder and rape. Shit. But what did he expect? This was one of the toughest maximum security penitentiaries. Did he think these inmates were going to be upstanding citizens? "MacNally. Guys call me Mac."

"MacNally. Like the road maps?" The two men laughed.

MacNally laughed along with them. "Rand McNally's Irish, like me. But he spells it differently."

"I'm Carl Wharton," the obese man said. "He's Kurt Gormack."

MacNally sat down on his bunk. "What about you, Kurt? What are you in for?"

"Lots a things, I guess. Take your pick."

"Kurt beat a man to death with his fists. Caved in his skull. But it was justified."

Justified? MacNally swallowed hard. What the hell had he gotten himself into?

Kurt shrugged. "He owed me some money, and it didn't look like he was gonna pay. I told him that wasn't the way it worked."

"How much did he owe you?" MacNally asked, at a loss as to how he should respond—but needing to say something to disguise his revulsion.

"Fifteen bucks. But the amount wasn't the point. You let some dipshit like that get away with stiffing you, it gets around and your rep's fucking shot."

"Yeah. Of course," MacNally said, hoping they would buy his weak attempt at giving the impression that he understood something he could not possibly comprehend.

Kurt sat expressionless, his thick chest rising and falling at regular intervals. He glanced up at Carl, who appeared to be studying MacNally's face.

"So what's there to do around here?" He wanted to get the hell out of there but didn't want it to be obvious that he found his new cellies appalling.

Carl answered. "It's fucking prison, Map Man. Take a hike around the cellhouse, get to know your new home. My guess, you're gonna be here a while."

"Forty-five."

A crooked, salacious grin broadened Kurt's face. "Then it looks like we're gonna have some fun."

MacNally didn't know what his new bunkmate meant by that—but based on what Voorhees had told him, it left him with a sense of foreboding.

And he suddenly realized that "fun" was a relative term.

THE NIGHT WAS NOT MUCH cooler than the day. But the temperature was not the reason MacNally had a hard time falling asleep. He had taken a walk around the rotunda, strolled along the different cellhouses, and got his bearings. He ate dinner in the large mess hall and kept to himself. For a first day in a violent place, amongst men who were some of the worst society had produced, he felt proud that he had made it through unscathed.

But as he was soon to discover, it was premature to have congratulated himself.

# 31

Vail and Dixon arrived at the crime scene. The sun was bidding a quick farewell, dipping below the high-rises and bouncing a blood-orange reflection off the windows of the nearby buildings.

Dixon double-parked her Ford and they were met at the curb by the first-on-scene officer. Vail immediately shivered from the chilled air that blew against her the moment she stepped from the vehicle. She held up her creds and Dixon her badge.

"It's still too shiny," Vail quipped.

"Doesn't bother me. What matters is what's in here," Dixon said, pointing to her head. "Deal with it."

"Burden or Friedberg get here yet?" Vail asked, wrapping her hands around her torso.

"Inspector Burden's en route," the officer said.

"What've we got?"

"Some old woman. Pretty badly beat up."

"How bad?" Dixon asked.

"Bad enough. She's dead."

"Hey. Vail!"

Vail turned and saw Clay Allman jogging toward them. His bushy hair was in flyaway mode, the wind whipping it in all directions as he ran.

"Congratulations. You almost made it here before we did."

"I was on my way to Bryant when I heard the call over the scanner. I wanted to find out why you guys kept things from me."

"It's not our job to feed you information," Vail said. "You know that."

"Except when it fits your needs. A favor here, a favor there."

Dixon wrapped her sweater tighter around her body. "There are times when we need your cooperation. For the greater good. It's all about catching these assholes, Clay. It's not doing us any favors. We get paid whether we catch the bad guys or not."

Allman poked at his wire-framed glasses and slid them up his nose. "So what was up with that piece in the *Register*?"

"Yeah," Vail said, "that's what we'd like to know."

"You helped out Scheer, but you won't help me? How's that helping the greater good?"

"We don't owe you any explanations," Dixon said.

Allman looked off, shaking his head. "I expected more of Burden. He's a stand-up guy. For him to screw me like that—"

"He didn't," Vail said. "Scheer didn't get his info from us."

"Bullshit," Allman said, his gaze boring into Vail's. "Where else was a guy like Stephen Scheer gonna get stuff like that? He's a hack."

A car pulling up behind Allman caught Vail's eye. "You don't believe me, ask Burden." She nodded at the Taurus.

Allman swiveled his body and moved toward Burden as he got out of the car. "I saw Scheer's article."

Burden sidestepped his open car door, then slammed it shut behind him. "What's the deal? Is this one of our vics?"

"Just got here," Vail said. "Where's Robert?"

"Following up with those ice cream vendors. He said it looks like a dead end, but he's crossing his t's. If he wraps it up soon, he'll stop by. But I don't think he's too eager to see another brutalized elderly woman."

*Who is?*

"You gonna help me out here, or is Stephen Scheer your new best bud?" Allman stood at the edge of the sidewalk, hands on hips.

Burden stepped onto the curb, placed a palm on Allman's shoulder, and said, "Clay. C'mon, man. Are we really doing this? We had nothing to do with Scheer's story."

Allman chewed on his cheek, then nodded. "So who's his source?"

"I was hoping you could tell us. So far we've hit a wall. What he got, he never should've gotten."

Vail harrumphed. *That's an understatement.* "It could end up costing lives. So if you've got any idea who he might be speaking to—"

"If I had any idea who he's talking to, believe me, Agent Vail, I'd be talking to them, too. But I've got no goddamn clue. I assumed it was you people."

"Enough of this," Dixon said. "We've got a victim in there waiting for us."

"Hang out here," Burden said to Allman, pointing at the spot as he backed away. "I'll give you a buzz when you can come in."

"I left you something at your office," Allman said. "More articles and information about cases that I think could be related."

"Thanks," Burden said.

"Just remember," Allman said, "I'll be standing out here in the cold. Waiting."

Vail glanced back at Allman. *I'll break out the freaking violins.*

AFTER SLIPPING BOOTIES ONTO THEIR shoes, they ascended the steps to the second-floor bedroom. A sitting room at the top of the stairs contained a stout oak rolltop desk, bearing a PC and an oversize 25-inch LCD monitor that was asleep.

They walked into the bedroom and stood there, staring at the bed.

*This is not good.*

"What the hell is this," Burden said.

Vail stepped closer to the body. It was an elderly woman, with scraggly steel-wool hair that was matted with blood. Her face had been beaten, almost crushed from the force of the blows. And the behaviors they had seen all too many times were present: The woman had been sodomized with an umbrella. And her blouse had been pulled up to the level of her chin.

"It looks like an angrier attack," Dixon said. "Karen?"

"It does look that way. Some psychopaths enjoy imparting pain and damage to the victim. But he hadn't previously beaten their faces like this. Not nearly this bad. At first blush, it seems like he's pissed off."

"Because of Scheer's article?" Burden asked.

"That's the million-dollar question," Vail said. "And that's why we need to control what we release to the media. When something like this happens, we have no idea what's driving what. Is the offender steering the ship, or are we?" She tilted her head, sizing up the trauma, then said. "Yes, if I had to guess, and that's what I have to do here, I'd say it's because of the article. That was a pretty bad insult to his ego. And the timing is too coincidental. This looks like a fresh vic, and Scheer's article came out hours ago. Yeah. Related."

Burden pulled three surgical gloves from his pocket and handed two to Vail and Dixon.

"Where's the key?" Dixon asked as she inserted her hand into the baby blue rubberized material.

They twisted and bent, peered and knelt, taking care not to disturb it before the criminalist had a chance to document the scene.

"Found it," Burden said, pointing to a spot beneath the victim's torso.

Dixon held her iPhone in front of it and snapped off a couple of photos from different angles.

Burden extracted the key and held it up. "Not the same."

Vail tilted her head, appraising it. "Just a plain brass key. Kwikset. One in...what, millions? Not the specialized shape like the other ones."

"So...what?" Burden asked. "He ran out of the other kind?"

*Or it's a different killer. The violence to the face. A different key. Is this a copycat who went by what's in that* Register *article? Or is it the same asshole, just fucking with us, trying to make me do what I'm doing now. Running in circles and getting nowhere....*

"Karen." Dixon waved a hand in front of Vail's face. "Hello, Dixon to Vail. Over."

Vail refocused her eyes. "Sorry. Running it through my brain."

"Care to share?" Burden asked. "Usually works better that way."

"Telling people what pops into my head sometimes gets me into trouble."

Dixon chuckled. "No argument there."

Vail took the key in her gloved palm and looked at it. "It's possible this is a copycat. I wanna go back through Scheer's article and see exactly what details he disclosed. If this offender painted by numbers based on what Scheer described, the chances of this being a different scumbag go up. Could be he's the same guy, trying to throw us off. Playing with us."

Burden craned his neck and studied a letter laying on the dresser. "Just a guess, but I think our vic is Roberta Strayhan."

"Hey, you guys up here?" A voice from the hallway.

"In the bedroom," Burden said.

Rex Jackson walked in with his kit. He noticed the key in Vail's hand. "Couldn't you have waited? You're making my job harder."

Vail handed Jackson the evidence. "I'd apologize, but I don't want to be disingenuous."

Jackson chuckled a humorless laugh. "You're a piece of work."

"Hey," Dixon said. "You're getting a more civil, diplomatic Karen Vail. A few months ago, her response wouldn't have been so nice."

"Thanks," Vail said. *I think.*

Jackson pulled his camera from its bag. "I guess I should feel fortunate. But I don't."

Burden took a long look around the room, and then said, "Clay Allman's downstairs waiting to come up. How long?"

Jackson thumbed a dial on his Nikon. "Give me thirty. And make sure he's escorted, I don't wanna be responsible testifying about what he did or didn't see."

As Jackson began snapping photos, Burden, Dixon, and Vail left the room and let him work his magic. They exited the building and joined Clay Allman by the curb, right where they had left him, hands in his jeans pockets and flexing his legs in place. The temperature had dropped a few degrees and dusk had crept in.

"You didn't have to stay in the exact spot," Burden said. "I was only kidding."

Allman spread his arms. "I aim to please."

"My mother had a sign like that in the bathroom," Vail said. "Over the toilet. I aim to please, so please aim."

"Sounds like you had a strange childhood," Dixon said.

"You don't know the half of it."

"Give it another thirty," Burden said to Allman, "then head on up with Sanchez. Sanchez," he called to the cop standing at the building entrance. "Thirty minutes, take Clay Allman up to the crime scene. And don't leave his side."

Sanchez raised a hand in acknowledgment.

"How about you come by after, walk us through those cases you dropped off."

Allman consulted his watch. "I've gotta file a story, but I can come by tomorrow morning, spend a little time." He backed away, then said, "Good?"

"That'll work," Burden said.

"If it isn't my new favorite asshole," Vail said.

Pulling up to the curb was Stephen Scheer. He shoved the gearshift to its endpoint, and then got out of his Honda.

Burden extended an arm to block Vail's path. "I think I've gotten to know you pretty well, Karen. Leave him alone. Let me handle this."

Vail kept her mouth closed, but the firm set of her jaw and narrowed eyes spoke volumes.

Dixon came up beside Vail. "Think he's gonna look at us?"

"I wouldn't invite eye contact if I was him."

"Inspector," Scheer said, doing as Dixon had predicted and behaving as if the two women were not present. "I'm told you've got a new body."

"I can't confirm or deny," Burden said.

Scheer's gaze flicked over to Allman, who was standing thirty feet away, beside Officer Sanchez.

"So is that how this is going to be? Silent treatment and a barrage of 'no comments'?"

Burden cocked his head. "What do you want me to do? You've put us in a very, very tough spot. But yeah, there's a new body. That's all I'm gonna say."

"And get this, dickhead," Vail said. "Your bullshit article might be responsible for her death. Print that."

"Don't give me that," Scheer said.

"We warned you," Dixon said. "Did you think we were bullshitting you?"

Allman was standing by the doorway, his chin tipped back, watching the scene play out. Vail figured he must be enjoying it, though he displayed no overt signs that it brought him any pleasure.

"You still have a chance to make this right," Dixon said.

"It's beyond fixing," Vail said. "But you can prevent the guilt from keeping you up at night. Tell us where you got that info. Who's your source?"

Scheer poked his tongue against the inside of his cheek. He looked at Allman and held his gaze, then turned and stormed back to his car. A moment later, he burned rubber away from the scene.

Vail watched him peel away and began to wonder if they would ever learn who was sabotaging their case. If he didn't reveal himself soon, she was going to have to quit being so nice and do more than merely ruffle a few feathers.

# 32

MacNally had finally fallen asleep. He was dozing and dreaming of Henry when he felt a firm hand clamp down on his mouth. His eyes shot open—but before he could react, two arms swung him onto his stomach and his head was buried in the pillow. A heavy weight climbed on top of his legs.

A hand grasped the waistband of his pants and yanked hard, nearly ripping the fabric and pulling them down. His legs were pried apart.

MacNally tried to twist his neck, to free it, to call out, to bite—something defensive—but whoever had a grip on the back of his head had his face pressed so firmly into the pillow he had tremendous difficulty breathing. His attacker's other hand was applying such a powerful downward force between his shoulders that fighting back was impossible. He was, essentially, locked down in place.

Voorhees's words echoed in his mind, and he instantly knew what was coming. A second later, he felt something hard penetrate his anus. And it hurt, ripping pain as he tightened and tried to fight it—but with his legs splayed apart, he couldn't muster any strength to keep the sphincter closed.

MacNally swung his elbows back, hoping to make contact with something, to just get him to stop, but he struck hard objects—muscle, he figured—and the attack continued. Finally, minutes later, the rapist shuddered and his body stiffened, and then all movement ceased. The man pulled out and the weight lifted from MacNally's body.

He was able to lift his head—but a different set of hands immediately took over, shoving his face down into the pillow.

No air, can't breathe—

And another body mounted him from behind.

This time the rape was more forceful. MacNally now had a sense as to whom had gone first—Carl—and now hard-bodied Kurt was taking his own ride.

MacNally was as Voorhees had predicted. A lop.

Carl and Kurt were predators. And he was locked in a cell, imprisoned in more ways than one, with no end in sight.

In fact, it was just beginning.

# 33

Vail had an idea, and acted on it swiftly. "Get in the car, Roxx. Burden—your keys."

"My— For what?"

"Quick," Vail said, running over to the driver's door. "I'm going after Scheer."

"For what?" He tossed her the keys. "You sure that's smart?"

Vail didn't answer. She was busy turning over the engine. Dixon was pulling on her seat belt when Vail peeled away from the curb.

She leaned forward as she accelerated, struggling to keep an eye on Scheer's disappearing vehicle.

"Find the light, Roxx. Flip it on."

Dixon bent over and felt around, then found the round, magnetic device. She rolled down the window, turned it on, and then stuck it on the roof. "What do you have in mind?"

"A little blackmail. You in?"

"That's kind of ambiguous, Karen. And blackmail is, uh, well, illegal."

"Not real blackmail. Just some…creative coercion."

"'Creative coercion.' Sounds to me like the new PC term for blackmail."

Vail swerved around a car and accelerated. "I think we should use it, start a trend."

Dixon grabbed onto the seat as Vail yanked the wheel hard to the left. "How about not?"

Vail had closed the gap between their Ford and Scheer's Honda and were now forty or so feet behind him. The reporter's brake lights flickered, he appeared to glance in his rearview mirror, and then he slowed his vehicle. A Prius to his right pulled to the curb and allowed Vail to pull up directly behind Scheer's bumper.

As both cars came to a stop, Scheer remained in his vehicle.

"I don't think he realizes it's us," Dixon said.

Vail shoved the gearshift into Park. "He's gonna shit when he sees that it is."

"Getting pulled over like that, he's probably already shitting."

Vail grinned. "Even better." As she walked toward Scheer's car, his expression was evident in the sideview mirror. He popped open his door and got out.

"Don't you know that when a cop pulls you over, you're supposed to remain in your vehicle?"

Scheer folded his arms and leaned back against the Honda. "What do you want?"

Vail looked across the car at Dixon. "A bit testy, brash...even arrogant. Don't you think? Not the reaction we expected." She turned back to Scheer. "How about showing some respect for a federal law enforcement officer?"

"So is that what this is? You pulled me over to harass me? Fine, go on. Have your fun."

"Stephen," Vail said with a pitying shake of her head. "I'm here to help you. We wanted to make you an offer."

Scheer looked from Vail to Dixon. "What kind of offer?"

"I've got a story that's surely front page material. And," she said, rotating her watch to catch the streetlight, "looks like there's still enough time to make your deadline."

"Let me get this straight. You want to give me a story. After what you said to me yesterday? That's a bit hard to believe."

"It is hard to believe. No, I was thinking of making *you* the subject of a front-page article. The reporter who, pissed off at his former friend and colleague, decides to write some bullshit story that includes dangerous and irresponsible information that sets off a serial killer."

"We hear your job's in a bit of jeopardy," Dixon said. "A piece like that might not sit well with your editor. Or the paper's legal team. Might just put you over the edge."

"You wouldn't do that," Scheer said, his glance rotating between Vail and Dixon, no doubt gauging whether or not this was a joke. Or a bluff. "I've got a family to support."

Vail took a step forward. "Tell you what. We'll ask the woman whose house we just visited back there, and see if she's in a forgiving mood. Oh, wait. We can't ask her. She's dead. Because of you."

The muscles in Scheer's jaw contracted, bulging from side to side.

"But," Dixon said, "if you cooperated and helped us out, tell us who your source was for that article…" She shrugged.

"Then there'll be no story," Vail said. "Nothing will jeopardize your job. And you get to keep working at the *Register* until you fuck it up on your own, and get fired."

"What do you say?"

"I'd say this is blackmail."

"No, no," Dixon said. "Creative coercion."

Vail lifted her brow. "See? Has a nice ring. Don't you think?"

Dixon bobbed her head. "I didn't at first. But it's growing on me."

"So, Stephen. What'll it be?"

Scheer looked up at the black sky. Puffs of white were barely visible, and the moon was somewhere beyond, a glowing disc of stark brightness set against the mottled darkness. "I don't know who my source is."

Vail shook her head. "I'm disappointed. I thought he was gonna help us, Roxx."

"I'm telling you the truth. I don't know."

"What'd you do, meet some guy on a dark street corner? I think you've been reading too many spy novels."

"I got a text. A series of texts."

"From who?" Vail asked.

Scheer closed his eyes. "I don't know."

"How'd you confirm the information?" *I feel like a trial lawyer. I already know the answer to that question.*

"I didn't."

*Bingo.* "So you get a few texts from an anonymous source, and you run with it? You write an article based on unconfirmed and unsubstantiated claims?"

"I don't believe him," Dixon said.

"We're not convinced, Stephen. You've been a journalist a long time. Do you see why that'd seem like bullshit to us?"

"It's not bullshit. You were…you were right. My job's on the line. I needed something big. And I needed to get the jump on Clay. This first text came in, and I…I jumped on it. I've never done that before. I'm sorry."

"You're sorry?" Vail looked at Dixon. "He's sorry that he incited a serial killer to kill an innocent woman. And her husband."

Scheer threw his arms up. "Why do you keep saying that?"

"Because," Vail said, "that's what happens with this type of killer. The worst thing you can say to him—let alone in a national newspaper—is that he's of below average intelligence. That'd incite him, big time. A guy like this, he'll act on it."

"He may even come after you," Dixon said.

*Good touch, Roxx. But I think he's freaking out enough.* "Give me your phone."

Scheer jutted his chin back. "What for?"

"I'm gonna check out your story. He sent you texts, I want to see them."

Scheer bowed his head. "I deleted them."

Vail slapped her hand against her temple. "Why the hell would you do that?"

"I didn't know—I didn't want to get my source in trouble. I didn't want any record of it. Normally we don't have to disclose our sources. You know that. Even in a court of law, we're protected. But carrying it around on my phone all the time freaked me out."

"What was the number?"

Scheer slowly shook his head.

"You don't even know the number."

He sighed deeply. "I don't." He turned to face Vail. "Please. I'm really, really sorry. I didn't mean for that woman to get killed. I didn't realize—I thought the info was legit. I just wanted the story…"

"You hear from him again, we want that number—as soon as you get it. And don't delete it. You hear me?"

Scheer nodded, but kept his gaze on the ground.

Vail gave Dixon a look of consternation, then headed back to their car.

"I'm sorry," Scheer called after them.

Once in the car, they both slammed their doors.

"You believe him?" Vail asked.

"Yeah."

"Me, too." Vail watched as Scheer got back into his Honda.

"So what does this mean?"

"That's a good question. Who's leaking that info? I guess we can look into Scheer's cell number. His carrier will have a record of the numbers of his incoming texts. Even if they don't store the content, they'll have the sending numbers."

"If it's not a throwaway, it's worth a shot."

"Text Burden, pass on what we discovered, and tell him we'll meet him at the station, give him his car back."

WITH THE TIME CREEPING PAST eight, they dropped off Burden's Ford at Bryant Street, discussed Scheer's anonymous tipster with Burden and Friedberg, and then the two inspectors called it a night. Vail caught a cab back to the Hyatt while Dixon met a friend of hers who lived in the city for a drink.

Vail walked into the Hyatt and took the escalator up to the seventeen-story lobby, where the atrium's angular lines, pinpoint lights and expansive grandeur still grabbed her attention each time she returned to the hotel.

Resigned, Vail settled her back against the elevator wall, then rotated her head left and watched through the curved windows as the cylindrical car rose smoothly, the lobby diminishing in size as she ascended to the fourteenth floor. The doors slid apart and she made her way down the long open hall to her room. She dialed her son as she walked, and was surprised when he picked up on the first ring.

"Hey, honey. I was just checking in. How are things?"

"Fine."

*He's going to grow out of this one-word teen-answer phase, right?*

"You have everything ready for space camp?"

"I'm not some little kid, Mom. It's not space camp, it's Aviation & Space Challenge. It's an engineering program."

"I know, I registered you, I paid the bill. I just thought—I'm sorry, Aviation & Space Challenge." *And they say girls are temperamental?* "Did you see where I packed your toothbrush? Oh, and don't forget your raincoat. The intro packet said it rains a lot there—"

"I got it, Ma. I'll be fine."

Vail slid her card into the slot and the green light flickered. She pulled down on the handle and walked into the dark room. She ran her hand along the wall, fumbling for the light switch. A floor lamp by the window popped on.

"Is Aunt Faye there? I just want to go over a few things with her about getting you to the airpor—"

"She went to bed already."

"Maybe she's still—all right, whatever. Forget it. Do you know what time you're leaving?"

"Early. We've gotta be on the road at seven."

"Then you'd better get to bed."

Silence.

"Jonathan, you there?"

"Here."

"Did you call Robby, say good-bye?"

"He came over tonight, we had dinner."

"That's great. I'm glad you spent some time with him. All right— enough talk. Go to bed, get a good night's sleep. I don't want you getting sick your first day of camp." *Shit.* "I mean Aviation Challenge." *Jesus Christ. This is painful.* "Call me if there's a problem. And have a great time. I wish I could be there to see you off."

"I'll call you when I can."

"Don't forget your phone charger."

"Ma?"

Vail set her key card on the dresser. "I just want to be able to reach you if I need to."

"Don't worry. I'll be fine. I'll talk to you in a few days, okay?"

"Yeah. Yeah, that's great. Have a great time. Love you."

"Love you too." And then he hung up.

Having her aunt living with them since her ex-husband's death was a blessing in more ways than one. Being in a career where travel was a reality of the job made it difficult having a teenager, especially one in today's times where there were so many avenues for a young mind to go astray. Faye's continuous and steady presence in the house was an unforeseen benefit of all she had endured while handling the Dead Eyes case. She had no idea that Faye's presence would have such a positive impact on her life.

She realized she was still standing there, staring out the large window at the nightscape and sparkling lights of the Pacific Ocean below her. Looking at it but not seeing it. She reached down to plug in her BlackBerry on the desk to her left—and froze. Lying beside the charger was something that should not have been there.

An oddly shaped brass key.

# 34

MacNally lay on his cot the rest of the night but did not sleep. His rectum felt like it was on fire, and his groin and legs ached. He understood what it must feel like for a woman to be forcibly penetrated.

Carl and Kurt smiled at him when they got up to go to breakfast. They gave him a pat on the shoulder as they left the cell.

Carl winked at him. "Good job last night."

"Nice ride," Kurt said. "Maybe tonight we'll try something different."

MacNally didn't know what the appropriate response should be. Incite them, stand up for himself—or take it and not say anything that might antagonize them? He chose the latter. He needed guidance, someone who could tell him how to avoid being a lop. He had no interest in being a predator, but there had to be a middle ground...some way he could be left alone to serve out his time in peace.

Forty-five years. *Time?* More like a lifetime.

The way things were now, he would not last a year, let alone forty-five. He would seek out Voorhees. At least he had been straight with him once. Maybe he would be again.

"WE SHOULDN'T BE TALKIN' OUT here in the open," Voorhees said. "Go to the ladder room." He gave MacNally instructions on how to get there, told him he would leave the door unlocked, and that he should wait ten minutes before joining him.

Once inside the room, which did, in fact, contain ladders, MacNally presented his predicament as a hypothetical situation.

"Hypothetically," Voorhees said, "Let me tell you how this goes down. It's our job to protect inmates that've been assaulted or prayed on. So if we weren't talking about a hypothetical situation here, I'd lock you up in protective custody. And that, well, may not be such a good deal for you. So keep one thing in mind: if all you do is run to me, then you're gonna be turned out."

"Turned out?"

"Word's gonna get out—if it hasn't already—that you're a lop, a whore, a prison punk that's the lowest piece of shit. You'll be sodomized and traded like a fucking sex slave."

MacNally started to speak, but Voorhees held up a hand.

"I know what you're thinking. Do the protective custody thing and we can send you to another prison where they don't know you." Voorhees shook his head. "Won't matter. What happens in one makes its way to another. Cons have ways of communicating. Coded messages in letters home to girlfriends. Classified ads in known magazines where cons send messages to each other."

"So what the hell am I supposed to do?"

"First, you're taking a huge risk even talking to me. Something like this can catch you in the ass big time. No pun intended."

"Too late. I'm here."

"Look, MacNally. I'm at the Big L for an eight-hour shift. The other sixteen hours, you're on your own. See what I'm saying? I can't protect you."

"I'm not asking you to protect me. I'm asking—I don't know what I'm asking. I don't know how to survive. I'm not like these guys here. I robbed a couple banks, yeah, but I…I'm different. I was doing it to survive, for my son. This may not come out right, but I'm not a bad person, I was just an average family guy who had no—"

"Then you gotta figure out what you gotta do in here, to survive. Some ways, bein' in here ain't much different from being out in the real world. Society's got laws on the outside. In here, we got laws, too.

Not just the laws of the prison, but con law. A code. You'll figure it out. Maybe someone here'll give you some guidance. Just be careful. They give you something, they're gonna want something back in return."

"Anyone ever get killed here? I mean, rape's one thing. But..."

"It ain't an everyday thing, but does it happen? Hell yeah. Look at what we got here, MacNally. Murderers, sex deviants, rapists, child molesters, kidnappers, drug addicts, armed robbers, mobsters, bikers. Bad shit's gonna happen when you put crap like that under one roof. All trying to prove how tough they are, who's got the most power. The biggest dick. That's why they're here. They do bad shit, and if they cause problems at other prisons, they send 'em to us. So. Murder in the Big L?" He chuckled. "Bet on it."

"I'm just trying to make sense of it all, figure out how I can find my place."

Voorhees laughed, a rough, uneven smoker's rasp. "Boil everything down, it's about power. And fear. And anger. Keep those three things in mind, and you may get some kinda understanding of what these assholes are after."

MacNally nodded.

Voorhees lowered his voice. "I can't be your friend, MacNally. People'd find out, they'd think you're either my snitch or I'm fucking you. And it ain't good for me because I'd look weak to my colleagues." MacNally started to object, but Voorhees stopped him. "Ain't important for you to understand. Just telling you like it is." He shrugged. "Now, you want to feed me stuff, things cons are planning, maybe we can work something out. Shift around your living arrangements. Wouldn't be hard. We could communicate through kites—"

"Is that what this whole thing's been about?"

"What whole thing?"

"You people know what Wharton and Gormack are. You see a skinny guy like me and you think, *We can use him.* Put him in with those animals, they'll fuck him over. Literally. And then if he doesn't like it, he'll come crawling to us because he can't take that kind of abuse. So you turn me into a snitch."

"Hey," Voorhees said. "Those are your words. I'm just offering you an out. That's what you want, ain't it?"

"Sounds like something that can get me killed."

"Play it real careful, might get you a ticket outta here."

"Out, as in released?"

Voorhees frowned. "Transferred. Maybe to a place that's a little more to your liking."

MacNally chewed on that.

"If you want a shot at this, you gotta be smart about it. Keep your ears open, your eyes open. Learn prison life, who's who. If you're gonna do this, you gotta know what you're talking about, you gotta know that what you're seeing is what you think it is. We can't move on a guy for some bullshit thing. Because you give us shit, you get shit from us in return. And that for sure will get you killed."

"Sounds like a long-term proposition. I don't have long term. I've gotta end this now."

Voorhees shrugged a shoulder. "Fine. Bottom line, then. You don't wanna be fucked like that again, stand up for yourself. Today, before your rep is permanently thrown under the truck."

MacNally nodded.

Voorhees leaned in closer. "The cons, they talk. I hear shit when we shake guys down, pressure 'em. You want advice, you want a taste of con law, here it goes. Every inmate has three choices." He counted them off his thick fingers. "He can fight—meaning make the guy pay who gets in his face. Hard—so he doesn't even think again about hurting you."

Second finger went up. "He can hit the fence—escape." Third finger. "Or he can submit and get fucked. Now, I gave you a fourth choice, help us out. Doesn't look like it's gonna solve your problem. So you're left with three. But I didn't tell you any of that. I find out you repeated it, and I hear you said it came from me, you and me will undergo some thump therapy in a dark cell. You get me?"

MacNally had an idea: he'd be beaten.

"I were you," Voorhees said with a tug on his belt, "I'd grow a set of balls. Fast. As in five minutes after you walk outta here."

MacNally shifted his feet. Now? Take care of this now?

"Don't let yourself be a victim. Even if it doesn't work out, you'll feel better about yourself in the morning. Just be careful—guys make alliances, they look out for each other. You may think you're taking on one guy, but suddenly you're lookin' at three."

MacNally tried not to let the building anxiety register on his face. He squared his shoulders, nodded confidently, and said, "Okay."

"You're gonna need a weapon. A shank—a homemade knife. Be smart about it. And be efficient. Show no mercy, because they ain't gonna show you any."

Voorhees grabbed the doorknob. "Wait ten minutes, then get outta here."

He left MacNally alone with his thoughts. That wasn't the type of advice he'd been hoping for. Actually, he didn't know what he was expecting. He was looking for a solution. Voorhees had no doubt gone the extra mile, probably with some risk, to give him an honest view of his situation.

But as he was now learning, the only true solutions to his problem—this one and those that would undoubtedly surface in the future—could not be found by talking to, or relying on, others.

The answers had to come from within.

# 35

Vail whipped out her Glock and threw it up in front of her, her forearms taut and her pupils dilated, taking in everything and anything. She swung the weapon left and right, looking at the room, her eyes scanning systematically from right to left. *Clear.*

Vail moved into the angled bathroom, grabbed the pocket door to the water closet and shoved it hard to the right, more forcefully than she should've because it bounced with a deep thud and started to close. She toed it back and, with her Glock in her right hand, grabbed the tall shower curtain and swung it to the side. Nothing—no one—in the bathtub.

She swung back around, then pulled her BlackBerry with her left hand and dialed Dixon. "Get back to the room. Someone's been here. The offender."

It was noisy in the background. Vail remembered she was in a bar.

"How do you know?" Dixon shouted into the phone.

"He left something. A key."

"Did you clear the place?"

Vail's eyes kept scouring the room. The bed. She hadn't checked under the bed. "Working on it."

"Be right there. Hang tight."

Vail shoved the BlackBerry into her holster, then knelt down to inspect the king mattress. It was a platform bed, so no way could anyone be underneath it.

She moved to the closet and pulled open the door. Just her clothing.

*Fuck. How did he find out where I was staying?* She walked back toward the desk. *Not impossible. But this asshole's smart.*

She wiped a layer of sweat from her face with a sleeve, and after one more glance around the room, double-locked the door and then settled into the web-backed office chair. She reholstered her weapon. Looked at the key. It was the same wide, unusual shape as most of the others they had found. *He wants me to know, without a doubt, that he's been in my room. Power. Definitely fucking with my head. Anything missing?*

As she turned away to check her suitcase, she noticed something on the Hyatt pad beside the phone. A typed note, in large caps.

### I KNOW WHAT YOU DID IN NY

A new wave of perspiration pimpled her forehead, scalp, and chest. *New York. Not just New York. What I did in New York. How could he know about New York? There are only three people who know about that. Me, my confidential informant, and my former partner.*

Vail hadn't seen either one in years. Six or seven. Last she knew, Mike Hartman was still a special agent somewhere on the east coast. She thought it was New Jersey, but she wasn't sure.

*How is he connected to this? How's he connected to the offender?*

The informant…Eugenia Zachry… She had thought of her from time to time over the years, but had never initiated contact. Once she left the woman's life, it was better to maintain distance.

Vail sat there staring at the note. *Think, Karen. What should I do about this? Bring it to the office. Show it to Burden—no. I can't. Tell Roxx? How can I do that? She's a friend…but…shit.*

*How does this asshole know about it?*

Minutes passed as she tried to clear her head and think this through. Just then there was a rapid series of knocks on the door.

*Roxxann.*

Vail's heart jumped a beat as she looked at the note.

"Karen. Open up!"

# 36

MacNally looked around the ladder room. He wondered if Voorhees had chosen this place for a particular reason. Or was he reading into it?

He doubted inmates were permitted to be in here unsupervised. If caught, he could not disclose that Voorhees had suggested they meet for a counseling session. Per the officer's orders, he had a few minutes before he could leave, so he set out to locate something he could use as a weapon.

There was nothing overtly obvious—no knives, no ice picks or awls, hammers—no tools of any sort, for that matter.

MacNally crouched down, then pressed his stomach flat against the floor and brought his eyes from the furthest left wall across to the— Wait.... In the corner, something thin, oblong, and brown. He knelt in front of a tall, wooden ladder, reached under the bottom rung, and wiggled his fingers. He caught the item with a fingernail and flicked it toward him.

A rusted ⅜-inch bolt, roughly five or six inches in length.

It wasn't sharp, but it definitely could serve as a weapon. He shoved it into his pocket, then gave one more look around the room. There were no other devices, utensils or hardware he could find. The bolt would have to do.

MacNally pulled the door open and walked out, then headed for A-Cellhouse to find Gormack and Wharton. He did not have to go far: both were in the yard having a smoke.

MacNally walked into the hot sunshine, then stopped. He needed to think this through. He had never attacked anyone—had never even had a bar fight—but he had seen a few. His observations told him that the victor wasn't always the best brawler, but the one who hit hard and fast, aggressively, and unrelenting... The man who was possessed and who did not stop until forcibly yanked away.

He reached into his pocket and felt the ribbed threads of the thick screw, then approached his adversaries. Gormack was the bigger threat: the one to neutralize first.

MacNally took five steps—and stopped. Two men were approaching his targets. They laughed and started jawing at one another. The odds were no longer in MacNally's favor. Despite the need to act fast, it would be foolish to force his hand. Acting prematurely could—likely would—get him killed—in which case, his damaged reputation would be moot. As problematic as being labeled a lop would be, he had to exercise restraint. At this point, an hour or two's delay would not matter—and might, in fact, be time well spent.

He had to channel his anger and use it effectively. Given what he had been through the first night in his new cell, summoning up his rage was not difficult. If there was any doubt that he could raise a weapon and drive it through another man's skin, it vanished each time he flashed on what his cellmates had done to him. The anal soreness would likely not subside for weeks.

But the emotional scar would remain long after his torn rectal skin had healed.

# 37

"Be right there," Vail called to Dixon. She grabbed a couple tissues from the bathroom vanity, wrapped up the note, and slipped it into her jacket pocket.

When she pulled open the door, Dixon was standing there, her blonde hair disheveled and concern evident in fisted hands that were wrapped around her SIG Sauer handgun. She glanced around and behind Vail, into the room.

"Everything okay?"

Vail stepped aside. "It's clear. He's—he's gone. Key's on the desk."

Dixon squinted at Vail, then moved into the room. Convinced all was okay, she holstered her sidearm, then walked over to the far end of the room and placed both hands on her hips. "Jesus Christ. He was in our room."

"Yeah, Roxx, I know that."

"That's it?" she said, her eyes scanning the room. "Nothing else— just a key?"

*The key and an incriminating note that relates to information he somehow got about my past.* "What do you think it means?" Vail asked, skirting Dixon's question. She hated lying to her friend. Omission of information was as much of a lie as answering her with a fictional response. But it didn't feel quite as dirty.

"I think it's pretty goddamn obvious, don't you?" Dixon looked around the room, moving things aside with her shoe. "Did you call Rex Jackson? What did Burden say?"

Vail jutted her chin back. *Shit. I've totally blown this. Where the fuck is my head? I know where it is. Where it was.*

"No, I—I didn't," she stammered. She pulled out her BlackBerry and started punching numbers. "It kind of rattled me. I wasn't thinking."

"It took me fifteen minutes to get here. You just sat here the whole time? What the hell were you doing?"

"I don't know, Roxx. I— It—" Burden answered. "Yeah, Burden, listen. I've got a situation here." *A situation?* She mentally slapped herself. "I got back to my room, and I found—there's a brass key on the desk. Just like the ones we found before."

"In your hotel room? The scumbag was in your room?"

"That's what I'm saying. He— It's all clear. Roxxann's here now. You want to get Jackson over here? Dust the place?"

"I'll call him. Meantime, get out of there, wait in the hall."

"Yeah. Right." *Of course. What the hell's wrong with me?*

Vail hung up and shoved the phone in her pocket. "He wants us to—"

"Get out of here. What you should've done," she said, walking toward the door. "Get your head screwed on, Karen. I've never seen you like this."

*That makes two of us.*

# 38

MacNally wished he had access to tools like the ones he had used on the Flaherty construction job. His momentary reflection on his time in Alabama only set him back to thinking about Henry. Although the First National robbery had gone as horribly sour as a glass of turned milk, he realized he had enjoyed working with his son—as perverse as it now seemed—while planning the heist and then executing it.

MacNally had no one… With Doris dead, his parents long gone and no siblings he kept in touch with, his existence was unusually solitary. It was not something he thought about when he and Doris had gotten married at such a young age—they had known each other since grammar school and had always assumed they were going to spend a lifetime together—the dreams of young lovers, with everything ahead of them, a future full of optimism and hope, plans for travel and a family.

With nothing left but Henry, he yearned to somehow reunite with him. Legally or illegally, he intended to find a way back to him. That his previous unlawful tactics were responsible for separating them in the first place was not lost on him.

Still, the bank heists were things they had done together, experiences they would always share. He wondered if Henry looked back on the events that landed them in their current predicament.

How did he see them? Was he was able to claw through the negatives to reflect positively on his father?

Since the moment Henry ran off as the police cruisers descended on them, MacNally could not stop thinking—and worrying—about him. He had been informed that his son had been made a ward of the state and placed in an orphanage, a thought that bothered him as much as the concept of getting into bed across from Wharton and Gormack. He didn't know much about such institutions, but he was certain they weren't desirable places in which to grow up. And it would only get more depressing as a boy matured into a young teen.

MacNally shoved his new weapon in his pocket, in case he needed it when he least expected it. Rapes did not only occur in your cell; he imagined the community showers were also a likely place for such transgressions because of the number of inmates in one room, in close proximity, without immediate access—and direct supervision—by guards.

As MacNally pondered that, he realized that the very reasons that made the showers dangerous for him would also make it a reasonably favorable place for him to launch his attack. Other inmates would see what he had done, accomplishing the goal of establishing his reputation and—hopefully—reversing any damage caused by the stories Wharton and Gormack had undoubtedly unleashed in the cellhouse.

It was not without risk—as Voorhees suggested, guys like Wharton and Gormack had friends and established alliances, and if anyone stepped in, MacNally's attack would end quite differently than he planned. His strategy demanded a fast and decisive approach—before they, and their buddies, realized what was going down.

He dropped his clothing off at the laundry, and trudged, naked except for his underwear, into the large tiled room. Water spouted from dozens of overhead faucets; vapor rose from the floor and migrated in billows ceilingward.

In front of him, Wharton walked up to his shower head; Gormack was behind him. As MacNally stepped under the water, his shank curled beneath his right hand and wrist, Wharton turned toward him.

Smiled. And then he felt a hard, calloused hand clamp across his mouth from behind. Gormack.

Wharton stepped toward him with a suddenly visible erection.

MacNally threw his head backward as hard as he could, smashing his skull into Gormack's nose. Wharton lunged forward, but MacNally swung and connected with a vicious right-handed uppercut, the bolt tearing into the obese man's chin, ripping skin and sending a spatter of blood into the cascading water.

MacNally slammed his right foot against Gormack's shin to knock him back and gain some space, then whirled to face him.

Gormack's fist was coming forward to throw a punch, but MacNally blocked it with his left forearm. Before the big man could respond, MacNally swung wildly with the bolt, catching Gormack's right eye socket.

The bolt penetrated the soft tissue, but got stuck on the bony orbit. He yelped—MacNally yanked it out—then stabbed again at Gormack's face, catching part of his other eye.

Gormack squealed like a wounded animal and stumbled backwards, falling onto the slippery tile.

Yelling—guttural fury—spilled forth, echoing as surrounding inmates scattered to the periphery.

Off in the distance, angry shouts to break it up.

Chest heaving, face spattered with blood, and water spraying his eyes, MacNally turned to confront Wharton. But Wharton wrapped both arms around him, preventing him from raising his arms.

MacNally, possessed by rage of an intensity that he had never experienced, freed his right arm and swung upwards with vicious ferocity. The bolt penetrated Wharton's groin. His eyes bulged and his body froze, then fell backward to the wet floor.

MacNally drove onto his knees—and stabbed wildly in the direction of the man's chest. He missed and struck the tile—and then flesh—and Wharton screamed. He wrapped his thick hands around MacNally's throat and squeezed.

But MacNally did not yield. He dropped the bolt and grabbed Wharton's hair, then lifted his head and smashed it down into the tile.

Again.

And again.

His breathing was rapid. Despite the water and humidity, his shallow breaths came in dry, raspy gasps.

*MacNally swung around*
*eyes bulging—*
*saw the muscled torso of Gormack lying in*
*a diluting pool of blood,*
*water raining down on him.*

Three loud whistle blasts blew, once, twice, three times—but no guards came running. It was only then that MacNally realized the wild beast-like screaming he had been hearing was coming from his own throat.

He stood up and kicked at the bolt, sending it skittering across the floor. Men were staring at him, standing against the walls, keeping clear.

More whistles. Footsteps, yelling.

MacNally turned into the shower and washed the blood from his hands and face, arms and torso.

Through the cascading sheet of water, he caught a glimpse of approaching officers.

Orders were called out, loud and aggressive:

*"Back the fuck up!"*

*"Shut the goddamn water!"*

*"Stay back!"*

MacNally continued his shower…heart racing…intensely focused…

And numb.

A second later, he was pulled away and brought down hard to the tile by two or three officers.

"Jesus Christ!" Another guard came up along the periphery, taking in the bloody carnage. "MacNally, you do all this?"

The cons looked at the officer, as if he was speaking a foreign language. No one moved. No one spoke.

The guard walked over to a nearby phone, dragged an index finger around the metal dial, then turned to face the bodies of Gormack and

Wharton. "Two down in the showers. Send medics." He listened a second, then said, "Pretty bad."

MacNally was handcuffed, hustled up, and then led out of the room, the surrounding inmates gawking at the intensity and violence of the attack, which had—in actual time—lasted mere seconds.

Seeing his fellow inmates' faces as he was pushed out of the room, MacNally felt a broad grin spread across his face. In that moment, though he did not know what his fate would be, he felt certain of one thing: no one at the Big L was going to mess with him again.

# 39

As the door clicked shut behind them, Dixon looked at her partner. "What the hell's gotten into you?"

*A serial killer with a secret from my past, that's what.*

"Nothing. It was just unnerving to see that key. In our room."

"Give me a break. Karen Vail doesn't get unnerved by that shit. She gets angry. And then she gets even."

*That'd be about right. Except for this other little detail I haven't told you about.*

"Yeah, well..." Vail turned away, put her hands on the wood banister and looked down to the floor of the lobby, at the suspended sheets of lights, at the metal globe sculpture, at the conical glass elevator cars that were rising and falling on their tracks. An architecturally stunning view. But she wasn't seeing it.

Vail turned and saw Dixon staring at her. No, studying her. Hands on her hips. "What?"

Dixon shook her head, then took up a position beside Vail. "So what do you think the key is all about?"

"He's sending me a message. That he can violate my space and there's nothing I can do about it. No place is safe."

"Why not just kill you? If he can find out where you're staying, if he can get into your room, why not lie in wait and then do to you what he's done to all his other victims?"

"Because it's not about me. And if he kills me, he's losing his playmate. He doesn't want to do that. He's having too much fun fucking with us. With me. Allman did us a good goddamn favor by printing my name in that story. He made it all about me."

"Any way we can use this to our advantage?"

Vail snorted. "If I can clear my head and think straight, yeah, maybe I can come up with something."

"In the Crush Killer case, you established a line of communication with him. It was important."

"But this offender isn't like the Crush Killer. He is in some ways, but he's also very different. What worked for him won't work for this guy. We need to think this through. *Let's start with figuring out what the connection is to my former partner. And where did Stephen Scheer get the information—who's the leak?*

Ten minutes later, Vail saw Rex Jackson come up the escalator into the lobby. "He's here."

The sight of the criminalist trudging along, toting his kit, was one she had seen too often of late. For all involved, the Bay Killer was wearing out his welcome.

BURDEN AND FRIEDBERG WERE NEXT to arrive, and they spent fifteen minutes speaking with the concierge, hotel management, security, and the bartender and waitresses in the lobby restaurants. Vail figured it would yield nothing of value, but realized it was standard procedure and good police work to proceed according to accepted case management.

Dixon worked the phone. And Vail, after waiting for Jackson's cue, returned to the room. "May I?" she asked, picking up his latent print kit.

Jackson was on his knees with a small vacuum, hoping to find errant fibers. "Knock yourself out. I've already lifted a few dozen."

"No doubt mine and the prior week's guests." She took it over to the desk, removed the notepad from her suitcase, and quickly twirled black powder across it with the brush. Seconds later, she sighed and curled her lips. Nothing. Not even a partial. But not surprising, either. This offender had been far too careful to leave a meaningful forensic at numerous crime scenes; it wasn't likely that he would slip up on a simple note that he knew would rattle her.

She brushed off the powder, then rewrapped the note and slipped it into her pocket.

"Anything?" Dixon asked.

Vail spun, guilt sprouting from her pores. "Me?"

"No, Jackson. Anything?"

The forensic scientist swiveled on his knees. "Just about done. I've collected lots of stuff, but I won't know if I've got anything till we process it all. With all the budget cuts and the vics and crime scenes this guy's left us, we're already so backed up I've got no idea when I'm gonna come up for air."

Burden appeared in the doorway. "No one saw anything. They've got security cameras and Robert's getting the digital tapes for us, they're burning a DVD. But a guy like this—"

"He's too careful," Vail said. "He knew about the camera at that palace place and he made it impossible for us to see his face. He's gonna know about the ones they have here, too. I'm not optimistic."

"Me either," Burden said. "But it's what we do." He stepped into the room and said, quietly, to Vail, "You feel more comfortable if we moved you? Another hotel?"

"Honestly? He found me here. He'll find me wherever you move me. But as I was telling Roxx, I'm not at risk. He wants me alive."

"How so?"

"If he wanted to, he could've killed me just like he killed the others. But he's playing with me. I'm more important to him alive than I am dead. And whatever the reason he's killing those men and women, I don't fit his fantasy."

"Excuse me for not being so confident, but I think it's safer to move you."

"We'll be fine. Roxx's here with me. He won't be able to disable both of us at once. And Roxx is no pushover in case you haven't noticed."

"I noticed," Burden said.

Vail tilted her head. "You have?"

"I'm a guy. We notice those things."

Friedberg poked his head in the room. "Anything?"

"Don't know yet," Jackson said.

"You wanna stay here," Burden said, "fine. But my recommendation is that you move."

"Roxx," Vail called to Dixon, who was standing in the bathroom. Dixon poked her head out, the phone still against her ear. "You wanna switch hotels?"

"Shit no. I'm not running from this bastard. What about you?"

Vail turned to Burden. "We're staying."

Burden gave a disapproving shake of his head, then tapped Jackson on the shoulder. "Get me something as soon as you can."

Jackson closed a couple of latches, buttoning up his kit. "Add it to the freaking list. Wish you guys would find this guy. You're giving me a shitload of work. If I was making overtime, that'd be one thing…"

Burden took a final glance around the room. "See you both in the morning. Don't forget. Clay's gonna walk us through those other cases."

Vail sat down on the edge of the bed. "Let's hope there's something there."

# 40

Three hours passed. Since the inmates who showered together lived in the same cellhouse, they were all taken back to their cells and the block was locked down. After officers examined each of the prisoners for injuries and traces of blood, they were taken individually to the lieutenant's office, where they were interviewed by counselors.

Based on the staff's initial investigation and what the officers had witnessed upon their arrival, MacNally was identified as the instigator and given a nonstop ticket to the Hole, which was located in the west yard of the penitentiary in Building 63, a separate two-story structure. MacNally had escaped relatively unscathed, and except for assorted abrasions and bruises—mostly from when he was being wrestled down and handcuffed—his injuries were nothing compared to those sustained by Gormack and Wharton.

MacNally was escorted to a three-man unit with cement walls, a narrow stall shower in the corner, and formed-concrete bunk beds—one along the left wall and two in a line along the right—suspended by triangular iron brackets.

There was already a man asleep on one of the cots when the officer shoved MacNally inside.

The inmate stirred, lifted his head, but did not get up. "Who the fuck're you?"

"Walt MacNally. You?"

"John," the blue-eyed, dirty-blond convict said. "John Anglin. Guys call me J.W." Anglin narrowed his eyes, then swung his feet over the side of the bed and sat up. "Wait a minute. MacNally— you're the guy from the showers? Gormack?"

MacNally could not stop a grin from spreading his lips. "That's me."

Anglin nodded slowly, holding his chin back and appraising him. "You're a fish. Got a lot to learn."

MacNally set his kit down on the bed, then said, "So? What's your point?"

"Things work a certain way here. You gotta follow the law."

MacNally shook his head. "Gormack and Wharton had to pay."

"Something like you did—it's gotta be approved by the guy who's running the place."

MacNally sat down on his bunk and faced Anglin. "You mean the warden?"

"No, asshole. Every prison's got gangs, that kinda shit. But nothing happens in a joint without first being ran past the main guy, the head inmate. You know, a guy who's been around the place a long fucking time, who knows the players and how shit goes down—but still young enough to be callin' the shots because no one ain't never gonna cross him."

MacNally did not think that an apology would be a response that would be respected. Instead, he said, "Didn't have a choice. They had to be put in their place. But I'll tell you this, J.W. Those fuckers aren't gonna move against me again."

Anglin locked eyes with MacNally, then lay back down on the bunk and drew the covers up to his chin.

Thus far, the Hole or not, his new living arrangements were working out far better than his first cell assignment had.

TWO DAYS LATER, MACNALLY AND ANGLIN were playing cards when they both sensed a presence by the bars. They turned and saw Voorhees standing there.

"Know what happened to your former cellies, MacNally?" No doubt noticing the inmate's blank expression, Voorhees said, "Gormack's had two surgeries, but looks like he's gonna be blind. You did a number on his eyes."

"Don't know what you're talking about."

"One of Wharton's testicles was too badly damaged to be saved, and he's got a fractured skull and some sort of raging blood infection."

Does he think I went overboard? Is he putting on a show for J.W. to cover his ass? "Sounds like whoever did this was pretty pissed off," MacNally said. "Wish I could say I'm upset by it. But I'm not."

Voorhees kept his gaze fixed on MacNally a long moment, then pushed off the gate and walked off.

MacNally tossed a card onto the pile, then smiled internally. This was the best he had felt in a very long time—since the day before he found Doris's body on the floor of his kitchen.

Soon as he got out of the Hole, he would need to construct a new shiv. Given what he had been able to do with the bolt, he was never going to be without a weapon again.

Vail slept fitfully, a direct result of the shock she had gotten last night. Her dreams were filled with memories of New York, her former partner, and the unrelated bank robbery shootout that accelerated her ascendance to the Behavioral Analysis Unit. The latter episode shook her awake in a drenched sweat at 4:20 AM. Fortunately, her thrashing and subsequent trip to the bathroom to wipe herself down did not wake Dixon.

Before returning to bed, she woke Dixon's laptop and, keeping the screen brightness turned down to its lowest setting, did a search to see what she could learn about Mike Hartman. She found a press release from three years ago. He was in the Elk City, Oklahoma, resident agency—a substantial step down from his New York assignment when she partnered with him. She was unsure what caused such a demotion; although Hartman was nowhere near the sharpest agent she had worked with, he was serviceable. He had faulted her for a prior hiccup in his career path. *Could he blame me for this one, too?*

There were no other references to him, which was not unusual. It was, in fact, what she expected to find. Unless agents made the news in a major case, they preferred to stay out of the media—and off Internet search engines.

Vail put the PC back to sleep—and attempted to do the same for herself—but found that simple task elusive. She lay awake for the next two hours before Green Day began blasting from KFOG, the radio station to which Dixon had set the alarm. Her partner wanted to wake up early to squeeze in a workout before heading off to the station.

Vail accompanied her, and while Dixon pumped iron, Vail pumped her legs on the elliptical. Keeping her quads and hamstrings strong, particularly following her knee surgery, was a pledge she had made after all the sprinting and climbing she had engaged in during her Napa exploits.

On the way up the stairs of the Bryant Street entrance, and running about fifteen minutes late, Vail told Dixon she needed to make a pit stop in the restroom. If Dixon thought it strange that she would need to go again, after leaving the hotel only moments ago, she did not let on.

"Make it fast," she said. "Allman's waiting on us."

Instead of walking into the bathroom, Vail exited the stairwell on the third floor and dialed a number she had called so frequently that it stuck in her brain like the hundreds of crime scene images she had been unable to scrub from her memory. A male voice answered.

"I'm looking for Eugenia," Vail said. "Is she there?"

"Who is this?"

"I need to talk with Eugenia Zachry. Is this her number?"

"I don't know who you are," the voice said, a bit more hostile now, "but Eugenia passed on six months ago." Click.

Vail's heart slowed and her eyes teared up. Still holding the phone against her ear, she wiped away the moisture with thumb and index finger, then put away her BlackBerry. She wanted to ask the details—how it had happened, what the disposition of Eugenia's daughter was—but it was best that the man had hung up on her.

Vail took a moment to compose herself, then brought her thoughts back to the present. Eugenia was not the offender's source of information. But would Eugenia have told anyone about what she had done? Eugenia was, at the end of the day, an informant who made stacks of money selling information of value to others. Or could she have crossed paths with the person who would come to be known as the Bay Killer? Though both were possible, neither was likely—yet at the same time, they could not be definitively ruled out.

Given the law of attraction—if you move in scummy circles, you attract scummy people—it was more than just possible.

She again dialed Eugenia's number. No answer, no machine.

There was still Mike Hartman. She glanced at her phone and noticed the time. *Crap*. Allman was supposedly upstairs going through the prior cases.

Vail walked up one more flight and entered Homicide, where the unofficial task force was already assembled and waiting, including Clay Allman.

"Nice of you to join us," Burden said.

"Sorry—I had to...sorry." She settled herself atop the worktable and took the manila file from Allman. "This is the first one?"

Allman looked up as he shifted the remaining folders in his hands. "I'd label that one the second. First being the one in '82. Edgar Newhall."

Dixon reached over and made a point of counting the files Allman was holding. "You're saying there are nine prior kills attributed to the same killer?"

"Whoa, hang on a second," Allman said. "No. That's not what I said. These are all cold, unsolved cases. I see a few things that are common in them. That's it. As to whether or not they're the work of the same killer, well, I think that's the job of Agent Vail here." He turned to her.

Burden sat down in his chair, backwards, his chest against the seatback. "Why don't you walk us through these? Capsule summaries."

"Fine." Allman took the folder from Vail, set it on the table and opened it. "You've got that '82 murder, Edgar Newhall, where the killer left the brass key by the body. Key type matches the one found on the current—"

"Yeah, we got that one."

"Right. So the second one." Allman slid the top paper aside. "Back in '84, Terry Lindahl was murdered and his body was found on a ferry at Pier 33. Killed during the night and discovered in the morning by a dock worker. He was tied to the mast."

"Really," Vail said. "That's interesting. Any brass keys?"

"No."

"COD?" Friedberg asked.

"Blunt force trauma to the face and head."

"Weapon?" Vail asked.

Allman flipped a page, revealing handwritten notes on yellow legal paper. "Wounds were jagged and bloody, consistent with a 'vesicular igneous rock' found at the scene." He turned the sheet over. "Oh— and there was a stab wound to the left kidney. Knife not found. Could've been dumped in the water."

Dixon said, "Occupation?"

Allman turned another page, then another. "Homeless. They were only able to ID him because his fingerprints were on record. He did time in the state and federal prison systems back in the fifties and sixties."

"Okay," Friedberg said, inserting an unlit Marlboro between his lips. "Next one."

Allman moved on to the next folder. "Oh, yeah. This was a strange one. You may remember this one, Birdie. It was a front-pager. Donald Wright, '87. He was found in front of an Army surplus store."

"I do remember that one. Investigation led nowhere."

"COD?" Vail asked.

"Strangulation. Manual, according to the ME." He glanced through the file. A yellowed newspaper clipping from the front page of the *San Francisco Tribune* was preserved in a plastic sleeve. Allman moved it gingerly aside. "And before you ask. No key."

"And who was this Wright guy?"

"Postal worker." He moved another newspaper clipping aside. "Oh, yeah. This guy—he was one of the survivors of the shooting when that gunman opened up with a submachine gun in the Oakland sorting facility. That was back in '85. I think you guys looked into a possible connection, but nothing was found."

"No stabbing and no head trauma?" Vail asked.

"Nope."

"Then why did you think this was related to the others?"

Allman sucked on his teeth and stared at the open folder. "Not sure. Can't remember. Maybe because the body was found in a strange place, like the others? You tell me."

"Hell if I know," Vail said with a shrug. "Nothing I see here that would link them."

"What else do you have?" Dixon asked.

Allman closed the Wright file and spread open the next one. "Billy Duncan. Carpenter. Found with his tongue excised and his mouth propped open by an ice cream stick."

"Someone didn't like what Billy had to say," Vail said.

"No key. COD was…" Allman flipped through the file and found his notes. "Gunshot to the abdomen. He bled out."

Burden leaned back in his chair. It popped out from underneath him, but he caught himself in time to keep from landing on his rear. He swung the chair around and sat properly in the seat. "Where was Billy found?"

"In a school recreation yard in Berkeley."

Vail, Dixon, Friedberg, and Burden exchanged shrugs.

"What else?" Vail said.

"How old are all these guys?" Dixon asked.

"Mid-forties to mid-fifties," Allman said. "I can look through the files and give you—"

"We can do that," Burden said. "Continue."

Vail's vision blurred as she focused on what Allman had just said. *That would put them around the same age as the current vics, if they'd lived. There's something with that. But what?*

"What do you think, Karen?"

Vail looked up. "Huh?"

"Any thoughts so far on linkage?" Dixon asked. "What's the common factor?"

"I'm not sure there is any. Not yet, anyway. I need to spend time with the files. Wait—we don't have crime scene photos or ME reports, do we?"

"Lost in the fire," Burden said.

"I've got some stuff in the folders," Allman said. "But nothing approaching what was in the original SFPD files."

"What year was Billy Duncan murdered?" Vail asked.

"Ninety."

"Hmm." *Every two to three years. Maybe there is a pattern here. Something I'm not seeing. What?*

"Then there's Martin Tumaco, owner of the Mercury Dream Research Lab. A life preserver had been overinflated and it choked him. His brain was deprived of oxygen and he basically died of brain damage."

Burden pointed. "I remember that one. A buddy of mine caught that case. He was found in one of the flotation tanks. Went nowhere. No forensics, no leads, no suspects. Zippo."

"And why did you pull that one?" Dixon asked.

"Just because of the unusual location of the body. And the COD. He was strangled, like the other vic. But it wasn't manual." Allman took a breath, then shrugged a shoulder. "I don't know. Maybe it's got nothing to do with the others. Maybe none of these are related. I just had a feeling these all have a connection. But I'm just a reporter covering a beat. You people are the experts. You might decide none of these have anything to do with anything."

"Did any of these vics have numbers written on their foreheads?" Friedberg asked.

Allman lifted his brow. "No. None of them. I'd definitely remember that."

"When was this last one?" Vail asked.

Allman pulled open the file again and peered in. "Ninety-five."

Vail sighed deeply and sat back against the wall. *So much for my theory...but then again, this whole exercise is totally inaccurate to begin with. These vics may be related, but they may not be. There could be others Allman missed or doesn't know about. Or the offender could've been in the joint for something completely unrelated, disrupting his pattern. This isn't helping.*

"What happened with that ice cream vendor?" Dixon asked. "The carts at the Palace of Fine Arts?"

Friedberg rubbed at his eyes. "Company called North Beach Vending runs the show. They keep the carts locked away in a storage area behind the building. One of 'em went missing a day before we found the body. They found it in back in storage the day after. I had it brought over to the lab, but we're not gonna find anything."

"Who has access to that storage room?" Burden asked.

"Anyone with a bolt cutter. Just a simple padlock."

Allman laughed. "If you aren't a serial killer looking to transport a body, I guess there isn't much of a market for beat-up tin boxes on wheels."

As Vail was about to suggest they move on, Burden's phone rang.

He listened, then said, "Yeah, okay. Got it." He hung up. "We found Roberta Strayhan's husband."

# 42

December 16, 1959

*Leavenworth*

Three months passed. The warden never did assign a third man to their Building 63 cell, which worked to MacNally's advantage since he and Anglin had been compatible roommates. He had told Anglin about Henry, and even showed him a dog-eared photo he had brought with him—something he never would've thought of doing with Gormack and Wharton.

Although Anglin had never been married and did not have any children, he seemed to understand the pain MacNally felt over being separated from Henry. Anglin's siblings included two brothers who had also found the life of crime attractive, tending toward bank robbery and assorted petty infractions. One of them, Clarence, was a recent arrival at Leavenworth.

Nearly a month after being released from the Hole, MacNally and Anglin were assigned a cell together in B-cellhouse. A week after Anglin introduced MacNally to Clarence, he noticed that Anglin began huddling with his brother each afternoon around the same time, talking in secret for about ten minutes before going their separate ways.

Back in the cell that evening, MacNally asked Anglin what he and Clarence discussed when they met in the yard.

Anglin, sitting on his bunk, faced MacNally and said, in a low voice, "Mac. My brother and me, we been in a lot of prisons. But we don't stay long."

"That's good," MacNally said, unsure where Anglin was headed. "Right?"

"No. No, I mean, we leave. We escape." He leaned toward the bars and let his eyes dart back and forth, scanning the cell block. "We got a way out of here. We could use another guy."

"I've been thinking about the same thing. Trying to figure a way to get out, find my son." MacNally scooted closer. "You said you need some help." He tapped his chest, suggesting himself as an option.

"It ain't something to take lightly. You get caught, they add time. We're here, in this shithole, because we're good at escaping. Got out of every damn place they put us. If we could just stop gettin' caught robbin' stupid banks, we'd be two fuckin' happy guys. But no. They always nab our asses and throw us back in the joint."

"How—" MacNally lowered his voice. "How do you think you're gonna get out of here?"

"Clarence works in the bakery, and I just got a job in the kitchen. Clarence reckons to hide away in a box, one of them big ones they use to bring bread into the kitchen."

"A breadbox? You're shitting me. That won't work."

"Oh, yeah?" Anglin's face hardened. "How many prisons you break out of, Mac?"

MacNally leaned back.

"Yeah," Anglin said, "didn't think so. From the day I got here, I been thinking about leaving. And I'm not just talkin' 'bout thinking of it, I mean really figuring it out. Watching, talkin' with guys, workin' through how things work. That's how I do it. I look for the weak points, the things the hacks don't think about. Human nature, people gettin' lazy and not doing their jobs. See?"

MacNally nodded. "I've been watching for stuff like that, too. Go on."

"The hacks count us four times a day, right? The one at four o'clock's a stand-up count, and that's a tough one to beat. So I reckon we don't try. Clarence'll be there for that one. But the next one, at ten, is a much easier one to beat. Prop up some shit in your bed, make it look like there's a body there, and you're good to go. That gives Clarence six hours to get himself into the back of that there delivery truck and hide. When they drive off, 'bout seven, he'll have a three-hour head start before they even know to start lookin' for him. Follow?"

"That's not bad," MacNally said. "I was wondering how to beat the count. That's where I kept getting hung up."

"Like I said before, you gotta look for the weak points. Like that bread truck. A buddy of mine knows a guy who did time here once. He built a fake wall inside the back, just for Clarence. If we can get Clarence into the truck, he can get behind that wall and drive clear outta here. We don't have to cut through no bars, beat on a guard, none of the shit that'd git us a year in the Hole."

MacNally considered the plan. "The beauty's in its simplicity."

"You want in, or not?"

"What do I have to do?"

"I've gotta get Clarence into that metal box. Then I gotta push him into the kitchen elevator. There's a guard nearby, so we need to take his mind off things. Create a diversion."

MacNally thought about it a moment. If the Custodial Associate Warden sensed that he was involved, he'd be heavily disciplined. How bad, he had no idea. Time in the Hole, for sure. Of course, more than likely they wouldn't be able to prove he was mixed up in the escape attempt, and if he handled the diversion properly, he could make it look like it wasn't of his doing.

"What's in it for me?" If MacNally hadn't asked the question, Anglin would've been suspicious. Cons formed alliances, but there was a world of difference between pacts for convenience sake—and loyalty. MacNally had been told that even brothers snitched on one another in prison.

Anglin said, "I help you plan something. You're smart about it, you get to be with your son."

MacNally found himself nodding before he could speak or even think it through.

"Tomorrow. During dinner. Gets dark early, good time for Clarence to blow this joint."

"How do you know," MacNally said, "that they won't lock the place down and search the truck?"

"Won't matter. They did a good job with that fake wall. They won't find him."

"You sure?"

Anglin ground his jaw. "Let me worry 'bout that shit."

MacNally went over more details with Anglin, and then laid back on his bunk to figure out his diversion. He knew it had to be good, and it had to be clever. He fell asleep working those thoughts through his mind.

IN KEEPING WITH CLARENCE'S ESCAPE, the diversion MacNally sketched out would be as simple as possible to ensure a successful implementation and to reduce the risk of something going awry.

They were on the yard, amidst inmates who were lifting weights, smoking, and telling stories. Anglin closed his eyes and craned his neck skyward, the sun fully on his face. "What's your plan?"

MacNally spoke in hushed tones, his face canted toward the ground to prevent an officer or a snitch from reading his lips. "Get into an argument with someone. Loud, aggressive. I can sell it pretty good, I think."

"Keep going."

"If I can make it seem as if it was started by the other guy, and it's convincing, even if they suspect I was involved, they'd never be able to prove it. By keeping it 'in-house,' between me and you, there's no way for the hacks to prove it was a setup."

"They don't need no proof to throw you in the Hole. Suspicion's enough for 'em."

"If they had proof, it'd be much worse."

Anglin bobbed his head, his eyes darting from side to side as he processed what MacNally had told him. Finally, he nodded his approval.

The following day, MacNally shuffled into the dining hall along with his cellhouse's complement of inmates. John and Clarence Anglin were already in the kitchen on duty, as they were supposed to be. MacNally figured the best place for him to be was nearby, because when the shouting started, inmates would either stay put or leave their seats, anxious to put distance between themselves and the altercation. Being a witness to even the most minor incident can result in a quick death at the hands of the head inmate's enforcers.

Once the commotion had started, Anglin and another inmate could load the box containing Clarence into the truck. It would be heavy, but if the guard watching them was properly distracted, they could get it into the back without the officer realizing that it weighed substantially more than it should.

MacNally took care to choose an unwitting partner. He asked Clarence who would make a good victim—someone who was not connected to a gang that would take retribution against MacNally for what he was about to do. Clarence selected a fish, a new inmate who hadn't had the opportunity to make friends or forge alliances: Neil Wallace, a slightly built white-collar criminal who did not appear to have the constitution or stature to defend himself.

Clarence pointed out Wallace earlier that afternoon, and as they entered the dining hall, MacNally engaged the man in conversation while steering him toward the preselected location, near the kitchen.

Two minutes after getting their food, MacNally continued his discussion with Wallace before abruptly slamming his fork down. "What the hell did you say, motherfucker?" He jumped up from his seat and leaned across the table. "Go on—say it again."

Wallace leaned back, his mouth agape, hands splayed in surrender.

Feigning an unsatisfactory response, MacNally tossed his bowl of chili into Wallace's lap. The inmate reflexively sprung up, the shock of MacNally's unexpected aggression—and the pain of the burning liquid against his skin—registering in the contortion of Wallace's face. It was the sort of spontaneous reaction that was not possible unless it was a genuine response.

MacNally reached across the table and slammed a fist into Wallace's jaw, and the man tipped backward over his bench, arms flailing in the air before he landed hard on his back. He shook his head to get his wits about himself, then tried to scramble away in retreat, his feet sliding against the slick ground.

But MacNally knew the altercation hadn't lasted long enough to buy Anglin sufficient time to get Clarence loaded into the truck, so he clambered over the table and threw himself atop Wallace.

Shouting erupted from across the cavernous room: guards yelling orders to MacNally and Wallace to break it up; at each other to communicate what was going on; and at surrounding inmates to stay put.

MacNally drew back and punched Wallace repeatedly in the face until two correctional officers approached from opposite sides. While one guard fought his way through, the other grabbed MacNally by the collar of his shirt and yanked him to the side.

MacNally lunged at his prey—lest there be no question he was sincere—and landed another punch before the guards got a firmer hold. A kick to Wallace's face served as MacNally's parting shot as the officers slammed him to the floor, face first. They snapped handcuffs around his wrists while four other guards, who had just arrived, searched him for knives or shivs.

Wallace rolled along the floor, swiped at his bloody face with a sleeve, then looked up at MacNally, who was on his feet and being hauled away.

FOLLOWING THE DINING HALL INCIDENT, MacNally had been sent back to the Hole, a part of the institution with which he was unfortunately becoming familiar.

It would be his home for the foreseeable future while he awaited a disciplinary hearing to determine what punishment would be meted out. As MacNally stared at Henry's photo, lost in thought, he heard a noise.

Voorhees was standing at the bars, a clipboard in his left hand, his jaw tight. "Let's go."

"Where?"

Voorhees did not answer, but led MacNally into an office off the corridor. The door had barely closed when Voorhees spun on him. "That was a goddamn bullshit stunt you pulled."

"What are you talking about?"

"Clarence Anglin was caught. Goddamn idiot—thought he could sneak out in a box. A guard saw his brother and another inmate trying to lift the thing, which was supposedly filled with bread. A body weighs a whole lot more than fucking bread. Must've thought we're all stupid or something."

MacNally attempted to keep his face from betraying the intense sadness that flooded his thoughts. All that for nothing. He had done his part, though he doubted Anglin would help him now—or even be in a position to do so.

"Those Anglins aren't too swift, 'cause if they were, they'da known that when there's a fight in the dining hall, the rear gate's immediately shut down. Any vehicles in the institution would be searched by several guards before it'd be let out off the grounds."

"Good to know," MacNally said impassively.

Voorhees lowered his voice. "Did you know they were gonna do this?"

MacNally forced a chuckle. "Why would they tell me anything? And why would I help J.W.'s brother escape—what's in it for me?"

"Don't play stupid with me, MacNally." He was now speaking just above a whisper. "I'm giving you a last chance to work with me. Give me something I can use, and I'll see what I can do for you."

"I can't tell you what I don't know."

"Remember what I told you that first day? Your time here's gonna be defined by choices. Choices you make—good ones and bad ones."

"I remember everything you told me," MacNally said. "And you also told me you can't protect me. And you told me I gotta learn con law. And you told me that if I don't wanna get fucked again, I gotta stand up for myself and grow a set of balls. Do you remember telling me all that?"

Voorhees's face burned red. Through a muscular jaw, he said, "That fight was all just a bullshit act to distract the guard and let Anglin get his brother loaded into the truck. Wasn't it?"

MacNally looked down at his red and swollen hand. He held it up. "An act? I might've broken my hand, and you think it was bullshit?"

Voorhees refused to let his eyes find the inmate's hand. "I don't know if they're gonna be able to prove it, but I know what you did."

He shook his head. "Fucking broke Wallace's jaw and sent him to the hospital. Guess I'm the goddamn fool. I thought you were different from all these scumbags here. I even bought that sob story about your kid."

At the mention of Henry, MacNally stepped forward—but Voorhees stood his ground, lips tight.

He felt bad that he had deceived the officer; the man had been straight with him since he had arrived. As much as he was able to, Voorhees had attempted to help MacNally navigate the difficult transition to incarceration in a place like this. He surmised now, in retrospect, and being less green than he was when he arrived, that Voorhees was probably taking substantial risk in striking up a relationship with him. But this place, he was learning, was not a place of friendships—it was a place of survival. You helped those who helped you, and the rest of the population could go to hell—until you required their assistance, and then you became their best buddy and screwed over the guy you had been friends with.

Deception and subterfuge were the method of operation—and currency—of penitentiary life. If MacNally was ever going to see his son again, he had to choose a side, and as well as Voorhees had treated him, there was a limit to what the guard could do. Anglin was going to help him escape, whereas the "value" of his relationship with Voorhees had already reached a pinnacle and, unless he turned into his snitch, would only diminish going forward.

"You're just as fuckin' bad as the rest of 'em," Voorhees said.

"That's not true. And you know it." It *was* once true. Was it still?

"Apparently, I don't know nothing." Voorhees shook his head, his face contorted in contempt.

He grabbed for the door, flung it open, and shoved MacNally into the corridor. "Get back to your cell. I'm done with you."

# 43

Burden steered the Taurus along the winding, tree-canopied Telegraph Hill Boulevard, negotiating the curves until he came to a full stop behind a long line of cars.

"Shit, I should've thought of this," Friedberg said.

"Tourists," Burden said, in explanation for Vail. "They jam up the approach to Coit Tower, it's like a freaking parking lot." He swung the car around and did a three-point turn on the two-lane road. Following at a close distance was Clay Allman, mirroring Burden's maneuvers.

Burden led them around and brought them up Filbert, an intensely angled street that tested the Taurus's anemic horses trapped under the hood.

With the sedan's engine groaning, Vail said, "Why don't you let me out? I can probably walk it faster. And it might help you get up the hill."

Burden ignored her dig and eventually got them to the base of the Filbert Steps, where he parked the car at a ninety-degree angle to the curb.

Vail surmised that on a street of such intense incline, the parking brake and transmission weren't sufficient locks against a runaway vehicle.

As they unfolded themselves from the Ford, a steady wind blew against them. The air was crisp and the sun was bright, with scattered, yet plump stark white clouds sliding rapidly across the deep blue sky.

Allman got out of his car and began digging around in his trunk for something.

Vail craned her neck as high as she could see. Looming above her was an imposing, sand colored, architecturally modern cylindrical structure. Cypress trees surrounded the base, and an American flag fluttered strongly above a California state flag.

Burden gestured at a green sign twenty feet ahead of them that read, Stairs to Coit Tower. "We'll walk it. Much faster."

"You've gotta be kidding me," Vail said, taking in the multiple flights of endless stairs staring back at her. An exercise session on an elliptical was one thing, but with her surgically repaired knee only recently beginning to feel fully healed, she didn't feel like testing it on what surely looked like a million steps.

"C'mon," Dixon said. "Time to move beyond that wimpy elliptical stuff. This'll be a good little workout for you. I stair climb at the gym every day."

"I'm sure you do," Vail said. "But I don't."

Burden and Friedberg had already passed the green sign when Burden swung his head around. "Quit complaining. You're wasting time."

Vail and Dixon followed, with Allman bringing up the rear, heading up the staircase that ran along a wall of townhouses on the right, before turning left and crossing Telegraph Hill Boulevard, where the cars were still at a standstill. They continued up additional flights of steps that were fronted by bricks engraved with what appeared to be donor names.

*Probably some* Save Coit Tower *movement, and a fundraiser run by vegans and alternative energy nuts.* Vail chuckled. *A few months ago, I'd have said that aloud.*

They continued along an asphalt-paved, tree-shaded path that led to…more steps.

"I think this qualifies as a week of workouts," Vail said.

Dixon snorted. "Give me a break. Have you even broken a sweat?"

Vail pulled at her blouse. "Haven't you?" She instantly realized the answer to her own question. But she could see Burden and Friedberg slowing down, pausing every dozen steps or so before proceeding. "So what is this place?" *I don't really care. But it'll slow 'em down.*

"It's a tower," Friedberg called back to her.

"No shit, Inspector Sherlock."

Friedberg stopped and turned to face her. He took a deep breath and bent over to rest his hands on his knees. "It was built in '33, a monument funded by a wealthy, eccentric woman named Lillie Coit for the volunteer firemen. They fought fires before the city had a real fire department, which was a big deal back then because all the buildings were made of wood. She actually hopped on their truck and helped put out fires decades before women did that stuff. She's now the patron saint of the city's fire department."

"Really," Vail said with admiration. "Sounds like my kind of woman."

"I think she lived around here. She left instructions in her will for the tower to beautify the city. The view from the top of Telegraph Hill, where we're headed, is—well, you'll see. You get a panorama of the Bay and the city that's worth cramming yourself into that tiny elevator."

"Just so you know," Vail said, looking up at the massive structure. "Using 'tiny' and 'elevator' in the same sentence is about as appealing to me as using 'serial' and 'killer' together. Nothing good comes of it."

Burden turned and continued up the steps.

Vail opened her mouth to ask another question—to give herself one more moment to breathe—but nothing came to mind. *The one time I want him to give me a freaking dissertation and he's actually brief. Can't catch a break.*

They reached the base of the tower and Burden led the way around the front. To the east, the Bay was stunningly clear, the wind having blown away all fog and clouds, highlighting the expansive Bay Bridge, not unlike the view she had from her hotel room.

A steamboat sat moored in the foreground at a pier, a large sign atop the vessel reading *San Francisco Belle*. Vail thought of Robby, and how fun it would be to get a room on the ship, then cruise around the harbor. The last trip they'd taken had turned into a disaster. A wave of superstition suddenly enveloped her, as if uttering the word "vacation" would cause things to blow up into a serial killer nightmare.

She stopped and took a deep, cleansing breath of the cool sea air. To her left, the north and west areas of the Bay, a dense bank of fog obscured all that lay before them.

"Nothing quite like it, huh, Agent Vail?" Allman asked.

She had to admit that the panorama before her was exquisite. "Virginia's pretty special in its own right."

"I don't doubt it. But…" Allman gestured with a sweeping motion of his hand. "This is like paradise.

*Paradise. I probably wouldn't use that term while a serial killer ran wild through the city.*

Burden led them around a circular path that brought them to the front entrance of Coit Tower. He stopped at the top of a small staircase, then led them down toward a circular parking lot—and the reason for the traffic jam.

"I thought it was typical tourist traffic," Friedberg said. "Apparently, it was us."

An SFPD cruiser sat at the lot's mouth, its lights swirling silently. Two cops were outside the car and standing near a large statue that rested in the center of the paved rotunda.

"Not us," Vail said. "Him." She gestured at the front of the statue, where a male body was strapped. Erect. Serene.

And dead.

February 19, 1960

*Leavenworth*

MacNally was sentenced to ninety days in segregation, a fair punishment, he had to admit, given that he had assaulted an innocent man and had been strongly suspected in aiding the attempted escape of another inmate. Although none of that could be proven, he had to give the warden and his executive staff credit for their even-handed treatment of him.

Segregation gave him time alone with his thoughts, which were focused on reuniting with Henry. He realized he had graduated to thinking like a convict, a shift in attitude necessary for survival at an institution like Leavenworth. As Voorhees had told him, and as he had come to learn, the rules of society did not apply inside prison. There was an entirely different set of laws that governed inmate behavior behind penitentiary walls.

In the outside world, if you had a problem with someone, you'd report it to the police. In the slammer, you couldn't run to the correctional officers—because, like Voorhees had said, they're off-duty sixteen hours a day. You had to settle it yourself.

If someone hit you, you had better hit them back. Even harder than they had hit you. You had to convince them you were the baddest, meanest son of a bitch that existed in your cellhouse so they wouldn't bother you again. They had to know—or believe—that if they bothered you, you were going to make them pay twice as hard.

The goal was to make them think it was not worth starting up with you.

And part of that was developing a rep, the power to invoke the fear he had sought to establish since his rape at the hands of Gormack and Wharton. Between his shower attack and the dining hall charade, which had been witnessed by dozens of inmates, word of what he'd done had wormed its way through the institution like a virus, cementing his reputation as an aggressive, loose cannon. For now, he was safe.

UPON RELEASE FROM SEGREGATION, MACNALLY picked up his new bedroll kit and returned to his cell to find that he and Anglin had inherited a new cellmate. The man was asleep, curled into a ball under the blanket.

"Hey, wake up," MacNally said as he tossed his bag on his cot. Receiving no response, he kicked the bunk's metal framework. "Who the hell are you?"

The man startled, then lifted his head and looked at MacNally.

"I said, 'Who the hell are you?' And what are you doing in my cell?"

"Rucker. Harlan Rucker. You MacNally?"

"You realize you're in John Anglin's bed?"

Rucker sat up. "First of all, J.W.'s still in the Hole for another three months. Word is he ain't comin' back here. Been moved to another block, if you can believe rumors. But makes sense. They didn't want you and him together no more, is my guess." Rucker pushed off his bed, mumbled something about having something to take care of, and then walked out of the cell.

MacNally snorted. A transfer of Anglin was an unavoidable result of their suspected collaboration. He wouldn't be surprised if Voorhees was behind it. But it didn't matter—during the three months in the Hole, he had devised what he thought could be a viable escape plan. He had implemented the first phase during those four weeks—which entailed a workout regimen to get into the best physical condition possible. He reasoned that because of the route he had chosen, he would have to be able to run and jump in order to elude police and search parties. And he might have to survive on a minimal amount of food and water for prolonged periods while on the run.

More immediately, if he could get himself physically fit enough and lose excess body fat, then he could squeeze through barred windows and other narrow places—and have the endurance to climb the forty foot perimeter wall without struggling. The longer it took, the greater the chances of a tower guard seeing him.

Despite a lack of formal training, he designed a protocol that he thought would yield results: high leg-kick running in place; pushups; sit-ups; and leg lifts that entailed lying on his back and repeatedly lifting his bunk with his feet. He also restricted his caloric intake, and when it came time to leave Seg and return to his cell, he was substantially thinner and sported more lean muscle.

But his plan required the assistance of another participant. And that was an obstacle for which he had yet to find a solution. Although John and Clarence Anglin were possible conspirators, given Clarence's failed escape, he was likely out of the equation. Postponing it until Anglin was released from the Hole would set him back another three months minimum—but because of Anglin's pivotal role in his brother's escape attempt, he was going to be watched more closely than he otherwise would have been. Teaming up with Anglin would mean MacNally would have to wait until the increased scrutiny subsided—several months, if not longer.

And while MacNally's aggressive behavior had the benefit of making him less of a target among the inmate population, that rep had a flip side, as well: the officers also knew who he was, and, as a result, he was on their short list of problem children.

Fortunately, his escape plan had the benefit of working even though the hacks might be scrutinizing him more closely. Bringing Anglin into the equation, however, would be unwisely tipping the risk scale into the red zone of danger.

MacNally lay back on his bed, brought both hands behind his head, and glanced over at his new cellie's empty bunk. Perhaps the answer lay a few feet away.

Still, trust was an uncertainty with inmates you knew well. With a con you just met, there needed to be some kind of third-party verification. Rucker apparently knew Anglin; that would be as good a place as any to start.

# 45

Vail stood beside Dixon, looking up at the ten-foot-tall bronze sculpture. "It's Christopher Columbus," Vail said.

"I can see that. His name is carved in large letters around the base."

"You think Chris was as fit as the sculptor made him out to be?"

Dixon tilted her head as her eyes moved up and down the icon's body. "I always pictured him as a plump, ruddy old explorer. Obviously, that's not what they wanted to depict with a humungous monument in front of Coit Tower."

"Which begs the question of why Columbus is even here."

"I think you should ask Friedberg."

Friedberg and Burden were talking with the SFPD officer twenty feet away. Allman was a foot back of them, pen and pad out, furiously taking notes.

"We're avoiding the dead body in front of us," Dixon said.

"I know," Vail said with slumped shoulders. "I've seen too many the past few days. If I ignore it—"

"It won't make it go away."

"No," Vail sighed. "It won't." She stepped closer to the edge of the planter, within five feet of Raymond Strayhan. Vail decided that Strayhan was not in as good physical condition as was Christopher Columbus—though one could argue both were past their prime. The Bay Killer's latest victim looked to be about five foot five, and as a result, was dwarfed by the enormity of the statue. Both were atop a four-sided pedestal, around which blossomed a planter with colorful, leafy vegetation.

A numeral, 122, was printed on Strayhan's forehead.

"Another number," Dixon said.

*Another number. Another victim. More puzzles. My brain hurts.*

Vail pointed at a section of disturbed soil. "Over there."

Dixon leaned over to get a better look. "Impressions in the dirt. A ladder, maybe."

"He needed to get Strayhan up onto the pedestal. Do you see any yellow rope?"

"Isn't that what was used at Palace of Fine Arts?"

Vail hiked her brow. "You've read the files."

"What little there is, yeah." Dixon moved around the statue's circular base. She stopped on the other side, at Columbus's backside, then pulled a pen from her coat.

"Find something?" Vail asked.

"Think so." She moved a section of the foliage aside and revealed a coil of rope. "Make that a yes."

"Yellow?"

Dixon leaned in closer. "Nope. Just plain old braided cord. Tan. Why?"

Vail furrowed her brow, then knelt beside Dixon. *What the hell's going on here? Roberta Strayhan's crime scene was different than the others. Purposely? Now her husband's scene...subtly different. A different killer, who read Scheer's article? Or the same asshole, just screwing with us?*

"You're obsessing over something," Dixon said.

"Yeah." Vail stood up. "The pedestal's only a couple of feet off the ground, but he needed a pulley system. Strayhan's only about five-five, can't weigh more than, what—?"

Dixon moved back around to the front to appraise their victim. "Maybe a hundred fifty, hundred forty. But even for someone who's physically fit, a dead body's a tough thing to lift. It flops all over the place, and the UNSUB's gotta keep it upright while he's tying it to the statue. If there's no one helping him, there's really no other way of doing it. The rope made it easy."

"So he wrapped it around Columbus's shoulders or neck, then hoisted up the body. Anything else?"

"Until we can cut the body down—"

"That'd be my job."

They turned around and saw Rex Jackson, kit in hand. He set it down and slung the Nikon from around his shoulder. As he lined up his first shot, Burden and Friedberg joined them.

"None of the staff saw anything," Burden said. "Probably because that statue is so freaking big."

"That 'statue' is a studly Christopher Columbus."

"Columbus?" He looked up at the monstrosity. "Looks more like Hercules."

"We've already been through that," Dixon said.

"Robert," Vail said. "What's Columbus doing here? If there's some reason why this statue is here, it might also tell us if the offender picked this spot for a reason."

"It's Pioneer Park. More than that, I don't know."

Vail contorted her lips. *Pioneer Park. Something with that? Does he see himself as a pioneer of some sort? How does that fit with the other vics and dump sites? And what the hell does it have to do with what I did in New York? New York...there has to be something with that. That's the key—*

"Karen," Dixon said. "You okay?"

Dixon's voice knocked Vail out of her reverie. She covered her concern. "I'm staring at another dead body. No, I'm not okay."

"Anyone have any thoughts on what we're dealing with here?" Burden turned suddenly, apparently realizing that Allman was standing directly behind them. "Clay, give us a minute, okay?"

He looked disappointed. "Yeah, sure."

Allman walked back toward the officer as Friedberg tapped out a cigarette. "He left the body in front of Coit Tower. Maybe the UNSUB's a frustrated volunteer firefighter."

Vail said, "Probably better to leave the psychoanalysis to me."

Burden turned to face the Bay. "Fair enough. So what do you think?"

Vail looked out at the fog-socked ocean as well. "Robert may've been right."

Friedberg cupped his hands and lit the cigarette. "You think the guy's a frustrated volunteer firefighter?"

Vail swung back and squared her jaw. "No. That the offender chose this location for a reason." She faced the water again. "What's special about this view?"

"From here?" Friedberg puffed on the lit Marlboro and looked out at the blanketing foggy white landscape in front of them. "Nothing that's materially different from the other crime scenes. The Bay. The Pacific Ocean. Islands. Sailboats. Ships. Cargo boats. Two bridges. Well, the Bay Bridge is still visible," he said, cocking his head east, to the extreme right. "Basically, it's just another vantage point. Beautiful stuff, but it's pretty much the same thing as what we've seen before."

Two women and a man on Segways rolled by, on some sort of guided tour.

"Do you think the UNSUB meant for it to be this foggy? Did he mean for the view to be obscured?" Vail asked.

Friedberg took a long drag, then spoke while the smoke streamed out of his mouth. "Hard to say. Depends on the day. This time of year, fog like this is common. Sometimes it burns off, sometimes it doesn't."

"And the 122?" Burden asked.

Vail only shook her head. "The numbers seem to be all over the place. What if you add up the first three?"

Burden looked at the sky a moment, then said, "Whoa. One-twenty-one."

"Well," Dixon said, "121 is not 122."

"No, it's not." Vail thought a moment, then said, "It's reasonable to assume he killed Strayhan sometime after his wife, then posed him under the cover of darkness." Vail craned her neck to take in her surroundings. "And the location was carefully chosen—a perfect spot, really, to place a dead body. No security cameras. When the public arrives in the morning, none of the staff is going to see the body because he's blocked by the statue. But like you said, soon as people start arriving in the parking lot, bam. Max impact."

"You had a problem with something," Dixon said. "You spaced out on me when I pointed out the rope."

"The rope," Vail said with a nod. "There were some things at the wife's crime scene that varied from the other vics. And there's rope here, just like the one at that Palace place, but—"

"Palace of Fine Arts," Friedberg said.

"Yeah. That one. The rope we found there was a specialized type that a climber may use. But the one he used here, it's just plain old rope."

"So things are a little different," Burden said. "What are you saying?"

"It could be a copycat, going off what he read in Scheer's article. Or it could be the UNSUB screwing with us. That's what this kind of killer would do."

"How can we be sure?" Dixon asked.

"Absent identifying forensics, behavioral analysis may hold the answer. Let's refocus our efforts, drill down a bit, start with the basics."

Friedberg blew out a plume of smoke and watched it zip away on the breeze. "And what are the 'behavioral basics' in a case like this?"

Vail spread her hands. "It all starts with the victims. Why these people? Why now?"

Burden glanced around the parking lot, then at the tower, then at Rex Jackson, who was processing the body. "So let's go back to the war room and plot this out." He nodded at Friedberg. "Where do we stand on the backgrounders you were putting together?"

"I've got the first four vics done. I was just getting started on the Ruckers."

"What happened with your chat with that retired guy, Inspector—" Vail waved a hand, the universal sign for assistance. "The one who handled the '82 Newhall case."

Friedberg pulled the cigarette from his mouth. "Millard Ferguson. He's not doing so good. Throat cancer, looks like shit."

"Sorry to hear the guy's dying," Vail said. "But the case. What'd he have to say about the case? Maybe we can prevent others from following him to the grave."

"That's cold," Burden said.

Vail hiked her brow. "Am I wrong?"

"Not wrong…just…cold."

Vail turned to Friedberg. "Did he give you anything we can use?"

"He only remembered certain things. Like that key. Thought there might be some connection to the building they found him in front of. But nothing panned out. They had a few suspects, nothing that excited them."

"So a dead end," Dixon said.

"A dead end," Friedberg said. "For now. Maybe one of those old cases Clay's got will pop up on our radar."

A phone began buzzing.

Friedberg wagged a finger at Burden's pocket. "You're vibrating."

Burden pulled his cell, read the display. He looked over at Allman, who was still standing beside the cop. "Text from Clay. Wants to know when he can come over, see the body."

They swiveled their heads to look at Allman, who had his hands spread in anticipation.

"I think we can use his assistance," Vail said.

Burden waved him over.

Vail held up her BlackBerry. "I'll be right back, gotta make a call." She moved away from Columbus and walked toward the edge of the parking lot, where it met the vegetation that led to the coastline. A wall of fog—of nothingness—stared back at her. A moment later, her phone connected to the Behavioral Analysis Unit.

"Lenka, this is Karen. Can you look something up for me?"

"How are things going in San Francisco?"

*Now there's a loaded question.* "I'd rather just discuss happy things."

"That bad?"

"There's a fresh dead body about thirty feet away. If you can look up Agent Mike Hartman and tell me where he's assigned, it'll make my day a little brighter." She heard Lenka tapping the keys.

"Then this may make the sun shine. He's right in your backyard. San Francisco Field Office."

Vail felt a cold sweat break out across her forehead. "You're shitting me."

"Just emailed you the phone number. You'll have it in a sec."

Vail thanked Lenka, then scrolled to her email. She clicked on Hartman's number and got his voicemail. "Mike, it's Karen Vail. Can you give me a call? It's very important." She left her number, then hung up and stared off into the fog a moment.

*What does this mean? Can Mike Hartman be the offender? No. He wouldn't implicate himself by leaving that note. And he can be a bit of an asshole, but he's no psychopath. No, either Eugenia told somebody—the Bay Killer?—or it's gotta be someone Hartman knows, someone who talked to him.*

*But why would Hartman tell anyone about me, and what I did in New York? Unless he's trying to embarrass me, cause problems. If it's someone Hartman talked to, the offender's gotta know I'm gonna call up my former partner and ask who he told about it. Unless he doesn't know Hartman's the only living person who knows. Or the source was someone who bought the info from Eugenia.* Vail sighed. *Shit.*

Vail turned and headed back to the knot of colleagues. Off in the distance, Vail saw Stephen Scheer approaching the officer who was maintaining the crime scene boundaries. She came up behind Allman and said, "You want to print something?" She did not wait for a reply; she knew the answer. "The offender missed something. He made some mistakes and we're keying in on him."

Allman's gaze swung over to Burden, then back to Vail. "Really? I can print that?"

*He missed the pun, the play on "key." If he'd been listening closely, he would've realized I'm bullshitting him. Tough.* She plowed forward, because she did want him printing the fact that the offender had missed something. "Yeah. Really. You can print that."

"Thanks," he said, scribbling on his pad.

"But next time don't use my name in an article without asking first."

Allman looked up and did a quick study of her face. "Just a guess...you weren't happy with that."

"You're a word guy, so I think the proper adjective would be 'pissed.' Not as pissed as I was at your buddy, Scheer. But pissed."

"Scheer's not my buddy."

"What do you know?" Vail said. "We've got something in common." She forced a smile. "I don't like him either."

# 46

August 31, 1960

*Leavenworth*

MacNally ruminated on his escape attempt for another three months, until John Anglin was let out of segregation. During that time, he observed the institution's physical layout, lighting, officer routines—anything that would give him an added advantage. He also spent time with Rucker and got to know him, as much as two inmates can when their only common link is that they're both criminals sharing a cell in a maximum security penitentiary.

Anglin remained MacNally's best option as far as determining if Harlan Rucker was someone who could keep his escape aspirations a secret; preventing their lips from flapping was a notoriously elusive trait that did not bless many inmates.

MacNally casually met up with Anglin in the recreation yard, out of view of the guards. They made small talk for a moment, sharing thoughts on their time in the Hole, before MacNally brought up the failed escape.

"Wasn't your fault," Anglin said. "Word is you really got into it. Sent Wallace to the hospital."

"It was pretty convincing." A damp sweat had erupted under his clothing, a factor of the stifling Kansas humidity. "Broke a bone." MacNally lifted his hand, which sported a knob on the middle knuckle. "Kind of lost myself there, actually. Took out some frustration, I guess. Poor bastard didn't know what the hell was going on."

Anglin glanced around, clearly checking on the guards. "I know I said I'd help you out, but things've changed. Risky even standing here talkin'. They gonna think somethin's up."

"What do you know about Rucker?"

"Decent guy. In for dealing heroin and robbing a five and dime. Beat the owner pretty bad."

"Trust him?"

"Much as anybody here in this place can be trusted. Really. I mean, we're all fucking criminals, right?" He laughed. "But even if they break the laws out there, knock off or kill a straight john, in here it's a different deal. You don't want no trouble? Don't rat out other cons. It'll get you in the ass. Really—it will. That's a good one." He laughed again, this time louder. "Rucker's never been a problem for me. Haven't heard no bad shit 'bout him, neither."

MacNally looked around, his eyes darting across the compound. He needed to end this and get away from Anglin before they attracted attention. Despite what Anglin had just said, there were rats in Leavenworth. Just like Voorhees offered him the chance to tip him off to stuff, other officers had presented the same deal to other cons.

He'd heard some prisoners talking in A-Cellhouse about guys they suspected of being informants. They decided to set up one of them, planting bogus information to see if the guards acted on it. They did—and there was no longer any doubt who their source was. The snitch was shanked in the right kidney the next morning during breakfast. No one saw anything—and by the time the medical staff tended to the inmate, he had bled out.

MacNally was not integrated well enough into the population to know who could be trusted and who was working with the officers. That meant he had to take on some risk. Rucker was lean and looked to be in pretty decent condition, so he could fill the role as well as anyone else he could choose.

"How well do you know him?"

"Good enough." Anglin grabbed the front of his denim shirt and pulled it away from his damp skin, then flapped it a few times to generate a breeze. "Goin' back to Florida. Both did time in the joint there. He won't hurt ya."

MacNally pursed his lips, then nodded. "Catch you later."

He walked back to his cell and found Rucker reading a book. He sat down on the edge of the bed and, in a low voice that required Rucker to lean close to hear, he said, "I'm interested in gettin' out of here. J.W. says you can be trusted. Interested?"

Rucker indicated he was—and MacNally outlined his plan.

After listening carefully to what MacNally laid out, Rucker cocked his head to the side. "Not bad."

"The towers on the west wall are pretty far apart, right?"

"But there's a guard in them," Rucker said. "An armed guard. And no matter what they say, they've got orders to shoot to kill."

MacNally nodded thoughtfully. "That's why we're not gonna let them see us. Now—along that wall, looks to me like the lighting's gotta be kind of shitty. And because we're so close to A-Cellhouse, the laundry, and the segregation building, I think this has gotta be the best place for us to get out—"

"Between the two towers? You crazy?"

"Think about it. We go at night, it's pretty dark. The buildings are close to each other—and close to the wall. Tower five—you know which one I mean?"

Rucker nodded.

"It sits on the northwest corner of the wall and tower six sits on the southwest perimeter of the prison. And it's not attached to the wall. You see what I'm saying?"

Rucker's eyes moved back and forth a few times, then he said, "Makes it easier for us to get out without being seen."

"Exactly."

The two men discussed it a while longer, at which point Rucker gave his approval—and appeared to be energized by the prospect of breaking out.

MacNally was now committed.

The plan had merit on paper, and John Anglin had vouched for Rucker. The only remaining questions required careful consideration: when they should do it—and whether or not they could pull it off.

# 47

Vail wearily sat down at the long table where their case files were arranged. She had spent the afternoon pouring through them, looking for commonalities, hoping she could find linkage in one or more of them. Although there were some promising possibilities, it wasn't anything definitive.

Complicating the task was that she was not working with full homicide case files—it was a mishmash of a journalist's musings, unofficial and substandard crime scene photos, and excerpts from interpretive writings. It was so far from the objective summaries, analyses, and formal reports she was accustomed to reviewing on cases that she concluded the exercise carried only limited validity.

An hour ago, one of the inspectors had come by to report that he had obtained and executed a search warrant for Stephen Scheer's cell phone logs, and that the anonymous texts in question originated from two different throwaway phones.

At that point, Vail made a point of noting that she was tired—tired of getting nowhere in identifying the Bay Killer.

"Agent Vail."

She looked up with bleary eyes. Clay Allman was standing there, hand in a pocket, leaning against the doorjamb.

"You look beat," he said. "Wanna join me for some coffee downstairs in the café? A little caffeine could do your brain some good."

Vail made no effort to stifle a wide yawn. "Yeah, fine."

"Burden or Detective Dixon want to join us?"

Vail glanced back at the room. "They're with the CSI. You just get me."

They took the elevator down in silence, Vail too tired to object and too tired to climb the stairs. They grabbed two coffees—which Allman insisted on paying for—and started toward a table.

"Let's walk. You okay with that? It'll help get my blood moving."

"So what's it like?" Allman asked as they headed toward the stairwell. "Being a profiler."

"Is this on the record?" Vail asked as she adjusted the corrugated jacket surrounding her hot cup.

"Nothing's on the record here. In fact, there is no record. We're just two people talking. Actually—to be honest, I came up because I wanted to apologize. I didn't realize mentioning you in the article would upset you."

"It's not that it upset me," Vail said as she pushed against the fire door. "There are certain ways you handle a serial offender. And certain ways you don't, depending on the type of killer you're dealing with. Mentioning my name and my position was not the best way to deal with this guy."

Allman kept his gaze ahead as they climbed the steps. "And what is?"

Vail hesitated. Off the record or not, she did not feel that chatting idly with a reporter was good form. Despite Burden's vouching for him, nothing good could come from it, and more likely than not, bad would result. "Clay, no offense, but I'm not accustomed to talking about active cases with anyone, friend of the department or not."

Allman faced her with a wide grin. "Can't blame a veteran reporter for trying. No worries. I get it. I've been around this block—around this building—a really long time. I didn't expect a pro like you to actually give me an answer." He grabbed the handrail as they turned to ascend the next flight of stairs. "Can you at least tell me what the killer missed—what mistake he made?"

"No. Did it make it into your article?"

"Story's filed, already up on the website." Keeping his eyes focused ahead, he said, "You know, I was serious. About the apology. Sorry if I put you in a tough spot."

"Tell me about yourself." Vail patted herself on the back. A classic—and effective—tactic for switching gears, even if he was keenly aware of what she was doing.

"Myself." He chuckled. "I'm usually probing others for information. Very few people ask me questions about…me."

"I'm not like most people."

Allman hiked both brows. "Yeah, no shit." They reached their floor and he pulled open the door. Vail stepped through and Allman followed.

After a long pause, she said, "Married?"

"Nope. Never. No kids."

"Brothers? Sisters?"

"One of each. They're back east. We Skype. My sister's got a teenager. My nephew's a pretty good writer, actually." He chuckled. "He emails me stuff to edit at least once a week."

"And you?"

"I think I'm a pretty good writer, too."

Vail couldn't help but smile. "I meant you, tell me about you."

Allman was grinning, as well. "Well. I've always loved English. I went to a small college in Washington—the state, not the district—and was editor-in-chief of the school paper. Wish I could say it was a life-altering experience, but I just liked the idea of digging to find the story behind the story. I graduated, nothing special—no honors or anything like that—but I landed a job here, in the city. In the *Chronicle*'s mailroom." He chuckled. "Four years of college so I could sort mail. At least I was sorting mail at the *Chronicle*. And I actually picked up a lot of stuff just by hanging out with the reporters. But six months later I hooked on with the *Tribune*."

"And what was the *Trib*'s mailroom like?" Vail asked with a grin.

"I didn't realize profilers had a sense of humor." He took a drink. "I was writing articles. At first, it wasn't anything earth-shattering, but I kept flooding the city editor with story ideas. I got shot down a lot—I was just a cub reporter, what the hell did I know—but he liked me, I guess, and he ended up teaching me how to pitch in the morning sessions. Pretty cool stuff."

"When did you meet Scheer?"

Allman glanced sideways at her, then took a sip of his coffee. "How'd we get on this topic?"

"I asked."

"Yeah, right." He tipped the cup back again. "I had a knack for crime reporting, so my editor paired me up with Stephen. He'd been covering the crime beat for about three years, so the feeling was Stephen'd teach me the ropes."

"But he didn't."

"Oh, no. He did."

Rather than walking back into Homicide, Vail continued down the hallway. "I'm sensing there's more to this."

Allman drank again. He thought a moment, then said, "Stephen was great. He taught me a lot of stuff. Got me into places I never would've gotten into. Like SFPD. Back when I started, things were more relaxed than they are now. Reporters had better access to people and things. Made our jobs a whole lot easier. We lunched with the dicks, we made their coffee in the break room. Things were good."

"But," Vail said. "There's a but."

Allman chuckled sardonically. "There is, in fact, a but." They passed the photography lab on the left, white-collar crime on the right. "My editor liked my style better. And he kind of didn't hide the fact he really dug my writing. Somewhere along the line I learned how to tell a story. Not just the typical journalistic pyramidal structure, but an actual story. Anyway, I got a line on a case in '82, and I sold my editor on it. He trusted me. Led with it, in fact, and put it on page one. Turned out I was right. And we beat the *Chronicle*. In my editor's eyes, I looked like a freaking genius, even though Stephen and I co-wrote it. Couple months later, I was promoted. Stephen got nothing. Actually, he got angry. Big time. And he bolted."

"That was the case in San Bruno?"

"Yep."

They reached the end of the hall, turned back and headed for Homicide.

"And you haven't spoken to him since then?"

"Kind of. A thing here or there if we met up at a crime scene. Occasionally at a bar around town. But we've kept our distance. He's still got a lot of animosity, all these years later."

"Long time to hold a grudge." Vail realized she had hardly drunk her coffee. She took a sip. "You really have no clue who his source is on that story?"

"Not even a suspicion." Allman nodded at an inspector who was hurrying down the hall in the opposite direction. "Do you really have a line into the killer?"

Vail smiled, then sipped her drink.

"Hey, can't blame me for trying. I'm on deadline."

They arrived at Homicide. "You've got enough to run with. Give me some time, maybe I'll be able to give you more. Just not yet." Vail placed a hand on the door.

"Fair enough. Catch you later."

Allman backed away, leaving Vail alone as she pushed through the entrance. Dixon was visible in the back room.

"Anything?"

Dixon turned. "Lab's still working shit up. They're backed up big time. You get anywhere?"

Vail set the coffee down on the table. "Nothing earth shattering. If we had actual case files, maybe I'd have a shot at something. There's just not enough info to link these cases together. There are some similarities. But to do it right, we need to look into the victims."

Burden came up behind them. "I think I've got a way for us to do that. Budget's a disaster, but I've got a line into some college students, criminology majors. I spoke to their class a couple months ago. If I can get my lieutenant to sign off on having them do some Internet and microfiche work for us, they may be able to put together your victimologies much faster than we could."

"That'd be extremely helpful."

"That's what I thought. Wish me luck." He moved past them and headed for his boss's office.

Friedberg leaned back in his seat and called across the room. "Karen. I picked up a disk from Rex with the crime scene photos, all the way through this morning. You wanna look through 'em?"

Vail pushed up from her seat. "Don't have to ask twice." She walked over and snatched up the CD. "Nothing else is working. Wading knee deep in the blood and guts may just get the juices flowing."

"Anyone ever tell you," Friedberg said, "that you've got a way with words?"

# 48

October 1, 1960

*Leavenworth*

MacNally and Rucker had spent the better part of the next four weeks working through each step of their plan. During that time, MacNally had been told that John Anglin had been transferred out of Leavenworth—where, no one knew. But MacNally did not concern himself with those details: he was planning to be far away from this place, with the likes of Gormack and Wharton and the Anglin brothers, and even Voorhees, a distant part of his past.

As to the escape, it turned out that Rucker's three years worth of varied experiences at Leavenworth proved invaluable because he knew details about the penitentiary and hack procedures, work schedules, and yard layout that MacNally had only been able to surmise based on what he had observed.

Their plan would begin in the same manner that Anglin had outlined—but that was where the similarities ended.

When all of the prison departments closed for the evening and the cellhouse officers made preparations for shutting the institution down for the night, MacNally and Rucker dressed up their beds with "imposters": they positioned jeans and shirts beneath the bed covers in their bunks in the shapes of legs and torsos, then overstuffed underwear into a sock, giving a fair approximation of a head—with the covers drawn high and assuming the guard did not scrutinize their "bodies" as he passed the cell.

They then made their way to the chaplain's office, in the second floor recreation area, where they hid out until the staff left at 9:00 PM. With some difficulty, they forced their thinned-down bodies through a barred window and then proceeded towards the laundry. There, they waited until 10:00 PM before continuing on to the west wall.

As Rucker told MacNally, 10:00 PM counts were conducted by the evening watch officers. The men coming on at midnight did an immediate tally and then assumed their graveyard shift duties. If the guards did not detect anything untoward, the count was declared "clear" and all supplementary staff went home.

"That leaves two officers per cellhouse," Rucker had said during their earlier discussions. "One officer each on the west yard, the east yard, the Centerhall, and in Control. Best odds we'll have in a twenty-four hour cycle."

"How do we know the guards won't decide to do another pass of the cellhouse?" MacNally asked.

"'Cause they're kickin' back. Things are quiet, cons are goin' down for the night, listenin' to music, playin' board games. The hacks go through inmate mail and sort it for delivery. Think back to other prisons you've been at. Nighttime hacks pass the time, just tryin' to stay awake. The cons are sleepin'. Fucking boring as shit, but some of them wimps like that shift 'cause it's the safest one."

MacNally didn't bother to tell his cellie that this was his first penitentiary experience. If their escape attempt failed, he did not want to diminish his hard-won rep.

"So we make our move once they call the all clear," Rucker said. That was consistent with what MacNally had planned before he disclosed his scheme to Rucker.

Now, after leaving the laundry at 10:14 PM, they exited in the west yard part of the institution. MacNally inched forward and peered around the edge. The yard officer was letting the guards out of segregation, the brick two-story Building 63.

MacNally held up a hand, telling Rucker to wait. He watched as the officer followed the guards to the rear corridor, where they would be keyed into the main prison building.

It was common knowledge among the inmates that these particular doors were twice-secured, requiring the officer on either the east or west yards to unlock them from the outside while the Centerhall guard performed the same task on the inside.

He and Rucker stayed where they were, in a corner joint formed by the intersection of two twelve-foot heavy-gauge cyclone slow-down fences that were topped with barbed wire. MacNally motioned to Rucker, who opened a pillowcase they had brought with them and passed him a shortened broom handle. MacNally slipped the wood stick through the chain links, then used it as a step. Rucker handed him a wool blanket, which he then threw across the protruding wire's prickly sharp points.

Once they had both scaled the slow-down fencing, they low-crawled twenty-five feet to the perimeter wall, a much taller and imposing structure: it was rumored to extend forty feet into the air and an equal distance below-ground to prevent a prisoner from going over, or tunneling underneath it.

MacNally and Rucker set their kit down at the base of the west wall where it joined with A-Cellhouse. Based on the location of the towers and the lighting fixtures, as well as the configuration of the buildings, MacNally had suspected this corner area would be the darkest section of the barrier. But until he was in that spot at night, he could not be sure. Fortunately, his educated guess turned out to be accurate.

Rucker withdrew from the pillowcase a homemade rope they had fashioned from various pieces of clothing they had tied together. It wasn't elaborate, but it didn't have to be. All it needed to do was hold their weight during the climb. They had checked a short length in their cell during the night by pulling on it at various points, and it appeared to be sufficiently strong. Testing it in combat, so to speak, was another matter.

Complicating the issue was that they had assembled the longest part of the rope during their time in the laundry room, when they had access to bushels of additional articles of clothing. Working in the dark, they had tied shirts and sheets together, attaching at the end a metal cleat they had fashioned out of parts appropriated from the innards of the industrial dryer.

They modified the crude-looking device into the shape of a jagged claw so that, when tossed over the side of the rough brick masonry, it would grab onto the wall's exterior surface. If all went according to plan, it would latch on sufficiently to support their weight as they made their ascent. Once one of them made it to the top, he could stabilize it for the other.

As MacNally stood there looking up at the wall, he had to admit, the penitentiary designers at the turn of the century understood human nature. It was an imposing obstacle—four stories high—and he and Rucker needed to scale it with only the assistance of a handmade rope. If it were not for Henry, he would think twice about attempting the climb. He looked over at Rucker, who was likely thinking the same thing as he peered up into the darkness.

"We're not gonna get over it by staring at it," MacNally said. "Let's get going."

After they scaled this barrier, there was yet another perimeter fence to defeat. But it would be a simple task compared to the daunting structure in front of them. Once over it, the massive prison buildings and tree line would provide adequate concealment as they made their way through the surrounding roads that would take them into the city.

There they planned to steal a vehicle or find a garage for cover. Although most escaped inmates attempted to put as many miles and angles as possible between themselves and their pursuers, MacNally reasoned that they should do the opposite—and remain in the neighborhood until the search parties had passed them by and the manhunt expanded into adjacent states. Then it would be safe to move.

MacNally gave the cleat a twirling heave, and it soared up and out of sight. They felt the slack go tight, then heard a clunk as the metal claw struck the other side of the wall. MacNally tugged, and then, convinced it had sufficiently secured itself somewhere on the masonry, nodded at Rucker.

But as he gave Rucker the signal to proceed, he heard the crunch of footsteps on fine gravel. They both spread their bodies against the cellhouse limestone, and waited, hoping the officer would not look in their direction.

They were wearing standard issue dark blue prison jeans, and the area in which they were standing was poorly illuminated—the reason why MacNally had chosen this spot for scaling the wall. As long as they did not move, shuffle a foot, sneeze, or cough, the approaching officer might merely pass them by.

MacNally's heart thumped in his ears as he awaited a shout, a spotlight—anything to go wrong. But the footsteps faded, and once they had vanished completely, he pushed away from the cellhouse wall and silently signaled Rucker to get moving.

Finally, as planned, Rucker began his ascent, moving upward, hand over hand, footstep after footstep, deeper into the darkness until MacNally was no longer able to see him. But the rope kept swaying and jiggling. When it went quiet, that would be MacNally's silent cue that Rucker had made it over and was ready for his partner to begin his climb.

It felt like several minutes before the rope stilled. As MacNally was about to tighten his grasp for the ascent, he heard noise behind him. He dropped to the ground, burying his face in the dirt, and waited. Seconds became a long minute. But all appeared to be quiet.

Finally, he rose and grabbed hold of the rope. He pulled down toward him and started to bring his foot onto the rough face of the wall—but instead of the line tightening, it went limp—and he fell backwards, onto his side. "What the f—"

MacNally got to his feet and pulled some more, trying to generate tension. If the rope did not go rigid, there would be no purchase, and he would not be able to climb. He continued to yank, the line falling impotently at his feet as yards of the knotted cotton accumulated on the ground.

He wanted to yell—scream—at Rucker, demand to know what had happened. The milliseconds passed and the homemade cord continued tumbling down against his ankles. He realized this could mean only one thing.

Rucker had screwed him.

He must have cut the line at the end, and removed the cleat. The question of why he would do that flittered through his thoughts—but he dismissed it as quickly as it came, because all that mattered now was getting over that wall—before he was caught.

MacNally gave his last yank—and the remaining rope flew down at his face. He ducked—then scrambled to find the end. It had been severed—just as he had feared—and the cleat was gone.

MacNally looked around in the near darkness, trying to locate something else he could tie to the end, a jagged device that had enough mass that it would grab the other side of the wall and hold his weight as he climbed. But there was nothing.

He peered further into the dim, humid surroundings—and saw a freestanding structure. There had to be something in there. He left the line where it was, then ran the two dozen feet to the building's entrance. It was locked—not surprising. He examined the door, but it was solidly built. There was a window—but he did not want to risk the noise it would make. Even if this was the darkest area of the grounds, a stray and unexpected crash of glass would invite trouble.

But each minute MacNally was in the open, outside the institution building, he was in danger of being discovered. He had been willing to accept the consequences when he launched the escape—because he was in charge of his own destiny and he felt confident he would be able to make it. But he had not planned on being double crossed by his co-conspirator. Now, with the chance of failure increasing with each passing second, the risk seemed far greater than it had when he sat down to plan it.

He circled the building, but found no other means of ingress. The window had to be it; he pulled the tail of his thick cotton shirt from his pants, then balled it around his left hand and punched it through the glass. It shattered as expected—and made as much noise as he had feared. Nothing he could do about it but get inside and find something that would help him climb that wall.

He hoisted himself up and through, and landed hard on the ground, amongst the broken shards of glass. He felt warm blood oozing from his cheek, but he didn't care. He stumbled over haphazardly placed equipment of some sort, then groped in the darkness for something that he could fasten to the rope. A moment later, he found a rough, rusted rake. He stamped hard across the wood handle and the brittle wood snapped after three blows.

Drips of perspiration rolled off his brow, stinging his eyes. He wiped a sleeve across his face, and then examined the tool. It showed promise, but needed to be more rounded, like a hand. Anything he could use to bend it—a sledgehammer or other weighted device—would make substantial noise. Although his night vision had adjusted to the unlit interior, he could not find anything to reshape the hardened metal.

He tossed it out the window, then climbed up and out of the building. He picked up his new cleat, and cradling it like a football against his forearm, made like a running back and took off for the wall.

# 49

It was creeping past the end of the workday by the time Vail had started looking through the crime scene photos with Friedberg and Dixon. They had not gotten past the Anderson crime scene when Burden came running into the room.

"He left something for us." Burden had a sheet of paper cradled between the thumb and forefinger of both hands. "Stuck it under the windshield wiper of my car."

"He knew which car was yours?" Dixon asked.

"Apparently. After I spoke with Hayes—our lieutenant—and he gave me the go-ahead to use those interns, I had to get their names from a file in my car. And I found this." He held up the document.

"Does SFPD have cameras in the lot?" Vail asked.

Friedberg stifled a laugh. "There are some out front, and some strategically placed around the building's exterior. But the parking lot's low priority. And we've had very few problems so there's no incentive to spend money on that. You know how government works—we fix a security hole *after* we have a breach."

"What's it say?" Vail asked.

"It rambles a bit, kind of sounds like a manifesto."

They gathered around Burden's desk and huddled to read the letter.

> You think I made a mistake? Right. That's why I'm locked away
> in a jail cell. Oh, wait. I'm not. You people are a horrible waste

of our tax dollars. Are you all so stupid I have to spell it out? Society functins by rooles and laws but they don't apply to me. I don't respect author-ity. Never did when I was growing up. My parents taught me to question author-ity. So why should I respecdt it in prisin son of a bitch bastards all they want to do is stick you force you to become someone your not if thts not a crime what is. I ask you agent vail what does all this mean. What does life mean if a man does all he can but cant make it work in society. It makes you think doesn't it? If you still dont get it Agent Vail your not worth shit. I mean if all the philososphors and experts give us references for the trends of society what does it all mean if goverment doesn't respect an individuals rIght to live in peace. I am a weakish speller but don't take it for a fault. Underestimate me, you will be badly disappointed.

"I'm gonna take it over to the lab," Burden said. "Have them do the usual workup, see what they can tell us. Karen?"

Vail was reading it a second time. They waited for her to finish, at which point she sat back in her chair. "There's a lot of anger. It looks like his grammar is atrocious, which would indicate a lower level of schooling. But I don't think that's what's going on here. There's a purpose behind it. And he specifically warns us not to underestimate him."

"What else?"

"The writer appears to have done time in prison. He obviously refers to it and implies he's had experiences there. I assume being 'stuck,' in that context, refers to being raped. And he asks why he should respect authority in prison if his parents taught him not to respect it when he was free. That could merely be bullshit, but he does describe an attitude toward authority that's common among violent offenders: a lot of them don't think the laws of society apply to them. So I think there's a good chance our writer's been incarcerated."

"That could help us out big time," Friedberg said.

Burden leaned toward Vail. "He mentions you twice, as if he's talking directly to you. What do you make of that?"

"That would be what our UNSUB would do. Same with his opening—he puts himself out as the smart one, us as the dumb ones."

"You think this really is from the Bay Killer?" Dixon asked.

"That's a much more difficult question to answer." Vail sat forward in her chair and carefully slid the paper toward her using the eraser of a pencil. "It could be someone who read Allman's article. He mentioned me, so this crackpot could be trying to get his fifteen minutes of fame, if tomorrow's newspaper, or the paper's website, mentions the letter. Or it could actually be our guy—but he could be deliberately altering things to throw us off."

"Throw us off, how?" Friedberg asked.

"Reading this, you might think he doesn't appear to be too bright, with all the grammatical and spelling errors and run-on sentences. But hints of his intelligence come through when he makes his point, however circular and pontificatory he made it sound."

"Pontificatory?" Burden said.

"Yeah," Vail said, "pontificatory. You got a problem with that?"

"Go on," Dixon said.

"There appears to be a cogent message beneath the surface, if we read between the lines. I said before that he's angry. He's pissed about something that happened in prison. It might be a rape, but I think it's more than that. Sounds like he got out of prison and tried to make it work, but he couldn't survive in society.

"This is also a recurring theme with criminals—they do their time or get paroled, and then get released—and are completely unprepared for how society functions. They can't get jobs, or they get one and can't relate to people and they get into trouble, get fired—and then have no money and no way to get another job. So they turn to what they know, or what they learned in the joint, and that's robbery, or theft, or drugs. And they get caught and tossed back in prison again." Vail slid closer to the letter, took another look at it, and said, "There's more here, but that's a start."

"So what do we do with this?" Friedberg asked. "He didn't give us a way of responding."

"But he did," Vail said. "He wants the attention. So if we want to reply, and we do, we have to do it publicly."

"And what reply do we 'want' to send?" Burden asked.

"Appeal to his grandiosity. We should make it all about him. He's the ultimate, super important. All our efforts are focused on him. We're blown away by his intelligence. But at the same time, we have to challenge him so he doesn't get bored with us."

"Bored with us?" Burden asked. "You've gotta be kidding me."

"Psychopaths get bored. It's a part of who they are, their personalities. We're finding they'll even vary their crimes just to keep it interesting and different. That could explain why the new crime scenes are slightly different."

"But if he gets bored with us," Friedberg said, "and stops communicating, then what?"

"Nothing good from our perspective. Unless we handle it right, he could quickly lose interest in me. I have to let him think he's in control. Some detectives who had a dialogue with a serial killer want to talk to them after they're caught. They think they've got some kind of 'special' relationship with this killer, but the killer doesn't give a shit about them. It's all about how the serial killer thinks he can manipulate and use the detective. And then he spits them out.

"If I go to visit an offender in prison, someone I've spoken with a number of times in the past, he won't have warm, fuzzy memories of talking with me—even if we did have productive chats. These assholes don't form a bond with me or anyone else. There's just no loyalty there because they're not capable of it. Our UNSUB's contacting us—me—because it's exciting to contact 'his' profiler. But I could lose him really fast if I don't handle it right."

"I say we just tell him to fuck off," Burden said.

"First of all," Friedberg said, "other than quotes in an article that we plant, we have no way of reaching him."

Vail said, "He's set this up as a one-way conversation, which fits—his opinion is all that matters."

"What about TV? Would that be better than a newspaper or website post?" Dixon asked.

Vail cringed. "TV's bigger, more grandiose. We definitely don't want to go there unless he forces us to. So far that hasn't been an issue."

"So we build up his ego," Dixon said. "How would we simultaneously challenge him to keep his interest?"

Vail rose from her chair and walked over to the murder board where the photos were displayed. "We ask him to help us out, because we're not getting what he's trying to tell us. We understand he had a tough time in prison, but we sense there's a bigger picture, that there's a message here we're not capable of seeing without his help."

Burden slapped a hand on the table; the pencil jumped. "So you're saying we should play dumb and ask this fuckwad, who's murdered several people, to help us out because we're incompetent and we can't catch him?"

Vail tilted her head. "Do you see him behind bars, Burden? Because I sure don't. So check your ego at the goddamn door so we can do what we need to do to keep this guy contacting us. Sooner or later, if we play it right, he's gonna tell us something that will give us a direct line to him. Get it?"

Burden tightened his jaw. "Whatever."

"I'll take that as a 'yes.'"

"Karen," Dixon said, then gave her a slight shake of her head.

*Cut it out.* Vail took a deep breath. *You're letting the offender get to you.* She closed her eyes and cleared her mind. When she opened them, she realized her team was looking at her. "All right. I don't see where we have a choice. This asshole wants to play." She shrugged. "Let's play."


AT VAIL'S URGING, BURDEN CALLED Allman and told him to meet them at the Tadich Grill, a four minute ride from the station. They hadn't eaten in several hours, and with Burden looking to avoid his lieutenant's overtime budgetary wrath, they decided to extend their day by meeting, unofficially, offsite.

"Tadich is the oldest restaurant in the city," Friedberg said. "It may even be the oldest business, period. Dates all the way back to the Gold Rush days, 1849."

The neon sign that protruded perpendicularly from the emerald-toned building front confirmed Friedberg's information. Apparently, the establishment was proud of their heritage, as it was also emblazoned across the transom over the doorway. And on the glass storefront.

Vail pointed to the text. "Actually, it says they're the oldest in the state, not just the city."

Friedberg hiked his brow. "Whaddya know. I'll have to remember that."

"Please do," Vail said. She leaned back and looked accusingly at Friedberg. "Is the rest of your info that faulty?"

"Did you notice the name of this building?" Burden asked. He pointed to the sign above the Tadich entrance. "The Bitch Building. Guess it's only fitting that you're eating here."

"It's B-u-i-c-h," Friedberg said, spelling it out. "I'm not sure I'd pronounce it 'bitch.'"

"Karen might," Burden said.

Vail jutted her chin back and looked admiringly at Burden. "Good one."

Dixon pulled open the polished copper door and they filed in. Ahead of them stood an expansive bar that dominated the right side of the long and narrow restaurant. A silver-haired man in a white jacket and black pants greeted them and led them across the white tile and paneled walls to a series of private booths that lined the left side of the interior. Quarter loaves of round sourdough bread sat on a plate on each empty table, along with a bowl of sliced lemons.

"In a few minutes this place is gonna be packed," Burden said.

"Food's that good?" Vail asked.

Burden bobbed his head from side to side. "It's more...the experience of eating here."

"The *experience*," Vail repeated. She turned to Dixon. "I think we're in trouble."

The waiter gave Vail an unsavory twist of his face, set down the cardstock menus, and pushed his way toward the front of the restaurant, where more diners were entering.

Their table was separated by a tall wood divider that gave them a sense of isolation. Stacks of white linens were piled atop each of the dividers, which extended into the distance.

"I figured this would be the best place to discuss serial killers without pissing off the customers," Burden said.

Dixon pulled out her wood chair, then nodded at the front door. "There's our guest."

Clay Allman followed the same path the others had a moment earlier, then pulled over an extra chair and placed it at the end of the table. "I haven't eaten here in years."

"I hear it's quite the experience," Vail said.

Allman pursed his lips as he snagged an extra napkin from the divider and unfurled it with a flick of his wrist. "That's a good way of putting it."

"So remember we talked about helping each other out?" Burden said.

"That's what I do, Birdie. And have done, for twenty-five years. You know that—what's this about?"

"We've got something that needs to appear in tomorrow's paper."

Allman stole a look at his watch. "You did say, tomorrow, right?"

"I did."

Allman sighed heavily and sat back in his chair. "We missed the 5-star deadline, but I can probably make the 8:30 '1-dot' edition. What's so urgent that it has to get into the paper?"

Burden looked at Vail, who picked up the conversation.

"We got a letter from the offender."

"What's it say?"

Vail glanced at her task force colleagues, then said, "It reads like a manifesto. Off the record, it seems like he's done time in prison."

"And that's off the record? Give me a break, Karen." Allman leaned closer. "Can I call you Karen?"

"Call me whatever you want. But we need you to print something for us."

"How 'bout I print that for you and you let me see this manifesto—and let me mention that prison thing in the article?" Allman twitched his brow.

"How 'bout we buy you dinner," Vail said. "And you mention that we received a letter from the offender."

Allman tilted his head in thought. "How 'bout—"

"Clay," Burden said. "We're up against the wall here and we need you to do this." He looked at Allman, his gaze steady—and intense.

"Evening everyone," the waiter said. "May I take your order?"

They pulled the menus up to their face, selected quickly—Pasta and Clams for Burden, White Branzino Sea Bass for Friedberg, Bay Shrimp Diablo for Vail, and Pacific Oysters Rockefeller for Dixon.

"You're buying?" Allman asked.

"If we've got a deal," Vail said, "we're buying."

Allman groaned. "Fine." He looked up at the waiter. "Lobster thermidor." He glanced again at his watch. "Not that I'll have much time to eat it…"

The server collected the menus and left.

Allman pulled out a spiral notepad from his leather bomber jacket. "So what do you want this to say?"

Vail looked off at the rapidly filling restaurant. The scent of fresh fish sat heavily on the air, the sizzle of frying food off somewhere in the distance. *Appeal to his superior intellect.* "Try this: A letter was received today by the investigating detective on the Bay Killer case. The task force is awed by the killer's intellect, and by his insights on the rules of society." *We have to challenge him.* "But I'm asking him to be more forthcoming about what his intent is, and what it all means, because even with the mistakes he's made, I haven't been able to figure it out."

Allman stopped writing, then looked up. "You want this personal. You used the first person. Is that the way you want it? A direct quote?"

"I want him knowing it came from my mouth, yeah."

"Want to clarify what you mean by 'the mistakes' he's made?"

"Just go with what I gave you, Clay. But don't post it online tonight. Let it hit the paper in the morning. I want to control when he sees it in case he feels the need to act. I'd rather it be daylight."

Allman again consulted his watch. "If I'm going to make tomorrow's edition, I'll have to leave here in fifteen, twenty at the most."

He began jotting notes on his pad and had filled the third page when their food arrived. Allman ate quickly, periodically checking the time. Finally, he asked the waiter to box up the remaining food on his plate, then left.

"You think that'll get a reaction from the offender?" Dixon asked.

"I know it will," Vail said. "He's shown a pattern of monitoring the media for information dealing with his handiwork. We're going to hear from him. I just hope it's not in the form of more bodies."

Friedberg scooped the last forkful of his sea bass and held it in front of his mouth. "Amen to that."

Vail crunched on her shrimp, wondering what the connection was to her past... How the killer could know about what she had done in New York... How he had managed to get inside her head—not to mention her hotel room last night. But he had. And somehow he knew the right button to push that would prevent her from sharing this key piece of evidence with her colleagues. It was a brilliant move on his part. But what did it mean?

"What's on your mind?" Burden asked.

*Lots.* "Nothing."

He regarded her a moment, then nodded slightly and directed his attention back to his food.

It was clear that Burden knew something was up with her, but didn't know what it was. And, unfortunately, Vail found herself rowing in those same shark-infested waters.

# 50

MacNally tied the rake head to his line and began windmilling his arm to send it soaring into the darkness—and hopefully over the wall. He did not have a watch, but his internal clock told him that Rucker had abandoned him about twenty minutes ago. It was a head start that would likely make it impossible to catch him. Because if he did, he would—

Stop. He focused his thoughts. First he needed to get his tool to catch on the other side of the masonry. Then he needed to climb over the wall. Then he could let his anger boil and entertain thoughts about what he would do to Rucker should he find him.

The rake clanged against the wall and came flying back down at him. It struck the dirt and buried itself an inch deep. It was heavier and larger than the cleat, and that meant it was more difficult to arc forty feet into the air. He pulled it from the ground and tried again.

On the fourth attempt, it cleared the top. MacNally pulled and brought tension to the rope. He started to laugh—a nervous, anxious energy that told him he was confident he would get out of there.

He gave it a firm tug to test its viability, and using the knots as grab points, he began the climb. His injured hand still ached, and each grasp-and-pull maneuver sent pain shooting up his arm. But he'd have plenty of time to worry about that once he was en route to Henry.

He had made it about twenty paces, his humidity-induced sweaty palms chafing against the cotton, when an alarm sounded—followed instantly by two bullets that buried themselves in the brick wall, inches to the right of his torso.

"Stop right there!"

"Don't move!"

"Not one fucking muscle, you hear?"

Different voices. Multiple guards. He did not dare turn around because he did not want to lose his balance. But he did as ordered, and froze in place.

"Get down here. Now," said one officer.

"Slowly," yelled another.

MacNally descended the wall and dropped the last ten feet. His ankles burned, but his heart ached more. Henry. That was all he thought of as four men converged, shoved his face into the dirt, and snapped metal handcuffs and leg irons on him.

"Where do you think you were going, asshole?" a guard said by his ear.

MacNally was yanked to his feet by two of the officers.

"Where's your buddy?" another hack asked.

"On his way to hell."

The man stepped closer, his jaw set. He apparently did not care for that answer.

"Gone, over the wall. That's all I know. He screwed me. I hope you find him, because I'm—" He stopped himself. He needed to contain his anger, because anything he said could cause more problems for him. And as it was, he was now in enough trouble.

MACNALLY SAT IN SEGREGATION, HIS head bowed. The morning came but he had not slept. He cried silently much of the night, knowing that he had lost his best shot at getting out of Leavenworth. Once he was released from the Hole, he would be watched more closely. If he was released. He had no idea how seriously they would treat his offense. Probably very.

Three days passed, but they seemed like weeks. He didn't need the prison counselor to tell him he was in a bad way emotionally. He had stayed in bed most of the time, trying to sleep. Rather than bars and masonry and homemade ropes, this was an escape of a different sort:

something less concrete… He was attempting to avoid his thoughts. And consciousness. Or perhaps life itself.

As he lay on his bed, he heard the click of an officer's boots on the glossy cellhouse floor. Voorhees appeared, an open envelope in hand.

"This just came." He slipped it through the bars and held it out for MacNally.

MacNally lifted himself up and swung his legs off the cot—which took all his energy. He tore open the letter and pulled out the single piece of paper. The note read:

> I figured this was better revenge than just killing you for blinding Gormack. He sends his regards. Have a nice time in the Hole, motherfucker.

Hatred surging through his veins, MacNally looked out at the officer, doing his best not to react. Revenge, that was what this was about. Did Anglin know that when he vouched for Rucker?

Voorhees stared back, but did not speak. MacNally had to give the man credit: though he knew what was in the letter and knew what it meant, he was not gloating. He did not use the opportunity to lecture him. Then again, he had already expressed his thoughts the last time they had spoken. What more needed to be said? What more could be said?

Voorhees maintained eye contact. "You're being transferred this afternoon."

"Transferred," MacNally said. "To a different cellhouse?"

"Different prison."

MacNally stood up and grasped the bars, the letter in his hand crumpling around the curve of the metal. "Why?"

"When a guy gets outside the institution like you did, he's considered an escape risk. Adding in your attack on Wharton and Gormack and the Anglin escape attempt…" He shook his head. "The warden'd had enough. He figured you were too big a risk to stay at Leavenworth."

"What the hell does that mean?"

"Means your time here's done. Officers'll be by in thirty minutes to get you. You've got an afternoon flight." Voorhees turned to walk off. "You've been a big goddamn disappointment, MacNally. Good luck where you're headed. You're gonna need it."

"Hang on," MacNally called to the back of Voorhees, who was already moving down the corridor. "Where am I going?"

"End of the line, a place you'll never escape from," he yelled back. "Alcatraz."

# 51

Vail and Dixon returned to the Hyatt and spent the remainder of the evening in their room gathered around Dixon's laptop, pouring over the crime scene photos Friedberg had given them. They had a pad full of theories and notes, but nothing that took them in a particular direction worth pursuing.

Vail had been tempted at various points in their brainstorming session to confide in Dixon about the private note the killer had left her last night. But she could not get herself to broach the topic.

Dialing up her stress—as if it wasn't high enough—Hartman had still not called back. If she didn't make contact with him in the morning, she would go through the switchboard operator and have her walk the message over to his desk—or she'd have to pay him a visit in person.

She slept fitfully that night, her mind unwilling to shut down and her heart rate breaking speed barriers. She finally rolled out of bed, careful not to wake Dixon, and went down to the lobby. She sat there for an hour, staring at the lights. At one point, she laid down on the cold tile floor beneath the rows of bulbs and let her eyes roam them, counting them, hoping that sleep would come to her.

Fortunately, no one ventured into the lobby—because it would've been difficult to explain her behavior to a rational human being. Finally, at three o'clock, she lifted herself off the ground and rode the elevator back to her room. The last time she looked at the clock it was 3:49 AM. She fell off to sleep shortly thereafter.

Now, as she and Dixon drove back to Bryant Street, Dixon turned to her and said, "I know you, Karen. Something's bothering you. Wanna talk about it?"

Vail did not look at her. "Tell you the truth—" The vibration of her phone made her jump. She pulled the BlackBerry off her belt. "Robby. What's up? How are things going?"

"I'm about to head into a stakeout so I only have a minute. But everything's good. I took Jonathan to dinner a couple times, we played some Xbox. I helped him with a math project, and now he's off to that Aviation Challenge thing. How's your case going?"

Vail's eyes slid over to Dixon. She desperately wanted to tell Robby what was going on—what was really going on—but she couldn't, not now, and certainly not over the phone. She wasn't proud of what had happened back in New York—more like how she had handled it—and it was something best discussed in person, not over the phone. Robby would understand. How could he not, given his background?

After a long hesitation, Vail said, "It's going."

"What's wrong?"

"Why the hell is everyone asking me what's wrong?" *Because something is wrong.*

"Do I really have to answer that?" Robby asked. "Come on."

Dixon brought the car to a stop at a red light and turned to face her.

"We've got what I think is a fairly accurate profile coming together, but we're not very far into figuring out who this asshole is. And I feel like I'm missing something. I know I'm missing something. More than something."

"You'll eventually figure it out, Karen. You always do."

*You always do. I do, don't I? But I'm not Wonderwoman. What happens when I hit a case where I don't?*

"And when the time comes that you don't," Robby said, "what do you think will happen?"

*Did I say that out loud?* "I'll feel like a failure."

"That may be. But you'll really just be human. I seem to remember you telling me something about that."

A smile lifted the corners of Vail's mouth. "I miss you, Hernandez."

"Tell Robby I say hey."

Vail turned to Dixon. "Roxxann's with me. She says hi."

"Tell her I still hope to get back out to Napa for a real vacation with you. We'll kick back, taste some wine, do a mud bath—"

"I told you. I'm not lying in horseshit again. Once I found out what it was…I just can't get past it. Besides, you'll have to carry me kicking and screaming back to California."

"Kicking and screaming, huh? Sounds like just another day in the life of Karen Vail."

Dixon pulled into the SFPD parking lot and found a spot near Burden's Ford. At least, it looked like Burden's—there were about a dozen Tauruses, and they were all blue or gray.

"Gotta go," Robby said.

"Call me when you get a break." They said good-bye and she hung up, then got out of the car with Dixon.

"Did you leave the room last night?"

Vail glanced at her partner as they walked toward the building. "You're a light sleeper. Yeah, I was tossing for a couple hours, so I finally gave up and went down to the lobby."

"And did what?"

"And…I lay down on the floor and gazed at the lights."

Dixon looked at her friend with squinted eyes. They went through the magnetometers and nodded at security as they passed through the lobby. "Should I be concerned about you?"

Vail stifled a wide yawn, then waved a hand. "Let's solve this case. Then everything will be fine."

As they walked into Homicide, Vail told Dixon she needed to make a call, then ducked back into the hallway. She sent Robby a text telling him to give her a call when he had a chance. Then she phoned Hartman. It again went to voicemail and she left another message, then redialed and worked her way to the operator, who placed Vail on hold before she had a chance to explain what she needed.

After a moment's wait, the man returned to the line.

"This is Special Agent Vail out of Quantico. I'm trying—"

The Homicide door flew open and Burden emerged. "New vic," he said. "C'mon."

*Crap.* "I'll have to call you back." Vail disconnected the call, then fell in behind Dixon.

"Where's Robert?"

"Following up with Scheer's cell carrier on the way in. Hoping to get us somewhere on that anonymous informant buddy he had." Burden shouldered the stairwell door and started galloping down the steps. "I texted him, told him to meet us there."

"Where is 'there'?" Vail asked.

Burden grabbed the handrail as he turned and headed down to the next floor. "Inspiration Point."

"Then maybe we'll get lucky," Vail said. "And inspired."

THEY ARRIVED AT THE PRESIDIO'S picturesque overlook to find Stephen Scheer already onsite. A United States Park Police vehicle was parked at the mouth of the minimalist parking lot, blocking its entrance. News vans were parked on the side of the road. Two cameramen, their tools of the trade balanced on a shoulder with cables snaking along the floor at their feet, stood at the ready. Primped blond and brunet reporters waited outside the crime-scene tape beside Scheer.

"So much for avoiding TV," Dixon said as they pulled to a stop a few dozen feet from the news vehicles.

Burden slammed his car door and asked, "What are you people doing here?"

Scheer stepped in front of the TV crews. "I was at the Presidio on another story when my editor texted me. Apparently, your killer called it in to the papers and TV station himself. He obviously wanted us all here."

Vail frowned. "Obviously." She grabbed the thin plastic tape and pulled it above her head, then she, Burden, and Dixon slipped beneath it.

"Mind if I tag along?" Scheer asked.

Vail faced him with narrowed eyes. "What do you think?"

"Hey, this one you can't blame on me," he said.

Forty feet away, on a semicircular slate tile plaza, a tall black man in a well-tailored dark suit and bright red tie chatted with a woman wearing an FBI jacket, "Evidence Response Team" emblazoned across her back.

A narrowed walkway split the terrace down the center, with a wood bench on either side of its entrance facing outward, providing a spectacular view of the Bay. The glowing sunburst dome of the Palace of Fine Arts stood out in stark contrast to the surrounding bed of richly hued evergreen and cypress trees that lined the hilltop. A light haze hung over the mountains in the distance across the Bay, but the water was a deep baby blue.

The Evidence Response Technician pointed her Canon at the left bench, where an elderly man sat, seemingly staring ahead at the scenic view.

Vail, Dixon, and Burden stepped alongside the criminalist and made introductions to the suited man, United States Park Police Major Crimes Detective Peter Carondolet. They explained that this victim was likely part of a case they had been working in the city.

"Looks like we got a new member of our task force," Burden said.

Carondolet held up both hands. "No. Wait. Hang on a minute— I'm buried in a huge case. I'm here as a favor to a buddy. I'll— Why don't we play it by ear. Keep me posted if you come across useful info, and I'll do the same with you people."

Vail, Burden, and Dixon shared an uneasy look.

"Detective," Vail said, "the offender, the guy who killed the victim in front of us, has murdered several men and women, and just might be responsible for a number of others going all the way back to '82. It's a major case. You work in the Park Police's Major Crimes division, no?"

Carondolet shifted his feet. "I'm not saying I won't help. But I— I'll do what I can. Let's leave it at that for now. Why don't we just focus on what we've got here and now? We can always reassess. I mean, we're not even sure it's the same killer."

Vail appraised their latest victim. A number 25 was scrawled on his forehead. She swung her head back to Carondolet. "Yes, Detective. I'm sure. Same killer."

Carondolet regarded her with a twisted frown. "You look at the vic for five seconds and decide it's the same guy?" He snorted. "I don't think we pay you profilers enough."

"I don't like to waste time dicking around," Vail said. "And I'm very, very good."

"She is," Dixon said.

Carondolet's gaze shifted between Burden, Dixon, and Vail. He chuckled mockingly and said, "If you say so."

Burden turned back to the victim. "Interesting." He nodded at the body, which was decked out in a black shirt and Roman collar. "A man of the cloth."

Vail frowned. "What was your first clue?" She shook her head. "And they call you a detective?"

"Actually, they call me an inspector."

"Whatever."

Burden turned to Dixon. "What's gotten into her?"

"Something's bugging her."

"Hello?" Vail said, waving a hand. "I'm right here. You got a question, ask me."

"Fine," Burden said. "What's bugging you?"

Vail banded her arms across her chest. "Nothing."

Burden threw both hands in the air. Can't win.

"Are you people always this dysfunctional?" Carondolet asked.

"You want to know what's bugging me?" Vail gestured at the body. "He's sitting. All the other males were tied to a column or a pole or a post of some sort. Why is this guy on a bench?"

Dixon rotated her head, taking in their surroundings. "No poles. Maybe he had no choice."

"Maybe," Vail said. *But I don't think so. Something's different about this victim.*

"Do we have an ID?" Burden asked the criminalist. "You are?"

"Sherri Price. And no, no ID yet."

The slam of a car door caused all of them to look up. Clay Allman had arrived.

Price said, "Go on. I've processed the body but I haven't checked his pockets."

Burden slipped a gloved hand inside the man's coat and removed a worn wallet. "Ralph Finelli. Father Ralph Finelli."

Dixon knelt in front of the bench, to the left of the man's right knee. "Rosary beads still in his hand."

"Any thoughts on what that means?" Burden asked.

"Where do you start?" Vail said. "It could be another taunt. It could be referring to the Mysteries of the Rosary. The mysteries recount the life of Jesus—but the UNSUB may be using it to thumb his nose at us... The mysteries he's leaving behind for us that we've been unable to solve."

"Where's Robert when we need him?" Dixon said.

"You texted him, told him to meet us here," Vail said. "Right?"

"I did." Burden consulted his phone. "He didn't reply." He began tapping out a new message on the keypad.

"Who's Robert?" Carondolet asked.

"Another member of our team," Burden said.

"I think there are twenty mysteries." Vail looked at Burden and Dixon for confirmation. They shrugged.

Dixon pulled out her iPhone and began a search. "I hope those twenty mysteries don't correspond to the number of vics he's planning to kill."

"Amen to that," Burden quipped.

Vail scrunched her face. "That was awful."

"You're right," Dixon said, reading off the screen. "Twenty mysteries. Joyful, Luminous, Sorrowful, Glories—"

"Penance," Vail said. "Maybe the father's holding the rosary to signify that he's done penance after confession. His penance being his murder."

"Speaking of awful," Burden said. "Killing a priest, a man of God..."

Dixon leaned in closer for a look at the rosary. "I don't think this offender's concerned about heaven and hell."

"I'm sure there are other explanations and religious undertones," Vail said. "Friedberg can probably give us a whole freaking recitation on the history of the rosary."

Burden squinted. "Don't count on it. He's Jewish."

"Did he say when he's gonna be here?"

"Still hasn't responded." Burden shook his head and reholstered his phone. Before he moved his hand aside, the device began vibrating. "Hang on—" He lifted it from his belt. "Robert just texted me. Says he's tied up at the moment."

"Great." Vail tilted her head and looked at the body, then stepped back a few steps to get a broader perspective. "Something else is different." Her eyes moved from shoes to head and— "That's it. He's wearing a hat. Do priests wear hats?"

"No idea," Burden said. "But why not?"

Vail shook her head. "It's more than that. None of the other males had hats on." She stepped up to the body, then stopped. "Price— gloves?"

Price pulled out a couple from her kit and tossed them to Vail, who stretched them across her hands. She lifted the hat—and a note fell into Father Finelli's lap. Vail carefully unfolded it. In printed computer text, the note contained one sentence:

where is inspector friedberg?

# 52

November 21, 1960

*United States Penitentiary - Alcatraz*
*San Francisco Bay*
*Alcatraz, California*

The cold, damp fog blasted MacNally's face as he debarked from the white wooden launch inscribed with the name *Warden Johnston*. The boat rocked a bit as he stepped onto the swaying gangplank. Ahead of him, a large black-on-white sign stared at him, informing him of the obvious:

UNITED STATES PENITENTIARY
ALCATRAZ ISLAND
ONLY GOVERNMENT BOATS PERMITTED

There was other text on the sign, but the rest of it did not matter. He was here. On an island, in the middle of the Bay in the Pacific Ocean, a long way from shore. One of the officers on board the ship told him there were sharks in the choppy, gray waters, but MacNally did not care to look. It was an ocean; he did not doubt it.

Ahead of him stood a five-story cream-colored brick structure—an apartment building, he guessed. To his right, a black steel guard tower rose from the dock. An armed officer stared down at him, a high-powered rifle cradled in his hands. Daring MacNally to try something.

By the look on his face, his morning had been as exciting as the desolate waters around him, and a little action would be welcome. MacNally decided to move along as instructed and not give the hack any chance to relieve the day's boredom.

Then again, he was wearing leg irons and handcuffs, and he was surrounded by three officers. If he was going to attempt an escape, this would not be the time or place he would choose.

From the Bureau of Prisons's perspective, Walt MacNally was a man who had robbed two banks at gunpoint, kidnapped a child, participated in one escape attempt at Leavenworth, engineered another, and had been strongly suspected in the brutal attack of two other inmates.

MacNally did not blame them for moving him to a prison island and taking stringent precautions. To them, he was a dangerous convict capable of heinous things. And he had to admit, who he was a year ago and who he was now were as different as summer in Spain and winter in Siberia.

"Move it," the officer said with a shove.

A transport bus's rough diesel engine idled impatiently as MacNally ascended the steps as best he could with his ankles fastened together. He took a seat and the vehicle lurched forward. A moment later, it strained to climb the steep switchback roadway that led to the prison building.

Seagulls swooned and dove above and around the truck, and their droppings littered the pavement and penitentiary's exterior brick facing. Even inside the bus, he heard the large birds' screams. He had a feeling this was a sound with which he would become intimately familiar.

Through damp and dirty windows, the institution loomed before him. He craned his neck and looked up at the building. Three or so stories. Barred windows. The design was not as elaborate or grandiose as Leavenworth. More stark, prison-like. Dreary.

Vegetation was everywhere, however. The hillsides were well planted and lush, and as the bus chugged up the incline, he saw a garden of some kind along the roadway. The transport hooked another left, and then headed up again, toward the entrance to the penitentiary.

Finally, the bus screeched to a halt.

"Up," the guard said.

MacNally pulled himself from the seat and slowly stepped down the stairs, stooping his tall frame to avoid striking his head while taking care not to trip over the leg irons. The wind was blustery, fiercer here at the top of the island. He took a moment to glance at the Bay view.

"Get a good, long look. That's what you'll be missing out on."

"Incentive to keep your nose clean here," one of the other guards said. "We don't tolerate bad behavior, MacNally. We've seen your sheet at Leavenworth. That shit won't fly here. You're on The Rock now." The officer gave him a shove forward.

MacNally walked into the sally port and stood before a barred metal gate.

"Opening up," the duty officer said.

A buzzer sounded and a metal plate slid aside electronically, baring a lock mechanism. The guard removed a key and inserted it into the opening.

The uniformed men led MacNally through an additional gate and then down a hallway before turning left into a large room. To his side stood a long row of shower heads; in front of him, a caged area where two men folded clothes.

One of the guards pulled a key from his pocket and gestured to his feet. "Be still. No fast moves. Understand?" MacNally agreed, and the officer crouched down to unlock the irons. He handed them to his colleague, who headed off the way they had come.

MacNally and his escort continued ahead about thirty feet, stopping at a wire mesh gate with a pass-through opening.

Two trustees dressed in denim shirts and white pants asked him his shoe and clothing sizes, then turned to the wood wall-mounted bins and selected the appropriate items. The inmate tossed it into a neat pile, then added a shaving kit: mug, brush, and soap. "You gotta shave three times a week, no exceptions. No beards, moustaches, sideburns. Nothing. From 5:30 to 8:30, Tuesday, Thursday, and Saturday, guards'll come around and pass out razors. They collect 'em when you're done." He grabbed a printed booklet from a stack and slapped it atop the pile. "It's all in here. These are the rules. Read 'em. Learn 'em. Things go easier that way."

He handed it all to MacNally through the opening in the metal mesh wall. MacNally took it and looked down at the thin blue-on-white printed manual titled *Institution Rules & Regulations.*

"Your new name's AZ-1577," the trustee said. "You'll be in cell C-156." He turned and walked back to the bins.

MacNally took a moment to glance around. "You been here a long time?"

"Five years, nine months. Six days."

"How is it?"

The man glanced sideways at the correctional officer. "Some guys here call it Devil's Island. How do you think it is?" His eyes slid over again to the guard, then back. "You're in the middle of one of the most beautiful places on earth. Most of the time, you can't even see it 'cause you're either locked in your cell or you're workin' in Industries. But you can hear it. When the party boats pass by on New Year's, you can hear the people laughing. When you go out to the yard, if it's a clear day, you'll see all the pretty women in bikinis cruise by in them fancy boats. You can look but you can't touch. You're stuck here. On a fucking rock in the middle of the goddamn ocean."

He looked at the officer again, then leaned in closer to the mesh wall. "Watch yourself, MacNally. Evil lives here, always has... There's a reason why these guys are on The Rock."

"One inmate, he called it Hellcatraz," the other trustee said from across the room. "Seems about right to me. The boredom, day after day, the same routine." He nodded slowly. "You'll see."

"Enough." The officer grasped MacNally's left arm. "Let's go."

MacNally looked the guard over as he led him out of the room, then up the mint green metal staircase to the main cellhouse. He wore a charcoal double-breasted suit, baby blue shirt and red tie, with a matching gray pentagonal policeman's hat. A silver badge was pinned to the front of his cap—but otherwise, there were no nametags or other designations on the uniform.

"What's your name?" MacNally asked.

The officer gave his arm another yank, leading him up the steps. "What do you care?"

"Just two people talking."

"You ever kill anyone? 'Cause if you did, this conversation's over. I'm the CO and you're the convict, you do what I say, and that's that."

MacNally stopped. The officer did, too—and he quickly swung his head toward his prisoner to see if he was going to have a problem.

"No. Never killed anyone."

The man nodded slowly, examining MacNally's eyes. Then he said, "Name's Jack Taylor. Call me Officer Taylor, or officer or Mr. Taylor. Never Jack. You got that?"

"Got it," MacNally said.

Taylor led him up the steps and through another locked gate beneath the West Gun Gallery at B-Block. "Over there's the dining hall," he said, tilting his head to the right at the gated room. An officer was sitting at a duty desk a few feet away.

"Hallway here's Times Square," Taylor said, "because of Big Ben up there." He motioned MacNally along. "On your right, that metal door there goes to the rec yard. You get two and a half hours Saturday and Sunday. Softball, handball, shuffleboard, weights. If you sit up on the top of the stairs, you get a view of the Bay and the Golden Gate Bridge. What 1161 was talking about in processing."

MacNally said, "1161?"

"The inmate. That's who gave you your stuff." He led MacNally down a main corridor between the cell blocks. The floors were spit-shine clean and glossy, and the area was unusually quiet save for the hacking cough of a man who was lying on the bed of his ground-floor cell.

"This is Broadway," Taylor said with a nod of his head. "Next block over to the right, Seedy Street and Park Avenue. To the left is Michigan Avenue."

"Seedy?"

"It's where C and D blocks are. C, D... Seedy."

"The cells are locked during the day?" MacNally asked. At Leavenworth, the doors remained open, allowing prisoners freedom to roam the cellhouse.

"Unless you've got a work detail, that's where you spend twenty-three out of every twenty-four hours. Don't wanna go stir crazy, get yourself a job. Otherwise, those cold, shark-infested waters will look mighty inviting after a few months."

As they continued down Broadway, MacNally glanced into each of the cells. Along the bottom, a dark green stripe served as a baseboard. Gloomy mint paint extended halfway up the wall, and white finished it off, up to and including the ceiling.

Some cells were stark, with no personalized décor—just a white towel, a shaving kit, a toilet paper roll, and a chocolate brown wool blanket thrown across the bed. Each cell had two small metal shelves, mounted in tandem one above the other, placed opposite the mattress, with another two above the toilet, which sat beside a compact porcelain sink and a cross-hatched air vent opening in the cement wall.

"Are all these singles?" MacNally asked.

"That's all we got here. Some think having your own cell's better than a place like Leavenworth where you always got five or ten cellies living with you. Others think it's more lonely."

MacNally knew which he preferred. If he'd had a single at Leavenworth, things may've turned out differently for him. And he would not now be in the middle of the Pacific Ocean, over a mile from land in a place known for its cold, foggy, and windy weather. An institution considered the last stop, living amongst the most incorrigible, most dangerous, and most unruly criminals the United States' criminal justice system possessed.

As MacNally walked past a few more cells that were unoccupied, he slowed as his eyes locked with a man sitting on his bed.

John Anglin.

MacNally did not know if he should acknowledge him—if Anglin had been a model prisoner at The Rock during his brief tenure, associating with him would be a positive; but if he had been a troublemaker, the opposite would be true. He decided on a gentle lift of his chin, then brought his eyes forward and continued walking beside his escort toward the far wall.

They hung a right and came upon another series of cells. "Welcome to C-Block and Park Avenue. Your new neighborhood."

"That a library?" MacNally asked, gesturing ahead and to the right.

"Off limits. You want a book? A trustee'll bring by a push cart filled with 'em. You can have three in your cell at a time. Well, three and a Bible. Magazines, too. *Popular Mechanics, Time, Life, Popular Science,* that kind of stuff. You want, you can buy a subscription."

"You said this was Seedy Street. C- and D-Blocks. This is C. Where's D?"

"Glad you asked." Taylor grinned. "D's in the room next door. Our Treatment Unit."

"Hospital?"

"Hospital's upstairs, above the dining hall. No, Treatment Unit's solitary confinement. Segregation. The Hole." Taylor stopped in front of C-156. "Best you stay out of there, MacNally. Trust me on that one." The officer leaned back and faced another guard, who was standing a hundred or so feet away, at the end of the cell block. "Rack 'em, 156!"

A moment later, the officer pulled out keys and appeared to be accessing what MacNally assumed was some sort of control box. The man reached inside and after a series of arm gyrations—he pulled down, then up, then grabbed something else—a *click* sounded above the barred door for C-156. A loud *clunk* echoed, followed by the gate in front of him sliding to the right.

"In," Taylor said. "Morning gong's at 6:33. At 6:50, second gong goes off. Stand right here, by your bars, fully dressed, facing out. At the whistle, the lieutenants and cellhouse guards do a standing count. Next whistle's at seven sharp. That's when you'll be turned out to the dining hall for chow. Rest of the daily schedule's in your book. Page four and five. Oh—and pay attention to the diagram on page eight."

MacNally stepped into the confining, five-by-nine foot chamber. "Diagram? Of what?"

"Your cell. Everything's got a place. Towel, jacket, toilet paper, books, calendar, soap. Shows you where everything's got to go."

"You're joking, right?"

Taylor's face thinned, his jaw muscles flexing. "No. I'm not." He turned to his colleague and yelled to the far end of the cell block. "Rack 'em!"

More clicks...a solid metallic crunch...and then the door slid closed in front of MacNally. A lonely, bone-jarring slam echoed through the cellhouse.

Taylor's shoes crunched quietly on the polished cement floor as he walked away. MacNally watched the officer's shadow disappear, a chill shuddering through his body.

Despite its reputation among cons, MacNally could not imagine how Alcatraz could be worse than Leavenworth. But he had a feeling he was going to soon find out.

# 53

V ail handed the note to Price, then pulled out her BlackBerry. "That text—who was it from? The one that said he's tied up."

Burden looked at his phone. "Robert. Why am I not understanding what's going on—"

"I'm calling Friedberg," Vail said. *I have a feeling I know exactly what's going on, and it ain't good.* "Call your department, get every fucking cop mobilized in the city looking for his car. And see if they can get a fix on his cell signal."

Seconds later, Vail gave up. "Went right to voicemail."

Burden hung up, then began pacing. "All right, let's clear our heads. Think this through. He was stopping at Verizon on the way in, to see about those text messages Scheer got." He looked over at the reporter, who was standing a few paces from Allman, beyond the crime scene tape.

"We know what's going on," Vail said. "Our UNSUB's got Friedberg."

"Let me get this straight," Carondolet said. "The killer's got an SFPD Inspector?"

"You got it," Dixon said. To Burden: "Call Verizon and see if he made it there, and if he did, what time he left."

Burden pulled out his phone and made the call.

A text hit Vail's BlackBerry. She still had the device in her palm when it began vibrating. She rotated her hand and read the message. "Son of a bitch."

"What?" Dixon asked.

Vail showed her the display.

> lotsa bodies werent motivation enuf
> need one of ur own on the line
> want to know what this is all about
> pay attention u have ten mins
> think history
> ur answers in the place where
> violence and sleep come under watchful eyes

Burden ended his call abruptly and joined the huddle. His brow hardened. "What the hell does it mean?"

"You're the puzzle guy."

"Sudoku," Burden said. "Numbers. Not goddamn riddles."

Dixon stepped to the left and cupped her hands around her mouth. "Clay! Bring your colleague over here. Now."

"What are you doing?" Vail asked.

"We've got two guys fifty feet away who ply their trade using words," Dixon said. "And they also happen to know the city inside and out. Got nothing to lose by using their brain power. Friedberg's life's on the line—do we really care what the press knows?"

"Worry about it later," Burden said.

"Exactly."

"You're bringing two reporters into the crime scene?" Carondolet said. "Are you crazy?"

Allman and Scheer slipped under the tape and ran through the parking lot.

"What's going on?" Allman asked as he approached.

"Let's also see if we can get a fix on those texts," Vail said. "One was from Friedberg's but the other was from a different handset. I'll send you the number. See what they can do with it. Every carrier's different, but even if they can't localize it better than a few miles, we'll at least know if he's in the city."

"Got it," Burden said. He started to make the call.

"So here's the deal," Vail said to Allman and Scheer as she played with her BlackBerry keypad to send the phone number to Burden. "Killer's got Inspector Friedberg. He just used Friedberg's phone—and then what I'm guessing is a disposable—to send us messages."

Scheer and Allman both reached for their pads.

"Fuck the story," Burden said, rotating the phone away from his mouth. "We need your help. He sent us a riddle."

"Is this on or off the record?" Scheer asked.

Carondolet shook his head "I can't believe you're involving these guys."

"Don't make us sorry we brought you over here," Dixon said to Scheer. "Put that shit away. And don't ask again."

Both journalists reluctantly shoved their pads and pens into their jackets.

"How can we help?" Allman asked.

Vail stole a look at her BlackBerry, "The text says, 'Think history. Your answer's in the place where violence and sleep come under watchful eyes."

"Isn't Friedberg the historian?" Scheer asked.

Vail's gaze flicked over to Father Finelli, then back to Scheer. "That's right, dipshit. And he's not here. So what does it mean? Any thoughts?"

No one answered, as all stared off in various directions, working it through.

"What kind of place comes under watchful eyes?" Vail asked.

"A police department," Burden said.

"Surveillance would qualify as watchful eyes," Allman said.

Dixon snapped her fingers. "So that'd bring us back to law enforcement. A stakeout. Violence, sleep."

"Hopefully little of each," Burden said. "But what do we do with that? Too general."

Scheer looked up. "Wait a minute. I wrote something like that once. In one of my features, years ago. Something about violence and sleep and watchful eyes."

Vail stepped forward. "Are you saying this text is a quote from your article?"

Scheer bit his lip, his eyes moving left, right, up and down as he thought. "I can't remember. Something like that."

Burden combed through his hair with his fingers. "C'mon, man. We've only got eight minutes. Think."

"I am thinking," Scheer said slowly, emphasizing each word. "I just—it was a long time ago. It seems like it's... Yeah, that's what I wrote. Close."

"We know the UNSUB's from around here," Dixon said. "And if this is the guy who's killed repeatedly in the Bay Area, as Clay thinks, then he's likely followed all the newspaper articles on murders and violent crime in the city. Maybe he saw Scheer's article."

"What was it about?" Vail asked.

"A bank robbery," Scheer said. "The robber shot and killed a security guard."

"What's sleep got to do with it?"

"The guard had fallen asleep in a back room where they had the surveillance cameras. The gunshot woke him up and he hit the silent alarm, but it was too late. They got away." Scheer rubbed a hand across his cheek, then continued. "The long delay between the robbers entering the bank and the trip of the alarm was a big problem. The FBI investigated the guard. Like, maybe it was an inside job. They leaned on him pretty hard. He finally admitted he'd fallen asleep. And that was that. No inside job, just—gross incompetence. And they never caught the robbers." He shrugged. "So, whether it's an exact quote or not, violence and sleep came under watchful eyes."

There was quiet. Finally, Vail said, "That's not exciting me."

"Me either," Burden said. "Clay, you got anything?"

"I'm thinking."

Dixon checked her watch. "Think faster. We've only got five minutes."

"Fuck me," Burden said, kicking a rock into the slate wall. "How the hell can we figure this shit out under pressure?"

"A sleep lab," Allman said. "You know, they hook you up to sensors so they can diagnose sleep disorders. Sleep under watchful eyes."

"No violence," Dixon said.

"The bank's not far away," Scheer said. "A few blocks. Maybe we should go check it out. We can think on the way."

"I'm with Karen here," Allman said. "I think that's a waste of time."

Burden worked his jaw, then said, "We've got four minutes left. Let's go. If we think of something better on the way, nothing lost."

"You coming?" Vail asked Carondolet.

"I'll finish with this DB, you go on ahead and…solve your riddle."

They ran to Burden's car and piled in. "Where we going?"

Scheer leaned forward in his seat. "Corner of—" He put his head down.

"Scheer," Burden yelled. "Now's not the time to have a brain fart."

"Presidio and Sacramento. Yeah, that's it—"

Burden accelerated and spun rubber, then the Taurus rocketed forward, briefly losing grip in its rear wheels on a slick surface before once again grabbing pavement and jolting them on their way. Burden hung a sharp left onto Jackson Street as Vail slapped the flashing light atop the car. "We should be there right at the deadline. Anyone else got any better ideas?"

Vail tried to concentrate, but watching Burden swerve his way down Jackson, she found it hard to think about anything other than surviving the ride. She did not want to close her eyes—but that was the only way she could get her mind to focus.

*How's the offender gonna react if we're wrong? How will he know? He gave us a ten- minute window to find this place. Wherever it was he wanted us to go, he knew where we were starting out. It had to be in a ten-minute radius. In a city, what is that? A mile?*

"Not sure this helps," Vail said, "but the place he sent us had to be in a ten-minute radius of Inspiration Point."

"It doesn't help," Allman said. "That's a shitload of potential places in a city like this."

"It's the bank," Scheer said. "Has to be."

"Wish I could be so sure," Burden said under his breath. He screeched the Ford to a stop in front of Sutter Savings Bank. They jumped out and headed toward the corner building.

"Now what?" Dixon asked, rotating her body in a circle.

Vail stood back and took in the entire location. "No idea. Look around. Anything that seems like it might be meant for us—"

"I'm going in," Burden said. He pushed through the front doors. Dixon followed, leaving Vail with the two journalists.

"See anything?"

"No," Scheer said. He looked over at Allman and pointed an index finger. "Don't give me that."

Allman spread his arms. "Give you what?"

"I know what you're thinking."

"The only reason you know what I'm thinking, Stephen, is because I already told you this was a waste of time."

"You didn't offer anything better. So just—just shut the fuck up."

Allman shook his head, then waved a hand. "Whatever."

Scheer walked off, down the block.

*Maybe involving these guys wasn't such a great idea.* Vail headed into the bank and locked gazes with Dixon and Burden, who shook their heads. A man in a suit standing with them looked puzzled by all the attention, while several customers at the teller window looked on with concern.

"We got nothing," Burden said.

Vail's phone vibrated. *I don't want to look.* She pulled it from her belt. Dixon and Burden huddled around her.

> no no no
> ur friends life depends on it but ur clueless
> those intended to heal
> may give life but drown truth
> cant sink or swim can float
> mission st

clocks ticking

figure it out or im done with you


"No." Burden shook his head. "I'm done playing games."

"Burden," Vail said in a low voice. "We talked about this. Psychopaths get off on feeling superior. And they get bored easily. This is a game to him, to prove to us—and to himself—how much smarter he is. By tricking us, he's able to gloat. It builds him up and knocks us down. At the same time, we've gotta make some headway in these clues to hold his interest. If we don't prove a worthy challenge, we'll lose him. And if we lose contact with him, we lose any shot at finding Robert."

"C'mon," Dixon said, then led the way outside.

Burden slammed the door with his hands and it flew open. He let it swing closed behind him, nearly striking Vail in the face. "Asshole better realize I'm losing patience, too."

"What's on Mission?" Vail asked.

Allman and Scheer came jogging over from opposite directions.

Burden threw open his car door. "Lots of things are on Mission."

"Let's take a minute, break it down."

"We get another message?" Allman asked.

Vail held it up for the two reporters to read.

"What's 'intended to heal'?" Dixon asked. "A medical clinic? A doctor? Surgeon? Acupuncturist? Chiropractor?"

Burden shook his head. "Probably all of that on Mission. It's a long freaking street. You've got businesses, seedy areas, banks, office buildings, a BART station—"

"Then let's go to the next clue," Vail said. "May give life but drown truth. Doctors give life. We're back to doctors."

"God gives life," Allman said. "Strictly speaking. If you're a religious sort."

"A church?" Dixon asked. "Doesn't fit with drowning the truth."

"Now there's a whole other philosophical question," Allman said.

"Hell with philosophy," Burden said. "Forget religion. None of that fits. Read the rest. What's it say? Can't sink or swim, but you can float?"

"A bath tub," Scheer said. "Too small to sink or swim in. But you can float."

Burden gave him a dirty look.

"Hey, I was wrong about the bank. I get that. But what do you want from me? I'm just trying to help."

Vail held up a hand. "Let's go with that." She checked her watch. How much time they had left, she had no idea. "A mud bath. You can't sink, you can't swim in it, but you can float in it."

"No mud baths around here that I know of," Dixon said. "Back home in Calistoga, but nothing here in the city. You guys know of any?"

Allman, Burden and Scheer shook their heads.

"Wait a minute," Dixon said. "Float. You can't sink in a flotation tank. And you can't swim in it, but you do float because of the salts."

"Come again?" Vail said.

"Alternative medicine clinics. There are a couple on Mission, I think. They put you in sensory deprivation tanks. You float in heavily salted water for hours."

Vail shuddered while thumbing her BlackBerry. "That would definitely creep me out. Why would someone want to do that?"

"Didn't the *Trib* do a story on that once?" Burden asked.

"A few years back," Allman said. "When that sort of thing was big."

Dixon held up her iPhone. "It's supposed to reduce the levels of stress hormones in the body, according to Wikipedia."

"There's the medical angle," Vail said.

Dixon tapped and scrolled. "We've got one on Mission. SDL Incorporated—Sensory Deprivation Lab, 2944 Mission."

"Let's go." Burden got into the car, twisted the key and turned over the engine.


SENSORY DEPRIVATION LAB'S FACILITY STOOD in a nondescript brick building that looked like it had been a remnant from decades past. They entered through worn wood doors and consulted a posted sign that directed them to Suite 201.

Vail held out a hand. "Why don't you two wait down here."

Allman tilted his head. "But—"

"There's no reason for you to come up. This is still an investigation. If we're on the right track, we'll let you know. If not, we'll be back down in a couple minutes because we—and Inspector Friedberg—will be in deep shit."

Neither Allman nor Scheer appeared pleased with this arrangement—or they were not happy with the prospect of having to keep one another company while they waited.

"I'm gonna go take a walk," Scheer said.

*That answers that question.*

Vail encouraged Burden and Dixon to take the stairs, and moments later, they were heading into an office with a scripted "SDL" in gold leaf, above the phrase, Empowering your health through sensory vacuum therapy.

"No one's vacuuming *my* senses, thank you very much," Vail said. "I mean, really? Who thinks that shit up?"

Although the building's shell and lobby showed its age poorly, the clinic sported high-end granite counters, sleek stainless steel wall accents, and halogen downlighting. "Apparently," Vail said, "sensory deprivation therapy not only vacuums your senses, but your bank account, too."

"Can I help you?" Walking up to the front counter was a woman in her thirties, with radiant skin and a natural beauty that Vail instantly found unfair.

"Yes," Burden said. He stopped and looked at Vail and Dixon, apparently unaware of where to begin.

"We were told to come here," Dixon said, "by a friend."

"We certainly appreciate referrals. And who might we thank?"

Vail held up her creds. "Special Agent Karen Vail. Look, Miss—"

"Veronica."

"Veronica. We're working a case. And honestly, we can't tell you why we're here. But we need to ask some questions and they may seem a bit odd. Go with it, okay?"

"Are these questions about patients? Because Dr. Tumaco set some very progressive rules many, many years ago about the sensitive nature of doctor-patient confidentiality. He was ahead of his time in many ways. I'm afraid we can't disclose that type of information."

*That name's familiar. Tumaco. Where've I heard it?*

"We don't need patient information," Dixon said. "We just need you to answer some questions." She hesitated, then said, "Did someone tell you to expect us? Or—did anyone leave a message for us?"

Veronica shook her head. "I'm sorry—I don't know what you're talking about."

*Unfortunately, neither do we.* "Tell us about your facility," Vail said. "Actually—tell us about Dr. Tumaco."

"Oh," Veronica said, her face brightening. "One of the pioneers in the field of flotation sensory deprivation therapy. He first realized the benefit of meditation and sensory attenuation about thirty years ago. The pioneer, John Lilly, started the movement in the mid-1950s and did much of the groundbreaking research on the origin of consciousness."

*This isn't helping.* "Okay, yeah," Vail said. "That's great. But I think I may've heard Dr. Tumaco's name before. Any idea why?"

Veronica nodded silently, then took a seat behind the granite desk. She leaned forward and spoke in a low voice, prompting Vail, Burden, and Dixon to move closer to hear.

"Dr. Tumaco was found in one of his flotation tanks. The police believed he'd been murdered."

Vail slammed a hand down on the granite counter. "That's it!" She turned to Dixon and Burden. "One of the old cases Clay gave us. Martin Tumaco. Killed in '95. Strangled with a life preserver." She swung her head back to Veronica. "Right?"

Veronica, her head bowed, nodded without comment.

"But wasn't he found at some other place? Something with 'dream' in the name?"

"The clinic's name was changed when Dr. Tumaco was killed," Veronica said. "People were freaked out about getting back in a flotation tank after someone had been found dead in one. It hurt the business. So Dr. Tumaco's wife changed the name, and she changed the focus of the facility from dream and sleep research to a therapeutic-based referral business."

Dixon gestured with her head for Vail and Burden to join her a few paces out of Veronica's earshot. They huddled in the far end of the waiting room.

"I think we're on the right track," Dixon said. "But—now what? How would the UNSUB know? It's not like we can call him up."

Burden jutted his jaw forward. "That's a great goddamn question. How did he know when we ended up at the bank? Was he watching?"

"Obvious explanation is he was waiting where he wanted us to go, in a high rise, on an apartment roof, in a car—whatever—and when we didn't show in ten, fifteen minutes, he knew we went to the wrong place."

"So what's with the riddle?" Vail asked. "Those intended to heal— Tumaco—may give life—he's a doctor—but drown the truth." She thought a moment. "Was Tumaco involved in a cover-up?"

"Of what?" Burden asked as his phone vibrated. He grabbed it, answered, and listened. "Got it— Yeah, no, that's fine. About what I expected." He shoved it in his pocket. "They can only tell us that those texts that came from Robert's phone are in a two- to three-mile radius. They're putting a trap on the phone, but it's off."

"I doubt the offender'll use that phone again," Dixon said.

"Violence and sleep come under watchful eyes," Vail said. "Now I get it. He meant here, where a man was killed in a flotation tank under watchful eyes."

Burden huffed. "Apparently, no one was watching."

"Wrong," Vail said. "The killer was watching." She turned and walked back to Veronica. "Can you give me one of your cards—and jot down your direct line on the back in case we need to reach you?"

Veronica did as requested—and handed it to Burden as Vail's phone vibrated.

A text.

> this one comes from on high
> the other mission
> where darkness reigns
> seek not the son but the father
> make haste

Vail looked at her partners. "Let's take this outside."

They ran down the stairs to the street. Allman was on the phone, leaning against a tree. Scheer, also on a call, saw them first and trotted over.

"Different cell," Vail said as she thumbed her BlackBerry. "Sending it on to your office for a trace. Probably a throwaway."

Burden nodded at her phone. "The text. Break it down like we did before."

"Another message?" Scheer asked as he approached.

Vail read it to them.

"Mission District," Burden said.

Allman shook his head. "No—it can't be."

"Why not?"

"Read the rest of it. He wrote, the *other* mission."

"Yeah. So what?" Dixon asked. "What other mission is there?"

Scheer looked up. "The Mission—as in the church. San Francisco de Asís. *In* the Mission District."

"We already pissed him off once by getting it wrong," Vail said. "On your brilliant idea. I'd like to avoid a repeat performance, thank you very much."

"How sure are you about this?" Allman asked.

Scheer's lips tightened. He looked at Allman for the first time. "Pretty sure, Clay. Sure enough to risk embarrassing myself in front of you. Again."

Clay threw up both hands—an *I give up* gesture.

"I think it works," Burden said. "I don't see the 'where darkness reigns' part. But I'm not hearing anything better."

"Then let's go," Vail said. "'Make haste.'"

THEY ARRIVED AT THE CHURCH, LOCATED on Dolores Street near Sixteenth. A two-story white adobe structure with four columns dominating its front and a simple cross at the pinnacle of its pointed roof sat beside a tan, ornate dual-spired basilica. Two young pine trees rose from a grass strip in front of the mission.

Burden led the way up the burgundy tile steps of the smaller structure. The interior was long and narrow, with a floor-to-ceiling mural dominating a wall to the right. Pews lined both sides of the room, with a center aisle leading up to the front. A striped, multicolored wood-beamed ceiling ran the entire length of the ground floor.

"Anyone know anything about this place?" Burden asked as they all cleared the wood front doors.

"I think it's one of the original missions," Allman said. "If I remember, Father Junipero Serra officiated here, back in the 1700s."

"That would be 1782, and that's correct. One of only two remaining missions that can say that."

The group turned.

To their right stood a bespectacled, well-coifed man in dark robes, his hands clasped in front of him. "May I help you?"

Burden held up his badge. "Lance Burden, SFPD. And you sure can."

"Then I am at your service," the man said with a slight bow.

"We were sent here by someone…pertaining to a case. Is there anything you can tell us about your facility that might…well…" Burden turned to Dixon and Vail.

"That might involve violence, or murder," Vail said.

Burden brought a hand to his forehead. Apparently, he was uncomfortable with her direct approach.

"No offense intended, sir," Scheer said. "But time is of the essence."

Vail turned slowly. "Thanks. Now keep your trap shut."

The man's eyes moved back and forth between Vail and Scheer, clearly unsure what to make of this tightly wound redhead—and her direct and offensive question. He finally said, "Nothing to my knowledge, Officer."

"Any idea why someone might refer to this as a place where darkness reigns?" Dixon asked.

The man took a step back. "If anything, Miss, this is a place of light. Enlightenment. Fulfillment, and repentance."

"I meant no disrespect. We're just…"

*Fishing. Clueless. Desperate. Pick any of those adjectives. They all fit.*

"…working a case," Dixon continued, "and it's forcing us to ask some uncomfortable questions."

"Holy shit." Vail clapped a hand across her mouth. "Sorry, I didn't mean to say that out loud. Holy—father." *Is that better? Jesus Christ, I don't think so.* "I—uh—I just had a thought," she said to Burden and Dixon. Then, back to the increasingly insulted clergyman: "Did a Father Ralph Finelli ever work here?"

"Finelli…" The man's brow furrowed and he looked off into the distance. He finally shook his head. "I'm nearly certain he has never ministered here. I have a listing of all the priests who have been a part of the mission since its founding—"

"This would be much more recent. Say the last fifty years or so."

"Then the answer would be no."

Vail looked at Burden and Dixon. "You guys want to ask anything?" She then turned to Allman and Scheer, who were a few paces back. "What about you?"

They both shrugged.

"Thank you for your assistance. And please accept my apologies for…well, everything."

They walked outside. "You guys give us a minute?" Dixon said to the journalists.

The men walked off in different directions, down the sidewalk.

Once they were out of earshot, Vail said, "I really thought I was onto something with Father Finelli."

Burden glanced around at the street. People strolled by, turning their heads to take in the historic mission and its ornate neighbor. In a low voice, he said, "So what do we do now? Wait around till he texts us again? I gotta tell you, Karen, this doesn't sit well with me. Pisses me off to have my chain yanked by a goddamn lowlife. Psychopath or not, I think we should tell him to go fuck himself. We should be calling the shots, not him. I mean, what's it gotten us?"

Vail folded her arms across her chest. "Are you done? Because if not, go ahead and get it out of your system." She widened her eyes. "Well?"

"I'm done. For now."

"Good. Because we don't have any other options other than working the case the way you normally would. And we've been doing that. If you think we've been wasting time, go back to Bryant and do your thing. I'm fine with that. I'll play his stupid games until it yields something useful—because I think, ultimately, he's going to give us something we can use. He may already have."

"At the sleep deprivation center? Or the mission?"

"*Sensory* deprivation. And both." Vail nudged Dixon's arm. "What do you think?"

"I don't like getting jerked around either. But I trust your judgment. If you're confident he's going to give us something—or already has—then I'd rather continue. But there are limits. I don't know how much longer Robert has. If he's even still alive. I wish we could communicate with the asshole, somehow get him to talk to us about Robert."

"He's basically made it a one-way conversation. I don't want to be strung along, either. If we don't get some sort of resolution, we'll have Allman and Scheer post an article to their papers' websites. Eventually, the offender may see it. But who knows how often he's checking?"

"Why wait?" Dixon said. "Why not do that now?"

Burden nodded.

"Fine." Vail leaned to the side around Burden and whistled to Allman, then turned and called behind her to Scheer.

"You said he may've already given us something," Burden said. "What are you thinking?"

"To start—"

Vail's BlackBerry buzzed. She made eye contact with her two partners, then pulled it from her belt. "Well. The game's afoot." She looked at Burden. "You want to play? Or ignore it?"

Burden grumbled, but he and Dixon huddled around her phone and read the message:

> 11th & folsom
> that which it contains not
> constricting restricting and single-handedly cold it has got
> see that which its not

Allman and Scheer joined their grouping.

Burden sighed. "Getting more cryptic."

"Let's do what we did before," Vail said. "Parse it, line by line."

"Another message?" Allman asked.

"Another message," Dixon said as she reread it. "I say we get moving toward Eleventh and Folsom, work it through in the car."

"How far?" Vail asked.

"Couple minutes depending on traffic," Allman said. "Less than a mile."

They got into the Ford and Burden took them down Sixteenth Street. "Read it to us," he said.

Vail consulted her BlackBerry. "First line. That which it contains not. Any ideas?"

Dixon leaned forward in her seat. The restraint locked; she sat back, let it tighten, and then pulled it back out. "How about this: whatever it is that we're talking about doesn't hold in, or contain, the object it's supposed to."

Scheer said, "So a fence that's supposed to hold a dog in a yard doesn't do the job. The dog gets out."

"Might be talking about us," Vail said. "We're supposed to contain him, prevent him from killing. But we're not. In which case it'd be talking about him."

Dixon was still struggling with her seatbelt, which again locked on her. "Since this whole thing is all about him, that makes sense."

"Why do you think it's all about him?" Allman asked.

Vail brought her gaze back to the riddle. "That's in the DNA of psychopaths. Everything revolves around them."

"I didn't realize we were talking about a psychopath. You sure?"

"Yes, Clay. I'm sure." She turned around to face him. "And no, you may not print that. We definitely don't want the UNSUB knowing we think he's a psychopath. In fact, none of this goes in anything either of you guys writes unless we read it first. Agreed?"

"A little late to be asking that question," Scheer said.

Vail twisted her body and faced Scheer, who was seated behind Burden. Dixon was the physical buffer between the two journalists. "Don't push us, Scheer. We will push back, and you'll be goddamn sorry. After that texting bullshit you pulled, be glad we're including you in any of this."

"What texting bullshit?" Allman asked, leaning forward to get a look at Scheer.

Scheer ignored Allman's question. "You needed my help, Agent Vail. Let's not forget why I'm here. It's for you people, not for me. What good is it to be riding around with you if I can't write a story about any of it?"

"Next line," Vail said, turning her eyes back to the phone, "is 'constricting restricting and single-handedly cold it has got.'" She shook her head and read it again, placing different emphasis on the latter part of the sentence. It didn't help.

Burden hung a left on Folsom. "He's clearly fixated on constriction and restriction."

"Maybe he's claustrophobic," Dixon said.

"I don't think that's it," Vail said. "Believe me, if he wanted an image for the anxiety of claustrophobia, I can think of a bunch more visceral adjectives."

"But it's not about you," Allman said. "It's about him."

Vail pursed her lips. "Good point. I'll give you that one, Clay."

"Almost there," Burden said, craning his neck to check the street sign.

"What about 'single-handedly cold it has got'?" *Maybe he's talking about the look Scheer's been giving me the past minute or so...*

Burden passed beneath the freeway, which ran perpendicular to Folsom, then gestured at the street sign. "That's Twelfth ahead. Almost there."

"No idea what 'single-handedly cold' is," Dixon said. "But he says it's *gotten that way*, implying it wasn't that way initially."

Vail turned and looked at Dixon. "Really?"

Dixon shrugged. "I gave it a shot."

Vail blew air through her lips. "I've got nothing better. Maybe the location will give us some idea of what he's trying to tell us."

Burden pulled the Taurus into a red zone in front of the Jackson Brewery building and they got out. "He gave us an intersection, which means what we're looking for could be on the four adjacent blocks. Fan out, make a survey of what you see. Meet back here in five."

They did as Burden instructed, taking in their surroundings, walking up each of their assigned streets. A minute passed. Two….three…and shortly thereafter, they began gathering, finding one another in front of an oversize mural of a beer bottle, above which a large bar sign read, "Caliente."

Vail looked at it. *Hot. Is that a comment on us—we're on the right track? Or just a coincidence and it means nothing?*

"Anything interesting?" Burden asked.

Dixon said, "Couple of restaurants. A few bars. Bus stop. People. Car repair shops. Buildings. Mercedes dealership. Graffiti. A homeless guy with a dog. I gave him a dollar."

"Don't forget Urban Cellular," Vail said, "across the street. Unlimited family and friends for fifty bucks a month. And to think I had to come all the way to San Francisco for a deal like that."

Burden gave her an icy look as he said, "Why'd the UNSUB send us here?"

Vail's gaze moved about the immediate vicinity, as if she would suddenly see something she had not seen previously. Nothing stood out. "He brought us to this intersection for a reason. He wants us to see something." *And if we don't figure it out soon…* "Have I ever told you I hate puzzles?"

"I love puzzles," Burden said. "But not when we're getting jerked around by a killer."

"Tough," Vail said. "Put your puzzle hat on, 'cause we got nothing."

"My puzzle hat," Burden repeated. "That's very helpful." He turned his head, scanning the area, as they had all done more than once. Finally, he rested his hands on his hips and shook his head. "Let's try something different. Call out the first thing that comes to mind. Don't think—just say it."

Construction workers. Traffic cop. Taxis. Bars. Storefronts. Asphalt. Mercedes dealership. Cell phone store. Car repair shop.

Vail stopped them. "This isn't helping. You word guys got anything?"

Allman and Scheer asked to see the message again.

Finally, Burden asked, "Anybody's phone shoot video?" They all answered affirmatively. "Okay, then. Take a couple minutes, go back to your street and shoot some footage of things that you see. Go slow so we can make out signs and other details that might be important. In case we need to take another look later."

They walked in opposite directions and started panning when Vail's phone nearly vibrated out of her hands. She fumbled to stop the recording and bring up the message.

> ive given u some latitude
> but youve come up short
> if u got it see u there 1 hr
> if not
> maybe ill give 1 last clue or
> maybe not

Vail felt like slamming her phone into the pavement. Instead, she walked back toward the car, where Dixon was waiting. Vail did not speak; she merely held up the BlackBerry.

Dixon read it, absorbed it, then turned away and leaned her back against the vehicle. "We'll find him, Karen. We'll figure this out."

Burden and Allman joined them, read the message and offered nothing of value.

Burden swore under his breath, then looked off down Folsom. "Where the hell's Scheer?"

Vail lifted her phone to call him—but before it connected, he appeared around the corner.

"We're leaving," Burden said. "I'll drop you both at work on the way back to the station."

"Did you get it?" Scheer asked.

"Did *you*?" Burden asked.

Scheer shook his head. They piled into the Ford and Burden drove off, headed back toward Bryant Street…tired, irritable, and no closer to finding Friedberg than they had been before.

# 54

November 21, 1960

*Alcatraz*

Walton MacNally shuffled into the dining hall in single file behind other cons who lived in C Block and the adjacent B Block. The rectangular room was large—but a fraction of the size of Leavenworth's outsized eating facility.

Barred windows lined both long walls, through which MacNally caught a glimpse of San Francisco city lights across the Bay to his left. The mint and eggshell color scheme he found in his cell must have been a favorite of the Alcatraz interior decorators because this room featured the same design treatment.

Ahead, dominating the hall's front area, was the kitchen, where two inmates, wearing white chef hats and aprons, appeared to be mixing large vats of soup in floor-standing stainless steel kettles. A guard stood watch inside a glass block structure, approximately twenty feet behind the cooks.

John Anglin was in line several men ahead of him, but watching how the other inmates conducted themselves—walking in an orderly fashion and talking in normal or low tones, MacNally resisted the urge to call after him. After seeing Anglin earlier, all he could think about was confronting him about Rucker.

The line worked its way toward a long, stainless steel buffet-style steam table. As MacNally neared, Anglin was at the far end, lifting a roll from a trough. Steam rose from the soup tureen, hot beef, and vegetable platters. MacNally lifted a ladle and began dishing out food.

An officer, arms folded in front of him and standing on the other side of the table, cleared his throat. "You're new."

MacNally looked up. The guard was nearly as young as he was. His tie was tightly knotted and drawn up flush against his buttoned collar. "Arrived on the boat about an hour ago."

He nodded at the food in front of him. "Take all you want. But eat all you take. That's the rule. No waste."

MacNally glanced over at Anglin, who was moving toward a table. "I had a long trip from Kansas—no problem with my appetite today." He smiled, trying to win some points. But the officer turned away to observe the oncoming inmates.

The dining hall was filled with long picnic-style varnished wood tables, accompanied by bench seats made with a thick, steel pipe frame. The furniture, which sat five men on each side, looked pocked and worn.

MacNally quickened his pace to where Anglin and two other men were settling themselves. They were already engaged in an animated discussion.

"J.W.," MacNally said, setting down his tray and not waiting for an invitation.

"Who the fuck are you?" the shorter man to Anglin's left said.

MacNally felt the muscles in his forearms tighten. He looked down. There were knives on the table within reach, but his adversary's fingers were already wrapped around one. "We gonna have a problem?"

Anglin held out a steady hand to calm his acquaintance. "Walt MacNally, this's Frankie. Frank Morris. Frankie," Anglin said, casually motioning with his fork. "Mac and me did time together at Leavenworth. Helped me 'n Clarence with an escape."

Morris, thin lips with dark, wavy hair, gaunt face and serious eyes, bunched his brow and relaxed—ever so slightly—his grip on the knife. "This the guy who started the fight?" he asked with a Louisiana twang. "The diversion?"

Anglin nodded. Morris set the utensil down.

MacNally turned to the man at Anglin's right, who possessed a more youthful, relaxed face, perhaps late twenties. He was not as intense as Morris, but just as slightly built.

"Allen West," the man said, not lifting his eyes from his tray.

"Carnes," another said as he took the seat next to MacNally. "Clarence Carnes." His skin was a shade darker than the others, and he had full lips and a broad nose. Moderately bald, his face had an exotic look to it.

MacNally nodded. "Good to meet you guys. Just got here this afternoon."

The men looked down and went about eating their chow.

MacNally realized they had been engrossed in conversation when he walked over, yet in his presence they had fallen mute. "You don't have to stop talking on my account. You want me to move," MacNally shrugged, "I will."

West leaned in to Anglin. Though he spoke in a low voice and near his ear, MacNally read his lips: "Can we trust him?"

Anglin, blowing on a spoonful of soup, nodded.

"You good at anything?" West asked. "Electrical, plumbing, that kinda shit?"

MacNally lifted a shoulder and pouted his lips. "Worked some construction. Good with my hands. I like to sculpt, build things. And yeah, I know electrical. And heating and ventilation. Some plumbing. I used to be a handyman, so I know a little about a lot." He let his eyes move from man to man in front of him. They all stopped eating and were staring at MacNally.

West suddenly looked down at his plate, swirled his fork, playing with the food, and then glanced around. MacNally figured he was about to tell him something significant, and he was assessing where the nearest officer was. "I been planning a break 'bout a year now. Got lots of ideas. We could use somebody with the things you know. Interested?"

MacNally slid his buttocks forward on the bench. "Hell yeah." He lifted a roll from his plate, then looked up and waited for West to bring his gaze back toward him. "What—when?"

"We're takin' our time," Morris said, his eyes moving from left to right across the room. "Goin' slow. Want to do it right. We've got a lot of shit to plan."

MacNally nodded. "Going slow's a good thing. I made a break myself, after the one we tried with J.W. and Clarence. His brother."

"Don't look like that worked out too good," Morris said.

Rather than responding to Morris's remark, MacNally turned to Anglin, hoping to tactfully broach the subject he had wanted to bring up since the moment he had seen Anglin. "I would've made it if Rucker hadn't fucked me over. He went over the wall, then cut my rope." He realized his fingers had squeezed through the roll, which he had crushed in two. The pieces fell to the plate. "If I ever find that guy, J.W., I'm gonna kill him." He began bouncing his knee, watching Anglin's reaction. He had none; his face was impassive, as if that kind of shit was expected to happen in a penitentiary filled with liars, cheats, thieves, and murderers.

And maybe that was the correct read of the situation. No doubt such a thing was commonplace. But it did not matter. MacNally would exact his revenge... Somehow, somewhere, sometime.

"Did you know he was buddies with Gormack?"

Anglin leaned back. "Fuck no. That the reason—"

"Yeah. He sent me a note."

"Who's Gormack—and Rucker?" Morris asked.

"Nobody important," MacNally said, his eyes riveted to Anglin's.

"You mentioned you did some work with ventilation," West said. "Carnes and I got an idea."

"Oh, yeah?" MacNally said, pulling his gaze over to West. "You three know anything about escaping?"

Carnes and Morris laughed.

"Carnes was involved in the Battle of Alcatraz in '46."

MacNally tilted his head. "Never heard of it."

West grinned. "Legendary shit, m'man."

Carnes waved a hand. "I was nineteen. Sometimes shit happens you can't anticipate, no matter how smart your escape plan is—and this one was well thought out. A key that was supposed to be in the gun gallery wasn't there, and we couldn't get out of the cellhouse. Six of us were involved, but Bernie Coy and Joe Cretzer led the thing. They offed two hacks, shot a bunch of others. Marines came, shelled the place, dropped demolition grenades into C-block." He looked down, stabbed a green bean with his fork, keeping his gaze on the plate. "Coy, Cretzer, and another guy, Hubbard, were killed. Two others were gassed at San Quentin for killing those hacks. I got a second life sentence and six years in Seg." Carnes looked up at MacNally, who was riveted by the story. "But Frankie here's a legend, too."

Morris stuck a small piece of meat in his mouth. "I've escaped from every prison I've ever been at," Morris said, his chewing and molasses-thick drawl making it a bit difficult for MacNally to follow. "You know what the warden's record on me says?" He laughed. "Under 'Occupation,' it says, 'escape artist.' He nodded. "I fuck you not."

"Since you're on The Rock, doesn't look like your record as an escape artist *worked out too good*," MacNally said, mimicking Morris's earlier dig, then flashing a smile to defuse the mocking sarcasm behind the comment.

"I'm better at escaping than I am at robbing banks."

MacNally nodded slowly. At least the man could admit his faults. "What'd you want to know about ventilation?"

"There used to be eight air exhaust blowers," Carnes said, "on top of the cell blocks, above the third tier. They were attached to ducts that vented to the building's roof. We looked at goin' out of 'em during the '46 shootout, but we couldn't get the scaffolding over there. After the hacks retook the cellhouse, most of the blowers were removed and they sealed off the vent openings with bars and concrete."

Carnes seemed to be articulate and thoughtful. MacNally found himself listening carefully to the man's soft-spoken delivery.

"But," West said, "I heard one of 'em's still there."

"Frankie and I work in the library," Carnes said. "I bring books around on a cart to all the guys here. It gives me a chance to look around, observe. And looks to me like that one vent is the one that's over the back side of B block."

"I just moved cells," Morris said. "To B-356. Right under the vent."

"This vent," West said. "It's round and pretty damn wide. There's a blower attached to it, with ductwork. If we can get that ductwork off, I bet it'd lead us right up to the roof. And once we get on the roof, it's a matter of getting off the island. The water presents other problems, but we're working on that."

MacNally said, "Ductwork's fastened with sheet metal screws. A wrench or screwdriver would do the trick. But—and this might seem like an obvious question, but how do we get out of our cells?" MacNally suddenly felt the presence of someone over his left shoulder. He shifted the topic. "What do you guys like to do out in the rec yard?"

"Baseball," Morris said. "Sometimes I just like to enjoy the sun, when it's out. And smell the sea breeze." He kept his head straight, on MacNally, but his eyes followed the officer as the man continued past them and then hung a left, toward the other side of the room.

"Those cross-hatched grilles under the sink?" Anglin asked. "You seen 'em?"

MacNally nodded. He had seen them—recessed, rectangular, eight-by-ten-inch grates that allowed air to passively flow from an area behind the cells into the cell block.

"We startin' to poke around at that there cement," Anglin said. "Frankie thinks we can dig 'em out, then crawl through."

"Through? Into what?" MacNally asked.

"Take a look when you're walking back to your cell," West said. "Between the cell blocks, between, say, B and C, there's a metal door. Behind it, a utility corridor. Water and waste pipes run through there. If you look up, it's a clear shot to the top tier of the cell block."

"A ventilation duct has to vent to the roof," MacNally said.

"Right," West said. "So if we dig out those grilles in our cells, we just crawl through the opening into the utility corridor, then use the piping as a ladder to climb up to the roof."

"How are we gonna dig out the cement around those grilles?"

"Inmate plumbers," Morris said. "Con I know, Billy Boggs, helps out fixing busted pipes. The plumbing was put in by the army back in

1900 or some shit like that. The sea water that goes through 'em rots 'em out. And when they burst, they flood that utility area and eat away the concrete walls. Billy says the walls look pretty bad."

"And those walls," West said, "are the walls of our cells."

MacNally absorbed what he was being told. Before he committed to the plan, he wanted to be sure he had a decent chance of making it out. The water—those sharks—was another problem.

But there were more immediate logistical concerns. "How can you dig out the cement without the guards knowing about it? They're pretty strict where you can put shit in your cells. You can't block that grille. They'll get suspicious."

"One of the oldest inmate tricks in the book," West said. "Wet some toilet paper, mix it with soap flakes, then force it into the holes you're making."

"Get a job," Morris said to MacNally. "J.W. works in clothing. I'm in the brush shop in Industries. Do what you're told and don't cause any trouble, they'll give you work. Take it. Best way to get the tools and supplies we need. They got everything in there: wire, electrical tape, varnishes, nuts, bolts, machines… Some of us are already gettin' stuff together."

MacNally nodded.

"Like I said," West added, looking across the room at an officer, who was approaching. "I been workin' on this a long, long time."

"What about the water?" MacNally asked. "The sharks?"

Carnes chuckled. "No sharks in the water, MacNally. They tell you that to keep your ass on the island."

"I just got the new *Popular Mechanics*," West said, then waited for the guard to pass. Teaches you how to make blow-up rubber geese. Works for life preservers and rafts, too."

MacNally shook his head. "You read something about making rubber duckies and you think you can build a raft out of that? One that'll hold up in that choppy ocean?"

"Trust me on that," Anglin said. "Clarence and me, we grew up swimming and rafting in Lake Michigan. The stuff they say in that mag, it'll work."

"We need raincoats," Morris said. "We can get 'em from Clothing, where J.W. works. But we need a lot of 'em. Maybe four dozen, way I figure. Maybe more. They're Navy jobs made of rubber backed canvas. We can cut 'em up and glue the pieces together with rubber cement, then sew the seams on the machines we use to make gloves in Industries." He winked. "Paddles we can make in the furniture shop. Smaller pieces, attached with nuts and bolts. Most everything we need's there in the shops. Biggest problem's smuggling the stuff out of Industries."

"A little bit at a time, under your shirts and jackets," MacNally said.

"As long as there's no metal," Anglin said. "Snitch box'll get us. Metal detector. You'll see. Gotta pass through it on the way out of Industries."

"We'll have to figure that out," West said. "Big thing is getting up to that vent blower."

The whistle blew: dinner over. MacNally had hardly eaten. He shoved some meat and vegetables into his mouth, then did his best to clean his plate. If there was one thing he took from this discussion, it was that he had to keep his nose clean and avoid segregation.

And he needed a job. But unlike his problems obtaining and holding one in the outside world, finding a position here at Alcatraz presented a much easier challenge.

# 55

Burden and Dixon took the elevator up to Homicide, while Vail said she wanted some time to think on her own and that she would meet them there in a few minutes.

Robby had not called back. More significantly, neither had Mike Hartman—so Vail called him, again, and left another message: "Very important— Call me soon as you get this. It involves the Bay Killer."

As she ascended the stairs, she tried the main switchboard. After being placed on hold, the operator told her that Hartman had been out of town, but that he was due to return tonight. Vail asked for his cell, and then left a message there as well.

She stood in the hallway, a shoulder against the wall, lost in thought, when the doors to Homicide swung open.

Dixon's head appeared and her eyes found Vail. "We're ordering in pizza. Good?"

Vail pushed off the marble facing. "Whatever. I'm exhausted, pissed, and frustrated. My mind's not on food." She followed Dixon back into the room, and then sat down hard in a seat by their worktable and murder board.

Burden grabbed his chair and sat down backwards on it, then rolled it over to Vail and Dixon. "You've said that playing the media's important. Back at the mission we talked about putting something out there. What do you think?"

Vail rubbed both eyes. "Not sure." She exhaled long and hard. "The offender's been in communication with us. But today he's been

305

dictating the terms of the conversation—basically, he talks, we listen and run all over the goddamn city like his puppets. A good psychopath is a puppeteer—he's skilled at pulling the strings of others because he's got exceptional manipulation skills. He uses them to dominate and exercise control. And all day, we've been dominated and controlled." She thought a moment. "I'm starting to doubt whether I'm gonna be of any value to this investigation. It's not like I've made a difference up to this point."

Burden took a moment to examine her face. Then he laughed. "I was waiting for some joke. Or maybe that was the joke. Because you've been real valuable so far. We know who we're dealing with, what type of guy to look for. You're an expert on psychopaths, Karen. You've studied them, you've researched them, you've sat across the table from—what, dozens? Right now, you're one of the most important forensic tools we've got."

"Never thought of myself as a tool."

"C'mon," Dixon said. "Sometimes you're a hammer. Other times an ice pick."

"Lovely image. Thanks, Roxx."

Burden stood up. "Enough feeling sorry for ourselves. We don't have time for that shit. We've got a man down, and we need to go after this fucker like a freaking tornado. I don't know about you, but I've had enough of his crap." He tossed the case files on the worktable. "I spoke to my lieutenant on the way up here. Overtime's authorized and he's working on getting us some extra manpower, on top of those interns."

"Has he issued a statement about Robert?" Vail asked.

"No. He felt it was better to wait before we release the fact that the killer's got one of our inspectors. He thought it'd spark a wave of fear."

Vail raised her brow and nodded. *If we can't protect ourselves, how can we protect the people?*

"So back to the nuts and bolts. Investigation 101." Burden took a marker and uncapped it.

Vail took a deep breath and mentally slapped herself. When someone close to her went missing, there was no time to rest, no time for self-doubt. She rose from her chair and literally rolled up her sleeves. Time to get back to work.

FOUR HOURS AND FIFTY-ONE minutes passed. Vail repeatedly kept looking at Friedberg's empty chair and abandoned desk, files piled on the right edge, a notepad front and center. And a thick book, *Complete History of San Francisco Bakeries,* on the left. *A history of bakeries?*

They still had no knowledge of Friedberg's whereabouts and no way of directly communicating with the Bay Killer, unless he texted them. And that was the way he wanted it. He wanted—demanded—control, and thus far had been successful in attaining all that he desired.

The tasks of many of the inspectors in the department had been diverted and a few were now working Friedberg as a missing persons case, engaged in various tasks along those lines. But they all knew it was much more than that. Knowing, and being able to do something about it, comprised an insurmountable gap.

The Homicide room was a flurry of people, phones and cells ringing, keyboards clicking and laser printers whirling. The law school, criminal justice, and sociology interns were in another room with the same information, making follow-up phone calls on the older cases; they were due to have a group conference in an hour to get briefed on any newly discovered information and to assist in integrating the material into their existing database of knowledge.

The latter text messages had originated from disposable cell phones purchased with cash at two different Bay Area electronics stores during the past four months. Even if they had surveillance cameras focused on their registers—which they did not—the video would have been written over many times since.

Hartman had still not called, but he was at least closer to returning to the office. Even if he hadn't gotten the voicemail she had left on his cell, he would soon retrieve the ones she had left on his work phone. She decided that, grudge or not, he would return her calls because of their volume—and urgency.

Vail rose and looked at the murder board. All the victims' names and locations, causes of death, occupations, photos, and key crime scene attributes stared back at her. It was talking to her, a constant chatter—but it was as if it was written in a foreign language. Perhaps there would be one new fact someone would discover that would pop the lid off the case. But she had the sense that all they needed to know was on the board in front of her.

Vail called over to Dixon. "You in the middle of something?"

Dixon pushed back from her makeshift desk. "What do you have in mind?"

"Let's go take a look at the video we captured. Maybe something will hit us."

They had asked Allman and Scheer to send the videos they had taken using the large file email service, TransferBigFiles.com. The photo lab informed them the footage was now available to view. Hoping to find something to stimulate her brain, the recordings represented an unexplored avenue.

They settled themselves in front of a monitor and opened the first file—Allman's video. Cityscape images scrolled by. They watched it straight through, then started it again. Vail yawned and reached for the coffee cup she had brought with her from Homicide.

"What do we see?" Dixon asked. "Restaurant. A bar." The scene panned slowly. "Another bar. A cell phone store—and another bar."

Vail took a drink and leaned forward. "Two auto body shops. Bus stop."

The sixty-second video ended and Dixon opened her own file. Repeating the process, they first watched it in its entirety, absorbing it all before calling out their observations.

As Vail sat there, deep in thought, her phone vibrated. She jumped—startling Dixon, as well. The number brought relief—and a slight lift to the corners of her lips. "Keep going with this. I'll be right back." She pushed through the door into the hallway, then answered the call. "Hey."

"Hey yourself," Robby said. "Sorry it took me so long to get back to you. That stakeout we were on turned into—"

"That's okay," Vail said. "It's fine. No big deal."

"You sound...stressed, for a change. Everything okay?"

Vail closed her eyes and took a breath. "I needed a favor and you're the only one I can trust. I had to find out where an old partner was assigned."

"This may sound like a really, really dumb question. But you're an FBI agent. All you needed to do is—"

"First of all," Vail said, "that's not a question. But you're right. It's dumb. I could've picked up the goddamn phone and made that call myself."

"You're cursing. And you're definitely stressed out. This isn't good, is it?"

"No."

"So what's the deal? Why didn't you want to make that call?"

"Robby. This isn't helping." *Maybe this wasn't such a good idea. Talking about this is difficult enough. But over the phone...*

"Sorry. I'm— I've only got a few minutes 'cause I'm still on that case and—"

The door opened and Dixon poked her head out. "You coming?"

Vail twisted the phone away from her mouth. "I'll be there in a minute."

The door closed and Vail turned her attention back to Robby.

"It's not earth-shattering. It's—it's something I'd much rather tell you in person, not over a phone. But—"

"Yeah," Robby said, his voice muffled. "I'll be right there. Put him in a room. Give me a minute." Then, back into the phone: "Karen. I don't mean to be short. But get to the point. What do you need help with?"

*Shit. I can't bare my soul and summarize this under pressure. If it would make a difference in the case, I'd do it. But it won't.* "It goes back to when I was a field agent in New York. But it's a long story. It'll have to wait."

"You sure? Seems that it—whatever it is—is really bothering you. I can probably break away in a couple hours. Will that work? Are you in danger?"

"There's really nothing you can do. I just wanted to talk things through. Besides, if the offender wanted to kill me, he could've done it already."

"Jesus Christ, Karen. I definitely don't like the sound of that. If your safety is—"

"Let's not do this," Vail said, pinching her forehead with two fingers. "I can take care of myself, you know that. Don't worry about it."

"Don't worry about it?"

"I love you, Robby. I promise I'll be okay."

"Love you, too. But if I can help in any way, you call me. I'll get someone to cover for me or—I'll work something out."

"You just started with DEA. I'm not going to jeopardize your job. I'll be fine. Really. I'll talk to you soon."

She ended the call, then wondered what gave her the confidence to guarantee that all would be okay. *Who am I fooling?*

Vail pushed back into the room and sat down beside Dixon in front of the screen, where urban scenes continued to roll by.

"Everything okay?" Dixon asked, keeping her gaze on the video.

"Yeah." *No.* Though she knew the only person who could help her was Mike Hartman, she had desperately wanted to share the story with Dixon. But Vail was no longer in the mood to discuss it because it would require an explanation that she did not feel like getting into. She would be talking with Hartman soon enough. Then, if it turned out to be significant, she would brief everyone on the task force. Maybe that would bring them the break they had been looking for. Or maybe not.

The door swung open and Burden stuck his head in. "Pizza's here—and we're almost ready for the meeting."

Dixon thanked him, then pressed Pause and the image froze. Vail almost screamed at the monitor. *What the hell am I missing?*

# 56

July 19, 1961

*Alcatraz*

Walton MacNally marked off the days on loose-leaf sheets stored in a binder he kept in his cell, beside his now dog-eared picture of Henry. He had been told the salt air would eventually ruin the photo, but it's the only one he had. And if their plan was successful, he would hopefully not be in his cell long enough for the corrosive environment to take its toll. Sitting beside his son on a dock, fishing, or shooting hoops, or fielding grounders... Was that too much to ask? Had the crimes he committed been so heinous that they needed to lock him away for decades? Prior to going to prison, he had never harmed anyone.

Just money. He just took money. And that wasn't even his fault, not really.

Or was it? Was Voorhees right, that life was about choices, and he had made the wrong ones? Choices that led him to this point in time, in a penal colony locked away on an island in the middle of an ocean, living among the worst of the worst.

He had already been told about those who had called The Rock home before him—the likes of serial rapists, killers, mobsters. And then there were others like him, armed robbers and bank heist offenders. Kidnappers. Psychopaths and sociopaths.

This was not the life he had envisioned when the idea of stealing money from Township Community Savings came to him. It was, in effect, a life of imprisonment borne from a need to provide food and shelter for his son.

But he could almost put the past couple of years behind him if he broke out of here. *When* he broke out.

He looked up from his reverie, standing behind his bars, waiting for the count to be finished so he could grab breakfast with Morris, Anglin, and Carnes. Anglin's brother, Clarence, had arrived on The Rock a few months ago with instructions that he not cell with his brother. At least, that's what Clarence said he overheard the officer telling the marshal during the handoff at the airport in Kansas City.

Thing was, despite Alcatraz's stringent rules, well-behaving inmates were largely given the freedom to choose where they wanted to live. With somewhere around seventy-five cells unoccupied at any one time at the penitentiary, it was common for convicts to move around from time to time—often as friendships and alliances developed.

But an apparent breakdown in communication on the part of institution leadership led to Anglin taking a cell adjacent to his brother's.

That fact facilitated the Anglins' drilling out their ventilation grilles with greater ease as they were able to hand tools from one to the other. While one worked, the other maintained a lookout with the assistance of foil fastened to a stick, serving as an offset mirror that could be inserted through the bars as an early warning system against advancing officers, whose crepe-soled shoes concealed their approach.

During the past three months, the men had been honing the details of their plan, gathering materials and assembling their tools. While Carnes decided to drop out of the group due to doubts they would be successful, the others became increasingly convinced they could pull it off.

MacNally requested a job in the glove factory, which gave him access to the industrial sewing machines they were going to need for constructing the life preservers and rafts. Although he had thought the *Popular Mechanics* "rubber geese" article was mere folly, when he saw the magazine and read the instructions, he realized that its method of vulcanizing the rubber, by heating it, could easily be applied to a much larger flotation device.

As it turned out, Morris's estimate of fifty rubber-backed rain garments was on the mark. They had sufficient time to obtain them, if they each participated. A general population inmate showered twice weekly; afterwards, they were handed freshly laundered clothing, towels, and bedsheets. Anglin, working in the clothing room, would slip each of the men two raincoats, which they would take back to their cell.

They also arranged for other prisoners to assist. Because of the seagull population on the island, cons often wore their rainwear to the rec yard as protection against falling bird poop. Their conspirators would wear their extra coat when they went outside, peel off the smuggled one and hand it over to Morris, West, MacNally, or the Anglins, who would put it on over their own.

For all their ingenious planning, they were presented with a daunting challenge that stumped them for a time: where to stash their wares while they awaited either assembly or implementation. West came up with a solution: he had heard that the officers were talking about painting the cellhouse—and he knew that A-Block, a remnant from Alcatraz's history as a Civil War fort and military detention facility, was used primarily for storage because its flat bars had never been replaced with the hardened tool-proof steel rods that now adorned the B-, C-, and D-block cells. Squirreling away their ill-gotten possessions under a paint tarp in A-Block would be ideal cover.

West fabricated a story of having once painted houses for a builder, and thus he knew his way around with a brush and roller. He would be willing to take on the job of recoating the entire cellhouse and kitchen areas. From the warden's perspective, the man who had been a pain in the ass to the staff since his arrival three years ago was asking for an opportunity to do something productive—a long-term task that the captain of the guards outwardly joked might keep him out of trouble.

MacNally pointed out that should West be given the job painting the cellhouse, not only would it provide them clandestine storage space, but it would give them access to the mint-colored paint they needed for wall touch-up each night to conceal the holes they were making around their ventilation grilles.

But carving holes in the cement was tedious work that required them to work after lights out for hours at a time, always exercising care not to drop their tools—heavy-gauge steel spoons they had smuggled out of the dining hall. With few exceptions, because inmates were prevented from having metal objects in their possession, the signature clank of metal on concrete in a prison facility stood out like a gunshot in a kindergarten class.

Now, as MacNally lined up with the rest of the workforce in the recreation yard, he felt the morning mist from a dense fog prickling his cheeks. It made him feel alive. The whistle blew and the men began moving through the steel door that swung open in the middle of the tall cement wall. From that vantage point, as he looked down the steep set of dozens of concrete stairs, he saw the trail of workers headed to the Industries entrance directly below him.

To the far right, beyond that structure, stood the old three-story Model Industries that housed all the prison's industrial infrastructure until 1940, when it was deemed an escape risk after a number of cons had gotten out of the building and made their way to the adjacent water's edge. Since the new factory had opened, the former facility remained vacant, though it served as the support base for the Model Tower, a guard lookout and catwalk that provided officers with a birds-eye view of that side of the island.

Ahead of MacNally, for those inmates who dared look, was the Golden Gate Bridge, a majestic span that reached from the city to his left across the Bay, to the toney community of Marin on his right. Each time the prisoners left the rec yard for their work detail, the postcard-perfect view of the city and bridge served as a powerful reminder of a vibrant life they were missing.

MacNally walked through Industries' second story doors and onto the shop floor. It was densely packed, with endless rows of machines and work tables, where inmates manufactured various products in the glove, brush, and tailor shops, and the furniture and wood-working factories.

Circular columns rose regularly across the floor, and tall sectional windows along the left wall brought a gray luminosity into the building. Pipes and wire conduits crisscrossed the ceiling, hanging down alongside single-bulb light fixtures that supplied readily available electrical outlets for the trade-specific machines such as drill presses, saws, specialized cutting tools, routers, and sanders.

Officers stood watch throughout the expansive, rectangular interior. Along the right wall, a guard's catwalk stretched the length of the building, patrolled by men with Winchester rifles slung over their shoulders and tear-gas guns at the ready.

MacNally took his place at the assigned station, where a long, thick bobbin of heavy gauge thread sat to his right, already spooled into the machinery, just as he had left it yesterday. He began the task of slicing the raw material canvas and leather sections that would then be cut into templates and sewn into gloves.

As MacNally reached into the bin to his left, he saw a blur coming at him out of the extreme periphery of his vision. He instinctively flinched and curled away as something razor sharp sliced into his side. He was body slammed toward the cold cement floor, but his hip struck the worktop on his way down, flipping him onto his back and spilling his metal glove-making tools all around him.

That's when he saw Harlan Rucker bringing up a glistening knife, about to plunge it into his chest.

"FUCK YOU!" RUCKER YELLED as he arced his weapon through the air.

MacNally kicked up his knee, catching Rucker's forearm and deflecting the blow. He slapped at the floor with his feet, trying to get up, or get away—but his leather soles kept slipping on the slick cement.

MacNally yelled, then flailed his left hand along his side, trying to grab something—anything—to defend himself. But his palm brushed clumsily against round tools, scattering them from his reach.

Rucker again jabbed the knife toward him, but MacNally twisted away and it struck the hard concrete floor. The impact sent the weapon skittering out of Rucker's hand. He dove sideways to gather it up, giving MacNally room to move.

Off to his right—a cold metal rod. He wrapped his fingers around it and whipped it toward Rucker.

The clunk of steel-on-steel reverberated throughout the room as Rucker's knife flew from his hand.

Rucker yelped, his hand paralyzed, likely fractured.

In the distance, shouts echoed from guards.

Again, MacNally swung his rod—

*violently*

*hard and*

*fast*

Then a thud—metal against bone.

And Rucker went down.

MacNally got to his knees and brought his weapon back—winding up for a full swing—then slammed it against the asshole's shoulder, then his cheek, then his nose, and then—

—someone grabbed MacNally's arm, driving him backwards and pinning him to the ground.

A guard? Or one of Rucker's lieutenants?

MacNally swung his head around and saw a fist blurring toward him. Before he could react, the punch landed on his right cheek and whipped his neck around.

MacNally struck out—a wild backhand with the metal bar—and landed a blow across the man's back. He stiffened, as if he'd lost his breath—and swung again, striking him across the buttocks—

"MacNally! Lindahl," yelled a voice from behind him somewhere.

Whistles blew, footsteps.

"Drop it! Drop your weapon!"

MacNally did not realize he was still holding the rod. He was hyperventilating, eyes wide, chest heaving, heart pounding in his ears.

A hand pried angrily at his fingers, and he released his grip. Two officers yanked him onto his stomach, then fastened handcuffs around his wrists.

"Rucker. He started it," MacNally said as they pulled him to his feet.

"You'll have a chance to tell your story," one of them said. "After we get you to the hospital."

It was then that MacNally felt the pain in his side, where his cleanly sliced blood-soaked denim shirt was adhering to his skin.

Rucker lay unconscious on the floor, blood oozing from his nose and a deep gash on his forehead. Lindahl, his buddy, was on his knees, writhing in pain as another set of officers gathered him up and snapped handcuffs around his wrists.

Dozens of nearby inmates appeared to be looking at MacNally with newfound respect—and fear.

"Everyone back to work," an officer called out.

As they led MacNally away, a man in a white medical coat with a black leather doctor's bag in hand was being ushered through the crowd of inmates.

"Watch it, clear aside," his escort, another uniformed guard, said. The two men huddled on the ground alongside Rucker.

"When did he get transferred here?" MacNally asked, his demeanor calmer, the adrenaline clearing from his system.

"Who?"

"Harlan Rucker. He escaped from Leavenworth."

"Transferred over directly into the Treatment Unit. Got out about a week ago."

Segregation. Apparently, either the US Marshals Service, FBI, or local police caught him at some point after he left MacNally at the bottom of the forty-foot Leavenworth wall. "You saw him attack me, right?" MacNally asked.

"Looks like you're lucky to be alive," the guard said. "That's all I'd be thinking about right now."

MacNally knew that to be untrue. He now had to worry that Rucker or his cohorts would find him again, at a time, and a place, when he least expected it.

MACNALLY WAS TAKEN UP TO the hospital through a staircase originating just inside the dining hall. He climbed the steps slowly, as it felt as if each flexion of his hip separated the wound's margins, causing more blood to seep out.

He was led to a large room outfitted like so many others in the institution: barred windows. Mint paint. Highly polished concrete floor. This, however, was an operating or trauma suite.

He lay down on an articulating metal table, where a massive track-mounted light fixture hovered above him. Stainless steel cabinets, stocked with medical supplies, boxes of gauze and bottles of saline solution, stood against the walls.

Within ten minutes, MacNally's wound was sutured with a dozen stitches. He was given penicillin and released to the officers, who had remained at his side. MacNally asked to be returned to his post in the glove shop, because he did not want to risk losing his job and he figured it might score points with the officer in charge: most cons, after an incident like that, would consider it an excuse to return to their cells and skip the rest of the workday.

Instead, he was placed in his cell pending an administrative hearing, which was expedited and held two hours later in A-Block. At a consular table pushed close to the cellhouse wall and facing the row of Civil War-era military cells, MacNally sat before Associate Warden Dollison, Industries Lieutenant Carson Eldridge, and two other officers. A brief discussion ensued during which charges of fighting and possession of a weapon were proffered. After listening to Eldridge's testimony, followed by one of the other guards, and then by MacNally's, Dollison nodded and held out a hand.

"I'm convinced that this altercation was brought on by Inmate Rucker and that you, Mr. MacNally, were an innocent bystander, attempting to defend yourself."

"Yes, sir," MacNally said.

"Your work record has been exemplary and you have been, for all intents, a model inmate. It's my ruling that you be spared time in the Treatment Unit. You may return to your job in Industries."

MacNally thanked Dollison, once again feeling as if he had been dealt with more than fairly. Often, a prisoner involved in a fight was automatically sent to segregation, as the facts almost did not matter. In reflection, he felt fortunate to have found both Voorhees at Leavenworth and now Dollison on Alcatraz. Reasonable and just treatment at a penitentiary was something MacNally had not expected.

When the dinner whistle sounded and they convened in the dining hall, MacNally recounted to his planning crew what had happened. Anglin claimed not to have known that Rucker was now at The Rock, and admitted the man had a proclivity toward seeking revenge. MacNally had wondered how much Anglin really knew about Rucker when he vouched for him back at Leavenworth. Was Anglin in on the setup to have him get caught?

Could Anglin be trusted now?

"Are we done with this Rucker thing?" West asked. He was squirming on his bench, leaning forward as if he had important news to share.

"What's the deal?" Morris asked West. "You look like you're gonna jump out of your pants."

"I got it," West said. "The job, painting the cellhouse. I start tomorrow. And that means our tickets out of here have been issued and punched. Now we just gotta do what we need to do, and be smart about it. If all goes right, we could be outta here in a few months."

MacNally gazed off at the far wall and thought again about Henry. He could deal with a few more months on Devil's Island with the Harlan Ruckers of the world if it meant he'd be getting out. He leaned forward, rejoined the conversation, and helped map out the details of what needed to be done next.

# 57

Vail tore off a bite of pizza, which was slathered with grilled onions and roasted tomatoes. But she was staring at the murder board, and did not taste any of it. The way this case was going, she was beginning to feel that she had bitten off more than she could chew. And it had nothing to do with what was in her mouth.

The photos and notes on the murder board dominated her thoughts. Along the left side, Burden had written pertinent key words: odd-shaped brass keys; flotation tanks; sensory deprivation; orientation of the bodies—facing the Bay; the numbers scrawled on the victims' foreheads; the Cliff House tunnel; bars; retail stores; Mercedes dealership; cell phone shop; Mission San Francisco de Asís; printouts of the text "clues" the offender had sent them. And so on.

Dixon was clicking through the crime scene photos on her laptop, zooming in on some, standing back and evaluating others from a distance. "I wonder if it's not necessarily the Bay, but the direction the vic was facing," she said. "Or the street. Burden. I wasn't at the Harlan Rucker crime scene. Which way was his body facing? Leavenworth?"

"Leavenworth's in Kansas," Vail said. "So that'd be east of—"

"No—no. I mean Leavenworth the street. Look." Dixon pointed to the photo on her screen, which was zoomed 50 percent. "He was found at the intersection of Leavenworth and Bay Streets."

Vail leaned closer to the picture. *Wait a minute.* "There's a Leavenworth Street in San Francisco?"

"Yeah." Burden pulled open the case file, then ran a finger across one of the pages. "That's right—Leavenworth and Bay."

They were quiet a moment. Then Vail said, "The Bay Killer leaves a vic at the intersection of Leavenworth and Bay. All his vics, except one, faced the Bay. There's something here."

Burden said, "Yeah. That is a bit weird." He rose and stood in front of the board, examining the posted city map.

"Not all the vics were found facing the bay," Vail asked. "Just the men."

"Except for one," Dixon said. "Russell Ilg. He was facing the end of a long tunnel carved out of the rock."

"One of you called it a hole," Vail said to Burden. "Right?"

"A hole in the rock, yeah. That's what it looked like when we were—"

"The hole," Vail said. "That's what segregation's called in prisons."

They were quiet as they processed that thought. *This is it. I can feel it. C'mon. Look. What are we missing?*

Burden looked at the board, then pointed. "Tumaco's place—SDL. Sensory Deprivation Lab. Think about it. Those flotation tanks. What is sensory deprivation?"

"Isolation," Vail said. She rose from her seat. "Isolation. Segregation. The hole. Leavenworth."

"Leavenworth's a key to this killer," Dixon said.

"Let's get a list of inmates," Burden said, "who did time at the penitentiary for—what? The past fifteen, twenty years?"

"I'd go farther back," Vail said. "These are all elderly vics and if they have a tie to the offender, he could be an older UNSUB. Go back…five decades; start with 1960—no, make it 1950 so we don't miss anyone."

"I'll get someone on that," Burden said as he pulled his phone.

"Can an older guy commit these murders?" Dixon asked. "Does that fit your profile?"

Vail turned to face the board. "In terms of the female vics, an older offender can easily incapacitate them using his intellect. Even more so if he knew them. It may be enough to keep them from freaking out when they made eye contact. There are a lot of ways to gain control over someone. A gun, a knife, a stun wand. Once he's got control, yes, very possible. As to the male vics, it'd require the UNSUB to be a fit older man. And remember, he used a rope for leverage. And the two that required a rope were slight, small men."

"So it's physically possible," Dixon said.

Burden had hung up and was listening to Vail's analysis. "What about your profile?"

"I would not have pegged this on an older offender. But that's why behavioral analysis is but one tool in the forensic kit. If he's disguised it well, I could've missed it."

"Knowing that, let's take a fresh look at these photos," Dixon said.

Burden was staring at the murder board. A few moments later, he said, "Those numbers on their forehead." He turned back to his PC and started clicking his mouse. "I may have something."

"We have background sheets on our vics?" Dixon asked as Vail moved closer to the board to examine Rex Jackson's photos.

Burden was now pounding the keys. "Robert was working on that. He had some stuff assembled, nothing detailed."

"Let's be smarter about this," Vail said. "Instead of trolling thousands or tens of thousands of Leavenworth inmates, let's take a shortcut. Any of our victims do time at Leavenworth?"

Dixon turned to Vail. "You mean, like inmates?"

Vail thought a moment. *It doesn't have to be inmates. Not inmates. Guards.* "Anything. Inmates, guards. Especially guards. People in positions of power."

"I'm sure Bureau of Prisons can get us that info, but we can't wait till tomorrow. I'll see what I can find online. Hopefully there's a publicly available database." He opened a new tab in the browser, then clicked his mouse.

"Those funky brass keys," Vail said. "Let's see if keys like that were used on Leavenworth during that same time frame. But how the hell are we gonna find that out?"

"We need an archivist," Dixon said. "Or a historian who specializes in US penitentiaries."

"I'll give a shout to the guys in the other room, in case they—or the interns—know of a way to find someone at this time of night." Burden lifted his phone and made the call.

"How does this get us closer to finding Friedberg?" Vail asked.

"Don't know yet," Dixon said, preoccupied. But she then pointed at the text message hanging on the board. "Folsom Street. One of those clues the offender texted us. He sent us to Folsom. Folsom's a state prison."

*Prisons. Segregation.* "There were, what, three bars at that intersection on Folsom? And what else was there? A cell phone store. Bars and cells."

Burden hung up. "I heard what you said—bars, cells, Leavenworth, Folsom. What if we're wasting our time? It might not be Leavenworth."

"I don't think it is. Right idea, wrong prison. We're in San Francisco." Vail rose and stood in front of one of the photos. "What's that in the middle of the Bay?" She stabbed at a spot on the picture with a finger. "We kept thinking the vics were facing the Bay. But that's not it."

Burden's phone rang. Keeping his eyes riveted to the murder board, he reached for the receiver, then turned back to face his screen. "You're shitting me." He twisted his mouth, said, "Thanks," then hung up.

His eyes shot over to Vail. "SFPD dispatch just got a call from a security guard. Guy found a DB."

"A security guard?" Dixon asked. "Where?"

Burden swallowed hard. "Alcatraz."

# 58

June 10, 1962

*Alcatraz*

Walton MacNally stood at the bars as the correctional officer moved along the B-Block cell fronts, doing his morning count. MacNally was hoping this would be the last one he would have to endure, as all the pieces were in place and now it was a matter of days—today, tomorrow—it was a function of when they could break through the blower vent above B-block.

Once West had completed painting all the individual cells, he informed the cellhouse duty officer that he needed scaffolding to reach the expansive ceiling, which had begun peeling in the caustic sea air. Shortly thereafter, West was climbing the metal framework, which gave him an ideal look at the area above the third tier of the institution—and the ceiling above B-block, in particular. It was a gated, locked area that would require an officer to provide admittance each day. But once he scouted the mechanism in person, West described to MacNally the blower and attached ductwork.

MacNally then set out to secure the tools they would need to disassemble the pieces—which would give them access to the metal tunnel that led to the roof. It was a process that demanded patience and extreme care. One inmate known to trip the metal detector due to a plate in his skull was often used as a conduit to pass through small tools and hardware that would've otherwise set the snitch box in a tizzy. Over a period that spanned eleven months, piece by piece, they secured their stash.

Finally, with everything falling into place, West explained in March that in order to work atop the cellblock in the evenings, he would need to convince the officer in charge that it was necessary to hang tarps along the interior periphery of the caged area.

None of them thought that was possible—but somehow, the credibility West had built during the past year of providing trouble-free, quality, and dependable craftsmanship while painting the cellhouse won him the benefit of any doubt the penitentiary leadership may—and should— have had. The tarps were permitted and the men got to work.

Their efforts were assisted by Alcatraz's music hour, a loosening of the once-stringent rules implemented by prior wardens charged with running the nation's toughest federal penitentiary. Playing an instrument thus became a popular pastime on The Rock, with inmates of all skill levels taking up the challenge of making music. Some of it was downright awful—and for those who were good musicians, it did not matter—dozens of men simultaneously playing different songs on wind and string instruments in a cement-walled structure blended the good and bad into an echoing disharmony of cacophonous noise.

But for Morris, the Anglins, and MacNally working on top of the cell block with tools, prying, screwing, at times banging—that noise was like a world-class symphony; it was, in a sense, music to their ears.

By now, MacNally, Morris, and the Anglin brothers had all dug out the concrete around their cell vents and constructed faux grilles out of cigar box interiors and binder covers, slathered with mint green paint courtesy of West's access to the A-Block storage area. They had also sculpted dummy masks from Portland cement powder, soap flakes, magazine pages, wire, and electrical tape.

Fellow inmate Leon Thompson taught Morris how to mix oil paints to create facial pigment tones, and Clarence Anglin had collected hair from the barber shop, where he worked on a daily basis. When inserted in bed, these surprisingly realistic masks, with the covers drawn up to the "chins," gave the illusion the men were asleep during the night counts. As a result, MacNally, Morris, and the Anglin brothers had been able to work all hours of the night on top of the cellhouse, removing the blower mechanism.

Once done, however, they discovered yet another challenge: a steel grate with cross bars blocked the opening.

"Now what?" Morris asked. He swiped with a shirt sleeve at the perspiration that poured down his face. It was sweltering in the small space with the tarps blocking the airflow through the cellhouse.

MacNally peered up at the grille. "Take too long to cut through those bars. But look here." He moved his body, careful not to fall off the disassembled blower housing he was perched on—and pointed. "Rivets along the edge. If we can get a flat slotted screwdriver in the opening, we can pry 'em off."

Morris nodded. "I should be able to do that."

"Get to work on that. I'm going back down to my cell."

Morris and MacNally had made progress over the course of two nights, defeating several of the rivets with the screwdriver. It was difficult, painful work. Their wrists were sore but they had no complaints: their goal was now within reach.

Morris had also purchased a concertina—a bellows-type accordion—that he was certain they could use, at the water's edge, to inflate the two rafts they had constructed.

Now, during the early morning hours of June 10th, nearly all their escape materials were assembled atop the cell block, beneath the blower vent, hidden by the tarps that were—miraculously—still permitted to hang from the ceiling.

MacNally and Morris returned to their cells, replaced the fake grilles, and crawled into bed.

Morris whispered to Anglin, who passed it on to his brother in the adjacent cell: "All set. Should have the thing out tomorrow night."

MacNally checked his clock: it was 3:00 AM. He closed his eyes, thinking of the escape, of all the things he had missed during his incarceration: Wilt Chamberlain scored 100 points in an NBA game; an astronaut orbited the Earth in a space capsule; and a massive wall was erected in Berlin, dividing the region and causing political and social upheaval. While he'd heard or read about each of them, he felt strangely detached, as if they were news items rather than historical events he had lived through.

Shortly before MacNally drifted off, his thoughts turned to Henry—which, above all, made him feel the most content. Everything else in life that he had missed certainly served as motivation to avoid imprisonment. But seeing—and holding—his son was a reason to risk his life breaking out.

The morning whistles blew, and MacNally dressed quickly. Despite being tired due to months of sleep deprivation while working nights atop the cellblock, he felt invigorated by the thought that in fourteen hours, he would crawl out of his cell through the wall vent, and never return.

Sunday morning breakfast went quickly, and as he walked into the recreation yard to relax, he took a long look at the city and Golden Gate Bridge. Though these sights normally brought sadness, today they infused him with energy. He would be amongst the masses in a matter of hours—in disguise and existing without money—but he would be free and on his way, somehow, to finding his son.

MacNally locked eyes with Morris, and then they headed toward each other to review the fine points of their plan one final time.

But as MacNally made his way toward the baseball diamond, he was shoved from behind as his ankle was hooked—and he went tumbling to the pavement. He quickly twisted his torso and saw a man he had seen around—Billy Duncan—a bitter, mean con who had a reputation for fighting. A baseball bat was dropped by MacNally's right side as Duncan pulled out a shiv and stabbed it toward him.

MacNally grabbed the bat and swung from the ground, not going for the knife but for Duncan's knees.

With a *smack!* across the bone, the big man crumpled, but not before lunging for MacNally and sticking the shiv into his thigh. MacNally cried out in pain and struggled to move—but the heavy Duncan had landed atop him and started beating him with his fist. On the second blow to MacNally's face, his hearing became muffled with an intense ringing—and the heads and torsos of the surrounding inmates went blurry.

MacNally threw up his arms, blocking follow-on blows, but he was in no condition to hit back. His head slammed against fist and pavement until—

*Whistles sounded, followed by*

*two gunshots*

The nearby cons hit the ground as several officers ran toward MacNally and Duncan. When they arrived, MacNally's jacket was soiled with spattered blood and his jeans were soaking in thick, oozing fluid from his thigh wound, where the sharpened-spoon-handle shiv was still protruding.

Duncan was pulled off MacNally and handcuffed by two guards. MacNally was lifted to his feet, searched for weapons, and then rushed to the hospital.

MACNALLY AWOKE VARIOUS TIMES, fading in and out before falling back asleep. At one point, he became aware of the fact that he was lying on a bed in a larger cell, a segregation unit in D-Block. He rotated his head to the right, saw the sun setting beyond the barred windows, then flittered off once again into a painkiller and concussion-induced slumber.

SHOUTING, OFF IN THE DISTANCE. His brain was slow to respond, and his eyes were shut. No—the people were not actually far away; as he regained consciousness, things became clearer. Voices were loud, urgent in their tone. Men were running—no, not men. Hacks.

Thumping overhead, coming closer…vibrating the penitentiary windows…then retreating. Helicopters.

MacNally lifted himself off the bed and a wave of dizziness struck him like a blow to the back of his head. He fell back toward the mattress, but threw out a hand to catch himself.

A sharp pain stabbed at his thigh—and his lips were swollen and cracked. And then he remembered. Billy Duncan. The fight. He was in Seg—he looked up at the windows and saw morning light.

The escape. No—please. No!

"They long gone," a voice emanating from the adjacent cell said. "Left without you, asshole."

He knew that voice.

*"Duncannnn,"* MacNally screamed, a guttural yell that carried the pain and sorrow of a man who had something of infinite value slip uncontrollably through his hands.

His chest was heaving, his body drenched in instant perspiration. He pulled himself erect, and he leaned forward into the wall of bars. He put his face up against the cold metal and forced his eyes to the extreme left, trying to see into Duncan's cell.

The man was standing there. Laughing.

"Who did this to me?" MacNally asked. "You started that fight on purpose. To keep me from getting out of here. Was it Rucker? Rucker, you bastard. I'm gonna kill you!"

"I'll kill you before you kill me, you son of a bitch," Rucker's voice answered back. "Much as I'd like to take credit, wasn't me."

"I'll find out the truth, Duncan, and then I'm gonna carve you up. Fucking pull your heart out of your chest. I will! I *will* kill you."

"Yeah, whatever," Duncan said. "You're all talk, MacNally. You ain't got it in you."

MacNally fell back onto his cot. The gash in his lip had reopened, and the stitches in his thigh were bleeding through his clothing. The pain, the swelling, the blood— He didn't feel any of it. Instead, he put his hands to his face and wept, silently.

TWO HOURS LATER, THREE MEN appeared at his cell: Captain of the Guards William Anderson and two FBI agents. MacNally was led to the warden's office, where he was placed in a chair and left in shackles.

"I'm extremely disappointed in you," Associate—currently Acting—Warden Arthur Dollison said. He wore a bowtie and a charcoal wool suit, and sported a calm demeanor. "I thought you had made tremendous strides, a concerted effort to follow the institutional rules. You've been a good worker in Industries. But now I'm told you were one of the principal architects of the escape. And to think you were no doubt planning this when you sat before me in A-Block at your hearing..." He shook his head, sighed deeply, then took a seat behind his desk. "Deeply disappointed."

"We know you were complicit in the escape," one of the agents said. "We're in the process of conducting a shakedown of the cellhouse and we just found the same kind of fake ventilation grille in your cell that we found in Morris's and the Anglin brothers' cells. We're going to need the details. Everything you know. Whatever you tell us will be kept confidential, and you will not be identified as the source of information."

"When did they leave?" MacNally asked, his gaze fixed on the warden's desk.

Dollison glanced at the agents, then decided to answer. "Sometime during the night. In his interview this morning, inmate West told us the three men left their cells sometime around 8 PM. But we've determined that they didn't leave the cellhouse roof until 10:30."

"West," MacNally said. He leaned forward in his seat. "Didn't he go with them?"

"He claimed that he couldn't get out of his cell," the agent said. "There was a hunk of cement he had a hard time removing. We checked the utility corridor, and confirmed a large chunk of concrete was lying just outside his cell. West stated he finally dislodged it around 1 AM, but by then Morris and the Anglins were gone."

"So," Dollison said, pinching the bridge of his narrow nose. "Now that we've answered your questions, it's time you answered ours."

MacNally looked at Dollison. "Warden. I'll tell you everything I know. But in return, can you go easy on me on setting my time in the Treatment Unit?"

"You were fighting in the yard a couple days ago. You're already likely to get a month just for that."

"I was attacked," MacNally said. "Just like last time."

"That, sir, seems to happen to you a lot."

"Mr. Dollison. I think one of the men who escaped got Billy Duncan to start that fight. Just so I wouldn't be able to go with them."

Dollison looked dubious, but nevertheless made a note on his pad. "We'll look into that."

"One other thing." MacNally looked from Dollison to the FBI agent. "Did they make it?"

Dollison held MacNally's gaze a long moment, then said, "They're not on the island. Whether they made it to shore, we don't know."

IN THE ENSUING WEEKS, MACNALLY would learn that all three men had made it off The Rock, as Dollison had said. The remnants of their life jackets were located floating off a beach in the Marin headlands, three miles north of the Golden Gate Bridge, along with one of the wooden paddles and two partially deflated life jackets, their canvas laces still tied—indicating they were discarded by the wearers; if they had failed while being worn, the preservers would still be attached to the bodies.

A waterproof wallet that Clarence Anglin had fashioned from raincoat material, containing a list of phone numbers and photos of relatives, was also found. MacNally laughed. Anglin had told his brother to construct two of them, one containing a number of pictures and an identical list of family contacts; he planned to drop the copy over the side of the raft to lead officials to conclude that they had drowned; the hope was that they would suspend their search. Morris had suggested they dump their life preservers when they made it ashore, lending credence to the authorities' drowning theory, which he figured would inevitably develop.

Perhaps more importantly, MacNally also had determined that Billy Duncan had been working on Anglin's behalf when he had him start the fight that put MacNally in the Hole. With Anglin long gone, Duncan no longer needed to hide his motives. He said that he had owed Anglin a favor dating back to their time while serving out robbery sentences at Raiford State Prison.

And he now surmised that Anglin had been working with Harlan Rucker in setting him up for getting caught. Rucker had also done time at Raiford—but why Anglin had something against MacNally, he did not know.

As he gathered information, in a subsequent interview with the FBI agents, he learned that the second raft had never been completed—and that the raft they had found was only designed for three men, four if they sacrificed safety. The triangular design described by the agent conflicted with the style the men had discussed constructing; perhaps the Anglins and Morris had never intended to take him along. He might never know for sure, but it did not matter. His best guess said that the Anglin brothers and Frankie were free.

And MacNally was still behind bars.

He was released early from the Hole, for "good behavior," he was told. After spending three months in segregation, leaving his cell only once a week for a visit to the yard and two showers a week, his only psychological escape was through reading. But it was not much solace to a man who sat in a cement room with only a 25-watt lightbulb and two enemies—that he knew of—close at hand.

He had withdrawn into himself, anger simmering like a frying burger left in a pan too long: well done, charred beyond recognition, and brittle to the touch.

MacNally was setting his new kit of supplies on the shelf when Clarence Carnes rolled the library cart up to his cell. He handed through a new *Popular Mechanics* issue, atop which was a postcard.

"What's this?" MacNally asked as he took the magazine.

"Can you read that scrawl?" Carnes asked.

"Gone fishin'," MacNally said. He looked up, his mouth agape. "Son of a bitch. The bastards made it." It was their prearranged code phrase, a signal that one or more of them had reached land.

"Looks like it."

Carnes slipped the postcard back in his pocket. "Except maybe Frankie. Word is a body was found floating off the island a week after the escape. Some freighter saw it and said it matched Frankie's description, down to his clothes."

MacNally sat down on his bed. "They fucked me over, Clarence."

"I know that. And I also know they were cons, and cons do shit like that. You're in goddamn prison, Mac. Accept it."

"I'm here. I understand that. But I don't accept it. Someday I'm gonna have my revenge."

Carnes chuckled loudly. Too loudly. He stifled his outburst, glanced down Broadway, then said, "If it makes you feel better thinking like that, good for you. But you're here for a long, long time."

"Not if I can help it."

Carnes eyed him, then looked off as an officer passed. When it was safe, he said in a low voice, "Don't do anything stupid. If you drown, or get shot trying to get over the wall, it ain't gonna do your boy any good, now, is it?"

"It's not like I'm doing him any good being locked away in here."

Carnes studied MacNally's face, then nodded slowly. "You have any idea on how you're gonna do it?"

The whistle blew, signaling the beginning of music hour.

"I had three months to think about it," MacNally said. "If there're two things I've got plenty of, it's time and ideas."

The sound of horns squealing and blowing echoed in the cavernous cellhouse. MacNally stood and moved close to the bars.

"I know a guy," Carnes said. "I owe him for something. He's got a big head start on planning something. And you know I've heard a lot of plans over the years. Had some myself, too. But this one…sounds like it could work."

"Can he be trusted?"

"Always consider the other guy's needs, Mac. He needs a partner. That's his motivation. Till you get to the water's edge, you'll have value to him. I think you'll be okay."

"Name?"

"Reese Shoemacher. One of the negroes."

"I don't care if he's purple, as long as he doesn't screw me. What's his plan?"

"He's been assigned to the Culinary Unit for about a year now, so he spends a lot of time down in the kitchen basement. Mostly unsupervised time. Says he's gonna go out the basement window. Been working on the bars for nine months with string, wax, and scouring powder—"

"A flexible file," MacNally said. He nodded slowly. The scouring powder acts as an abrasive and when you wrap the cord around the bar, then keep pulling it back and forth, you cut through the steel.

"That's the idea. Fills in the groove with soap and grease before he gets off his shift to hide it."

"Why does he need a partner?"

"Most guys don't escape alone; you need lookouts, help getting over fences, carrying your kit. Shoe was gonna go with another negro, Leonard Williams, but Williams's supposedly got something else cookin'. I happen to know Shoe's got a big hole in his plan—like what he's gonna do once he gets in the water. And you've got experience with flotation devices." Carnes grinned.

"Let him know I'm in."

"I'll bring you two together tomorrow, on the yard." Carnes grabbed the handle of his cart, then winked at MacNally as he pushed off toward the next cell.

# 59

"Alcatraz," Vail said. She sat down in front of Dixon's laptop and started a search. "There's been so much written about it that I have to think someone, sometime has listed the inmates that did time there."

As she began pounding the keys, a male voice yelled, "Birdie!"

Burden turned toward the administrative anteroom, where an inspector was approaching with a notepad in hand. "Got something. Your vic, Martin Tumaco. Found in that flotation tank in '95. Tumaco was a government doc—a Public Health Service physician—and a surgeon who worked on Alcatraz."

"Alcatraz," Dixon said. "We just found something, too, that led us there."

"That's not all. That other vic, Father Ralph Finelli—he was a seminarian back in '60." He consulted his notes. "Finelli unofficially worked at Alcatraz—Father James Raspa of that church you went to this afternoon—San Francisco de Asís—was the registered clergy on The Rock, but he brought along Finelli, his student, to get some experience working with some seriously bad dudes."

"What happened to Finelli after that?" Vail asked.

"Became a priest down south. He's done a series of interviews about his work at Alcatraz over the years. Talked about his relationship with"—another glance at his notes—"Jack Pallazo, and his work with two inmates in particular, Leigh Bosworth and Walton

MacNally. MacNally is the one that stands out because Finelli considered his work with MacNally such a gross failure that he would've left the seminary if Raspa hadn't talked him out of it."

"Is Raspa still around?"

"That's where we got this info. He's retired, lives in Concord. He was very upset to hear about Finelli."

"Great work," Burden said.

"Now that we've got a place to look," the inspector said as he backed out, "hopefully we'll have more for you soon."

"Check all the other vics," Burden called after him. "Find out if there's an Alcatraz tie-in. Inmates, correctional officers, support staff—anything."

Dixon swiveled her seat toward Burden. "Before your phone rang, you said you thought you'd figured something out."

"Yeah," Burden said. He turned back to the PC and, while alternating his gaze between the screen and his pad, scribbled some notes. He walked over to the murder board and began reordering the male victim photos. "Those numbers, the ones written on the vic's heads. I figured out what they are."

Vail's phone vibrated. She pulled it out and—*Holy shit.* She jumped up from her chair, which careened backward into the worktable. "New message." She read it aloud: "I'm stuck between a rock and a hard place, in the middle of fucking nowhere. You have twenty-nine minutes."

"The Rock," Burden turned back to the board. "So those numbers. Putting them in order of kill chronology, they read: 37, 49, 35, 122, 25." He held up his pad to check his information.

"And?" Dixon said. "I'm still not getting it."

"Me either," Vail said as she scanned the photos. "Spit it out, Burden."

"They're latitude and longitude readings. Of Alcatraz. I looked it up: 37° 49' 35" latitude, -122° 25' 23" longitude."

*Wish we'd seen that before.*

"We're missing a number," Burden said.

Vail stepped up to the board and jabbed a finger at one of the messages the offender had sent. "He wrote, I've given you some latitude, but you've come up short." She faced them. "One number short."

Dixon looked at the wall clock. "Here's another number we're gonna come up short on. We've only got twenty-seven minutes to get there."

AS THEY RAN DOWN THE stairs, Burden called the SFPD Marine Unit and told them they needed the Zodiac ready to rock and roll in ten minutes. They hit the lobby in single file and ran past security, then out the front door into the cold night air.

They dashed left, around the corner, and into the lot where the Taurus was parked. From there, Burden accelerated hard and screeched his tires, headed for Pier 39.

BURDEN SWERVED WIDE ON A turn and his rear fender caught the corner of a *San Francisco Register* street dispenser. Vail and Dixon grabbed for something to hold onto.

"Was the DB Friedberg?" Dixon asked.

"Don't know," Burden said. "Should've asked. Roxxann—get the goddamn light up there."

Dixon, riding shotgun, reached down and put the flashing dome atop the roof.

"Guard said it was a male, no ID."

"That fits the pattern," Vail said. "Doesn't get much more high profile than leaving a body on Alcatraz."

"No kidding," Burden said. "They get like five thousand visitors a day there. People come from all over the world. It's like mythic or something. People are fascinated by the place."

"How long till we get there?"

"We'll be at the dock in five, if I run some lights."

"And to the island?"

"No idea. I've only gone there by ferry. Fifteen minutes, maybe. I think we can do a lot better in the Zodiac."

"Either way," Vail said, "it's gonna be close." She thought a moment, then said, "Think back to all the victims. The way they were positioned. They were facing the Bay. But were they all facing Alcatraz?"

Burden thought a long moment, no doubt running the crime scenes and male victims through his memory. "Yeah," he finally said. "Except for Ilg, who was in the tunnel—the hole—I think they were."

Vail nodded. *Then we're right. Alcatraz is the key.* "This guy. Our UNSUB is likely a former prisoner there."

"And," Dixon said, "the vics are probably tied to Alcatraz in some way, too."

"Reasonable assumption," Vail said. "Other prisoners who wronged him. Or guards."

"The phone that text came from," Burden said as he swung a hard right onto Embarcadero. "Send a reply. We're on our way."

"He's not interested in hearing from us. He wants us there, to find what he's left for us. But I'll see if they can put a trap on the phone. He's too smart to get caught like that—but who knows."

Moments later, the Ford pulled up hard against the curb and they jumped out, making a dash for the small Zodiac inflatable, which was lit with spotlights and moored at the dock. An officer stood in the back, adjusting a setting on the Johnson outboard motor.

"Whoa." The cop held up a hand as they approached the Zodiac. "Not enough room to bring you all over. One of you's gonna have to stay behind."

Vail looked at Burden and Dixon, then said, "We're all going. Together." She stepped down into the inflatable gray craft, followed by Burden and Dixon.

"You heard the woman." Burden, perched on the elevated hump in front, gestured with his chin. "Move it!"

# 60

September 16, 1962

*Alcatraz*

The morning after his discussion with Clarence Carnes, Carnes introduced MacNally to Reese Shoemacher in the recreation yard. They talked about the progress Shoemacher had made in cutting through the bars, then, having finished their business, moved off their separate ways: Shoemacher to play dominoes with the other negroes, and MacNally to sit and think, alone.

MacNally closed his eyes and took a deep breath of salty, damp San Francisco air. The uncharacteristically sunny day gave him much needed light, and an equally uncharacteristic lift to his spirits.

He sat on the top step, his back against the penitentiary wall, symbolic in so many ways that he dared not explore it too deeply.

And then a man called his name. MacNally opened his eyes and saw a short, squat individual he had never before seen. He was not an inmate, as he was dressed in a black suit. As he approached, MacNally saw a roman collar. A priest—and he was now standing in front of him, blocking the sun.

"I was told I should come talk with you."

"That right?" MacNally said, turning his gaze away, toward the Bay. "And who told you that?"

"Warden Dollison. You apparently made an impression on him. He said he was concerned about you and felt you could use a friend."

"I don't have any friends."

"That's precisely why you could use one." He extended a hand. "Ralph Finelli."

MacNally examined the offer but did not accept it.

Rather than walking off, Finelli sat down beside him.

MacNally looked at him, his bewilderment likely showing on his face.

"I'm a seminarian," Finelli said, "at Mission San Francisco de Asís."

"You mean, like a sky pilot?"

Finelli smiled. He was obviously familiar with the prison term for a priest. "Not yet. But soon." He tilted his head and regarded MacNally. "You have a great deal of anger. And heartache. I can see it in your face, the way you hunch your shoulders. It's tearing you up inside."

"All due respect, Father. I'm not interested in religious discussions."

"Call me Ralph. And I'm not here to proselytize or talk with you about religion. I'm just here to listen, lend some advice if that's what you need, and to guide you through a difficult time."

"After what's happened to me the past few years, I can't say I believe in God."

"I'm only here to help," Finelli said, palms out. "That's it."

"I need to get out of this place, to see my son. He's living in some kind of orphanage. Can you help me with that?"

Finelli grinned broadly, as if MacNally had said something ridiculously humorous. To an outsider, it may have seemed like just that.

"I'm afraid that's beyond my powers of assistance. What's your son's name?"

MacNally clenched his jaw. He did not want to talk about Henry, unless it meant blazing a path for reuniting with him. But perhaps this man could help him in ways he did not yet understand. "Henry."

MacNally told him about his wife's murder, the fact that Henry witnessed it, the trial, and his subsequent difficulty in holding down a job. But more importantly, he talked about the guilt of not being there for Henry's formative years, of losing total contact with him, of longing to see him. He had to admit that his chat with Finelli was therapeutic. It lifted his spirits, as if the emotion of what had been building during his time in the Hole had been tamed by their ninety-minute talk.

"I'll be back tomorrow," Finelli said. "I'd like to talk with you some more. And I'll see what I can do about locating your son for you. Why don't you write a letter to him tonight? I'll make sure it gets to him."

"You can do that?"

Finelli bobbed his head. "Normally, I'd write it myself and send it on your behalf. But I can tell this means a great deal to you. And I'm a pretty persistent fellow when I need to be. Besides, that's why people like Father Raspa and I are here. The way I see it, if I can't make a difference in the lives of you men, my job is largely meaningless."

The whistle blew. MacNally gave him a nod, then rose from his seat. As he lined up to return to the cellhouse, he started composing the letter to Henry in his head.

HE WROTE SEVEN PAGES. It flowed like nothing he had written before: a heartfelt apology for doing the things that resulted in their separation, an accounting of what he had been through, of advice for his son on how to deal with adversity, and a plea to never allow himself to fall victim to influences that could land him in a place like Leavenworth or Alcatraz.

MacNally folded it in half, then half again, and brought it with him to the yard the next day. Finelli was already there, in the same location, waiting for him.

He handed over the letter, which Finelli took and slipped into his pocket. "All prison communication is supposed to be screened. But rest assured...the staff will not be reading this. I'm willing to trust that you don't have any escape plans sketched out amongst these pages." Finelli grinned.

MacNally looked out at the men in the yard, the ones playing shuffleboard in front of him and those to his right, choosing up sides for a baseball game on the grass diamond. "I have been thinking about it, Father."

"About what? What's *it*?"

MacNally glanced around, then leaned closer to Finelli's ear. "Escaping."

Finelli jerked back, seemed to compose himself, then said, "My understanding is that it didn't work very well for you last time."

"Worked better for the guys who got out, I'll admit that much." MacNally grinned—the first time he could recall smiling in years.

"I heard they're presumed drowned."

MacNally nodded slowly. "That's what the prison staff and FBI want to believe. But it's not true. At least one, maybe two of 'em made it. John Anglin sent a postcard."

"I see. Well, I would be remiss if I didn't seek to discourage you. How serious are you about doing this?"

"I've had three months to plan it. Solitary does that to you. It was either think of that, or think of Henry. Thinking of Henry is very painful."

Finelli's hand went to his pocket where the letter sat. "You have my promise that I'll get your note to him. But I would like you to give serious consideration to not participating in a foolish escape attempt. Eventually, you'll be released from prison. You got lucky the last time. Because of your cooperation, the Classification Committee didn't add time to your sentence. But if you make another attempt, not only will they increase your time—maybe even to life—but prisoners who've been caught in the act have been shot and killed by tower guards."

"The way I see it, I'm not doing anyone any good rotting away in this shithole. Pardon my language, Father. But I'm definitely not doing Henry any good. If I make the attempt and get shot..." MacNally shrugged a shoulder. "That's what's in the cards, I guess."

Finelli looked down, clearly disappointed in MacNally's answer. "You've obviously given serious thought to how you're going to do it. When would you leave?"

"Two or three months, if things work the way I think they will."

"Then I have some time to discourage you from making your attempt. You don't mind, do you?"

"How about you focus your energies on finding my son and getting that letter to him."

Finelli promised he would do just that—and each Saturday, when released out onto the yard, MacNally asked if the seminarian had made any progress. Three weeks later, he informed MacNally that he had located Henry in Peekskill, New York, and that he had mailed his letter.

"I think your note was beautiful," Finelli said as he gazed out at the Golden Gate. "Your son is going to be touched by what you wrote."

MacNally swung his head toward the man. "You *read* it?"

"In view of the comments you made about your desire to escape, I felt I had no choice. I told you I wasn't going to turn it over to prison officials, and I honored that vow. But I had a responsibility to…review it. If there had been something in it pertaining to your escape, I could be arrested for aiding in your felony."

MacNally felt his face turn hot, despite the constant chilled wind blowing off the Bay. "That was a violation of our trust, Father. You shouldn't have done that."

"I'm a seminarian, Walton. And I did not violate anything. I did what I felt was required of me, in keeping your private matters private, between the two of us. I did not share the contents of your note to Henry with anyone. And I will never speak of what you wrote. You have my word."

The anger MacNally felt building within was something he had not experienced since his time in isolation. He felt that his innermost feelings had been exposed, raw emotions he had reserved for, and decided to share with, his son. He had been violated. There weren't many things he had in prison he could call his own, but what he had written to Henry, the personal sentiments he had shared, were the last things he was able to claim as sacred.

MacNally rose abruptly from the cement step. "I need to take a walk." Finelli stood as well, but MacNally held up a hand. "Alone." It was better than assaulting a priest—or a seminarian—or whatever he preferred to call himself. If MacNally wanted to have a shot at implementing his escape—at seeing Henry again—he needed to keep his anger in check.

But as MacNally would soon find out, his failure to heed the wisdom Officer Voorhees had given at Leavenworth—the part about making the correct choices in life—would once again have catastrophic effects.

# 61

The Zodiac sped through the rough San Francisco Bay waters in the darkness, the lights of the city behind them attempting to poke through the misty fog that was hanging low over the tops of the buildings.

"ID yet on the vic?" Burden asked.

"Nothing, from what I heard over the radio," the officer yelled above the din of the engine.

"How old is he?" Vail asked.

"Pretty old."

Vail, Dixon, and Burden shared a glance: not Friedberg.

As the Zodiac ventured closer to the island, the vapor got denser, to the point where they appeared to be whipping through an undulating opaque curtain.

With visibility so poor, the officer slowed the craft and motored in blindly, as if approaching by braille. Finally, he called out, "There we go. Up ahead."

Vail craned her neck and saw what appeared to be a lighthouse in the front of the island, slinging its beacon around at regular intervals.

He brought the craft alongside the dock, behind a larger boat. He tied off the Zodiac, and then the three of them climbed up onto the dock. Vail looked over the area: multiple amber-lit buildings, some shedding their coats of paint and others burned out hulks, shells of what they used to represent.

And then, as they approached what appeared to be a windowed National Park Service booth, her eyes locked on the silhouette of two men: a National Park Police officer and a man she had not seen in years, dressed in a leather jacket and slacks: Special Agent Mike Hartman.

Vail couldn't make her way over to him fast enough. "Mike! I've been trying to reach you."

He turned to face her, but the brightness behind him prevented her from seeing his face. "Just landed in Oakland. ASAC told me to double-time it over here."

"Nice to see you answered your ASAC's call. You've been ignoring mine."

"Yeah, well, fuck you, Karen."

Vail jutted her chin back. *That's usually my line.* "You can't still be pissed."

"Don't you dare tell me what I can and can't be feeling." Hartman rubbernecked his head; the whites of his eyes seemed to settle on Dixon, before shifting to Burden. "This isn't the time. Or the place. We've got a DB and I'm goddamn tired." He turned to the Park Police officer. "Where's the body?"

"Hold it," Vail said, stepping forward. "I really need to talk with you. In private."

Dixon and Burden shared a look. "Can't that wait?" Burden said. "That DB may help us locate Robert."

"Actually," Vail said, "No. I need to find out—"

"We'll talk later," Hartman said. "Maybe." He turned back to the officer. "Where's the body?"

"This way."

"Inspector!" The Zodiac officer was approaching on the run. "Dispatch wants an ETA on my return. You three need me to hang around?"

Vail remembered seeing a boat at the far end of the dock. She looked over and saw it was a Coast Guard cutter, with a uniformed man on deck. "I don't think we need him hanging around. Who knows how long we'll be here. We'll find a way home."

"Agreed." Burden shooed him away with a hand. "Go on back, but stay on alert."

Vail, Burden, and Dixon turned—and saw Hartman heading up the inclined roadway in a red, two-seater Toro flat-bed vehicle.

"Gotta be kidding me," Vail said, her hands on her hips. "What an asshole."

"Just an observation," Burden said, starting up the hill. "He doesn't like you."

"No guessing required. Back in New York, after he was reassigned and given a new partner, I was involved in a bank shooting. He responded to my call for backup, his partner was killed, and Mike took some lead. Had nothing to do with me or anything I did, but I was a convenient scapegoat for him because I made the call. Anyway, he was laid up for months and thinks he got passed over for promotion because of it. Of course, none of this was an issue till I got the BAU gig. Then one day he goes off on me. Haven't seen or heard from him since."

As they trudged along the sharply inclined roadway at a quick pace, Dixon said, "You think the offender knows we're here? We're bumping up against the deadline."

"Depends on how he's tracking our movements. Out here, in the middle of the Bay, in a fog-socked night, I doubt he's watching from the mainland."

"Unless he's monitoring the radio band," Dixon said.

Burden swung his head over. "I'm him, that's what I'd do. No way for us to track that. But if that's the case, he knows we're here."

"It's possible he's here, too. On the island," Dixon said.

"Anything's possible," Burden said. "Let's see what we're dealing with, then we'll have a better idea as to when he killed this vic. I doubt he'd stick around, on an island. His getaway options'd be limited if the place was suddenly swarming with cops."

Sodium vapor lights provided barely adequate illumination along the roadway, which was steep and took a good few minutes of uphill hiking. "Now I know why you stair climb at the gym," Vail said between huffs. "So when you're trudging up the hills at Alcatraz in search of an UNSUB, you're able to do it without losing your breath."

"Exactly," Dixon called back, ten paces ahead of Burden and Vail. "Because I come here so often tracking serial killers."

Ahead, the small vehicle that had transported Hartman was parked outside the Alcatraz cellhouse, an imposing, and aging, prison structure.

When they arrived at the top of the hill, they hung a right and entered the building through the main entrance, where an arched, three-dimensional sign over the door read, Administration Building. An eagle protruded from above, perched atop a rendition of the American flag—though the vertical red stripes were modified to read, FREE.

"Someone has a sense of humor," Burden said.

They entered the facility where, ahead of them, a man in a suit held out a hand. Vail immediately pegged him as FBI.

"ID?"

Burden, Vail, and Dixon displayed their badges.

"This is federal jurisdiction," the agent said, his gaze dwelling on Burden's and Dixon's state credentials.

"They're with me," Vail said. "We've got reason to believe this vic was done by the same offender we're tracking in the city."

The man waved them through.

They entered the large cellhouse. Ahead on a flesh-toned wall, a tourist-friendly sign read B BLOCK. The interior was in decent condition, the ceilings bright white and the cell bars well worn but intact.

Off to the left, voices. They moved in that direction following another modern-era sign that read, Broadway. Down the main corridor, which featured cells on either side, stood a sharply dressed black man, US Park Police Detective Peter Carondolet, who was huddled with a suited Asian man. Mike Hartman was talking with a woman holding a camera—Sherri Price, the FBI forensic technician they had previously met at Inspiration Point.

Burden reached into his pocket and handed out paper booties.

"There's your buddy," Dixon said to Vail as she slipped a set over her shoes.

After heading down Broadway toward the knot of law enforcement personnel, they made introductions: the man they had not previously met was FBI Special Agent Ignatius Yeung, a field office colleague of Hartman's.

"Who's the vic?" Vail asked.

"Elderly male," Hartman said. "Looks to be late seventies, early eighties. No I.D. A full set of upper dentures and two partials on his lower. Callused hands."

"Is he in IAFIS?" Vail asked, referring to the FBI's national automated biometric database.

"Don't know yet," Price said. "I took a set of prints and emailed them to the lab. Because it's after hours, I don't know how long it'll take to get an answer. But I asked them to expedite."

Vail asked the men to move aside so she, Burden and Dixon could get a look at the crime scene. Staring back at them was an elderly male standing upright, his legs and arms handcuffed to the bars, facing forward. The numeral 23 was drawn on his forehead. "Looks like our UNSUB."

"As if there was a question?" Dixon asked.

"I meant the text he sent. He said he gave us 'some latitude.' I thought he meant he gave us some leniency, but there was a double meaning—those latitude/longitude readings. The missing number was 23."

"TOD?" Burden asked.

"Just a guess at this point—I can't even get to the body—but rigor hasn't yet set in, so less than three hours."

Hartman's phone rang. He pulled it from his pocket and moved off.

"Mike," Vail called after. "Hang on a sec—"

The BlackBerry pressed against his ear, Hartman held up his middle finger as he walked away, without turning around.

*Lovely.*

Burden pointed at the wall behind the victim. "There are things in the cell. Books, paintings. A magazine on the shelf." He twisted his head. "From 1961. Looks like this cell's a diorama of sorts, for the tourists."

"Exactly," Detective Carondolet said. "I got my start as a ranger here on the island when I was seventeen. Lots of stuff has changed, but I still remember a fair amount of my Alcatraz history and training."

Vail grabbed the bars and gave them a yank. "Can we open this thing?"

"Only way," Carondolet said, "is using those locked vertical closets at the end of each cell block. I checked, but the keys aren't where they used to keep them after hours. Dispatch is trying to find a ranger who can tell us where they keep 'em now. They're the original keys from back when the prison was open."

*Keys.* "Would those keys be short, stubby, funny looking things?"

"You've seen them?"

"Unfortunately," Burden said. "Killer leaves them at some of his crime scenes."

Carondolet said, "They sell facsimiles in the gift shop. Look just like the real thing."

"His clothing's a bit odd," Dixon said, nodding at the victim. "Don't you think?"

Vail turned back to the cell. "Deep creases in the shirt, sun bleached along the crease marks. As if it was folded and on a shelf a long time."

"Denim shirt and khakis," Dixon said.

"Prison dress," Carondolet said. "Posters—maybe you saw 'em on the way in. Photos of famous prisoners who did time here. Capone, Machine Gun Kelley, the Birdman—"

"You think the UNSUB dressed him in these clothes just for us?" Dixon asked.

"Bet on it." Vail knelt down and viewed the body from below. "Going with our theory, this vic either worked here or did time here. Way he's dressed, looks like the latter."

"Unless," Dixon said, "the UNSUB didn't like a particular guard and this is his way of finally getting justice. He puts the guy in a cell and handcuffs him to the bars. Treating him like the UNSUB was treated."

Vail pursed her lips. "That's good, Roxx. You might be right." She turned to one of the agents. "Are inmate and employee records still kept on the island?"

"I doubt it," Carondolet said. "Bureau of Prisons abandoned the place sometime after they shipped off all the inmates and closed it down. A lot of the laundry and medical equipment was sent to other penitentiaries and a chunk of the records were given to some doc for a research project, some kind of sociology study or some shit like that. He never returned 'em. About fifteen to twenty years later, I think a judge compelled him to turn everything he had over to the National Archives facility in San Bruno."

Vail stood up. "San Bruno. That's where the archives building is? And the Alcatraz records are kept there?"

"They've got all sorts of things, like evidence the Bureau found after the big '62 escape. The raft, paddles, tools, stuff like that."

"That vic, back in '82," Burden said. "Edgar Newhall. Wanna bet that building where he was found was the National Archives?"

"Things are starting to come together," Dixon said.

*Yeah, but are they coming together fast enough? Where the hell's Friedberg? How much longer does he have—if he's even still alive?* With that thought, Vail's BlackBerry buzzed.

"I'm gonna call the office," Burden said, "let 'em know what we've got here and see if they're anywhere on that roster of officers and inmates who served here."

Vail looked at the phone; it was her boss, Thomas Gifford. *Doesn't he ever sleep?* "Yes, sir."

"I don't like the sound of that," Gifford said.

Vail pulled the phone from her ear and looked at it. Then she brought it back to her face and said, "What are you, like a hound dog, sniffing out my emotional state?"

"So I'm right."

"Sir, no offense. But we're busy here. Is there a problem?"

"Not a problem," Gifford said. "For me, at least."

"Now it's my turn to say, 'I don't like the sound of that.'"

Gifford plowed ahead. "Just decided this evening. BAU's going through a reorganization."

"A reorg— Are you telling me I'm fired?"

"I'm not that lucky. No, nothing that radical. Years ago we were organized into regions. West coast, east coast—"

Vail looked at her phone. "Hello?" She moved back a few feet, then glanced at her handset. One bar.

Price's camera flash spread light across the front of the cell block.

"Sir," Vail said, turning again and taking several steps to her right. "You there?"

"Yes—yes. Did you hear what I said?"

"You winked out for a few seconds," Vail said. "But yeah. The regional setup. It went out the window right after I started."

"It's coming back in the window," Gifford said. "One SAC's failed policy is another's solution. So we're shifting back next month. And since you've done so well out west, you've been assigned that region."

"No, sir," Vail said. "Just… No." She rubbed at her forehead with thumb and forefinger, then glanced at Burden. He was still on the phone. Dixon was sticking her pen through the bars and moving aside the man's shirt, gesturing to Price about something.

"I know this is sometimes a hard concept for you, Karen, but when I ask a question, my voice rises at the end. When I give you an order, it goes down in pitch. In case you're not totally sure, my voice is going down now. Way down. You are going to be assigned to the west coast region. So when we get a case that's somewhere out west, it's yours—"

"Look, sir," Vail said. "I really can't deal with this now."

"I'll let you get back to work. You can go through all this with Frank when you get home."

"Del Monaco? Why should I talk with him?"

"He's your new partner."

Vail laughed. "Good one, sir."

"It could be worse."

Vail stood up straight. "How on earth could it possibly be worse?"

"Give me some time. I'll work on it."

"Is this really the way you want to treat the woman who's dating your son?"

"I did not hear that."

"I said, Is this—"

"Karen," Gifford said. "Get back to work. I just wanted to give you a heads-up so you can warm up to it. I was hoping to head off a confrontation."

"Don't you know better than to expect things like that of me?"

"Make nice with the agents in the 'Frisco field office while you're out there. You'll be making more trips out that way in the future."

"San Francisco. They hate 'Frisco."

"See?" Gifford said. "You're already learning the lingo. This is going to work out great."

"Yeah, well, you should've given me that heads-up a little sooner."

There was a moment's hesitation before Gifford said, "You've already managed to piss off—"

"Not my fault. The guy they've assigned to the case is... Well, we've got a history."

"My voice is going down here, Karen. This will not affect our realignment. You're just going to have to learn how to play well with others. And if you've already shit in your bed, well, it's up to you to clean it up."

"Great image. Thanks, Dad. Hey, who knows? One day I may say that and it won't be laced with sarcasm."

"God forbid," Gifford said. "Now get back to work."

Vail pressed END. "Shit."

Dixon turned away from the body. "You're lucky this isn't our cuss-free week."

Vail sighed heavily. "Your what?"

"California legislature can't pass a budget to save their lives, but they can pass a decree declaring that one week a year everyone should stop cursing."

Vail eyed her suspiciously. "You're shitting me."

"Just an observation here, but I think you'd have some difficulty with that."

"Damn right I would."

"Goddamn politicians," Dixon said. "Hell with all of 'em."

They both laughed.

Vail took a deep, cleansing breath. "Thanks, Roxx. I needed that."

Dixon gestured at Vail's phone. "Bad news?"

"I'll deal with it. Right now we need to get our heads around all this."

Burden hung up from his call. "They're emailing us what they've got so far. It's not complete—they've got a list of inmates, still working on the correctional officers."

"Something you should all know," Carondolet said. "Cell door's locked, right? And I told you the only way to get it open is by getting access to that closet. But what I didn't tell you is that the locking mechanism is a complicated gear and clutch job. I remember having a tough time learning it when I worked here."

Vail turned back to the victim. "So you're saying the offender has to know what he's doing. An insider?"

"I'm just saying. It might mean something."

"Actually," Agent Yeung said, "it's up on YouTube. Someone filmed a park ranger explaining how it works. My brother gave me the link after visiting from New York."

Burden sighed. "Is anything about this case easy?"

*New York.* Vail looked around; Hartman had still not returned. *Goddamn him.* She turned to Yeung. "I really need to ask Mike an important question. Any idea where he went?"

"I'll give him a shout." Yeung lifted his BlackBerry and dialed. A moment later, he said, "Went straight to voicemail. Coverage on the island's spotty at best."

Vail clenched her jaw. *Talk about delayed gratification. This is really pushing the limit.* "I'm gonna go find him." She walked out the way she came in and realized she did not know where she was, or where to begin looking. It was dark and the lighting was insufficient, at best. She thought of asking Carondolet to take her around, but she didn't want him there when she questioned Hartman. She headed back into the cellhouse and approached the agent who was manning the entrance. "You got a map or something I can use?"

"Just a tourist brochure I picked up on the dock when we got here." He reached inside his sport coat and handed it over.

Vail thanked him, and then walked back outside. Ahead, the lighthouse was whipping its beacon around at a regular interval. Off in the distance, straight ahead and cutting the fog, was the Bay Bridge, lit up and stretching from the extreme left, across an island, then traversing the ocean to the soupy murkiness of the city on the right.

A gull dove and pecked her hard on the head. "Damn bird." She brought a hand to the spot to check for blood, but found none.

The temperature had dropped and the wind was slapping rudely against the map she had unfurled. She took a moment to study the diagram of the buildings, then moved ahead a few paces onto a patch of grass and peered into the dark areas around her. To her left stood the burned-out remains of a building: the warden's house. She started in that direction, but her BlackBerry buzzed. A text from Dixon:

Get back here now.

Vail turned and trotted into the cellhouse, then back down Broadway. "What's going on?"

"Got an ID on the vic," Burden said. "And you're not gonna believe it."

"Why should this be any different from the rest of the case?" Vail said. "Who is it?"

"That, Karen, is John William Anglin."

# 62

November 9, 1962

*Alcatraz*

W alton MacNally and Reese Shoemacher had coordinated their plans for escape during each weekend on the yard. Shoemacher had nearly cut through the interior bars on a rear kitchen window, along the south side of the basement. Once through those, the window rotated inward, exposing a second set of flat, and softer, bars. He had cut through a substantial portion of these as well, leaving just enough to withstand the periodic "bar knocking" procedure the guards implemented throughout the cellhouse to ensure inmates were not doing what Shoemacher had done.

Due to the increasing risk of discovery with each passing day, he urged MacNally to move forward as quickly as possible with his role: devising a method of getting them safely across the Bay to land.

MacNally had never disclosed his role in the Morris-Anglin escape, other than telling the investigators that he had assisted in the planning and the gathering of certain materials, such as pilfering dining hall spoons that they used for digging out their ventilation grilles. Fortunately, Allen West did not implicate him relative to his work sewing the life preservers or rafts, and MacNally likewise took care to place a majority of the responsibility on the three men who had left the facility: no disciplinary action could be taken against those who were no longer behind bars.

As a result, MacNally was permitted to return to his job in the glove shop upon release from segregation. The flotation devices he planned to construct would be simple and easy to build, made from raincoat material that he secured from the clothing room on successive shower days, utilizing his Industries pay to compensate the con who passed him the attire. After cutting and sewing the pieces into two pant-leg shaped sleeves, he would manually inflate several rubber gloves another inmate had pilfered from the hospital, and insert them into the hollow tube he had created.

Once wrapped around their torsos, they would provide buoyancy, allowing them to ride the outgoing current—which, according to a prisoner who knew how to read tides from his time in the Navy— would take them west toward the Golden Gate Bridge and directly to the Marin Headlands, where they would make land.

There was risk—the water stood at around 54 degrees year round, so the amount of time they would be able to remain submerged was limited. If they did not get ashore quickly enough, their body temperatures would plunge, and they would perish shortly thereafter.

The crucial part of their plan required that MacNally request, and be granted, a transfer to the Culinary unit. He explained to the officer in charge that he had always wanted to learn how to cook and prepare meals, and since he had spent nearly two years working in the glove shop, he wanted a change of scenery while simultaneously getting the opportunity to acquire a new skill.

With the escape planned for this evening, he had awoken early, unable to sleep. He sat up in his bed and drew his knees to his chest. He reached over and took the photo of Henry and once again inserted it into the waterproof covering he had constructed for the last escape. The officers who searched his cell had not known what he intended to use it for, so they left it undisturbed. Also in the wallet was $31 in cash he had secured during his stay; it was money he had made trading items he had purchased with his Industries wages: a musical instrument he had no intention of playing, which he bought and then sold at a discount, and a magazine subscription that he handled in the same manner.

Once he made it off the island, he would need the money to buy food, a bus ticket—anything that would allow him to survive without having to break into a home or commit some other crime that would be reported to the authorities, giving them a bread crumb with which to locate him. He believed that not plotting ahead for the success of their own plan was a common mistake made by escapees.

MacNally placed the wallet in his shirt pocket, then grabbed his pad and pen to compose a letter that he was certain would be found. Upon discovery of his escape, the cell would be searched, and there were things he did not want left unsaid. He began writing, the words flowing freely:

*Dear Associate Warden Dollison,*

*I wanted to thank you for treating me fairly and with respect back in June, in the aftermath of the escape. By now you know that I have left the island. But I don't want you to take it personally; it is the unending desire to see my son, who I essentially but unwittingly abandoned, that has led me down this path. I have no desire to commit criminal acts with my freedom, but I would be lying if I didn't admit that the boredom, the rote mechanics of life on The Rock, the sucking of intellect and the loss of person...the loneliness, the violence that I have endured are also reasons for leaving. All have left a permanent mark on me.*

*I find myself in this place by circumstances not of my own creation. This is not to say I don't take responsibility for my actions. I was once told by a Leavenworth hack that life is a series of choices, and that I have made a number of bad ones. I've had time to reflect on that, and I don't feel it's quite that absolute, or black and white. I did rob those banks and I did take the money, but it was only to provide for my son. That said, I should've found a way to do things differently. I know that now.*

*My decision to leave your institution is based on my attempt to fix what I have mangled in my son's life, and, I guess, in my own. I have only been incarcerated for three and a half years, but it feels like a lifetime. I have become a bitter and broken man, and if I die amongst the waves of cold Bay waters, at least it was with the noble intent of looking after my child's well-being.*

*With respect,*
*Walton MacNally*

MacNally folded the letter and left it on his wall-mounted desk with "Warden Dollison" scrawled across the top. He sat on his bed, thinking of the last time he saw Henry, watching him run from the car into the blind area between the houses. Tears formed, then ran down his cheeks. He grabbed his hair in two hands and pulled, the pain he had attempted to hide instantly present, replacing the numbness he had sought to guide him through each day.

The wakeup whistle blew and MacNally jumped off the bed. He could not wait for the day to begin—because when it ended, he expected to be standing on land, two miles away.

His work request had been granted and he started in the kitchen on November 6. Two days earlier, he had passed the flotation devices to Shoemacher in the yard, who stored them behind one of the large refrigerators in the basement, trusting that his partner would not depart without him.

The day passed slowly. MacNally kept watch on the time, trying to go through his activities without exhibiting behavior that would arouse suspicion. When dinner ended at 4:45, the prisoners returned to their cells for the 5 PM count. MacNally, Shoemacher, and three other inmates had the assignment of cleaning the dining hall and food preparation areas, as well as wrapping and placing all uneaten food in the refrigerators. Though they were not in their cells for the standing count, Culinary Unit workers were accounted for by the correctional officer assigned to the kitchen.

On his way down to the basement, MacNally slipped a carving knife out of the deep sink filled with soaking pots, pans, and cooking utensils, and wrapped it in a soiled apron. Shoemacher joined him downstairs a minute later and they busied themselves with putting away supplies.

Once the guard finished his survey of the basement, he ascended the steps to check the remainder of his patrol.

Shoemacher grabbed a twelve-inch crescent wrench he had taken from an inmate's maintenance toolbox and then hidden behind a large fuel tank that stood by the window from which they planned to leave. Using the tool, he went to work prying loose the nearly severed bars.

MacNally, meanwhile, used the knife to slice off the long electrical cord from the industrial floor waxing machine. He quickly made a knot every several feet, then shoved the wire into one of two potato sacks along with the knife and the flotation devices that Shoemacher had squirreled away behind the refrigerator.

MacNally joined his partner by the window, ready to pass him their kits once they broke through to the outside.

But a loud clang that sounded like it emanated from the basement made both of them stop and turn in its direction.

"Go!" MacNally said, knowing they were now committed. They were in the southernmost portion of the room, and the tank provided reasonable cover should the guard unexpectedly appear. If the hack ventured too close, they would have to deal with him: splitting up and rushing him from different directions would prevent the unarmed man from subduing them.

"Fucking thing isn't giving!" Shoemacher said through clenched teeth as he pried against the bars with the wrench.

MacNally came up beside him and grabbed his partner's hands and pulled, tensing his muscles and leaning into it with his entire body weight. The metal fatigued—the severed joint gave way—and two crossbars popped free.

But the wrench slipped and struck the window casement with a clunk.

They looked at one another, wide-eyed. Had anyone heard that?

MacNally couldn't worry about it—he grabbed the wrench and leveraged it against the other two joints, and a second later had broken those free as well. They pulled open the window and then slammed the palms of their hands against the flat bars. Shoemacher had been able to do a more thorough job on these, and they surrendered more easily.

Shoemacher squeezed through the opening and reached down toward the wide sill on the outside of the cellhouse, but missed it and fell to the sidewalk below. He shook his head and rose slowly with a grimace and a bloody scrape on his forehead, but reached up and received their kits, which MacNally was pushing through the window.

MacNally then mimicked Shoemacher's movements, but learned from his accomplice's tumble and successfully righted himself before jumping to the ground seconds later.

With his back against the building, MacNally saw the Bay fading in the descending darkness. The carefree squeals of gulls emanated from somewhere down the hillside ahead of him, on the other side of a tall chain-link fence.

They could go right—away from their launch point—or left, alongside the building, headed toward it. There were advantages to both routes, but moving closer to their intended goal made more sense than taking a more circuitous course. The longer they remained on the island, the greater the odds their absence would be noticed and the officer corps would be mobilized.

They crouched down—passing other kitchen basement windows—and scampered along the building in the direction of the towering water tank that loomed a hundred yards ahead.

They reached the end of the cellhouse and stopped. Listened. Hearing nothing, MacNally peered around the edge. Directly to their left rose a staircase that led up to the hospital wing. They moved past it and stepped up to the sixteen-foot barbed-wire-topped cyclone fence.

MacNally slung his kit across his left shoulder, then began climbing. When he had reached the top, he tossed the sack across the spurred surface, then laid his body over it and pivoted to the other side.

Shoemacher followed, pulling their barbed-wire shield off the fence top and tossing it down to MacNally before beginning his descent. This time, his landing was more graceful than his clumsy exit from the kitchen's basement window.

They ran down a short flight of cement steps, then turned right—and saw a much longer staircase—that was bisected partway down by a tall chain-link gate, topped by yet another row of barbed-wire.

MacNally stopped and looked up. "C'mon, we're going back. Over that wall—"

"Back?"

"Up. Faster and easier than trying to get over that gate." He led Shoemacher back to a spot thirty feet from where they had traversed the sixteen-foot fence. In front of them stood a short, decorative cement wall. "Get the electrical cord."

Shoemacher rooted through the sack and pulled out the knotted wire. MacNally tied it around an opening in the concrete barrier, then tossed the long end over the side. "Follow me." He climbed over the edge and went hand over hand till he reached the stairs, on the other side of the chain-link gate, approximately twenty feet below. He waited for Shoemacher to reach his side, then headed down the steps.

He did not want to leave the electrical cord behind, if nothing else because it would provide an important clue as to which direction they were headed. But it couldn't be helped.

They ran past the old Army morgue building, then two large fuel tanks. Above and over their left shoulder was the border of the recreation yard.

MacNally led the way forward, beneath the massive, iron-footed water tower, then down a short set of stairs to a long, sloping, narrow sidewalk. In the near darkness, they had to be careful not to go off the edge—to their right was a sharply inclined hillside, which abutted the main road that either led down to the dock, or up toward the south end of the Industries building.

Running faster than was advisable down the steep sidewalk, MacNally struggled to slow his pace as he approached its end. He stopped, his shoes slapping against the pavement, and peered right, down the wide roadway. Directly ahead stood the Quartermaster warehouse, abutted by the three-story Powerhouse building, which contained the generators that provided the island with electricity.

Seeing no patrols, MacNally crossed the road, with Shoemacher maintaining his flank, their escape kits cradled across their shoulders.

To the left of the building's second floor entrance, a set of metal stairs rose to the flat rooftop. They quickly scaled the steps—the clanging causing MacNally to take two steps at a time to minimize the footfalls—then ran toward the back of the Powerhouse. He was hoping there was a way down, as they no longer had their makeshift rope.

MacNally stopped at the edge. Five feet below them, a metal vent led from the side of the Powerhouse building to the adjacent smokestack. He swung his legs over the side, then lowered his feet till they met the ductwork. The wind was aggressive and challenged his ability to maintain his balance. Not knowing how old or sturdy the six-foot horizontal structure was, he inched across it, arms extended at his sides as if traversing a high wire.

He reached the smokestack and hugged it, then stretched as far as he could around its right side, reaching for the metal grab bars that ran along its length from the ground as far up into the sky as he could see.

He climbed down, then removed the kit from his shoulder. As Shoemacher followed his partner's movements, MacNally looked out at the dark water. He heard it crashing against the rocks more than saw it, but he knew it was there; he smelled the salt, felt the dampness on his raw cheeks.

They were standing atop a cement slab that sloped down, away from its center.

"This is it," Shoemacher said. "The Caponier. Almost home."

"We're almost in the water. Home's still a ways off," MacNally said.

Ten feet or so below them lay the choppy waters of the Bay. To their left, the Powerhouse smokestack rose skyward, into the darkness. And to their right sat the short and narrow path that abutted the water's edge—their entry point into the ocean.

Directly behind them stood a back room of the Powerhouse, where the large boiler tanks were located.

Shoemacher turned his back into the wind, and his jacket caught the gust, ballooning out around him. "That water's gonna be a bitch. Sure we can do this?"

"We aren't going back, I can tell you that much. *I'm* not going back. You want to, your choice."

"Hell no."

"Then I'm gonna get out of the wind and start blowing up the gloves." MacNally took both sacks and stepped into the boiler room. "Watch out for patrols."

MacNally dropped to his knees and pulled out the raincoat devices he had sewn. As he put the first glove to his mouth, he heard a man shout.

"Hold it! Don't move—put your arms behind your head and get down on your knees."

MacNally knew that voice. Officer Jack Taylor. He instantly broke out in an aggressive sweat. His heart started racing, and he nearly whimpered anger and frustration into the night air. But he fought to keep his emotions muted.

What to do?

"Where's MacNally?" Taylor yelled.

"Who?" Shoemacher asked.

"Don't fuck with me, boy. You're in a whole lotta trouble." A second's hesitation, then, "MacNally! Where the hell are you?"

Taylor's voice rode away on the wind, but MacNally knew he did not have much time. Taylor was only feet away, on that sloping cement slab where he had been standing only a minute ago.

Could he reason with Taylor, explain why he was doing this? No— hacks have a job to do, and that's to keep prisoners in line and prevent them from doing what MacNally was attempting to do.

There was no way out. If he surrendered, he would be thrown back in the Hole. Dozens of years would be added to his sentence. When he did get out of Seg, he would likely not be granted work privileges again. The thought of a lifetime behind bars in a cell, twenty-four hours a day, some of it in darkness with little human contact... It was not something he could live with. He had nothing to lose.

MacNally slipped his hand inside the sack and pulled out the knife, then straightened up and put his back to the doorway. He heard Taylor key his radio.

And that's when he struck.

MacNally stepped out of the room and plunged the knife into Taylor's chest. The officer stiffened, dropped his handgun, released his radio, then looked at MacNally with wide eyes. Shock or fear, MacNally couldn't tell.

Taylor fell to his knees, gasping for breath, his hands grappling with the knife handle, unable to generate enough strength to pull it from his body. He fell onto his side and went still.

"The fuck did you do?" Shoemacher's disbelief was as genuine as Taylor's had been. "Are you out of your mind?"

Perhaps. And perhaps not. As Voorhees had once told him, life was about choices, and he had just made one. Good or bad, he didn't yet know, for his goal of reuniting with Henry was something that he valued above all else. It was all that mattered. But righting the wrongs he had done—including the one lying at his feet—that would have to be reconciled at a later date.

There was, however, one thing that could not wait for future evaluation and analysis. And that was the man standing five feet away: Reese Shoemacher. MacNally was amped up, huffing rapidly, puffing vapor into the chilled wind, which whipped its away around his neck. He reached down and lifted Taylor's .38 caliber Smith & Wesson revolver from the ground.

Shoemacher had gone into the room to grab his flotation device. As he stepped back onto the Caponier, he said, "You've lost it, man. I'm gettin' out of here."

"I didn't have a choice," MacNally said. "I'm not going back." He stepped closer to his partner and pulled the trigger, sending a round into the man's chest. And another. Shoemacher slumped forward, then fell face forward to the cement.

There could be no witnesses to Taylor's murder. If the failed escape of '46 that Clarence Carnes had related was an indicator of what would be done to him, should he and Shoemacher be caught, MacNally's killing of an officer would surely earn him a trip to San Quentin's gas chamber across the Bay.

MacNally's eyes darted around at the two bodies. He had to cover his tracks.

Fingerprints.

Then get the hell out of here.

He pulled the denim shirt out of his khakis and wiped the knife handle clean. Then he dragged Shoemacher's stilled body toward the weapon, pressed the man's fingers around it, and then did the same with the revolver, using Taylor's right hand. Need be—and he hoped it didn't come to this—his story was set in motion, and it would be bolstered by the evidence: MacNally was in the Powerhouse room preparing their plunge into the water when Taylor surprised Shoemacher, they struggled, and Taylor got off a couple of shots as Shoemacher plunged home the knife.

MacNally ran back into the Powerhouse and finished inflating his flotation device. He stepped out—and saw an officer. He reached back to throw a punch, but was struck from behind with a crushing blow to the head. It stung—his hearing winked out—and his vision went momentarily blank. MacNally went down hard to his knees.

*"The fuck have you done?" a voice yelled.*

*"He killed Jack."*

*"Son of a bitch. Who is it?"*

*"Negro's Shoemacher. This asshole's 1577. MacNally."*

MacNally shook his head, then cricked his neck to get a look at the men who were standing over him. Out of the corner of his eye, he saw a shoe moving toward his face. He threw up a hand, but missed. The foot did not.

The first kick to his head knocked him onto his back. The next one, and the ones after that, seemed progressively further away, the pain growing duller and more distant.

Until, eventually, he felt nothing at all.

# 63

V ail looked at Dixon. "Okay. John William Anglin. That's great." She looked sideways at Burden. "Who the hell's John William Anglin?"

"You never heard of John Anglin?" Agent Yeung asked.

Detective Carondolet cleared his throat. "John Anglin was one of the three men who escaped from Alcatraz back in '62. But their bodies were never found. The debate has raged for decades as to whether or not they made it. According to the FBI, they were assumed dead."

"Well," Vail said. "We all know what happens when you assume."

Carondolet frowned. "Marshals Service still has active case files on these guys."

Vail hiked her brow. "Looks like they can close one of them."

"So," Dixon said. "John Anglin. Fifty years or so later, he ends up right where he started. Just a guess, but I'll bet this was his cell."

Vail turned to look at the victim. "The UNSUB must've had some kind of beef with Anglin. He brought him back to Alcatraz as a gigantic fuck you—you worked so hard to get out of here, I'm going to lock you up in here—and this is where you're going to die. He got the last word. It took him a while, but he finally got even. We figure out who Anglin pissed off before he left Alcatraz, and we may have our offender."

"There was one guy, if I remember my history," Carondolet said. "MacNeil, or MacNally. Something like that. He was in on the escape but he thought Anglin cut him out at the last minute. True or not, who knows. But he'd be the first guy we should look at."

"Good," Burden said as his phone rang. "I think it's time you officially joined our unofficial task force."

"Come again?" Carondolet asked.

*MacNally. Where have I heard that name?* Vail looked around the cellhouse. *Why isn't Hartman back?* Vail turned to Yeung. "Still nothing from Hartman?"

Yeung's eyes narrowed. "No." He pulled his BlackBerry and hit a few keys.

Burden hung up from his call and said, "One of the students found a pattern in the vics' backgrounds. There were a few odd things that cropped up on two or three, but only *one* thing that's common to all of them."

"Let me guess," Vail said. "Alcatraz."

"You got it. Six were correctional officers. Two were former convicts."

"Why didn't this come up in our backgrounders?" Dixon asked.

"The damn place closed almost 50 years ago," Burden said. "The people on his kill list moved on with their lives. According to what I was just told, the younger officers took jobs in the civil service system, or they moved to other Federal employment or they went into the private sector and retired after another thirty, thirty-five years of work. They had whole other lives after Alcatraz. The two inmates paroled out, got married, straightened themselves out. Didn't happen often, but it did happen."

Dixon wiggled an index finger at Burden's BlackBerry. "Have them look up an inmate named MacNeil or MacNally. He would've been incarcerated here around the same time as John Anglin. Let's also see what inmates had a problem with these murdered COs and cons. If this guy keeps coming up, I'd say it's a bull's-eye."

Vail slapped a hand against the bars. "It's MacNally. The guy who worked with Father Finelli, right? They had some kind of problem."

She turned to Carondolet. "Who'd have those records, the Bureau of Prisons?"

"Yeah. But if you want an answer tonight, you might be able to dig up some stuff on the Internet. Depending on the inmate, there is info up there. May not have what we're looking for, but we could get lucky."

"Good," Vail said, "then let's find out if this MacNally guy is still alive. If he is, get an address, cell phone, credit card—anything that'd help us pinpoint his whereabouts." She looked at Yeung. "And where the hell's Hartman?"

"Not answering," Yeung said. "Went to voicemail. Probably in a bad zone, without cell service. I was warned about that on the way over from the city."

Vail shook her head. "If Hartman walked out of here talking on the phone, and he's not come back, either he's still on the phone—which can't be because he doesn't have service—or he's turned off his phone, or—"

"Something's happened to him," Dixon said.

Burden held up a hand. "Before we assume the worst, let's get all available personnel together—"

"Wrong," Vail said. "Assume the worst. The offender took Friedberg, and now he's got Hartman. Count on it."

Burden brought his fingers to both temples. "All right. We'll do a grid search of the island. Hell with the crime scene. Anglin's not going anywhere. Carondolet—you know this place. Coordinate."

"Roxx," Vail said. "Burden, you too. Can I have a word?"

"Now?" Burden asked.

"Now."

"Get it together," he said to Carondolet. "I'll be right there."

Vail led them down Broadway, to Times Square. Standing beneath the large clock and the West Gun Gallery, Vail took a deep breath and said, "There's something you two should know."

"I don't like the sound of this," Burden said.

"Trust me," Vail said. "It gets worse. There was a note. When the UNSUB broke into our hotel room, he left a note."

"No, he didn't," Dixon said.

"Yes, Roxx, he did." Vail locked eyes with Dixon, who was clearly not pleased. In fact, she looked angrier than Vail had ever seen her—and that was saying a lot. "Before you say anything, I apologize. I—I didn't say anything about it but I've got a good reason. No— I've got a reason, but it's not very good."

Burden folded his arms across his chest. "Karen, get to the goddamn point."

"Mike Hartman. He was my partner in New York, remember? Before I was promoted to BAU. Something…happened…during that time. No one knew about it except me and Mike."

"And?" Dixon asked.

"And the note. It said, 'I know what you did in New York.'"

"How the hell can the UNSUB know what you did in New York if only you and Hartman knew?"

"There was another person who knew. But she's out of the picture."

"And why's that?"

"She's dead. A few months ago."

"Who was she?"

Vail bit her lip. "My CI."

Burden held up a hand. "What the hell does an old confidential informant from New York have to do with a serial killer in San Francisco who did time on Alcatraz decades ago?"

"Nothing," Vail said. "Like I said, she's out of the equation. Which leaves me and Mike. And that really leaves Mike. That's what I was trying to ask him, down on the dock. Actually, I've been calling him for a couple days now, but he wasn't returning my messages. I called his field office and they told me he was out of town and due back tonight."

"So let's rule out Hartman as the killer," Dixon said. "Right?"

"Mike's got his issues, but he's not a psychopath."

"Okay," Burden said. "So what's the connection?"

"That is the question."

"That's not the only question." Burden's gaze was penetrating. "What did you do in New York? What's the UNSUB talking about?"

Vail curled a lock of red hair behind her ear and broke eye contact. "Eugenia. My CI. For over two years, I paid her by the book, two to three hundred at a time for info she gave me on illegal firearms, drugs—her info was always spot on. Bureau's very strict about how you handle, develop, and pay your CIs. Forms have to be filled out specifying the amount you're paying them—and the CI has to countersign."

Carondolet came jogging over. "I called for some backup, but it'll be fifteen to twenty before they get here. And we can't leave the Coast Guard cutter unsupervised, so there's seven of us, plus the island security guard. I'm dividing us up into pairs, and the island into quarters. This isn't gonna be easy without flashlights."

Burden checked his watch. "Where are you assigning us?"

"Just so you know, searching this place properly would take hours."

"We don't have hours," Vail said.

"Right. So we'll do what we can. Vail and Dixon, take the northwest quarter. Burden, you and the guard have the northeast. Price's coming with me to cover the southeast, and Yeung and the other agent have the southwest. The island's kind of a bird sanctuary, so if someone wandered into their nesting areas, we'd probably have heard a 'bird alarm.' I'm not sure if that means anything, but keep it in mind if you hear the gulls going off."

"I've seen one of those already," Vail said. "At that Palace thing."

"In the dark, it can just about give you a heart attack. Just warning you." Carondolet held up his phone as he started backing away. "Stay in touch, if you've got service. Regardless, let's meet back here in forty-five." The detective turned and jogged off.

Burden swung his gaze back to Vail. "Finish. And make it fast."

"This can wait—"

"Doesn't sound like it," Dixon said.

Vail sighed. "Fine. So Eugenia comes to me one day and tells me she needs nine hundred bucks. Her father has cancer and the drug he needs is expensive. She can't wait the two weeks it usually takes for the paperwork to go through channels. And no way would they've approved a nine hundred dollar advance. Mike told me not to do it, but…"

"You gave her the cash anyway." Dixon spread her hands. "But so what? Big deal."

"Wrong. A very big deal. The Bureau loves its procedure. Our Manual of Investigative and Operational Guidelines is four thousand pages long. Bottom line is I filed the paperwork anyway, for the usual amount—three hundred bucks—and figured I'd pay myself back after about three months. But Eugenia was busy with her dad, and for six months she didn't have any tips for me. But I'd already paid myself back. You see the problem?"

"You falsified docs," Burden said. "And you lied—"

"Fraud. It's called fraud. And all the while, Mike's on my case about it, and I couldn't get in touch with Eugenia… So on top of everything else, it looked like I'd taken FBI money without getting info in exchange."

"But you were just trying to help Eugenia and her dad. It's not like you benefited financially."

"Not the point. It wasn't kosher, no matter how you sliced it. Anyone ever found out, I'd have been censured. And forget a promotion to BAU. You know how many agents want one of those coveted spots? I get passed over, I probably never get another shot. And I needed the promotion because Jonathan was young and it was too risky being on the front line. I figured BAU would be safer. But a letter of censure—I would've been permanently fucked."

"So Hartman knew about this," Burden said. "And apparently he told someone else. Our UNSUB. Or he told someone who told our UNSUB."

"No way of knowing which," Vail said.

Burden cocked his head. "Given the tight timeframe, it's more likely that he told our guy directly."

"Why didn't you just level with us?" Dixon asked. "With me."

Vail knew what she was asking: given their friendship, couldn't she at least tell *her*?

"There was nothing anyone could've done. I tried reaching out to Hartman. He wasn't taking my calls."

"But you could've gone to his ASAC," Dixon said. "Hartman would've answered his boss's calls. And what could the Bureau do to you now?"

Vail chuckled. "When the shit starts flying, everyone watches their own ass to make sure it doesn't stick to them. Even if Gifford had my back, I committed fraud and broke vaunted FBI procedure, then knowingly concealed it for years. No offense, but I'd rather not hand them a gift-wrapped excuse to throw the only woman out of BAU— or even out of the Bureau."

Burden spread his arms. "Just so we're clear. You put your own interests ahead of Robert's life?"

"No— I didn't think—" Vail stopped. *Shit, that is what I did.* "I didn't think. You're right. If I had gone to Hartman's ASAC, we might've gotten an answer from him." She looked up at Burden. "I know this doesn't help, but I'm more sorry than I can possibly express with words."

Burden frowned and shook his head. "We'll discuss this later. Right now—"

The sound of footsteps coming down Broadway made them all turn. A man dressed in a security guard uniform was approaching on the run. "Here comes my new partner," Burden said. "Your chance to redeem yourself, Karen. Find Hartman. And find out who he's been talking to."

VAIL PULLED OUT HER MAP and consulted it for a moment to identify their area of coverage before they began jogging down the hill. In addition to the whipping, icy Bay winds, Vail was experiencing another type of chill: Dixon chose to express her dissatisfaction with Vail's poor choice by giving her the silent treatment.

They headed up the main road, past the burned-out Officer's Club, which was now a shell of a building. They rubbernecked their heads, looking left and right, ahead, and behind them.

*This is ridiculous. Dim light...an entire island, several large buildings, a bunch of small ones...he could be anywhere.*

"Roxx, I know you're pissed at me. And you have every right. But can't we deal with that later? We need to focus on finding Hartman."

"You're the one who seems to have a problem with priorities."

*Ow. Guess I deserve that.* But the hurt was blunted by the sight of something that lay ahead of them. Vail slapped Dixon's shoulder, then took off on a run. "Follow me," she said, heading toward a prominent smokestack that protruded into the foggy mist of an Alcatraz evening.

Down the road, off in the darkness, Vail heard the cry of gulls. They weren't swirling in a frenzy, but perhaps they had been earlier; in the cellhouse, toward the other side of the island, they may not have heard it.

Vail did not know what building this was until she pulled the map from her pocket and held it out so Dixon could look on. Vail stabbed at the paper with a finger. "Quartermaster warehouse on the right, Powerhouse on the left. Caponier behind it." She shoved the brochure back into her jeans. "That's it, Roxx. The smokestack."

Dixon craned her neck into the darkness. "You sure about this?"

Vail walked forward and ascended a metal staircase that led to the roof of a flat-topped structure. "About as sure as I can be, without having a clue what I'm doing."

"That's very confidence-inspiring."

Vail and Dixon climbed the steps, then ran toward the roof's edge—and the smokestack, which telescoped skyward from behind the building.

Vail peered down into the darkness. Although she could not see much, she saw enough. She bent over and rested both hands on her knees. "Shit."

Dixon pulled her phone and dialed Burden. "We've got him," she said. "Behind the Powerhouse building, on top of the Old North Caponier." Dixon shared a frustrated look with Vail. "No, Burden. He's tied to a smokestack. Dead, just like the others."

"THIS DOESN'T BODE WELL FOR ROBERT," Burden said, standing with arms folded, approximately ten feet from Mike Hartman's body. Burden had made it to their location in three minutes, followed a moment later by Yeung and Carondolet.

"Don't jump to conclusions," Vail said. "Hartman had information that we think could've revealed the offender's identity. So he was a liability. Far as we know, Friedberg had no idea who the UNSUB was."

Burden grumbled. "I guess that's something."

"He's tied around the smokestack with an electrical extension cord," Price said, bending and examining the binding with her flashlight.

"That's a new one," Burden said.

Vail stepped closer to check it out. "And possibly significant."

"And the body's still warm," Price said as she strained to see her watch in the scant light. "Which would make sense since he walked out of the cellhouse only about forty, forty-five minutes ago."

Burden swung around, his eyes probing the darkness. "The UNSUB's still on the island."

Carondolet held up a hand. "Not necessarily. Lots of places to land—and hide—a boat here. We take the easiest, most civilized way—the dock. But depending on how hard you want to make it on yourself, if you've got a small craft or even something like a Zodiac or a motorboat, there are plenty of spots to come ashore. Except maybe for the sea wall along the south tip of the island, almost anywhere else is possible. In the right spot, with some foliage thrown on top for cover, no one'd even know."

"His cell still in his pocket?" Vail asked.

"I searched, didn't find one," Price said as she leaned closer to Hartman's head.

"Can you get hold of his office LUDs and cell phone records?" Vail asked Yeung.

"I'll see what I can do." He pulled his BlackBerry and started dialing. "This time of night, who knows."

"Uh…just found something," Price said as she trained her flashlight on Hartman's lips. She used a tongue depressor to pry the teeth apart, then said, "Someone give me a hand."

Burden stepped forward to hold the light while the tech reached into Hartman's mouth and removed a piece of paper. She handed it back towards Vail, who opened the folded note.

Vail sighed deeply. "Got that light?" She held it toward the illumination that Burden diverted to her hand, then read it aloud. "'You finally got this one, so I'll give you one more shot. Look for an old cable in a small dark place, near where California bricks were found long ago. Be quick or bye-bye Bob.'"

"I assume that's a reference to your kidnapped guy," Carondolet said.

"At least we know he's still alive," Dixon said.

Vail snorted. "If you can trust the word of a psychopath."

Burden's gaze was on the ground, and he was mumbling audibly. He looked up and said, "California bricks…San Francisco…the Gold Rush…Gold bricks?"

"Back up," Dixon said. "Where's there an old cable?" She pulled the note back into the light. "An old cable in a dark place. What kind of cable? The old type of telegraph?"

"Cables are found, where?" Vail asked.

"The bridges," Burden said. "There are cables that suspend them. Robert once told me how many miles of cables made—

"Cable Car," Dixon said. "They run on cables below the street, right? That's a dark place."

"Yes," Vail said. "Is there a train depot for cable cars?"

"Something they call a barn," Burden said. "They park 'em there overnight."

"We don't have time to debate this," Dixon said. "I think we've gotta run with it."

"What if we're wrong?" Burden asked.

"Let's hope we're not."

Burden nodded at Carondolet. "Detective. Can you coordinate with my office and help them out with the MacNally backgrounder? We need to know everything possible about the guy. And familiarize yourselves with the file. Have the task force email you everything we've got. There's a bunch of vics to catch up on."

A boat appeared to be approaching at a good rate, a spotlight sweeping the north end of the island.

Dixon nodded toward it. "Looks like backup'll be here any minute."

Burden waved his arms and got a light signal in return. "Have them search the island, just in case he's still here."

"He won't be," Vail said. "But maybe we'll get lucky. God knows we need it."

"And I'll have an answer on Hartman's phone logs ASAP," Yeung said.

"Call us," Vail said as she backed away, following Burden and Dixon toward the roadway. "Soon as you've got something."

# 64

November 9, 1962

*Alcatraz*

Consciousness came in increments but remained far off and dream-like. Initially, MacNally became aware of lying face up on a table, staring at a light green ceiling. His lids were heavy; his thoughts as foggy as the Bay weather. His eyes fluttered closed and he drifted off to a semiaware state.

*two voices*
*far off*
*but nearby*

"Dr. Tumaco's on his way," a woman said.

"Finelli warned us he was going to escape," a male voice said with a Boston inflection. "We were supposed to keep a close watch over him. But someone screwed up and approved kitchen duty…"

*footsteps*
*fast*
*coming closer*

And then, a second male voice: "What have we got?"

The Boston man: "Inmate Walton MacNally. He was attempting to escape and injured himself out behind the Powerhouse."

"Vitals?"

The woman: "Stable, but pulse is rapid and he appears to have suffered substantial head trauma."

"Start an IV, saline drip."

Fiddling, metal clinking…movement. Air brushing by his face.

*fading into sleep*

*far off*

*nothingness*

*then a voice*

The doctor: "And you are?"

"Ray Strayhan."

"So, Officer Strayhan. What happened?"

"Like I said, doc, he was involved in an escape attempt. Killed Jack Taylor."

"I meant what happened to the patient, not Officer Taylor."

*fingers probing—*

*stomach*

*neck*

*head—*

*pain!*

*pain!*

"What's it matter?"

"Officer, I'm not going to ask you again. I need to know what type of trauma the patient sustained so I can properly diagnose his condition."

*eyelid pulled open*

*penlight flicked across face*

*pain!*

*hand on wrist*

*pinprick*

*pain!*

"He resisted, got violent, tried to punch Russ—Officer Ilg. I'm not sure what happened. We did what we had to do to restrain him. It was dark, we didn't know what weapons he had. Taylor was stabbed and his .38 was missing. We couldn't take a chance MacNally was gonna shoot or stab us. We weren't gonna show him mercy, if that's what you're thinking."

"I'm not thinking anything. I know you men have a tough job and these…these inmates here are the dregs of society. But right now this dreg is my patient. So I'm going to ask you again: what was done to this man?"

"He was kicked. A few times."

*hands around neck holding it*

*body turned to the side*

*body flat down on table*

"This is…my god. This is quite severe. I— Thank you, Officer Strayhan. You can go. Nurse, wheel him into x-ray and get me a skull series, stat."

"Yes, Doctor."

"Dr. Tumaco," Strayhan said. He cleared his throat. "I— We— Officer Ilg and me—we'd appreciate if you would be…careful with how you word things in your report. Hopefully MacNally'll be okay. But we both have families to support. And if the captain reads that our use of force was excessive, it could be our careers. The rocks—so you know, our official story is that while trying to escape, MacNally fell down the rock bed, banged himself up pretty badly. Nearly ended up in the water. Officer Ilg and me…we saved him from drowning."

*bumps*

*rolling*

*movement*

*pain swelling bulging*

*pain!*

The voices faded further into the distance.

"Thank you, Officer. I understand your concern. I'll take it from here. Rest assured…"

A FOGHORN BLEW IN THE DISTANCE. MacNally opened his eyes. A thick bandage was wrapped around his head and an IV snaked from his right hand. Moaning, he heard moaning. It was him. Pain.

"Pain!"

A man rushed to his side. "Okay, Mr. MacNally. Okay. I'll take care of it…"

Darkness muted his vision, and seconds later, he heard nothing.

"MR. MACNALLY. WAKE UP."

A hand rocked his shoulder and he struggled to pry his eyes open. Standing beside his bed was a man in a white coat.

"I'm Dr. Martin Tumaco. I operated on you. You were in pretty bad shape. Do you remember anything?"

MacNally opened his mouth to speak, but his tongue felt thick and parched.

Tumaco held a cup to his lips and he sipped water from a straw.

"That's enough," Tumaco said, then withdrew the drink.

MacNally turned his head toward the doctor. His neck was stiff. "Am I going to be okay?"

Tumaco turned around, grabbed a chair, and moved it to the bedside. "We had to do emergency surgery, but you've made an extraordinary recovery. A month ago, you were brought in with significant head trauma. You'd apparently had an accident, and you sustained damage to the prefrontal cortex and frontal lobe areas of your brain. I don't want to get too technical on you, but—"

"I'd rather you say it. Be honest with me."

"Right. Honest. Okay." Tumaco paused, nodded silently, and then said, "In a normal brain, those areas provide self-control. If it's damaged, you have less control and increased desire. It feels better for you to *act* than to stop yourself from acting, even if it's a bad idea or if it's likely to get you into trouble. And if you succeed—meaning you don't get caught—you want to do it again. The longer the reward is delayed, the more the brain produces the hormone testosterone, which—" The doctor stopped and frowned. "That's probably more than enough for now."

MacNally glanced around his hospital room: two large adjacent—barred—windows on the wall to his right, a radiator squatting below it. Gray light streamed in and fell across a table fan that sat atop a glass cabinet to his right. "Go on. What does all this mean?"

"There will be certain deficits, that much I'm certain of. But I'm afraid I don't know yet what they'll be."

"But you have a pretty good idea. My brain will want me to do things without me being able to stop it. Right?"

Tumaco hesitated. "You're in the right ballpark. Bottom line is that aggression and violence may be a problem. But—we'll see how things go. I wouldn't worry about it now. Just get your strength back so you can—"

"So I can go back downstairs to my cell. And live with violent men who do violent things. Like me. Sounds like a recipe for success." MacNally closed his eyes, then turned away from the doctor.

A moment later, Tumaco rose from his chair and left the room.

# 65

The Coast Guard cutter delivered them to Pier 33 fourteen minutes later. They ran to their car, Burden driving with Vail riding shotgun and Dixon in the back thumbing her iPhone.

Vail stuck the light atop the Taurus to ensure the ride did not take any longer than necessary.

"I've got it," Dixon said. "It's called the Washington/Mason Cable Car Barn and Powerhouse. It's on Mason—"

"I know where it is," Burden said. "We're real close—we'll be there in four or five minutes."

"It's the only transportation system listed on the National Register of Historic Places," Dixon read from her screen. "Been around since 1873."

"Almost as old as Robert," Burden said with a laugh. But his grin immediately faded as he—no doubt—realized that his friend and colleague wasn't in the car to offer a retort.

As Burden pulled down Jackson Street, Dixon pointed at an open rollup doorway on the side of the brick building. "There."

A painted sign on the gray steel framework above the tall maw read, San Francisco Municipal Railway.

Burden stopped in front of the entrance and they poured out of the car; the wall to the right was dominated by floor-to-ceiling corrugated metal with a freeway guardrail in front of it and two horizontal windows featuring closed cream venetian blinds. Above the windows was an old Market Street and Fisherman's Wharf Cable Car sign, advertising Rice-A-Roni. Notices and papers were posted across the glass: Authorized Personnel Only, Keep Out, and Cable Car Storeroom, Parts, Receiving.

Vail stepped up to the steel door—it, too, was covered with signs and employee-themed paperwork. She rapped on it. Seconds passed. She banged again, and it finally swung open. She held up her creds, as did Burden and Dixon. "We need to talk with someone in charge."

The woman's eyes flitted over their IDs. "You got her. Elise Cooper. I'm a supervisor. What do you need?"

"We're looking for cables in dark places."

"Excuse me?"

"Go with me on this," Vail said. "Don't think too hard. Just—whatever comes to mind first."

Cooper shrugged and said, "Well, there are the tunnels…that'd be the most obvious."

Vail swung and looked around. Large form machinery, humongous spools of thick, stranded cable and spare brakes and gears filled the space as far as she could see.

"Tunnels," Vail said. "Where?"

Burden scrunched his face. "Tunnels?"

"Yes," Vail said. "Cables in small dark places. From the note."

Cooper looked from Vail to Burden and back to Vail. "And then there are the blind channels."

"What are they like?" Dixon asked.

"Long tunnels. The sheaves run through them, carry the cables under the street."

Burden's chin jutted forward. "The what? Shivs?"

"Spelled s-h-e-a-v-e-s, pronounced shivs. Large spool-type pulleys that keep tension on the cables. They enable the cars to change direction, like around curves. C'mon, I'll show you."

"Shiv," Burden said to Vail. "Prison weapons are called—"

"I know. Something tells me we're on the right track."

Dixon looked at Vail. "Is that a joke?"

Cooper led them through, and past, what appeared to be a maintenance and repair facility. Industrial grinders, saws, drill presses—a gearhead's dream.

Ahead, four lengths of cable crossed above their heads from one end of the long room to the other. To the extreme left, eight large-spoked wheels driven by massive General Electric engines spun in unison, feeding the thick woven wire across the large, rectangular expanse that stretched about seventy-five yards to their far right.

"Those the sheaves?" Vail asked, pointing at the wheels as they walked past them.

"Some of them," Cooper said. "That whole thing—the sheaves, the engines, and the gears—it's called the winding machine." She continued across the wood plank and cement flooring, beneath the moving cable, to a series of window-fronted rooms.

"This is the control room," Cooper said, then knocked on the glass. "The engineer'll take you into the Sheave Room."

A man waved at her through the window, then opened his door. His tightly cropped afro was highlighted with a sheen of silver at the temples and sides of his head.

"This is Jerry Haywood," Cooper said, then turned to her engineer. "FBI Agent Vail, Inspector Burden, and Detective Dixon."

Haywood gave a stiff nod at them. "Sumthin I cain hep you with?"

"Take them down to the Sheave Room, will you, Jerry? To the channels."

Haywood bobbed his head, then took off down the hall. He was football player large, but walked with a substantial limp, which appeared to be due to one leg being noticeably shorter than the other.

"Thanks," Vail called back to Cooper.

Burden looked around as they walked. "What is this place?"

"This here building?" he asked over the din of the large machines, which were now directly to their left. "Car barn up top, powerhouse here and below us. See, there are four lines. Used to be twenty-two, but you know how that goes. Progress." He led them past the lunch room, to a locked door; he opened it and directed them down a staircase.

"Each line's a closed system run by a loop o' cable. The cable runs all the time down under the streets, below them rails. The cars grip the cable and ride it. Piggyback. That's how they move. The cars 'emselves don't have no engine. When the gripman releases the grip's hold on the cable, the car slows and stops.

"The cables, they have pine tar all over 'em, kind a like an oil. It liquefies and vaporizes from the heat, smoothes out the metal rubbing on metal. Follow me?"

"We follow you," Burden said, sticking close behind Haywood, who apparently moved well despite the limp.

The engineer reached the bottom of the stairs, and then led them into a long basement-style room that contained several pedestal-mounted horizontal and slanted sheaves, spinning and guiding cable into and out of the room.

"The cable runs in a loop below ground and ends up down here. This here's the Sheave Room. You saw them huge gears up there on the floor. The cables go from them winding machines to this here room, where they change direction and go out to the streets to run each of the lines."

Vail turned her body in a circle. "We're looking for a place where a man could hide down here. Someplace dark, where there's cable."

Haywood laughed. "Lots a places here like that. You described juss 'bout every inch of the cable car routes."

Vail looked out into the darkness ahead of her, where a fifteen-foot grooved metal wheel was rotating, serving cable into the darkness. "Ms. Cooper mentioned tunnels. Is this one of them?"

"It ain't no tunnel, it's a blind channel. Actually, we now call it The California Conduit. 'Blind' ain't po-litically co-rrect."

"Looks like there are two," Burden said. "Two blind—two conduits."

"Two. Yeah. This here one," Haywood said, pointing to the far end of the room, "it's California-Mason. Goes 'bout two blocks down, and the other, Washington-Powell"—his hand slid to the side, as if turning left—"it go 'bout a block."

"How big—how tall is this conduit?" Dixon asked.

Haywood led them to the end of the Sheave Room and gestured with his head at the dark area in front of them. "This the biggest it gets. Farther you get, smaller it get. Down to 'bout two and a half feet. You don't wanna be going that far."

"Yeah," Vail said. "I don't want to be going *at all* into either of them…" She stood at the mouth of the tunnels, which sat at ninety degrees to one another, and felt an unease fill her chest. She forced air into her lungs and said to Burden, "You go. I'll wait here. Coordinate."

"Coordinate what?"

"She can't go in there," Dixon said. "Claust—"

"I forgot. Fine. Roxxann, you take the Washington-Powell tunnel, I'll take the California-Mason conduit. Karen, you stay here and…" He shrugged. "Go coordinate yourself."

"Take these," Haywood said, reaching to a nearby box and pulling out two helmets with attached headlamps. "Stay clear of the cable. Plenty a room in there. Plenty a room. Just keep away from the cable."

Dixon and Burden fixed the helmets to their heads, then stepped in.

Vail turned to Haywood. "Do people go in there a lot?"

"People? Yeah, as in maintenance workers and engineers. People like you? Nope."

Vail looked in and watched as Dixon disappeared into the darkness. Vail took a step back then cricked her neck toward the engineer. "Anyone ever get crushed?"

"Crushed?" He laughed, as if she had asked something foolish. "Nah, nothin' like that." Haywood made a slashing motion with his hand. "Decapitated. But not crushed."

Vail rose to fully face Haywood. "What do you mean, decapitated?"

"Back in '79, couple a guys did sumthin' stupid, dint turn out so good."

Vail turned back and again peered into the darkness of both conduits. No sign of Dixon or Burden, or their headlamps. "How so?"

Haywood chuckled. "These guys, they were up by California and Mason, there's a pit there beneath the street. The Sheave Pit. They lifted the metal hatch cover and dropped down in there to make some repairs. They radioed in and we shut down the cable. Ain't enough room in there with the thick cable zippin' by. It's a real small place, that's why we call it the pit, ya see? Anyways, they made their repair then lit up a joint, smoked some weed. Well, some asshole figured they were done and started up the cable. Bam. Loss they heads."

"How? I mean—"

"You saw that cable up there. Big, thick, movin' fast. Tight space. Like I said."

"Wait a minute." Vail thought back to the text from the offender. *Look for an old cable in a small dark place near where California bricks were found long ago...Be quick or bye-bye Bob.* "Where's that Sheave Pit located?"

"Up the hill, at California 'n Mason."

Vail faced the engineer. "California bricks. Not bricks of gold, but a mason's bricks."

Haywood eyed her. "You 'kay, lady? Yo talkin' bullshit. No offense."

Vail looked back toward the channels. "That Sheave Pit. It's small. Is it dark?"

The engineer threw his hands on his hips. "Now whaddya think? You see lights in there? Pit's juss as dark." He walked a few feet and pointed to a sheave, which was still. This here's the cable that runs through the pit."

"How can I get to the Sheave Pit?"

Haywood lifted an arm and started to point. "Go back outside, then hang a right. Go two blocks or so to Mason. You'll see a metal—"

Vail grabbed his shirt and started to pull him along with her. "Take me there."

Haywood shrugged off her grip. "Must be outta yo mind if you think I cain leave my post."

"You're right." Vail pulled her Glock. "I'm out of my mind. Now get going. A detective's life depends on it, so double-time it." She gave Haywood a shove in the back and they ran up the stairs, headed for California and Mason.

AS THEY PASSED THE CONTROL room on the left, Vail pulled her BlackBerry and called Burden, hoping he could have SFPD send a cruiser over to the area above the pit to stop traffic. Just in case her hunch was correct. But the call went right to voicemail. *Probably no cell service in the conduit.*

Haywood took her back the way they had come in, past the maintenance area. Two flatbed utility trucks, with equipment and compressors of some sort mounted in the rear, sat in front of Elise Cooper's office. Haywood pulled a set of keys from his pocket and popped open a door. "Get in, this'll get us there faster."

"How far's the pit?"

"Couple blocks directly ahead." He pulled out onto Jackson, and then flipped a switch and swirling lights began flicking white and red hues above them.

"That cable you showed me. The one that goes through the Sheave Pit. It wasn't moving."

"Thas because I shut it down. I got an order for repair on the line this evening. 'Round 7:30. The engineer who had the shift 'fore me took everything offline." He pulled his eyes from the road to consult his watch. "Cable's due to start back up in 'bout four minutes."

"Four minutes—who's doing the repair?"

"Don't know. I assume one of the superintendents assigned a crew."

*And what do you want to bet there is no crew, and the order was bogus?* "Can you shut it down? Keep it from starting back up?"

"This point, don't think so."

He accelerated, turned right, and then swerved around a taxi—the heaviness of the truck chassis apparent in the vehicle's sluggish response. "See that tall hotel up ahead? That's the Fairmont, 'bout where we goin'."

A block later, he brought the vehicle to a screeching stop in the middle of the street.

"We here. Now what?"

Vail pushed against her door. "Show me the pit. Open it up."

"Open the pit?"

"You can open it," Vail shouted. "Can't you?"

Haywood leaned back. "Yeah, 'course. But—"

"Then open it. Fast."

Haywood got out of the truck and met Vail around back. He fiddled with an apparatus in the rear bed as Vail once again tried Burden and Dixon. Voicemail.

"How long till the cable starts up?"

Haywood stopped and glared at Vail. "Jesus, lady. Which you want me to do? Answer yo' questions or open the goddamn hatch?"

"Open the goddamn hatch." She glanced around, looked at her watch, grabbed her temples. *What do I have...a minute or two? Or seconds? If Friedberg's down there...*

Haywood reached into the truck bed and pulled out a carabiner-like clasp. Vail looked down and saw a steel access panel of some sort beside the rail, four feet long by five wide. "Do whatever you can to keep the cable from coming on, even if you don't think it's possible."

"This point," Haywood said, "time it take me to make the call, nothin' I cain do. What you expectin' to find down there?"

"A cop. A friend of mine."

Haywood's eyes widened. "Holy Jesus." He dropped the clasp and crossed himself.

"Get the fucking hatch open!" Vail grabbed the dangling hook and attached it to the loop on the metal panel. She pointed at him accusingly— "Now!"

Haywood pulled a metal lever in the back of the truck. A winch started vibrating and whining, and the heavy access panel started rising.

Vail dropped to her stomach and peered in. It was dark and she couldn't see more than a few inches below street level. She pulled out the small LED light fastened to her key chain and shone it inside. It was woefully weak. "Robert! Robert, can you hear me? You in there?"

*Nothing. Maybe I got it wrong. All this for nothing.* She moved her light to the left—and saw something. *Is that—* "Shit!" She stuck the light in her mouth and crawled forward, down into the hole, beside the cable—which had not yet started moving—and squeezed deeper in. Haywood yelled something at her, but whatever it was, she didn't care.

A wave of claustrophobic anxiety swept over her. Her breathing got rapid. And she couldn't move her shoulders, which were wedged against something hard on both sides.

Vail tilted her head back and moved the small light around—and saw Friedberg, wedged against the wall, the cable pressed against the right side of his neck. *They were decapitated. Not crushed. Decapitated...*

Vail tried to reach forward, but her arm was stuck. She maneuvered her torso, twisted and pushed with her legs against something and got her right arm free. Extending her hand as far as it would go, she grabbed hold of Friedberg's shirt and yanked hard. His torso jolted forward and his head fell against her hand. She twisted her body in the opposite direction and freed her other arm, but her neck and shoulders began burning. *You can do this Karen. Pull—*

She tightened her left fist against Friedberg's other collar and yanked. Once, twice, and again—and his torso tilted forward against her forearms. Sweat rolled down her scalp, then into her eyes. She blinked it away and tugged again, and his body moved. It was now as far forward as she could get him, lined up with the opening. All she had to do now was lift him up. *Piece of cake. If I was Roxxann.*

She twisted right as far as she could and yelled for Haywood to give her the hook. Almost instantly, she felt the cold metal strike her palm. She pulled the loose wire and struggled to wrap it around Friedberg's torso, beneath his arm pits, then snapped the carabiner closed around itself.

"Turn it on! Slowly—" Vail assumed Haywood heard her, but she couldn't be sure until she heard the winch start up and felt the wire pull taut. "Hold it… Just a sec—"

She maneuvered herself up out of the pit, then yanked and turned Friedberg's shoulders as best she could so they would clear the adjacent rail and asphalt wall. "Go!"

The winch whined and the thick cable jerked to life. *Jesus Christ—*

As Friedberg's body lifted out of the pit, his leg scraped against the stranded cable. It ripped off a section of his pants, but his hips were free and seconds later they cleared street level.

Vail yelled for Haywood to cut the engine. "And call an ambulance!"

She unhooked the carabiner, then gently lowered Friedberg's torso and head to the pavement. She grabbed his legs and pulled them out of the pit, one by one, then felt for a pulse.

Fast and thready, skin cool and clammy. *Shock. But he's alive.*

Just then, the cable ground to a halt. But Vail was too busy to care. There was blood—slathered over her hand and jeans.

Had she cut herself? No. She scanned Friedberg's body—and found his right pant leg soaked. She yanked off her narrow leather belt and tightened it around his upper thigh. She then lifted both legs.

"Hold them up," she yelled to Haywood.

"Got the cable stopped," he said, closing his cell phone. "Didn't think I could." He took Friedberg's legs from Vail, then said, "Ain't you gonna thank me?"

Vail moved between Friedberg's legs and laid on top of him—to passersby, it would be misconstrued as an explicit sexual act. But so be it. She needed to keep him warm until the ambulance arrived.

Vail laid there, body drenched in sweat, her heart pounding in her ears.

Cursing the Bay Killer.

# 66

February 1, 1963

*Alcatraz*

MacNally sat in solitary confinement—D-Block, the Hole, Seg, the Treatment Unit…whatever they chose to call it—and wept. He had much time to consider his actions, his choices, his life. During the past two weeks, after being returned to the cellhouse, he had come to realize that it was highly unlikely that he would ever see Henry again.

It was a painful thought, as painful as the intense headaches he had been having on a near-daily basis. He wondered if Henry had gotten the letter that he had given Ralph Finelli to mail.

He hoped he never saw Finelli again, because if he did, he wasn't sure he would be able to contain the welling anger he felt toward him. Not only had he violated his confidence in reading his letter, but he had apparently told prison officials about his plans to escape.

There would be a trial, he was told, when he was medically cleared to participate. He had met with a defense attorney, who told him that the evidence against him was inconclusive at best. It appeared that his accomplice, Reece Shoemacher, had murdered Officer Taylor, and that comported with the statement that MacNally had given while in the hospital.

Nevertheless, charges were brought, including conspiracy, assault, and escape. These were likely to result in added years to his sentence. How much remained to be determined.

In the meantime, prison officials had sentenced him to five years in solitary. He was unsure what that really meant, because he had heard a rumor from another inmate in the hospital that Alcatraz was due to close soon. That meant he would be transferred to a penitentiary somewhere else in the country. If true, he would welcome the opportunity to get as far away from this place as possible.

As he sat on the cold metal floor in D-Block's steel-encased Strip Cell—the mattress was removed in the morning and returned in the evening—he was alone with these thoughts, which were as dark as the cell. He was only supposed to be here for forty-eight hours, but as the days mounted, MacNally asked the lieutenant for permission to move into one of the regular cells in the Hole. He had yet to receive an answer, nor was he surprised. At best, he was involved in the murder of one of their men, and at worst he had committed the act himself. He did not expect to be treated well, let alone fairly.

The clanking of the solid metal D-Block entrance gate grabbed his attention. Even locked away behind a steel door, he could hear that someone had entered the area. A moment later, rusted metal hinges creaked and a slice of light cut into his room. He swung a hand up to his face to block the blinding glare. After spending days in the dark, normal light stung as painfully as if he'd looked directly into the sun.

A man blocked the entrance and MacNally lowered his arm. No, two men. William Anderson, captain of the guards, and an officer MacNally knew from his time in Industries: Carson Eldridge, who was holding what looked like a letter.

Anderson reached for the envelope, but Eldridge moved it out of his reach. "All I'm saying is, let me give it to him."

"Stay out of this," Anderson said. "That's an order."

Eldridge's shoulders slumped and he handed the document to Anderson, who snatched it away.

Anderson flicked his wrist and tossed it into the cell, several feet from where MacNally was seated. "Happy reading, asshole." He started to close the steel door, but Eldridge caught it before it shut.

"Lock it up," Anderson said, then walked off, his shoes squeaking against the slick, polished concrete floor.

Eldridge kept the door open an inch, then looked over his shoulder in the direction of his retreating boss. Through the slit, he said, "I'm sorry, MacNally. I didn't think it was right for you to find out this way."

"Find out what?" MacNally pushed himself off the cold floor and walked toward the envelope. As he bent down, he looked at Eldridge for an answer, but the officer was not offering any further information. "Can you turn the light on?"

"You know I can't do that."

"But I can't see anything," MacNally said as he tore open the flap. "At least tell me what's inside."

Eldridge sucked his bottom lip, then averted his eyes. "Your son. He jumped from a bridge, committed suicide. I'm sorry. Really, really sorry."

MacNally's eyes glossed over. His hands trembling, he pulled out the letter. A torn newspaper article drifted to his feet, as well as another, smaller, envelope. He stood there staring at the items that had fallen.

MacNally bent down slowly and picked them up. With moist, trembling hands, he slipped the letter out of its torn envelope. It was the note he had given to Finelli. All he could make out in the scant light was a postal service marking: "Return to Sender." Behind it, a newspaper article's large headline screamed at him. *Boy Jumps to Death from Bear Mountain Bridge.*

"No!"

The guttural, pained cry from a man whose life had reached the low of lows, from a man with weightier regrets than a human being was equipped to endure, echoed throughout the cellhouse.

MacNally threw himself at the bars. Eldridge, a tear evident on his cheek, flinched. And then he slammed the door shut.

MACNALLY'S WAILING CONTINUED UNABATED. After twenty minutes, Anderson pulled open the outer steel door. His lieutenant, Donald Wright, and a senior officer, Edgar Newhall, stood at his side. Wright turned on a water hose and blasted MacNally in the chest.

MacNally fell back to the ground, but fought his way to his feet, dodged the stream, and then charged the bars. He ran into them at full force—and continued screaming, a tirade fueled by anger and guilt and the short-circuiting neurons that now comprised his damaged brain's electrical system.

The water hose only fueled his rage.

"Open it up!" Anderson yelled behind him. "Bring him upstairs," Anderson said to Wright and Newhall. "He needs to be chilled out." The door was racked open seconds later.

The men unfurled a white sheet and charged MacNally, swiftly enveloping him and tightly winding his torso, arms and hands, in the cloth. Newhall stuck his foot behind MacNally's leg and brought him down hard to the cement.

While on the ground, the two officers snapped leg irons around his ankles, then pulled him upright and led him into the main cellhouse, into the dining hall and up the steps to the hospital.

But MacNally continued to thrash and yell, making it an adventurous journey—with the three men twice nearly tumbling backwards down the staircase.

They yanked and pushed and got him down the hallway, where they hung a right into a spacious, white-tiled room. Wright pulled while Newhall pushed, and they got him over to a free-standing white porcelain bathtub that stood against the wall, beneath a large window.

As they moved him to the edge, MacNally saw that it was filled with ice cubes. Suddenly, something slammed against the back of his knees, and MacNally's legs buckled. The officers guided him into the bed of ice and held him down.

Newhall brought his knee up to MacNally's chest and rested his full weight there. Wright did the same below, across his legs.

The cold was achingly painful—and eventually numbing. Finally, MacNally felt his anger fading, the draining tirade waning. His breathing slowed, and as he eased his body into the ice, he began to shiver.

"That's it," Newhall said. "We call this the chill out. You calm down, we'll get you out, warm you up, and take you back to your cell."

As he lay there, the fury seemed to melt from his body, replaced by sorrow and the realization that his only family—Henry, his son—was dead. The sadness he felt brought him back to Doris's death. Seeing her lifeless, bloody body lying on the kitchen floor was life-altering and emotionally shattering. As bad as that was, this seemed worse.

"Kill me," MacNally said as his teeth chattered.

Wright turned to make eye contact. "What?"

"Kill me. Choke me, stab me, shoot me. I don't care. Just put me out of my misery."

Wright looked at Newhall, who was frowning. *Pathetic*, his face said.

"Believe me," Wright said. "After what you did to Taylor, a lot of guys would be happy if we did end your sorry life. But some think that'd be a mercy killing. No. You're gonna do your time, imprisoned like some goddamn rabid animal, facing your punishment like a man, you fucking slug."

MacNally closed his eyes and he shivered, tears flowing freely, warming his skin.

Minutes later, as he began losing consciousness, Wright's voice roused his mind.

"Let's get 'im out. He's done."

The two men pulled MacNally out of the tub. Another officer entered the room holding a wool blanket, and they began unfurling the sheet. His arms and hands were free, but his body was trembling.

The rage welled up yet again, and he began swinging wildly. He connected with Wright's jaw, sending the man back against the radiator beneath the window.

The officers slammed MacNally facedown into the tub, then shackled his arms with handcuffs.

"I'm fucking done with you," Newhall said. "MacNally, you just bought yourself a ticket to the Bug Room."

They yanked him from the tub, then dragged him down the hallway, hung a right into a narrow corridor, and up three steps into an area with tan-tiled walls. The third officer swung open a thick door to their left, and Newhall and Wright shoved MacNally into the eight-by-eight room. He went sprawling face-first to the floor.

MacNally rolled over and lay there on his back: tiled walls, a glass-block window, and a hole in the corner to use as a toilet. That was it.

The men slammed the thick door closed and locked it.

# 67

Vail, Burden, and Dixon stood in the middle of the California and Mason intersection, which SFPD had closed off with squad cars and officers, diverting traffic to alternate routes. An ambulance sat parked near the still-open cable car hatchway, and a female and male paramedic were tending to Friedberg a few paces away.

"Why did he do it?" Burden said. "Why not just kill Robert like he did Hartman?"

"It wasn't about Robert," Vail said. "The other vics have some personal meaning to the UNSUB. Robert didn't. And..." Vail looked off at the Fairmont Hotel.

"And what?" Dixon asked.

"You're not gonna like it."

"Oh, okay," Burden said, nodding animatedly. "So don't tell us."

Vail managed a slight chuckle. "The offender probably did this whole thing with Robert for two reasons. One you know—to fuck with us. Show his superiority. The other was...to keep us occupied."

"Occupied?" Dixon asked. "Occupied while he did what?"

"Exactly," Vail said. "That's the problem. I have a feeling some bad shit's gonna go down."

The male medic who was hunched over Friedberg's left arm straightened up. "IV line established."

"Hang saline and give him O$_2$," the woman said as she applied a compressive pack to Friedberg's leg. "Neuro intact. No other wounds. Looks like he might've nicked the femoral." She turned to Vail while she finished wrapping the bandage. "The Inspector probably would've bled out if you didn't get him out of there when you did."

*Thanks, lady. But I was more worried about the goddamn cable severing his head.*

"Vitals stable." The male medic placed the oxygen mask over Friedberg's face. "Ready to transport."

The medics moved to either end of the gurney, released the legs, and then pushed it into the open ambulance bay.

As the woman grabbed the right door to swing it closed, she said, "Anyone riding with him?"

"Yes…" Friedberg said weakly, the clear plastic mask riding up and down with the motion of his jaw.

"I'll go," Vail said. "Burden—I think you should come too. Roxx, you wanna follow in the car? See if you can reach Carondolet and Yeung, maybe they've got something on Hartman's phone."

Vail and Burden climbed in behind the male paramedic, who sat at Friedberg's head. He immediately began adjusting the IV line and the two hanging bags.

"So weak," Friedberg said.

The man reached across Friedberg's body and reseated his oxygen mask. "You're one tough hombre, Inspector. To think clearly, let alone talk—pretty impressive. Soon as we get your fluid levels up, you'll feel a little stronger."

Vail leaned a hand on the gurney's frame. "Can you tell us what happened? Did you see the offender?"

"Smoke. Want…one."

The medic swiveled, nearly knocking out the IV. "A cigarette? Are you crazy?"

Friedberg lifted the left corner of his mouth in a one-sided grin, then rolled his head toward Vail. "Thanks. For saving my life."

She lifted the mask an inch away from his mouth. "Tell us about the offender."

"Hit from behind, never saw him. Woke up in a dark place. Never spoke."

"Any idea where he had you?" Burden asked.

"Oil smell, grease. Heard noises…but he had something over my ears." Friedberg closed his eyes.

Vail looked over at Burden. "The cable car barn?"

Friedberg said, "He moved me once—no, twice, I think. Gave me something, drugged me."

"How long's he gonna be laid up?" Burden asked the medic.

"The doc's gonna be able to give you a much better answer. But assuming no internal injuries, infections, or neurological damage, two to three days. Best case."

Friedberg closed his eyes again. "Sorry."

"You've got nothing to be sorry about," Vail said. She rested a hand on his shoulder. "Get your strength back. We need you. Apparently, the offender is fixated on San Francisco bakeries."

"Bakeries." Friedberg's eyes opened. "I'm reading a book—"

"I know." Vail grinned, then gently set the mask back in place. "Get better. And get back on the street."

# 68

Vail and Burden left Friedberg at the entrance to the Saint Francis Memorial Hospital emergency room. Dixon, following in the Taurus, swung by and rolled down her window. "Get in—we've got something."

She didn't need to say it twice. The moment Burden hit the backseat and Vail the front, Dixon accelerated.

"Yeung got Hartman's cell phone logs. He's working on it with our guys at Bryant Street, but I can tell you one name stood out like a bullet hole in the forehead."

"Someone we know?" Burden asked.

"Stephen Scheer."

Vail's mouth dropped open. She immediately held up her hands. "Hold on. Let's think this through before we pull the trigger. They both live in San Francisco, Hartman handled major crimes and Scheer's a police reporter for a major newspaper. Maybe Hartman had a case Scheer was covering."

Dixon, driving twice the speed limit and weaving through the light traffic, was nodding at each of Vail's suggestions. But then she said, "Certainly possible, and very logical. But it doesn't appear to be the case. The calls all came within the last few days. And all of them were before you got that note from the offender."

*That's not good.*

"As if that's not enough, his last call was tonight. While we were at Alcatraz."

Burden grabbed the front seat and pulled himself forward. "That's who called Hartman when he left the cellhouse?"

"Looks like it."

*Can that be? Was I standing right next to the offender and didn't see it? Is that possible? No. Yes.*

"Where's he now?" Burden asked.

"Funny you should ask," Dixon said, blaring her horn at a truck that pulled in front of her. "Yeung and Carondolet are on their way to Scheer's house right now. And, coincidentally, so are we."

THEY ARRIVED AT THE NARROW two-story home on College Avenue in Berkeley twenty minutes later. A Ford was double-parked haphazardly, blocking the narrow street.

"So they're here," Burden said as they got out of the Taurus.

They marched up to the door and were about to knock when Yeung pulled it open. "We woke his wife and sons. She went to put the younger one back to bed."

Vail, Burden, and Dixon walked into the entryway. It was a modest home with spartan furnishings. Children's toys littered the floor in front of an old tube television. Framed newspaper clippings of what were presumably Scheer's early articles hung over the couch.

A woman in her late forties walked in, pulling her auburn hair back in a bun. She stopped when she saw another three cops standing in her home.

Vail, Burden, and Dixon identified themselves. Vail asked, "Ms. Scheer, do you know where your husband is?"

"You can call me Kathleen." She bent down and began picking up the mess of toys strewn across the weathered wood floor. "What's Stephen done now? Drunk in public again? Peeing on some homeless guy?" She uttered a pathetic laugh. "He did that once." She stopped and put a hand to her forehead. "So embarrassing. I met the editor of the paper down at the police station and had to watch while he called in a favor so they didn't charge him. Just a misdemeanor, but it'd be humiliating to the paper."

"Kathleen," Burden said. "It's not like that. We think he can help us with a case he's been working on."

"Must be important if it can't wait till morning."

They stared at her, feeling their explanation was sufficient.

Finally, Kathleen straightened up and said, "I don't know what you want from me. Have you checked his apartment?"

"We weren't aware he had one," Yeung said.

"We separated last month. I'd had enough."

Burden asked, "Did he...abuse you?"

"He had an addiction problem, Inspector. Mostly alcohol, some drugs. He'd go through rehab, then start drinking and we were off and running all over again. It was a never-ending cycle. I finally played the only card I had. I told him I didn't want him around our boys if he couldn't keep himself straight. I changed the locks. He got the apartment, and hasn't stopped calling and apologizing."

"Can we have the address?" Dixon asked.

"It's in Rockridge," Kathleen said, then gave them the street and number. "Is he really a witness? Or a suspect?"

"We think he has answers to a case we're working and we really need his help," Vail said. *The truth.*

"Have you noticed any strange behavior the past couple of weeks?" Dixon asked.

She set both hands on her hips. "Now that doesn't sound like a question you'd ask about a witness now, does it?"

Carondolet checked his watch. "Please, Ms. Sch—Kathleen. Just answer the question."

"His behavior's always a bit strange. I mean, people with addictions aren't normal, are they?"

*Depends on your definition.* "Behavior that you'd consider outside Stephen's norm," Vail said.

"No. But I also have been trying to avoid him, so I'm not sure I can answer that."

*And that could've been his trigger.* "Is he an empathetic person? Does he socialize well, form bonds?"

"Stephen does what he needs to do his job well. So he socializes when he needs to. But it's an effort for him because he's always been a pretty closed person. Sometimes it's hard to get close to him. He shuts me out. And that was another source of frustration for me."

*She's holding something back.* Vail took a step closer. "Kathleen. Is there something else you'd like to tell us?" Vail held her gaze. *Talk to me.*

Kathleen looked beyond Vail at the men. They apparently got the message because Burden said, "We'll wait outside."

When the door clicked shut, Vail led her over to the couch. Dixon remained standing.

"There's more to it than Stephen just being antisocial, isn't there?"

Kathleen looked down and waited a moment before speaking. "Stephen has a dark side. That's really why I left him. I mean the addiction was a big part, but..." She bit her lip. "He's always been a little secretive, and when I'd call him on it, he'd explain it away. He's a reporter, he'd tell me, and reporters sometimes work all hours, and go away for days at a time while they're researching a story.

"I figured he was having an affair, but I found some...things in his locked drawer. He was in the shower and I grabbed his keys and looked. He had photos of naked women, as if he'd taken them with a telephoto lens. It looked to me like he was some kind of peeping tom. And then I found a ring. A diamond ring, from the looks of it. It could be fake, I don't know. But it wasn't mine, I can tell you that."

*A trophy? Or nothing?*

"I put it all back then found a divorce lawyer. He doesn't know about the lawyer, I just said I needed some time."

"Does he know what you found?"

"I haven't told him. I was afraid... I just didn't even want to know what it meant. I'd been hurt enough. Once I made the decision, it really didn't matter."

"Thank you," Vail said. "I know it wasn't easy telling us that. We appreciate it." She stood up. "Call us if you hear from him." She handed her a card, then walked out with Dixon.

They congregated outside in front of Burden's Taurus and Vail filled them in on Kathleen's disclosure.

"What do you make of that?" Dixon asked.

"Maybe nothing, maybe something. The voyeurism could go with the addictive personality, or it could be more significant. Some psychopaths are substance abusers. But here's where it's important. Their psychopathy becomes more pronounced and they become more aggressive when under the influence. That said, what we see most of are psychopaths using drugs and alcohol to manipulate and compromise their victims—like slipping Rohypnol into their drink at a bar. Either way, given what we now know, we've gotta look hard at Scheer."

"What about MacNally?" Carondolet asked. "We should have some stuff on him very soon, but I don't think we should eliminate him."

"Absolutely. We look hard at MacNally too." Vail grinned. "From no suspects to two in a space of a couple hours. This is a good problem to have."

"Let's go by Scheer's apartment, see what we find," Carondolet said.

Yeung's phone rang. He glanced at the caller ID and said, "Mike Hartman's section chief." He stepped away and answered it.

"We don't have enough for a warrant," Burden said. "If he's not home…"

"We may be able to get one," Dixon said. "If we get a judge who's willing to stick his neck out a bit."

Vail tapped Yeung on the shoulder, and then explained that they needed a warrant. Hopefully, the section chief had enough juice to get it for them.

Burden glanced around the quiet street. "At the very least, we should go over to Scheer's place and see what we can stir up, talk to his neighbors."

"A canvass at this time of night?" Dixon asked.

Yeung turned to face them. "His section chief said Mike had a personal phone. If we can't find his Bureau-issue BlackBerry, his other cell may have something. I've got his carrier. Why don't you three go to Scheer's apartment and we'll try to track down Mike's BuCar in case his phone's in there."

"And the warrant?"

"Chief said he'd make a call. No promises."

"We'll be in touch when we know something," Burden said.

They got in their vehicles and headed off.

As Dixon locked in her seatbelt, she said, "If Scheer's the offender, does that make sense? Does he have a connection to Alcatraz?"

"Send it over to the interns," Burden said to Dixon. "See what they can dig up."

"Does he fit the profile?" she asked as she thumbed her iPhone.

Vail grabbed the door handle as Burden swung out into traffic. "Before we had that hit on MacNally, I was thinking we were dealing with a middle-aged man. That matches up. He's educated and, based on what we saw of his workspace, it appeared to be neat. I didn't get a sense that he's psychopathic, but they can be very good at disguising it. His wife said he's a closed person, that it takes effort for him to socialize. That could be pathognomonic of psychopathology. But it can also just be that he's an introvert."

"So you don't know," Burden said.

"Off the top of my head, no. I mean, the offender's played it brilliantly. He kept us busy, he took our minds off the ball, processing and evaluating multiple vics, chasing cryptic clues that he kept feeding us, dealing with Friedberg's disappearance. He totally knew how to work us. And unless something stands out, unless you pick up on some warning sign, you don't think to look at the people around you.

"If it is Scheer, that's a very bold strategy because we've had a lot of contact with him. Shit, Burden, you've known him for years. Not well, but if he is the UNSUB, he's been killing in your backyard and you didn't know it. That'd certainly fit his ego, to be around us at the height of a crisis and we're still not seeing him. But I need time to look everything over, all the crime scenes, all the vics, and think things through. I'm a little overloaded with facts and the UNSUB's subterfuge. I've gotta cut through all the shit and boil it down to an offender profile."

"Is it even possible?" Dixon asked. "We were with him while those texts were coming in and we were running all over the city."

Vail considered that, working those incidents through her mind. "He wasn't with us the whole time. And when he was, how hard is it to pull your phone and type out a short text? If he already knew what he was going to write, why not? None of us was watching him. I'm not saying that nails it, but it is possible."

Moments later, Dixon pointed out the window. "This is it."

Burden swung the car into a hydrant space at the curb.

As they were getting out, Vail's phone buzzed. While climbing the steps to the brownstone-style apartment building, Vail stole a look at the display. "Carondolet got a tech to pull Hartman's phone logs. We've got the dates and times that his calls and texts were made and received. Scheer's number's there. Nine times during the past three days."

"Let's go see what we can find out," Burden said.

Visible through the exterior glass door was a small entryway that contained a telephone handset and a series of mailboxes with their corresponding buzzers.

Dixon set her hands on her hips. "Why is it that security measures don't have any effect on a crook but they stop us dead?"

"I think we're good," Burden said.

A man in his late twenties was approaching the building and fiddling with his keys. He excused himself and tried to walk between them.

But Vail blocked his way. "FBI. We need entry to your building." Before the man could object or pose a question, Vail asked her own. "Do you know Stephen Scheer?"

The man, still fixated on Vail's badge, met her eyes. "He's my roommate. Why?"

"Is he home?" Burden asked.

"I was bartending. I'm just getting back myself. But I wouldn't be surprised if Stephen isn't home. He's gone a lot, working stories."

"Can we take a look around your place?"

The man squinted and leaned backwards. "Uhh…"

"Not a big deal," Vail said, pulling her BlackBerry. "We can camp outside your door and get a warrant. Or you can let us in. You got drugs in there, whatever, we don't care. Stephen is working a case with us, and he may have some info that he meant to give us."

The man bobbed his head, then finally nodded. "If he meant to give it to you, then why—"

"We have reason to believe he may be in danger," Burden said. "And we don't have a lot of time."

The roommate's eyes widened. "Why didn't you just say that? Come on up." He unlocked the door and led them inside.

Burden winked at Vail and they ascended the stairs, which creaked with each step. Inside, there were boxes stacked along one of the walls.

"Stephen hasn't finished unpacking. I think he's still hoping he'll get back together with his wife."

"How do you know him?" Vail asked as Dixon and Burden began looking around.

"I was a journalism major. I've hooked on with the *Register* and Stephen helped me get the gig. He needed a place to crash, and I had a study, so…"

A moment later, Burden emerged from a small adjacent room holding up a thin cell phone. Vail nodded, acknowledging the significance of the find, while Dixon completed her sweep.

"How's it going with you guys?"

"Stephen's an awesome writer. I've learned a lot from him. I mean, you can't overestimate the value of all the experience he's got under his belt."

*Hate to burst your bubble, kid, but this guy may have a whole lot of other experiences hidden under his belt you probably don't want to know about.*

Dixon and Burden entered the living room, signaling they were done.

"Well. Thanks for all your help."

"Did you get what you needed?"

Burden pursed his lips and nodded. "I sure hope so."

OUT IN THE CAR, BURDEN SET aside materials he had taken, and bagged, from Scheer's room: items that were likely to carry his DNA and fingerprints, should they be needed. He handed the phone over to Dixon, who said she was familiar with the operating system.

"What'd you see?" Vail asked, settling herself in the front passenger seat. "Anything obviously incriminating?"

"Things were pretty neat. It's a small room, so I'm guessing most of his stuff is still in the boxes. No bloody clothing in the closet, no trophies, nothing that appeared to have any connection to Alcatraz or any of the vics."

"If he is the UNSUB," Vail said, "I'd expect him to have some kind of secret location where he keeps his stuff. Not in an open apartment he's sharing with someone. He's a smart SOB. Maybe a storage locker. And I wouldn't expect it to be registered under his name."

Dixon held up the phone. "Got his text messages. And whoa— okay, here we go. Several exchanges with Mike Hartman."

Burden turned around to face the backseat. "Read 'em out loud."

"Scheer was looking for info on Karen. Hartman responded, 'Why me?' and Scheer wrote back, 'You used to be her partner.' To Hartman's credit, he said, 'nothing to say to you.' And then it went back and forth: 'I think you do,' 'fuck off...'" Dixon scrolled and flicked her finger, then said, "Oh, here's a good one. Scheer: 'I'm a reporter, asshole. You're gonna tell me what I want to know or certain facts will come out about Candace.'"

"Who the hell is Candace?" Burden asked.

Vail said, "Mistress? Who knows—someone who knows things Hartman wouldn't want to be made public." She gestured to the phone. "Go on."

"Right. Next one is 'Meet me at the Starbucks at Market and Fell, 1:00.'"

"Any reply?"

"No. But I think we should assume he went."

"Why?" Burden asked. "Why not arrest the guy for extortion?"

"He's not asking for money," Vail said. "And there's no way for Hartman to know if Scheer's set the info to be released automatically, or by some accomplice, unless he cancels it. Best move is to meet with the guy and see what he's about. It's a public place, so it's relatively safe. I'd go, find out what his angle is. You can always try to bust the asshole later."

"There's a phone call," Dixon said, "which I think is—yeah, that's the one he made while we were on Alcatraz."

"How long did it last?" Vail asked.

"Three minutes."

"Long enough for him to lure him outside and blindside him," Burden said.

Dixon slipped the phone in her pocket. "Could be."

"Any record of those texts the UNSUB was sending us before? The clues?"

"No," Dixon said. "But those came from different numbers—untraceable disposables."

Vail's BlackBerry vibrated. "What do you think—good news or bad?" She looked at the display. "Yeung says Hartman's car was clean. No phone. But Carondolet got hold of MacNally's inmate file. Or, at least, part of it."

"Impressive for this time of night," Burden said.

Vail yawned. "Sorry. Speaking of this time of night." She shook off the fatigue and said, "Let's meet them. They're back at Pier 33."

Burden turned over the engine. "On our way."

WHILE EN ROUTE, VAIL DIALED Clay Allman. He answered with a groggy grunt.

"Clay, Karen Vail." Another grunt. "Sorry to wake you—"

"Wake me, yeah. What the hell time is—are you out of your mind? It's…3 AM?"

"Sounds about right. Listen, we've got a question for you. You happen to know where Scheer is?"

"Let me get this straight," Allman said. "You call me up at three in the morning, looking for the last guy in the world I'd want to talk to. And you're wondering if I know where he is?"

"Again, that sounds about right."

"Can I go back to sleep?"

"I take it you haven't seen or spoken to him."

Allman groaned. "Not since you dropped him off after our…hang on a minute. If you're asking about Scheer at this time of night, something's gotta be up. Where arc you?"

"Thanks, Clay. You've answered my question." Vail pressed END.

"You really thought he might know where Scheer was?" Dixon asked.

"No freaking idea, Roxx. I took a shot they were throwing back beers in a bar somewhere in the city. You know, friends become enemies, then enemies become friends again after we bring them together like brothers who've had an argument."

Burden chuckled. "What drug have you been smoking?"

"Like I said, I took a shot." Vail's phone began ringing—Allman calling her right back, the diligent reporter taking a shot to pry info from her. She ignored it. Instead, Vail dialed the task force, which, she was told, had thinned since Friedberg's rescue. But many were still in the office despite the hour, toiling away with several interns who were likely aiming to score points with the inspectors while devouring the thrill of the investigation.

Vail asked them to delve into Stephen Scheer's background. No detail was too insignificant: she wanted an unfiltered dossier of who this man was, where he came from, what college he attended, and what he did in the years after graduating.

While the volume of information would be less robust than usual because numerous agencies had closed several hours ago, there was still a fair number of online databases and external resources they could access.

Fifteen minutes later, as Burden was pulling up to the parking lot for Pier 33—with signs advertising Alcatraz Cruises—Vail received a return call.

"Karen, it's Robert."

"Robert," she said, sharing a look with Burden. "Where are you?"

"I'm at the station, working with the task force. It wasn't as bad as they thought—once they pumped in fluids and stitched me up, I was able to get back on my feet. Sort of. I had one of the interns come get me. As long as I don't get up from the chair too fast, or go chasing our UNSUB down the street, I can function."

"I hope you know what you're doing." She paused. "I guess that goes for us, too."

"You asked them to put together a backgrounder on Scheer. They called his wife and got his social and such—which, I gotta tell you, she wasn't too happy we woke her again—but it was worth it. We hit some interesting stuff, but we just found it and I'm not sure what to make of it."

"Go on." She placed her BlackBerry on speaker.

"So Scheer was born and raised in San Mateo. First thing we did was log onto vital records, to start at the beginning and see where it led us. And it stopped us dead."

"How so?" Burden asked.

"Birdie!" The smile was evident in Friedberg's tone. "Good to hear your voice. Okay, so the problem is that we found two birth certificates. We're not sure what to—"

"He was adopted," Vail said. "When you're adopted, they assign the adopting parents' names. Then they destroy the old certificate. But once in a while, the original hangs around. What's the name on the original one?"

"Baby Markley. Markley would be the mother's maiden name if she wasn't married—which might be why she put the kid up for adoption."

"What does that get us?" Dixon asked.

Burden shrugged. "Not much."

Vail asked, "Can you pull the court records and see if the mother was married? That'd get us a last name—"

"Already checked," Friedberg said, the rhythmic tap of a keyboard coming through the speaker. "The records only go back to 1950. I think I might—hang on a second. Yeah. Here's something." More clicks. "Hmm. He's got a sealed juvie record."

Vail sat forward in her seat. "This is starting to sound interesting. Except that we've hit another roadblock."

"Maybe not," Burden said. "Sealed file—but there's no gag order on the investigating detective. Track down the guy who handled that case and we may get an answer as to what Scheer did to land his young ass in jail."

"I'll get on it. Call you as soon as we have something."

They met Carondolet and Yeung in front of the hood of their car. Yeung had his laptop open, and a warden information card filled the screen. A mug shot showed a man wearing a red, white, and black placard around his neck, identifying him as ALCATRAZ 1577. Walton MacNally.

"So this is our guy," Burden said.

Vail placed both hands on the car's hood and leaned closer to the PC. The screen's brightness, amidst the dark parking lot, played harshly across her face. "One of them."

"You've had time to look this over," Dixon said. "What's the big picture?"

Carondolet folded his arms across his chest. "They had MacNally pegged as a very bright guy, scored a 135 on a prison IQ test. Resourceful, motivated, hard worker. Did fifteen months at Leavenworth but was involved in two escape attempts and was suspected in the violent assault of two cons. After the second attempt, he was transferred here, where his history of violence continued. His intake card said he was considered a 'serious escape risk.'"

"What was the original offense?" Burden asked.

"Convicted of two counts of armed robbery and one of kidnapping. Oh, and he's listed as widowed. Get this—he was arrested and tried for murdering his wife but was ultimately found not guilty."

Vail pursed her lips. "Well, that's certainly…an impressive record. We'd be silly not to consider this guy a prime suspect."

"I thought we already did," Yeung said.

"We did. But we've been running all over the place tonight looking at Stephen Scheer."

"And?" Carondolet asked.

Dixon bent over the laptop beside Vail and scrolled down. "And he's looking guilty. Of what, it's hard to say. But something isn't right with him."

"How old is the guy?" Vail asked. "MacNally."

"Apparently," Dixon said, paging down a document, "a spry and fit 79."

"A few other things you should know," Yeung said. "He was involved in a number of violent altercations. One with a guy you're familiar with: one of our vics, Harlan Rucker, who he apparently had some bad blood with dating back to Leavenworth. Rucker and an accomplice attacked MacNally in Industries with a knife."

"I'm liking MacNally more with each passing minute," Burden said. "What else?"

Yeung cocked his head. "There was a clergyman at Alcatraz by the name of Finelli. He tried to pass a letter from MacNally to his son, but it apparently got returned unopened. The kicker is that there's a warden's note saying that Finelli tipped off prison officials about MacNally's plans to escape, and the attempt ended very badly."

"Badly for who?" Dixon asked.

"Everyone. An officer was killed, and an inmate who was in on the escape with MacNally also got killed."

"Who killed the CO and inmate?" Vail asked.

"The reports of the incident are sketchy," Carondolet said. "The file says it was unknown who killed the officer, MacNally or the other inmate. It also says MacNally fell down the rockbed during his escape attempt and the responding officers rescued him from drowning."

"But?"

"But when I was a ranger we were told that rumors were rampant at the time among the inmate population that MacNally killed both the guard and the prisoner. And that revenge was dished out by one of the guards who found MacNally in back of the Powerhouse, on the Old North Caponier. Tuned up MacNally pretty badly. The doc, according to the rumor, covered for the CO and wrote a bogus report."

"Let me guess," Vail said. "The doctor's name was Martin Tumaco."

"Give that lady a pat on the ass," Carondolet said. "And the officers involved were—ready for this? Russell Ilg and Raymond Strayhan."

"Holy shit," Burden said. "We've got our guy. MacNally is our fucking UNSUB." He looked at Vail. "Right?"

Vail pushed up from the hood. "Maybe." *Something's still not adding up.* "It looks that way. But...a couple of things are bugging me. MacNally is a violent criminal, I get that. But I'm not seeing convincing evidence he's a psychopath. The behaviors we've observed at the crime scenes, particularly what he did to the women… It doesn't fit, at least not given the information we've got."

Burden sighed. His frown telegraphed the disappointment that was now burnished on his face. "You said there were two things bothering you."

"Scheer. He threatened Hartman to get dirt on me, and when Hartman was all too happy to give it to him, that information ended up in my hotel room along with the type of key that the offender left at crime scenes."

"You're wondering," Dixon said, "what the connection is between a deadbeat journalist with a shady past—and present—and a former Alcatraz con."

"Shady past?" Yeung asked.

"Scheer's got a sealed juvie record," Dixon said. "And remember, his wife didn't exactly paint a Man of the Year portrait for us."

"Scheer's his son," Vail said softly.

"What?" Burden asked.

Vail curled some hair behind her ear. "MacNally had a son. Maybe it's Scheer."

"But I thought Scheer was adopted."

Vail shook her head. "We don't know that. It's a likely explanation for the two birth certificates. But it's just a guess."

"Even so," Dixon said, "big deal. MacNally's son could've been adopted."

"Could Scheer be a psychopath?" Bledsoe asked.

Vail sighed deeply. "Psychopaths are very skilled at deception, so it'd be possible for us not to pick up on it. Not to mention he had us running all over the goddamn city, keeping us busy while he readied his grand show: killing John Anglin and placing him in his original cell for us to find. Everything he's done has been planned, calculated. But he also works off what we do and shifts strategy on the run if he needs to." Vail massaged her forehead. "So yeah, it's possible. I need something to eat. And some coffee." *And some sleep.* "I'm having a hard time thinking straight."

"What happened to MacNally?" Burden asked. "Where is he now?"

Carondolet moved in front of his laptop and clicked, then scrolled. "Here it is." He read a moment, then said, "That head injury was pretty bad. He had brain damage to—"

"Brain damage?" Vail nearly shouted. "That could change everything. You numb nuts didn't think to tell us that earlier?"

"Excuse me," Yeung said. "You're not the only one who's been up all night. Back off."

Vail held up a hand. "You're right. I'm sorry. My ASAC wants me to play nice with you guys out here because I may be making more trips out to California. So let me rephrase. You numb nuts didn't think to tell us that earlier?"

Carondolet and Yeung looked at Burden, who was merely studying the ground, shaking his head. And doing his best to stifle a laugh.

"His injury was to the prefrontal cortex and frontal lobe," Yeung said with a tight jaw. "According to the doc's report in the file, that means he—"

"Suffered from severe impairments in judgment, insight, and foresight," Vail said. "My colleague's done a lot of research on brain trauma and violent crime, and this kind of frontal disinhibition syndrome was something he briefed us on a few months ago. If that's what MacNally has, that might explain a lot. I can dial him up, see if he can shed some more light on it."

"So where's MacNally now?" Dixon asked.

"After Alcatraz closed in '63, he was transferred to Atlanta, then to the new max pen at Marion when it opened a few months later. He served another fifteen years and was released in '77."

"Released," Burden said. "That's freaking great."

"We all know that's common," Yeung said. "Last known whereabouts, he was in Chicago. But that was back in '78. He fell off the radar after that."

"Please tell me one of you guys put out a BOLO," Vail said.

Yeung closed the lid of his laptop. "Done."

"All right, look," Burden said, rubbing his hands together as if trying to generate warmth. "We can't stand out here all night. Let's go back to Bryant. Get some food and coffee, give ourselves time to clear our heads, then attack it fresh."

It was approaching 4:15 AM when they walked into Homicide with several coffees and a selection of pastries from Sparky's all night diner.

Vail, Burden, and Dixon greeted Friedberg, who looked pallid and drawn, but otherwise appeared to be holding his own.

While the others settled in for an all-staff conference to review the latest developments and relevant case points, Vail called the profiler at the BAU who had written a number of research papers on brain injuries and their impact on violent behavior: her new partner, Frank Del Monaco.

"Frank," Vail said, moving away from the commotion of gathering inspectors and interns. "I've got a question for you."

"You mean you need something from me," Del Monaco said. "Admit it and I'll be more than happy to help you. Well, I'll help you. Let's leave it at that."

Vail rolled her eyes. "Yes, Frank. I need your help."

"Isn't it like the middle of the night in California?"

"Now *there's* the perceptive man I've come to know and loathe."

"Karen, I know you have a hard time with this. But when you call someone to ask a favor, you shouldn't start the conversation with an insult."

"Goes to my point, doesn't it? Your perceptive powers are truly exceptional. So. My question pertains to the research you've done on brain injuries. We've got a suspect we really like who suffered substantial head trauma that resulted in damage to the prefrontal cortex and frontal lobe. I remember you telling us about the inhibitory effects—"

"Wait, wait. Hang on. You mean you were actually paying attention to what I was saying?"

"I know," Vail said, "as hard to believe as that may be, sometimes you say something intelligent. So I have to be on my toes for that rare moment. Now, can you help me or not?"

"You know we're going to be working together, right?"

"If you're trying to piss me off by bringing that up, you've succeeded. Now, your research."

"There's actually a new study out of Israel that I'm incorporating into a paper I've been working on. I won't bore you with the details of the trial, but the bottom line is that the impairment patterns we see in the personalities of psychopaths are mimicked in individuals who've sustained frontal lobe damage. Very aggressive and highly impulsive and uninhibited violence."

"You're shitting me. You wouldn't joke about that, right? I'm serious—this could be huge."

"First of all, the frontal lobe symptoms they observed in the study were a bit different from the typical psychopath's instrumental, cold-blooded, and predatory violence. Second, just because such an injury *can* cause psychopathic-like behaviors, doesn't mean it *has to*. Third, no. I'm not yanking your chain. The study was conducted out of the University of Haifa and—"

"Was it good research? I mean, do you trust it?"

"The sampling's smaller than I'd like, but the study's sound, Karen. I think you can take this to the bank."

"All right, listen up, Frank, because you're not going to hear this often: Thank you."

Before Del Monaco could come back with a sharp retort, she disconnected the call and shoved the BlackBerry in its holster. She rejoined the group, related the information, and explained the implications of the new research. "I'm thinking this changes our focus. Or at least my assessment. It seems that MacNally could very well be exhibiting psychopathic-type behaviors."

"So you think he's our guy?" Friedberg asked.

Vail hesitated. "*Could* be, Robert. It's not a definite. But I'm fairly certain he's involved. Is he the offender? He fits the profile. I would've pegged the UNSUB to be a younger guy, no later than his mid-fifties. But given his long history of incarceration and everything that happened to him, the age can be adjusted."

"Adjusted how?" Carondolet asked.

"First of all, incarceration retards social growth, so even though we're looking at a seventy-nine year old, given that he spent almost twenty years in prison, that takes us down to the late fifties. And if we consider that the first murder we might attribute to him occurred in '82, I think we are definitely in the ballpark."

"Can a seventy-nine year old do the murders we've seen?" Dixon asked.

"Depends on the person," Burden said. "Some guys that old are frail, others are fit and pretty freaking spry. Done right, he can control the victim with a gun or a knife or even his words. The only question would be the way he's gotten the males tied to the columns and poles. But the rope and pulley setup he used could explain that."

"And he could've had help," Yeung said.

"Karen," Dixon said, "you mentioned Scheer could be his son. If so—"

"Negatory on that," Carondolet said. "I kept reading the file on the way back here. His son was placed in an orphanage in '59, committed suicide in '63. Jumped from a suspension bridge in upstate New York."

Friedberg said, "Another son, then? A nephew? Maybe on his wife's side of the family. Or he had a son by another woman and he didn't find out till later in life."

"See what you can find out," Burden said.

Friedberg conferred with an intern, who began tapping away on the inspector's keyboard.

Forty minutes later, they informed the others that there was no record of other children fathered by Walton MacNally. "At least, none in the available databases that can be traced to MacNally."

"So we're back to our two suspects, MacNally and Scheer," Burden said.

Carondolet's phone rang. He slid off the worktable and, forcing down a yawn, answered the call. A moment later, he said, "The teams are leaving the island. They just wrapped up their search. It's clean. Our guy's not there."

"No surprise there," Dixon said. "He killed a federal agent… He's gotta know the heat's been jacked up to the max. Why the hell would he stick around?"

"We had to check," Yeung said. "Now we know for sure."

"Here we go," Friedberg said. "Just got an email from the cop I asked to track down the detective who handled Scheer's case. The sealed juvie record."

"And?" Burden asked.

"And he was more than pissed we woke him in the middle of the night. But he remembered the case, even though it was thirty-something years ago." Friedberg scrolled down with the keyboard. "Scheer was sixteen when he raped a girl." He swung his eyes over to Vail.

"Two teens having a good time and then she said no and he didn't listen?"

Friedberg read a bit, then said, "Well, the detective didn't so much as remember the details of the rape as much as what the kid did to him. Guy said Scheer went into a rage when they arrested him, kicked him pretty badly trying to get away, and broke his wrist. Had to get it pinned and was on medical disability for a year before he was able to fire a handgun."

Dixon poured another cup of coffee, then set the pot down. "I think we've got a decent view of who Stephen Scheer was—and is. Between the rape and what his wife told us, he's not exactly the kind of guy you want to bring home to your mother."

"But is he the kind of guy who could torture and murder several women and men?" Friedberg asked. "Is he the Bay Killer?"

"We've got that video of our UNSUB from the Palace of Fine Arts," Burden said. "Now that we've narrowed our suspect pool, how about we take another look at the tape?"

Fifteen minutes later, Friedberg had called up the footage on his PC and was scrolling slowly through the dark and grainy image of their hooded offender. Carondolet and Burden felt it could be Scheer; Yeung, Vail, and Dixon thought it was impossible to reach a conclusive determination. The others either shrugged or walked away without rendering an opinion. Friedberg kept looping the excerpt. Finally, ten minutes later, he pressed Stop and buried his face on his desk.

THEY SPENT ANOTHER TWO HOURS reviewing the files, discussing the timeline and the victimologies. With the morning sun hiding behind thick, low-hanging fog, and the first support personnel beginning to filter into the office, Vail pulled her feet off the worktable and sat up straight. She felt like crap, and thought she probably looked like it, too.

Just as she was entertaining the thought that they had not heard from the offender—nor had they been able to find any trace of Stephen Scheer or Walton MacNally—her phone began vibrating. Vail yawned and reached for the BlackBerry at the same moment. But what she saw on the screen nearly knocked her back into the chair.

"Hartman's phone." She looked at Dixon, then brought it to her ear. "Vail."

But she realized it was a text, and instantly pulled it away from her face. *Jesus. I really need some sleep.*

> did you miss me
> oh yes you did
> because im still doing my thing

"That's it?" Vail stared at the screen. "What the hell do we do with that?"

Burden, Friedberg, Carondolet, and Yeung had joined Dixon at Vail's side. The phone began trembling yet again.

> time has come to purge the evil
> meet me where the devil still resides

"Devil's Island," Friedberg said. "A nickname for The Rock. What else could he mean?"

"He *who*," Burden said. "Gotta be Scheer. Hartman's phone was missing when we found him tied to the smokestack, and Scheer was the one who left that note for Karen—"

"But if we're convinced it's Scheer," Yeung said, "what's his connection to MacNally?"

"Without more facts," Vail said, "we can fall back on the kindred-souls-find-each-other scenario. Whatever the reason, we've got to find him—them—fast. If we can believe his text, our offender's back on Alcatraz."

Burden swung around. "Robert, get us a helicopter. Faster than taking that Zodiac and we can land somewhere central, like maybe the cellhouse roof."

"Bureau's Regional Aviation Assets might have a chopper," Vail said, "but I'm not sure if San Fran—"

"We just got one," Yeung said. "A Bell 407, all tricked out. Staged at Crissy Field."

"Perfect," Burden said. "Get it hot. We're on our way."

Dixon rose from her chair. "So what's the plan?"

"Plan?" Burden harrumphed. "We don't have a plan."

Vail tucked in her blouse as she moved for the door. "Sure we do. And I can sum it up in three words: Catch this asshole."

Dixon grabbed her jacket off the back of the chair. "Works for me."


THE BELL MOTORED OVER THE fog-socked Bay. Visibility was almost nil, with white enveloping the helicopter's windows and increasing the confining feel of the chopper's modest compartment. Vail closed her eyes and tried to calm the anxiety, focusing instead on what their next steps would be.

Dixon, Burden, Carondolet, and Yeung sat alone with their thoughts until Vail tapped Carondolet on the knee. They were all outfitted with headsets tuned to the same channel.

"Any agents still there from last night?" Vail asked.

Carondolet shook his head. "They left on a cutter this morning. Around four or five, if I remember. Soon as they cleared the island."

"How many armed LEOs are normally on the island?"

"None. There was a law enforcement ranger there for a few months once, but it wasn't a permanent position. Just no money for it. Park Service has got the same problem Bureau of Prisons had with Alcatraz—costs a goddamn mint to maintain the buildings and keep that place in one piece. The salt air's a killer. And cops just haven't been necessary."

"Until today," Vail said.

Carondolet, seated beside the pilot, shrugged: What do you want me to say? "Park Police and FBI's got people en route. I'll get an ETA." He twisted the radio dial and began speaking into his mike. A moment later, he tuned back to their channel and then turned his torso to face his task force members. "Backup should arrive about ten to fifteen minutes after we do. But you're not gonna like this. It's Alumni Day."

Vail leaned closer. "What the hell's Alumni Day?"

"Once a year deal. Former correctional officers and their families—and ex-inmates—go to the island. Have meals, reminisce, give talks for the tourists."

"Inmates and officers, socializing?" Vail asked. "You've gotta be shitting me."

Burden said, "And that's today?"

Carondolet nodded. "And tomorrow. It's not publicized. The tourists who come this weekend just luck out."

"I don't think 'luck' is the right word," Vail said. "Call it off, turn the ferry around—"

"They're already there. Probably in the hospital by now. That's where they eat and hang out. They close off the whole floor from the public."

The helicopter swung left, circling from over what Vail presumed was choppy Bay water, inward toward the island.

"I'm gonna land us on the fresh-water cistern," the pilot said. "Better access to all the buildings than the roof. Assuming I can see it."

Vail nudged Dixon. "This guy's got a sense of humor."

The FBI pilot swept around in a tight arc, then hovered and slowly descended, as if the agent was holding out a hand and feeling around for the ground. A moment later, with a slight jolt, he brought them to rest on a large, flat, cement area just north of the cellhouse and water tower—both of which were barely visible in the fog. Dozens of seagulls scattered, vacating the improvised landing pad for a much larger bird.

Carondolet pointed as he spoke. "We're near the north tip of the island. Industries building and the Golden Gate are to our right." Their heads swung in that direction. "Trust me, behind that wall of fog, they're both there. Cellhouse and rec yard's in front of us, which you can kind of make out. Powerhouse is to our left, down the hill."

"There's the smokestack," Vail said. "Or, part of it." *Looks a bit different without a dead body tied to it.*

"How do you want to handle this?" Yeung asked.

"First question to ask is why Scheer brought us here," Burden said. "We figure that out, we'll have a course of action."

"Another body?" Dixon asked.

Vail shrugged a shoulder. "Maybe. Maybe more than one. I think everything he's been doing, it's all been leading up to this. He chose today, and this place, for a reason. He wanted all the ex-officers and inmates on the island. And this Alumni Day gives him what he wants."

"Why?" Burden asked.

"I can guess, but I'm sure we'll find out." Vail's BlackBerry buzzed. "Apparently sooner rather than later."

welcome

"He knows we're here," Dixon said.

Vail frowned. "We flew in on a goddamn helicopter, Roxx. Fog or not, *everyone* knows we're here."

They jumped out of the Bell and pivoted, taking in what they could see of the structures Carondolet had mentioned.

Dixon put her hands on her hips. "He could be anywhere. We should get everyone off the island until we get things under control."

"The ferry's back at Pier 33," Carondolet said. "It's loading up. They'd have to get everyone off, then it'd take at least twelve minutes to get here, and then another ten to fifteen to load it."

Yeung, who was peering into the thick soup, swung around and said, "We should leave everyone where they are, in the hospital. Soon as backup gets here, we put an agent at each entrance. Right now keeping things simple will keep everyone safe."

"Fine. We need to focus on finding Scheer," Vail said. "You were him, where would you be?" Just then, her phone vibrated. "Here we go."

> i would give you a clue but
> ur time is running out
> go to the diesel tank

Vail turned to Carondolet. "What diesel tank?"

"There are several tanks on the island, some of them hold fuel and others water, so it's har—" He stopped and swung around, then peered into the fog in the direction of the smokestack. "Wait a minute. There is a diesel tank." He walked to the furthest edge of the landing pad, then held out an index finger and settled on a location. "There."

Carondolet took off along the left side of the helicopter, leading them toward the water tower. Just before they hit its stanchion, he hung a left down a series of cement stairs. The steps ended at a lengthy, deeply sloping sidewalk that paralleled the cistern where the chopper had set down.

As they ran along the path, to their right, the Powerhouse and Quartermaster warehouse rose from below the adjacent East Road.

Carondolet led them up East Road and through a cyclone fence sally port, just past the end of the Powerhouse building. A chain-link gate, its lock forced open, blocked the entrance to a steeply sloped steel gangplank that spanned a gully below. The metal footway led down to a sizable cement slab that contained pipes of varying sizes and stainless steel hatches. A white, black and red warning sign stood sentry where the bridge ended:

DANGER

COMBUSTIBLE LIQUIDS

DIESEL FUEL

A large cylindrical tank the color of a fire engine and marked Diesel Fuel stood on wide rails at the far edge of the concrete base, seemingly at the edge of the island. Barely visible beyond the red tank was…nothingness. Regardless of the fog, Vail still heard it: crashing waves of the ocean.

"There," Carondolet said.

Vail pulled open the gate and grabbed the railings of the narrow gangway, then headed down, followed by Burden and Dixon.

She stood in front of the massive tank, hands on her hips. "Now what?" She pulled her phone to make sure she had not missed a text from the offender. Nothing—but with the crappy cell reception on the island, she wondered what he would do if his messages weren't getting through. How would he react? *Not well.*

"Anything?" Yeung called out, standing watch with Carondolet at the gate, handguns at the ready.

Dixon jumped down to the ground about five feet below the concrete support base, which stood beside the Powerhouse's exterior wall. A moment later, she called up to Vail from the other side of the tank. "You wanted to find Scheer, right?"

Vail looked down in Dixon's direction, though she couldn't see her. "Uh, that'd be affirmative."

"Well, we found him."

Vail and Burden jumped off the foundation, then climbed over a series of yellow pipes that protruded from the cement base. Dixon was standing on the other side of the tank…where Stephen Scheer was seated.

"Is he—"

"No," Dixon said. "He's alive. Unconscious, but breathing. Drugged, maybe."

Burden craned his neck and reached across the top of the base. "He's chained to the tank." He leaned in closer, then said, "And not to dampen the spirit, but we've got another problem." He leaned against the edge of the foundation and pointed at a box to Scheer's left.

"Yeung," Vail yelled. "We've got an IED!" *A bomb. A goddamn bomb—*

Yeung, standing behind the cyclone fencing thirty feet away, pulled his phone and began dialing.

Vail climbed atop the cement base and knelt next to the device. "Timer—set for…holy Jesus—three minutes."

"Active?"

"Two minutes fifty-eight seconds. Yeah, it's active."

Carondolet ran halfway down the gangplank. "Get out, we need to get away from here!"

"Can you raise EOD—maybe they can talk us through deactiv—"

"Karen, that's a bomb attached to a diesel tank. And the slab you're standing on? It's a storage receptacle filled with fuel. Not only that, see that yellow piping?" Carondolet gestured at the tubes that snaked up the side of the Powerhouse building. "It runs the entire length of the island. All the way to the dock. This bomb goes off, it'll take half the island with it."

*And that's the offender's plan. Kill all the former guards and cons.* Vail rose and, among the many valves protruding from the back of the tank, chose one that was perched above a coupling pipe.

"What are you doing?" Dixon asked. "We've gotta get out of here."

Vail began turning the burled knob. "Burden—try to reach someone on the dock, have 'em find a valve on the yellow pipe and open it full bore."

Burden pulled his phone and ran up the metal bridge with Carondolet.

"Karen," Dixon said. "We've gotta go."

"We leave, Scheer dies—"

"If we don't leave, we *all* die." Dixon grabbed Vail's arm, but she shrugged it off.

"See if you can get him free," Vail said as she continued cranking the knobbed wheel atop the valve. "We've still got time."

Dixon moved to Scheer's body and began inspecting the bindings. "I can't—chain's tight. We need a hacksaw or bolt cutter—"

A loud hiss, indicating tremendous pressure—blew back at Vail. She yanked her hand away at the instant a thick stream of diesel fuel blasted outwards, cascading out of the mouth of the coupling pipe in a downward arc toward the ocean below.

The acrid odor constricted her throat. She twisted away and buried her nose in the crook of her elbow.

Dixon, her face likewise shielded, asked, "What good is that?"

"Emptying the tank," Vail shouted. "Concrete slab might dampen the explosion. Maybe it won't ignite the fuel underneath us."

"Now can we leave?" She leaned in close. "Ninety seconds left."

"What about Scheer?"

"Not happening. He's chained down. Unless you have a bolt cutter in your back pocket, there's nothing we can do."

*Shit.*

"Karen," Burden yelled from above. "Let's go—now!"

Dropping her arm and holding her breath, Vail climbed around the tank to leave—but gave one last look back at Scheer's chain.

But she suddenly found herself hefted up onto Dixon's shoulder.

"Roxx, what are you doing? Put me down!"

Dixon made it onto the gangway and did her best to run uphill. As strong as she was, moving up a narrow path on a steep incline with a grown woman over her shoulder was difficult even for her.

"Put me down, I'll go—I'll go!"

Dixon lowered her to the metal bridge's surface, and then gave her a shove. Vail made it through the fence and continued across East Road, following Burden up the sidewalk they had come down earlier, toward the landing pad/cistern and cellhouse.

"Did you reach someone on the dock?" Vail asked.

"They found a valve and opened it up. Whether it's too little, too late—"

The explosion was concussive, an eardrum-pounding blast that shook the bedrock and sent the three of them sprawling to the ground. Vail lifted her head and saw, through the dusty fog, daylight showing through the left portion of the Powerhouse. From what she could see, the remainder of the island was largely intact.

As they glanced around, surveying the damage, Dixon gave Vail's shoulder a shove. "That was brilliant. Brilliant, but incredibly stupid."

"Thanks, Roxx. I think."

Carondolet and Yeung came running down the sidewalk toward them, sidearms and cell phones in hand.

"You all right?" Yeung asked.

"We're fine," Vail said as they got to their feet. "Everyone safe?"

"Scheer's obviously toast—uh, literally. Everyone else seems okay. We've got a fire running the length of the pipe," he said, gesturing to the east side of the island.

Flames licked skyward from behind the foliage and brush along the coastline, extending past the vacant Officer's Club, and beyond.

"Backup saw the explosion and called the Coast Guard. We're heading down to the dock to help with deployment."

"If we've got service," Burden said, "we'll keep you posted."

The two men moved off. And Vail, Burden, and Dixon looked at one another. *Now what?*

They didn't have to ponder that too long, as another text arrived:

> probly confuzed abowt nowe
> you weakish speller ;-)
> i can see clearly now
> im on top of the world

"What's the deal with the misspelled words?" Vail asked.

"Who cares about—"

"No, Roxx—it's significant. He did this once before, in the—"

"That manifesto," Burden said. He pointed at her BlackBerry. "You have it on there?"

"I got it," Dixon said. She brought it up on her iPhone, and Burden and Vail crowded around the small screen.

Burden reached into his coat pocket and pulled out a pad and pen, then began scribbling. "Shit..." he whispered. And then his face went ashen, his skin instantly pimpled in sweat.

"What's wrong?" Vail asked, reexamining the document.

"This sentence. It's an anagram, a classic example. And I missed it."

"What sentence?" she said firmly.

Burden jabbed a finger at the screen. "He wrote, 'I am a weakish speller.' And then he just wrote it again. Do you see it?"

"I've played enough word games, Burden. Just tell me."

"Puzzles, right? I do *number* puzzles, but I started out doing word pattern games. Palindromes, metonyms, pangrams, all that shit. But I got bored with them, and then a buddy turned me on to Sudoku. I didn't get those clues before because they were cryptic riddles. But this one was so goddamn simple, I should've gotten it. It was right in front of my eyes. 'I am a weakish speller' is a classic anagram. Rearrange the letters and you get *William Shakespeare*."

"So?" Dixon asked. "What's Shakespeare got to do with this? The answer's in one of his plays?"

"No," Vail said, "maybe he left other anagrams or word patterns for us. And we missed them." She wiggled her fingers at the pad. "Let me see that."

"Give me your BlackBerry," Dixon said. "I'll pull up all those texts he sent us."

Vail handed it over and started writing down possible clues from memory. "No, this isn't right." She looked at the phone in Dixon's hands. "It'd be something more significant. The 'weakish speller' thing was aimed at you, Burden. To clue us in, a slap in the face to pay attention. But it wasn't the answer. And I don't think the answer's in those messages he sent us. Maybe…"

Burden looked at the pad, then the BlackBerry. "Maybe what?"

Vail wrote on her pad, Walton MacNally. "MacNally's our prime suspect—with Scheer dead, our *only* suspect. What if…" She started drawing slashes across the name and writing something below it. But then she stopped. "Doesn't work. Not enough letters."

"What doesn't work?" Dixon asked. "What are you thinking?"

Burden brought a hand to his forehead. "Oh, my god."

Vail looked at him. "If you've got something—"

"Yeah, I've got something. It's been there, right under our noses." Burden kicked at a rock and sent it skidding down the sidewalk. "Son of a bitch! For me. It was meant for me."

He turned away from them, but Vail grabbed his shirt. "Burden, so help me god. Tell us what you're talking about or I'm gonna wring your neck."

Staring into the fog's suffocating cover of homogeneity, he said, "I know who the killer is."

# 69

Burden clasped his hair in both hands. "I didn't see it! Why couldn't I see it?"

"Who's the killer, Burden?"

"Goddamn son of a bitch!" Burden spun back toward her. "It's Clay."

Vail stood there staring at him. Then she looked down at the pad, at Walton MacNally's name.

"It's an anagram," Burden shouted. "Walton MacNally—"

"I tried that," Vail said, studying the pad. "Not enough letters. Clay Allman—"

"That's because his full name is Clayton W. Allman. Remember? You saw it on his byline in that article we read."

Word play wasn't Vail's game, but one particular four-letter noun flooded her thoughts.

She grabbed her phone back from Dixon and dialed Yeung, hoping the call would go through. "We need all available agents, cops, inspectors, everyone—looking for Clay Allman. I'm betting he's somewhere on the island. Use extreme caution—he's the Bay Killer."

After a beat of silence, Yeung said, "Come again?"

"You heard right. Clay's our UNSUB." Vail pressed END, then started up the hill toward the cellhouse. "There was more to his message." She tried to steady her hand long enough to read the text: "'I can see clearly now' is another dig at us—can't we see what we've been missing? But he's 'on top of the world'..." Vail craned her neck up at the structure that stood on the highest point of the island. "The cellhouse roof. Yes?"

"Yes," Burden and Dixon said simultaneously.

They took off running, toward the building's entrance.

# 70

"There," Dixon said, pointing to an open set of barred doors along the side of the institution. Above the entrance, a green sign read, Main Cellhouse.

They jogged through what was once a sally port and saw a park ranger standing at the end of the long hallway that led to the Showers and Clothing room.

"FBI," Vail said, holding up her creds. "What's the fastest way to the roof?"

"East Gun Gallery," the woman said. "Why?"

"Take us," Burden said. "Fast."

As they ran up the adjacent staircase and entered the cellhouse at Times Square, Carondolet appeared. He jogged with them down Broadway and over to the corner of Park Avenue and the end of C-Block. They entered the East Gallery via a ladder, then climbed three more flights before emerging on the roof, handguns drawn.

The fog was beginning to lift, as Vail saw the city poking out across the Bay. Behind them, the lighthouse was working overtime.

A blast from the foghorn sounded off in the distance, and the scream of scattering gulls filtered up from the old parade ground below.

Using hand signals, the four of them spread out in a V formation, Burden and Dixon on Vail's and Carondolet's flank, slightly ahead of them. They advanced slowly, toward the north end of the roof.

To their left stood two massive, horizontally mounted black metal cylindrical water tanks perched atop concrete stands. They moved past them onto the largest, and widest, section of the roof.

Carondolet held up a hand and they stopped. He pointed at the brick and glass structures that extended into the distance lengthwise along the roof and said, in a near whisper, "These are the cellhouse skylights over Broadway, Seedy Street, and Michigan Avenue. And there's the vent Morris and the Anglins climbed through in '62," he said, gesturing at a flat, welded-shut metal plank.

"Can the Park Ranger tour," Vail said. "Useful information only— what are we looking at with this roof?"

"I'm getting to it," Carondolet said.

"Get to it faster."

He frowned at her and continued: "The height of the skylights on the east and west ends limit our fields of vision to only what we can see in that particular aisle. There are also pipes that run the length of the roof, circular vent outlets, and two large skylights down there, over the hospital. Plenty of places to hide behind."

Vail did not think Clay Allman was interested in hiding—that's not what this was about.

"And the roof drops off up ahead, over the hospital wing," Carondolet said.

Vail peered into the thinning fog. "So there's a big blind spot."

"Exactly."

Vail tightened her grip on the Glock. *Now that's useful.*

Burden looked over the area in front of them, then said, "Let's each take an aisle and move forward, toward the hospital. Roxxann, clear that east section. It's blind from here, so we'll wait for your signal."

Dixon moved to her right and pushed her back up against the flat end of the skylight. While the others waited and stood at the ready, eyes prowling the remainder of the expansive rooftop, Dixon spun toward the hidden section, her SIG extended, knees bent, anticipating—anything. But seconds later, she gave them an all-clear hand signal.

They shifted left, toward the west end of the building, and headed down the remaining three aisles: Burden to the left, Vail along the middle section, Carondolet one section over to her right, and then Dixon. They moved slowly but methodically forward, toward the narrow portion of the roof, which at that point spanned approximately forty yards in width and about a hundred in length: the hospital.

Carondolet's description was correct: there was a substantial drop-off in the roofline. As they approached, the skylights ended and the four cops had a view of one another.

Vail held up a hand and they all stopped; she pointed at the hospital roof, fifteen feet ahead, then held out her Glock in a Weaver stance.

"Come out, Clay. Slowly."

Clay Allman backed away from the blind spot. "About fucking time. You people are so damn stupid, you know that?"

Allman was holding a pistol in his right hand and what looked like a Boker stiletto knife in his left. But he was not making any threatening moves.

"Clay," Burden said. "What the hell?"

Vail knew that to get the most out of this discussion, she needed to play to his grandeur. But she was not interested in learning about Clay Allman...or whatever he chose to call himself. At the moment, all she really wanted to do, deep down, was put a bullet in his brain. She shoved those visceral thoughts aside and said, "You understand you're not in control anymore, right, Clay?"

"Depends on how you look at it. I've accomplished most of what I wanted. I blew up the island. Officers, cons, didn't matter to me. They were all here today. It was, I have to say, a perfect day to take care of business. I've been planning this for a long, long time, Vail."

"But you didn't blow up the island. You can't see what's going on down there, but we drained the tank before the bomb went off. You caused some damage, yeah. But when the fog burns off, you're gonna see. Everyone's safe—the former prisoners, the officers—they're below us, eating breakfast."

Allman's face stiffened and his grip tightened around his pistol.

Vail knew he was using every bit of self-discipline to keep from lashing out at her—because that would, in effect, give credence to what she was saying: that he had lost control.

And she knew he would not yield that power to her.

"Let me describe it to you, Clay. You knocked out the corner of the Powerhouse, and there's a brush fire. But the buildings are still standing. No one died." She tilted her head. "You accomplished nothing."

"Scheer's dead. That's something. I saved the city from a second rate reporter who got his lunch handed to him by a crime-writing serial killer." He chuckled—a forced attempt to cover his anger. "What kind of headline would that make?"

"I have to give credit where it's due," Vail said. "You had me. All of us—we had no clue. And that thing with Mike Hartman. That was very, very smart."

"I figured you'd make that connection, and I also knew you wouldn't ask him about it. According to him, it was pretty embarrassing for you. And it posed a bit of a risk to you and your cushy career. It was patently obvious that you two didn't like each other. It was a calculated risk for me, but I know you better than you know yourself."

*Don't bet on it. You guessed right this time, but that's it, pal.*

'So I established a connection between Scheer and Hartman, so that you'd see they talked. Because I knew you'd look at his phone logs. See, I've been hanging around Homicide for thirty years. I know how you people think, how you run investigations. I knew what you were going to do before you did it."

*You framed Scheer. And you ran us ragged because you knew we couldn't help ourselves. Texting us right under our noses, a dozen, two dozen feet away. Fuck you, asshole.* She wanted to say that—but held her tongue. Instead, she pursed her lips and nodded slowly. "I have to give it to you Clay, you got us good. Even faked your own death. That was particularly astute— for a kid, that's impressive." *Actually, it's goddamn scary.*

"I still remember that day, when I figured it out. What an awesome feeling, to know I could set things in motion and then observe the cause and effect. That's when I realized the power of the media. I could make people do things, lots of people, all by myself. So I acted distraught for a few days. Didn't talk to anyone. Then I told a couple kids I was gonna jump off the bridge, where and how. Then that night I snuck out of the orphanage, and waited. They went ape-shit looking for me. They finally must've questioned those kids, because they swarmed the bridge and the water. Pretty funny to watch."

"I don't think they found it funny," Vail said.

Allman contorted his face as if she had just spoken gibberish. "They didn't give a shit about me. I was a bastard of a kid, no one liked me. But people did come. I watched what happened, how the cops showed up, how the reporters came, too, scribbling on their notepads, taking photos. And the article in the newspaper the next day. The town, coming out and laying flowers on the bridge. The power! What a fucking rush. Do you understand what I'm saying?"

Vail nodded. "Yeah, Clay. I get it."

"Do you really? The media ruled. A journalist—he writes something and people believe it. Right? I mean, now we have the Internet and blogs and anybody can write shit and the idiots of this country think these 'experts' know what they're talking about. But!" he said, raising the knife as if to make a point, "until a few years ago, the journalist—the *real* journalist—interpreted. Analyzed. Composed. And controlled the news.

"I knew then, back in 1963, that I could do what I wanted. I dreamed of working alongside the police and killing people—and laughing at the cops' ignorance. And then to have the ability to legally return to the crime scenes and see everyone's reaction, to objectively view my work—and then write about it afterwards for hundreds of thousands of people to read. How fucking awesome would that be?"

Allman held up the hand with the stiletto. "Don't answer. I'll tell you. *Very* awesome. It's what I've lived for. It's what's kept me going, day after day, year after year…plotting, waiting, planning." He grinned slyly. "But it turned out to be even better than I'd fantasized. Having drinks with the detectives the same night that I killed someone." He chuckled and locked eyes with Burden. "And they had no fucking clue! No one would suspect me; I had the perfect cover." He looked up at the sky. "I get goosebumps even now, just thinking about doing it again."

Vail heard Burden's shoes crunch against the roof's loose gravel. She extended her left arm and held him back.

Allman canted his head in mock sympathy. "Sorry if that hurts your feelings, *Birdie*. You know how many times I walked into Homicide after murdering someone? And not one of you had a clue. You and I sat down over lunch an hour after I killed Billy Duncan in '90. Remember that? When I told you I was late because I got *tied up*? I thought you'd key in on that when I sent the text at Inspiration Point about Friedberg. But you disappointed me. I thought you were a better detective than that."

"That's what happens when people we care about are involved," Burden said, his voice tight, intense restraint evident. "We don't think clearly. We don't suspect those close to us because we don't want to think they're monsters."

"Aww," Allman said, tilting his head in mock sympathy. "I understand. But...actually, I don't. I don't know love. Or friendship. Or guilt. I realized a long time ago I'm not like other people—how they feel things, how they get hurt by things, how they love things. I know what they're saying, but I don't understand it."

*So true. The failings of a psychopath. No emotions other than periodic anger and rage.*

"No emotional attachments, no bonds, with anyone." Allman looked off for a second, as if pondering his own self. Then he turned back to Vail.

"You can fake it, but you can't feel it," Vail said. "So why'd you do it? Why kill all these people, Clay? Or should I call you Henry?"

A loud banging noise—from behind Allman.

"What's that?" Burden asked.

Allman looked over his shoulder, behind the large skylight several feet behind him. "Oh, someone's awake. Let me show you."

Vail raised her Glock, but Allman did the same as he backed away.

"I've got someone here you're gonna want to meet."

Vail, Dixon, and Burden shared a quick glance.

*Another officer? Another con...or another...con?*

Allman reached behind the skylight, grabbed hold of something, and dragged a man toward him, in front of the outcropping. His hands were fastened behind him and his mouth was stuffed with a rag.

Allman grasped the end of the duct tape and yanked it off his mouth, pulling out the gag.

The elderly man moaned.

Using the stiletto, Allman sliced through the ropes binding his wrists and ankles. "Hey, gang. I want you to meet my father. Walton MacNally."

*Of course.*

MacNally rolled to his knees, then, unsteadily, stood up and faced his son. "Why are you doing this?"

"Why? Why?" Allman tilted his head, as if MacNally was a child who could not understand that which should have been a simple concept. "All these years, I've been showing you what you haven't had the guts to do. I was showing you how to be a fucking man."

MacNally squinted anger; his face reddened.

"But you haven't been paying attention," Allman shouted. "Have you? Have you been following it in the newspapers? I sent you all the articles!"

MacNally blinked and recoiled his head at Allman's raised voice. "I didn't—I didn't know who they were from," he said quickly. "It didn't have your name on them. I didn't understand."

"Then you're as stupid as the people who imprisoned you. As stupid as the cops who were my best buddies while they were investigating—and I was writing about—the people I'd just killed."

MacNally shook his head, as if doing so would jar something and bring things into focus. "I don't think as well as I used to—my brains were scrambled, I'm—"

"Pathetic, that's what you are," Allman said. "If you were a real man, you'd have taken care of all these jerkoffs yourself. They wronged you, they abused you. They beat you, they threw you in a goddamn sensory deprivation cell and drained your soul. Total darkness, never seeing the sun, twenty-four hours a day. Day, after day, after day."

"And how would you know about that, Clay?" Burden asked.

"I read the goddamn books. All of 'em. And I've watched the interviews with the guards and the cons. And I read the warden's records in the San Bruno Archives. It's all spelled out there in detail. What a fucking wimp my father was. What an embarrassment." He turned back to MacNally. "But what did I expect? If you'd been a man when I was young, you wouldn't have ended up in jail on some stupid plan to rob banks. Banks! What a pathetic excuse you were for a father. You couldn't even do that right."

"I tried to be a good father. That's the only reason why I did it, why I destroyed my life." MacNally's face crumpled in pain. "You know that. I only wanted to give you food, a house. A bicycle…"

"And did I ever get that bike?" Allman leaned into MacNally's face. "Answer me!"

MacNally recoiled, raising a shoulder as if it could provide a defense against painful vitriol.

"You're a failure, *Dad*. Always were."

"Not true!" the muscles in MacNally's neck went taut, the veins in his forehead bulged, spittle flying forth from his lips as he spoke. "I had a job. A family. A wife, a beautiful soul. And I was a good man." Tears flooded his eyes and he fell to his knees. His voice rose in a painful whine as he craned his neck toward the sky. "Doris… Why'd you have to die?"

Allman spit on his father. "You're a pathetic old man. Clueless to this day. All that time to think, and you still don't know."

"Mr. MacNally," Vail said gently. "Henry killed your wife. He killed Doris." She turned to Allman. "You never had the courage to tell him, did you? Go on, Clay. Tell him."

Allman glared at her, his eyes black…no reflection. Soulless. She had seen this many times before when a psychopath felt threatened. Snake eyes.

MacNally looked at his son, perhaps putting events together in combinations he had never thought to do—could never *think* to do.

"You killed her," Vail said firmly. "Didn't you?"

Allman's face relaxed, broadening into a grin. "She was my first. It made me who I am."

MacNally pulled his gaze up to Allman. "How could you?"

"Mom knew I was different. She didn't know why or how, but she knew. It was you that was the problem. You didn't want to hear it."

MacNally looked at Vail, his eyes glossing over.

Despite the anger and blind rage that Walton MacNally had built up over his years of incarceration, deep down, Vail believed he regretted having to kill to survive; that he would not have taken a life had he not been placed in the do-or-die situations he had undoubtedly confronted in prison. He killed out of necessity. MacNally was capable of emotions, of bonds, of deep love for his son. He was not a psychopath, even with his brain injury. Vail was sure of that.

But he gave birth to one.

MacNally brought his sleeve up and dragged it across his face.

Henry MacNally—Clay Allman—was a sexual serial killer who did not need a reason for killing—but in his distorted view of things, his father presented him with one that brought cohesion and purpose to his murderous ways.

MacNally looked at Vail—his face pleading disbelief. Wanting an explanation.

"You probably didn't know what you were seeing, Mr. MacNally, but I'm betting that Henry showed some early signs as a child...inappropriate sexual contact, maybe even sexual aggression."

MacNally swallowed hard. "Doris—his mother found him with a girl about a week before she...before Doris was killed. Henry was holding her down, touching her breasts." He shook his head, looked up at the sky, then sniffled. "Doris was very upset by it. I told her he's just being a boy, he's curious." He turned to Allman. "I talked to him, told him that it's not right to touch other people's bodies like that."

Allman laughed. "I remember that." He smiled. "You had no fucking idea what you were dealing with."

*You sure got that right.*

"I bet you even took something from your mother," Vail said. "A locket, an heirloom of some kind."

Allman smiled.

MacNally's eyes widened. "Her grandmother's brooch. He had it when I got home that night. I thought he wanted something from his mother, to remember her by. How—how'd you know?"

"That's what a young psychopath would do. He did take it to remind himself of his mother—but it wasn't an act of sentimentality. He took it to remember how he felt when he killed her. To relive that sense of power."

"I find it kind of *touching*," Allman said. "Don't you?"

"That bar of soap." MacNally's eyes filled with tears as his gaze canted up toward his son. "I thought you stole it from that store because the scent reminded you of your mom. But it was really some sick way for you to relive her murder."

"It's over, Clay." Vail steadied her Glock. "Drop the weapons and get down on your knees."

Allman frowned. "Go fuck yourself, Vail."

MacNally struggled to get to his feet. He again drew a sleeve across his face and he sniffed back a nose full of snot. "An officer once told me that life's a series of choices. I made some bad ones that landed me behind bars, decisions that were for Henry's benefit. But that guard was right. Yeah, I always had a reason or an excuse—we needed the money. Or it's prison, and you've gotta eat or be eaten. Maybe that's all true. But it was never for me, it was for my son." He turned to Allman, whose contempt-filled smirk indicated his indifference to his father's moral struggles.

"I regret just about all the bad things I've done in my life, Ms. Vail. The pain and death I've caused." He made eye contact with her, then Dixon, then Burden and Carondolet. "There's a lot of things I'm sorry about...but only one I can really atone for." He turned to Allman. "My biggest regret is creating you. Without you, your mother would still be alive. I'd never hurt anyone before you came along. Never took anything that wasn't mine. Me, I did bad things for the right reason. You...you've done bad things because you just didn't care."

MacNally lunged forward and grabbed his son by the neck.

But Allman shoved the stiletto deep into his father's abdomen.

And Vail shot him, twice. Allman recoiled—his eyes met Vail's— and in that instant, he seemed to grin.

But MacNally, stiletto still protruding from his stomach, drove his son backward toward the roof's edge, then over it.

*Both men tumbled out of sight—*

*and then—*

*a sickening thud.*

# 71

Vail, Burden, and Dixon ran to the edge and peered over. Walton MacNally lay atop his son, blood pooling on the concrete of the recreation yard.

Burden swung away and started dialing his phone. Carondolet ran off, back toward the cellhouse.

And Vail stood there, numb. No thoughts, other than perhaps sadness.

A hand on her shoulder. *Roxxann.*

"You okay?"

Vail slowly turned to her. "I—I need to sit." She helped Vail to a seat on the cold surface of the rooftop. "I had a flashback. My ex-husband. And my son. The arguments I had with Deacon over Jonathan—" She stopped and turned away. "The choices I've made in my life, Roxx. They haven't always been good ones. For Jonathan."

"Come on, Karen. I know you. I know you've been a good mother."

Vail faced Dixon. "Have I? My son was in a goddamn coma and where was I? I was out trying to catch a killer. Does a good mother do that?"

"I'm sure you didn't want other women getting killed. You did what you thought would save the most lives at the time. You made a tremendous personal sacrifice. That's what makes you such a good cop."

"But does it make me a bad mother? I made a sacrifice all right. But it wasn't the right choice."

Burden cleared his throat and knelt down in front of them. "Excuse me, ladies. But we just caught us a prolific killer. I think this moment calls for congratulations, no?"

Dixon got up, then extended a hand and pulled her friend to her feet.

Vail sighed deeply and wiped her eyes. "You're right. Congratulations, Burden. You did an awesome job. You're a hell of a cop, one who I'd go through a door with any day."

Burden looked at Dixon. "Is she—is she being sarcastic?"

"No," Dixon said, studying Vail's face. "I think she meant it."

Vail turned and walked away, away from the fallen bodies of Walton MacNally and Clay Allman. And as she did, she pulled out her phone to call Jonathan.

VAIL HAD HAD ENOUGH OF the confining cabins of helicopters. She wanted to feel the wind blowing in her face, through her hair. She needed something to reinvigorate her.

Dixon, Burden, and Vail boarded the Coast Guard cutter as it prepared to push off from the dock.

Burden leaned both forearms on the railing. "I feel like I should've joined them over the side. You know how many meals I've shared with Allman the past twenty years? The poker games, the nights in countless bars. The Giants games." He kicked the wall of the boat. "He was right. I was totally fucking clueless. What kind of a cop am I?"

Vail moved closer to Burden, up against his forearm. "You couldn't have known. You realize how many people have been fooled over the years by intelligent psychopaths? The list is long, and contains a lot of prominent names. You're looking at one of 'em."

Burden sighed long and hard, then hung his head.

Vail turned and looked at the Alcatraz cellhouse, the wind full in her face, the chill going down to her bones. But it didn't help. The numbness ran too deep. She needed Robby. She wanted to talk with him, to bare her thoughts, fears, and…guilt.

She needed to hug her son.

A few moments later, she stood up straight and looked out at the cellhouse as the cutter eased past it. "What is it about this place?"

Dixon followed her gaze to the top of the island. "What do you mean?"

"It's a legend, mythical almost. It housed the worst of the worst. Yet, I can't help but think that the criminals we turn out nowadays are more violent, malevolent, evil. And we don't know how to deal with them. Do we execute them? Lock 'em up? We can't release them, but sometimes…we do. And a lot of them kill again. Because that's the way they're wired. Others don't know how to survive in society and fall back on what they know how to do. What they find comforting."

Burden watched as the boat jolted a bit, and then with a roar of the engines, its speed increased. "It's always been that way, for as long as cops, and laws, existed. For as long as humans have existed."

The bellow of a fog horn blared in the distance. Vail closed her eyes and took a deep breath of cold, salty sea air. "I guess all we can do is keep on keeping on. They break the law, we track 'em down and throw 'em behind bars."

Dixon combed windblown blond hair from her face. "I have to think we'll find a better way. Someday."

They were silent as the place known as Devil's Island retreated behind them. Whether or not "a better way" would be found remained to be seen. The evil Vail had personally fought for so many years gave her substantial doubt as to whether they'd ever find an effective means of dealing with society's incorrigibles.

For the rest of her career, Alcatraz, and places like it, would likely remain the de facto standard. And for now, she was okay with that. Because at least behind bars, on rocks in the middle of oceans, or behind electrified fences and razor wire, the offenders could prey only on themselves. And the way Karen Vail saw it, that was the best she could hope for.

# *Acknowledgments*

As always, I've attempted to be as factual as possible in the writing of *Inmate 1577*. I've consulted professionals, historians, archivists, correctional officers who worked at Leavenworth, and officers and others who worked, and lived, on Alcatraz. I've read numerous nonfiction books, reviewed original prison records, and worked with my usual cadre of experts, many of whom are mentioned below.

The nature and pacing of a novel forced me to condense the real-life Alcatraz June 11, 1962, escape attempt. In some cases where it was unclear from the archival evidence which inmate performed certain tasks in the escape, I assigned those to Walton MacNally. A more detailed discussion of Alcatraz fact versus *Inmate 1577*'s fiction can be found on a special page on my website, at www.inmate.alanjacobson.com.

As mentioned in my opening Author's Note, this story was not an attempt to provide a factual depiction of the Morris-Anglin escape. Still, some of the Alcatraz inmates (and the associate warden) included in *Inmate 1577* were real individuals. I've attempted to capture their personalities based on what I read of these people, but I am in no way claiming to have accurately portrayed them. My creative reconstruction could deviate from who they were as real persons.

*Inmate 1577* was unusual for me because it spans five decades. As such, I had to write what was essentially an historical novel, which required me to seek out people who lived and worked at these locations in the late fifties and early sixties. I needed to know what the experience was like from multiple perspectives. While I spent a great deal of time at present-day Alcatraz (and even wrote some of the novel on the island), I've attempted to be as accurate as possible in both my physical descriptions and the conditions that existed there fifty years ago. To my knowledge, these depictions are correct.

I sincerely thank the following individuals who made it possible for me to write the story with the realism and credibility that I strive for in my novels:

**Mary Ellen O'Toole**, Senior FBI Profiler and Supervisory Special Agent (ret.) for her extensive assistance. I've worked with Mary Ellen for over fourteen years, and have always found her perspectives on her work as a profiler fascinating and insightful. She's been instrumental in helping me to understand Karen Vail's place in the unit and how others see her because Mary Ellen is the "real-life Karen Vail," doing in truth what Vail does fictionally. I've not only valued Mary Ellen's friendship, but her font of knowledge. In the case of *Inmate 1577*, it was particularly vital in helping me to get a handle on the psychopathic killer's motivations and how he would react to Vail's actions (and vice versa). Not only do I owe Mary Ellen thanks for her year-long feedback on the manuscript, but also for her thorough review of the novel after I'd typed the final period. If I can quicken Mary Ellen's pulse, I know I've nailed the scene.

**George DeVincenzi**, former Alcatraz Correctional Officer (1950– 57), for his anecdotes and honest appraisals of life on The Rock; his stories of his interactions with the inmates; his descriptions of what life was like as an officer; of what specific inmates were like as individuals; and for taking a trip with me to the island to retrace his former steps. George's recall was remarkable, and his stories brought the cellhouse, hospital, barber shop, kitchen, Industries building, and grounds to life for me. He was a tremendous resource and I feel fortunate to have made his acquaintance. Likewise, his review of the manuscript for accuracy was important in my endeavor to get it right.

**Jolene Babyak**, author and former child resident of Alcatraz. Jolene shared with me details surrounding the 1962 escape attempt, the Anglin brothers, her meetings and interviews with Clarence Carnes, and insights regarding her father, Associate Warden Dollison. Jolene also answered a variety of questions regarding the prison and the time she spent on The Rock, and provided helpful perspective on Carnes. The discussions I had with her were always fascinating and her numerous books about Alcatraz are absolutely worth a read.

**Constance Smith-Golda**, Alcatraz Civil War–era historian, for her tour of the Hospital floor and absorbing discussion about Alcatraz's diverse history.

Alcatraz National Park Service Rangers **John Cantwell, Craig Glassner, Al Blank,** and **Jayeson Vance.** John's behind-the-scenes tours of the island gave me the depth of knowledge and detail that I needed to write *Inmate 1577* with the realism it demanded; Craig answered my many and varied questions spanning several months about procedures on the island, the functioning of the penitentiary, National Park Service/US Park Police law enforcement jurisdictions and protocol, etc. Al provided important background and information on a variety of prison issues, including the original keys and locking mechanisms used in the cell blocks. Jayeson assisted me with Alumni Day logistics and information regarding the law enforcement presence on the island. In addition, Ranger **José Roldan** at the Presidio Officers Club gave me an overview of the region and the law enforcement patrol protocols that exist within the Presidio.

Thanks also to **Marybeth McFarland**, Acting Operations Supervisor, Golden Gate National Recreation Area, National Park Service, for her efforts in attempting to obtain island access as well as her follow-up answers to law enforcement jurisdictional issues regarding the Presidio's Inspiration Point and the Palace of Fine Arts.

Father **Bernie Bush**, former Alcatraz seminarian, for his perspective on life on The Rock, and the details of his interactions with the inmates during the time of MacNally's incarceration. As Father Bush pointed out to me after reviewing the pertinent *Inmate 1577* chapters, the fictional Father Finelli bears no resemblance (physically, in demeanor, actions, personality, or otherwise) to the real Father Bush.

Former Alcatraz Correctional Officers **Jim Albright** and **John Hernan**, for their perspective and input on their years on The Rock and an officer's duties; **John Jr.** and **Kathy Hernan** for their ancillary assistance.

**Kenneth LaMaster**, twenty-seven-year Leavenworth Correctional Officer (ret.), Institution Historian, and author, for his assistance with, and perspective on, prison life at the penitentiary, the institution's layout in the late fifties, and the nuances that accompanied MacNally's stay there—including his escape. My lengthy phone calls and unending emails with Ken spanned several months, and his very thorough read of the novel helped me bring stark realism to the fiction. Even more so than Alcatraz, Leavenworth underwent substantial changes in the intervening decades, and Ken made sure the references, physical layout, and slang were correct.

**Jerry Gelbart**, MD, for his assistance with head trauma and frontal lobe brain injuries, their symptoms and sequelae; and **Maury Gloster**, MD, for his thorough explanation of Inspector Friedberg's injury, treatment protocol, and recovery time frame; for the treatment Walt MacNally received and the medical terminology used.

Award-winning *San Francisco Chronicle* staff writer **Kevin Fagan** for his assistance with all things reporter-based in the manuscript—including newspaper industry terminology, the timing of deadlines, the journalist culture, their thought processes and approaches to stories, and their relationships with the police.

San Francisco Police Department homicide Inspectors **Antonio Casillas** and **Tom Walsh** for their background on the workings of the department, procedures for handling major crimes, resources available to inspectors, and for answering my plethora of mundane yet vital questions regarding SFPD capabilities, crime scene management, etc.

**Carol Wolther** and **Sharon Phelan** at the Cable Car Powerhouse. Carol, the San Francisco Municipal Transportation Agency Maintenance Superintendent of component repair and heavy repair rail transit shops, oriented me as to the workings of the Cable Car barn, and the maintenance and storage of the cars. Sharon gave me a terrific overview of the cable routes, the Sheave and Control rooms, and an explanation of how the sheaves operate.

**Jorge Beltran,** Coast Guard Agent, for assisting me with Coast Guard terminology and for serving as the conduit for obtaining agency clearance; **Henry Dunphy**, US Coast Guard Public Affairs Specialist 2nd Class, for information pertaining to the Coast Guard's policies regarding interagency cooperation; and for a description of its vast complement of vessels.

**Joe Sanchez**, Archives Technician, The National Archives at San Francisco, for educating me on the Alcatraz materials stored at the facility and the time frame in which the documents arrived there; and for providing me with the current disposition of former inmates.

**Roger Lamm** and **Bob Goldberg**, for sailing around the island and giving me difficult-to-obtain views of Alcatraz. Gaining perspective on an island requires not only being on it physically, but viewing it from the outside looking in.

**Mark Safarik**, Senior FBI Profiler and Supervisory Special Agent (ret.). The novel is dedicated to Mark, but without Mark's nearly twenty years of tutelage on behavioral analysis, I would not have been able to conceive of the story, let alone write it with any degree of accuracy. Mark also helped me with Vail's "New York problem"—and did his usual, detailed review of the manuscript.

**Jeff Jacobson**, Esq. My brother was my initial point of contact and answer machine for issues and questions pertaining to MacNally's legal problems and Scheer's sordid background.

**Scott Portier**, electrician, for instruction on how to torture someone using exposed electrical wires. That sounds odd, but it is what I asked him about, and it is what we discussed.

**Kevin Smith**, my editor. I'd like to say that after four novels, Kevin and I have fallen into a rhythm. But I can't—because we were in lockstep from the moment we started working together on *The 7th Victim*. In baseball, some pitchers prefer to work with certain catchers because they call a great game and coax the best performance out of that pitcher on a given day. Kevin is my personal catcher…helping me throw the well-pitched game with minimal errors.

On the topic of errors, kudos to **Anais Scott**, my copyeditor. I'm increasingly convinced that Anais is not really human. She sees things—catches things—that everyone else's brain slides past. When I think I've found something on which she goofed (we're all human, right?), she replies with a detailed explanation as to why I was wrong. So I stand corrected. She's right—and for that, I benefit.

**John Hutchinson** and **Virginia Lenneville** of Norwood Press for producing the classy Karen Vail trilogy boxed set and for being the driving force behind the *Inmate 1577* hardcover release. They are a class act, and I'm excited to be working with them.

**Daniel Tibbets, Thomas Ellsworth,** and **Hutch Morton** of Premier Digital Publishing. Their vision, vast experience, and enthusiasm for this project were instrumental in successfully launching me into the eBook realm. Special shout-out to **Lorianne Tibbets** for her authorly proofing skills and behind-the-scenes assistance.

**Joel Gotler** and **Frank Curtis**, my agents, for taking care of the business side of publishing so that I can spend more of my time doing what I do best.

**Jill**, my wife, who has put up with insane schedules, long hours, and the unrelenting stress of multiple deadlines. I look forward to spending more time with you.

Additionally, many thanks to my draft readers, whose sharp eyes caught a litany of typos: C. J. Snow, and Jeff and Danielle Jacobson.

Thanks, as well, to those who have helped me get my books into readers' hands: the awesome Tom Hedtke, Vicki Lorini, Keith Kilby, and Nathan Spradlin; John Keese; Valerie Burnside, Kara Schneider, and Jeff Bobby.

Marc Stiles; Patrick Malloy; Pam Woods, Kirk Pasich; J. B. Dickey, Fran Fuller; Joan Hansen; Patrick Millikin; Bobby McCue, Linda Brown; Jennifer Ballot; Scott C. Maynard, Amanda Kruse, Patrick McGhee, Sheree Tolman; Peter MacHott, Willie Davis, Jennifer Griffiths; Bonnie Lewis, Chris Bravo. Douglas Thompson; Russell Ilg; Jeane Coggan, Kristine Williams.

Ed Kauffman; Robert Snyder, Bob Blake, Francis Murphy, Ted Pelonis; Andrew Gulli; John and Shannon Raab; Terry Louchheim Gilman, Maryelizabeth Hart; Patrick Heffernan, Lori Burns, Linda Tonnesen; Chris Acevedo, Daniel Piel; Barbara Peters, Will Hanisko; Terry Abbott.

Stuart McMillian, Guy Farris, and Melissa Crowley (News10's *Sacramento & Co.*); Janice DeJesus of *The Contra Costa Times*; Elise Cooper.

Jane Willoughby and Ingram Losner; Wayne and Julia Rudnick; Len Rudnick; John Hartman; Andrea Ragan; Russell and Marion Weis.

Special thanks to Terri Goodwin Landreth and Sandra Clark Soreano for taking the lead to organize the entertaining "Fans of Alan Jacobson" Facebook group, which connects me with my readers and fans. To check it out, go to http://on.fb.me/ic8lVl.

## Fact vs. Fiction: Walton MacNally's Alcatraz escapes

The escape of John and Clarence Anglin and Frank Morris was a real event, and was the most daring, careful, and impressively planned prison escape in United States history. The actual timeline and events were more fantastic than portrayed in *Inmate 1577*; the breakdown of penitentiary rules and executive discipline was undeniably shocking, and each successive blunder played an increasingly important role in the success of the escape. Ironically, if any one of the lapses had been corrected, the attempt would have been foiled. *Please continue reading at* www.inmate.alanjacobson.com.

## About the Author

ALAN JACOBSON is the National Bestselling Author of the critically acclaimed thrillers *False Accusations, The Hunted, The 7th Victim, Crush, Velocity,* and *Inmate 1577*. Alan's novels have appeared on numerous "Best Books of the Year" lists, including the Top 10 for *Library Journal, The Strand Magazine, Suspense Magazine,* and the *Los Angeles Times.*

Alan's eighteen years of research and training with law enforcement have influenced him both personally and professionally, and have helped shape the stories he tells and the diverse characters that populate his novels. His books have sold internationally, and two of his novels are currently under development in Hollywood.

As part of his work with the FBI Behavioral Analysis Unit, Alan coauthored a personal safety booklet with senior FBI Profiler Mark Safarik that they are providing free on Alan's website, www.AlanJacobson.com.

Follow Alan on Facebook (http://on.fb.me/lFZoKP) and Twitter (@JacobsonAlan) or use the links posted on his website.